Cave of Little Faces

The House of Prisca and Aquila

Our mission at the House of Prisca and Aquila is to produce quality books that expound accurately the word of God to empower women and men to minister together in a multicultural church. Our writers have a positive view of the Bible as God's revelation that affects both thoughts and words, so it is plenary, historically accurate, and consistent in itself, fully reliable, and authoritative as God's revelation. Because God is true, God's revelation is true, inclusive to men and women and speaking to a multicultural church, wherein all the diversity of the church is represented within the parameters of egalitarianism and inerrancy.

The word of God is what we are expounding, thereby empowering women and men to minister together in all levels of the church and home. The reason we say women and men together is because that is the model of Prisca and Aquila, ministering together to another member of the church—Apollos: "Having heard Apollos, Priscilla and Aquila took him aside and more accurately expounded to him the Way of God" (Acts 18:26). True exposition, like true religion, is by no means boring—it is fascinating. Books that reveal and expound God's true nature "burn within us" as they elucidate the Scripture and apply it to our lives.

This was the experience of the disciples who heard Jesus on the road to Emmaus: "Were not our hearts burning while Jesus was talking to us on the road, while he was opening the scriptures to us?" (Luke 24:32). We are hoping to create the classics of tomorrow, significant and accessible trade and academic books that "burn within us."

Our "house" is like the home to which Prisca and Aquila no doubt brought Apollos as they took him aside. It is like the home in Emmaus where Jesus stopped to break bread and reveal his presence. It is like the house built on the rock of obedience to Jesus (Matt 7:24). Our "house," as a euphemism for our publishing team, is a home where truth is shared and Jesus' Spirit breaks bread with us, nourishing all of us with his bounty of truth.

We are delighted to work together with Wipf and Stock in this series and welcome submissions on a wide variety of topics from an egalitarian, inerrantist global perspective.

For more information, see our Web site:

https://sites.google.com/site/houseofpriscaandaquila/.

"*The Cave of Little Faces* whisks the reader into an adventure in the Dominican Republic. The Spencers truly are masters of storytelling. It feels like you are there. This story could easily be made into a movie. The characters are delightful, unique, and so real. The dynamics of Jo's family come across in full color and in a relatable manner, and even the scammers are memorable characters. The storyline is captivating, to say the least. I could not put this book down. The vivid descriptions carried me away to another world—one filled with beauty, intrigue, drama, and a few good laughs as well. Bravo!"

—**Jennifer Creamer**, School of Biblical Studies, Youth With a Mission

"From their intriguing title, through a roster of memorable characters, to a string of concluding surprises that crackle like fireworks, the Spencers take us on a spiritual roller coaster ride graced with suspense, humor, and dilemmas of high moral complexity. As their heroine, Josefina, finds her way through the forests and mountains of Hispaniola, we realize that hers is a metaphor for the journey we all share—the pilgrimage of life."

—Robert Boenig, author of the award-winning *C. S. Lewis and the Middle Ages*

"I enjoyed *Cave of Little Faces!* The storyline and the conflicts are great and the cross-cultural setting is one of the book's big strengths . . . I loved the theology and history the authors brought into the book, managing to make arguments about Christianity's place in history come off as natural arguments, and not advertisements for the faith inserted into the text—a rare feat indeed! I also love the way they did the character descriptions. Thank you so much for sharing this wonderful gift with me."

—Jasmine Myers, founder and director of the award-winning
Still Small Theatre Troupe

"Awesome characters! I couldn't wait to get home from work and get together with them again. Once I was getting near the end, I began to realize how much I was going to miss them."

—Dawn Samsel, reading specialist in the Beverly, Massachusetts
public school system.

Cave of Little Faces

A Novel

WILLIAM DAVID SPENCER
and
AÍDA BESANÇON SPENCER

WIPF & STOCK · Eugene, Oregon

CAVE OF LITTLE FACES
A Novel

Wipf & Stock
An Imprint of Wipf and Stock Publishers
199 W. 8th Ave., Suite 3
Eugene, OR 97401

www.wipfandstock.com

PAPERBACK ISBN: 978-1-5326-5082-6
HARDCOVER ISBN: 978-1-5326-5083-3
EBOOK ISBN: 978-1-5326-5084-0

Manufactured in the U.S.A.

Areyto to the Great Warrior

From the Mother of the Islands,
on the vast, forbidding highlands,
watching from the forest fastness,
eyes of iron, will of stone.

Futilely pursuing treasure,
for the distant monarchs' pleasure,
furtively, despite their crassness,
eyes of terror, all alone.

As their horses' panting quickens,
stumbling, as briar thickens,
whinnying in steps of last stress
eyes extinguish, falling prone.

Soon they all discard their armor,
drag their swords before their harmer,
craving water, past disastrous,
eyes of naught but skin and bone.

Now their vanquisher with kindness,
Holy Writ dispelling blindness,
binds their wounds, restores with largesse
eyes that pledge and plead for home.

William David Spencer

The Regions of the Western Lands of the South

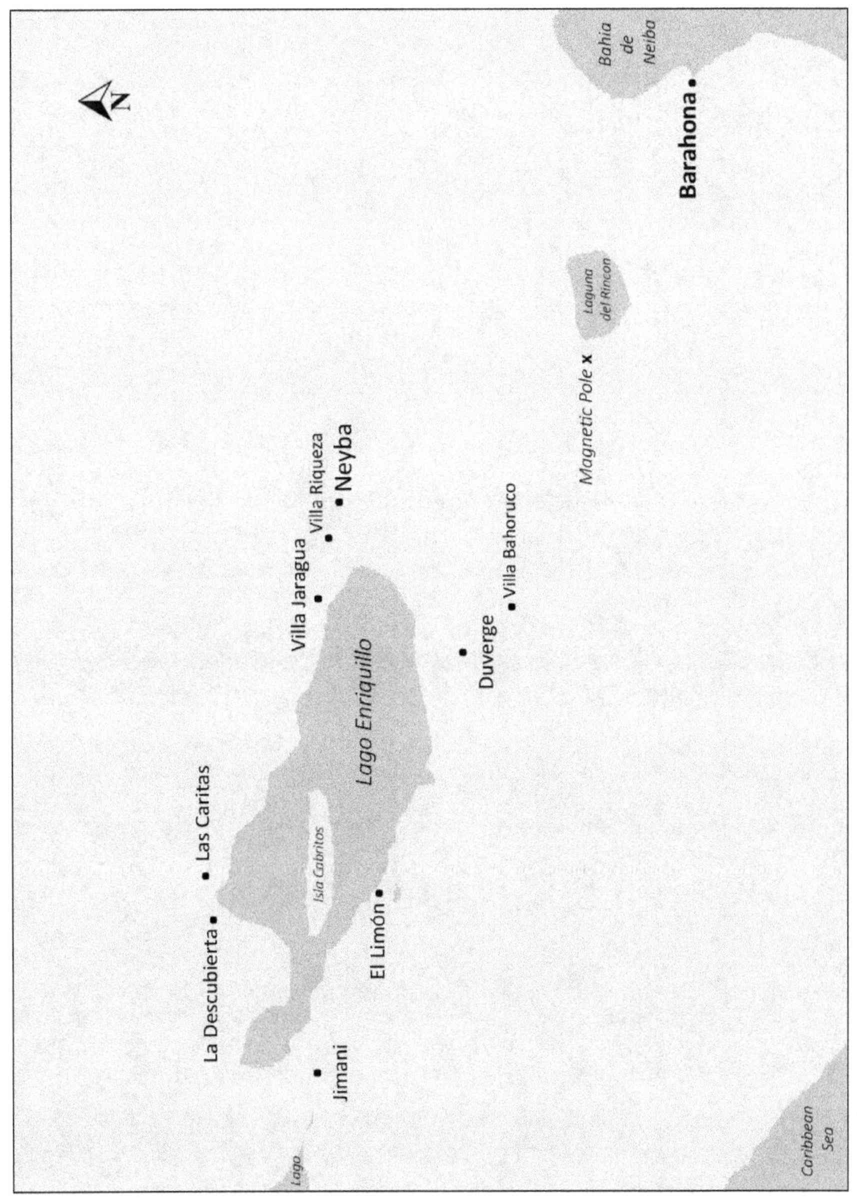

Prologue

"IT WAS AWFUL," said the man. "Those poor people!"

The woman shuddered. "They dragged them right out of their house—onto the lawn. It was so horrible." She began to cry.

The man put his arm around her shoulder and she turned her face into his chest and wept.

"Take some broth," said a kind voice. "You're both so cold and wet."

"Yes, the rain saved us—God's grace!" The man took the broth in his free hand and gently urged it on the woman, but she could not stop crying. He understood.

"It was so dark," he said, simply holding the steaming broth for when she would want it. "The darkness was our refuge as well. You see, it all came on so suddenly." He shook his head. "I guess *we* were the ones who came on so suddenly, they did not know at first we were there—the darkness was so complete. You see, the rain was impending. There was no moon, for the clouds were low. The road is so dark already, with no street lights until the towns on Route 28 and this stretch of road—after you make the left turn?—it is so dark at night anyway. . . . "

The woman was softly wailing interspersed by fits of shuddering. The man hugged her to him. "We're safe now," he tried to comfort her, but she kept shaking her head and murmuring, "Those poor people—dragged out of their home into the night and shot," and she would cry again.

"Did you get a look at the men at all?" asked the voice.

"Not clearly, but they looked like soldiers. They had uniforms, but not like ones we know. These were different—like camouflage."

"Camouflage?"

"Yes, like they were prepared for fighting in the woods."

"In the forest?"

"Yes, exactly—just like that. There were three vehicles." The woman shuddered against him and he held her more tightly to his breast and bent his head down on hers, kissing her gently. Then he slowly raised his eyes again and said, "They were all up on the lawn—one jutting out onto our road—all three of these large trucks. One was almost like an amphibious vehicle; the other two were like small troop carriers. The soldiers were all around the house—about twenty of them or so. We drove right up into the midst of them. I mean, we were on the road and they were shouting at the people and to each other and didn't even see us come up. But, we saw them drag out a man and a woman. They dragged her by the hair right out of the house and onto the lawn."

"And they shot them," cried the woman.

"Yes," said the man. "They shouted something I couldn't catch and then executed them both. I had stopped the car—I couldn't believe what I was seeing. Not here—not now. And then I realized—we needed to get out of there—whatever was happening. You know what the roads are like!"

"Yes," said another kind voice, "they are treacherous in the day, let alone night. Holes and rocks and speed bumps for no apparent reason. . . ."

"Exactly," said the man. "I didn't want to rev the motor so that we would attract their attention. I couldn't turn around, there were just ditches on every side, so I thought of backing up away, but, how could I K-turn? There's nothing there for purchase. So we crept into their taillights and began quietly to creep around them, and that's when one of them saw us and began shouting to the others. So, I gunned it then! I didn't care about the potholes or the speed bumps or the rocks or anything. I guess one of the trucks stayed with the bodies—the big awkward looking thing—but the other two started up to chase us. We were racing down the road. I knew if they caught up with us—that would be the end. It was us or the car."

"You did right."

"I know the road, but you have to drive it every day to know what's the daily condition, and we haven't been here for a while, so it was all guesswork. Well, I looked back to see where they were and they had dropped behind us. The first vehicle apparently had backed into a ditch and the wheel got caught. The second one had to lumber around it and that gave us our lead. I thought if we could just get ahead of them we might have a chance—I mean, we only had the little car and they had these all-terrain kind of vehicles, so I didn't know what was going to happen. And then the rain came."

"Thank God!"

"I do," said the man. "It was not, and then suddenly it was. Instantly, coming down in torrents. We could hardly drive, but they couldn't see anything either. We knew we were close, so my wife strained to see the turn and we saw it in time and made the sharp corner. She had the window rolled down and was leaning out in the downpour. She had the flashlight out the window and the light was bouncing up and down the side of the road. Then I took a gamble, figuring we were about at the right spot, and she found one of the little hidden entries—the footpaths. She spotted one—even through the rain," and he hugged her. "I slowed down and pulled the car in, off the road. It was bumping in over the branches and through the shrubs. I wasn't certain we would get enough of it off the road before it got stuck in the mud and the brush. I doused the lights as soon as we left the road and was driving blind, praying we wouldn't hit a tree. As soon as we both thought we were sufficiently off the road, we just stopped it—there on the path—and jumped out of the car and hid in the bushes and waited."

He hugged his wife more closely. She was quiet now and took the broth from his hand and sipped some of it.

"Well, in just minutes, they came careening by, skidding in the downpour, and then roaring up the road—both of them—right by us. We knew we had just a little time before they realized we weren't on the road anymore and they would begin picking their way back, searching for us. So, as soon as their tail lights disappeared, we hauled our suitcases out of the trunk and hid them in the bushes, hoping they wouldn't find them and know who we were. Then we put some brush over the car as best we could to obscure it from the road and then we left everything behind and worked our way up the path and came here—through the rain and all. And, you know, the downpour lessened just as we arrived."

"We will send out the young trackers who can find your suitcases and move the car before daylight," said another voice. The room was now full of men and women. Someone reached over behind them, put another blanket on them and hugged them both. "You are home and you are safe now. No one can touch you here. So, here you will stay."

"But, our children," said the woman. "They are on the next flight."

"I will send them an emissary," said the man. "They will be safe in his hands." And then he added, "I hope. . . ."

1

WHEN THE LETTER ARRIVED that would change her life, Jo was so busy she simply gave it a cursory glance and tossed it back on her desk. By the end of the night it was lost under a pile of Slossen literacy tests and English as a Second Language booklets. In fact, had Jo not needed to delve deeply into these reading assessment tools, digging for clues on how to help her students conquer the English language, the letter might have remained lost for weeks, like some forgotten artifact sifting down into a mound on which a new generation has built its own version of a city. After all, Jo was building knowledge into her students, and in that quest she was completely immersed. At the moment the envelope arrived, she was concentrating on the knotty problem of how to explain the letter *c* to a class of new English language learners, some of whom had perfect sound/symbol correlations in their birth languages.

"So, Professora Josefina," said Nilka, a pensive, thirty-something Guatemalan, currently toiling as a maid, but capable of so much more. "You are saying that *c* is both *s* and *k* in sound, but this poor little letter has no voice of its own?"

"Yes, yes, that's it," agreed Jo.

"So, then," pursued Nilka, "why not retire it? Let the other letters do their work. It would be so much more easy to read. When someone does not do their share, we let them go. It is not like in some countries where the *más viejos*—the oldest of the old—have no pension and must work on and on when they no longer can serve. Why must *c* remain on the job—on the page?"

Jo looked down at her teacher's guide. No help there. "I don't know, Nilka," she confessed. "We are kind of stuck with *c*. It is—well, it is . . . like a—ummm—chameleon. It changes color, depending on its surroundings. When it is—well, say, on the beach in Puerto Rico with the soft trade winds blowing, relaxing with its fun friends like the *i* and the *e*, then it is soft and relaxed, like it was 'sipping cider'—you see?—*c-i-d-e-r*—*cider*. But, if it's in downtown Santo Domingo, struggling next to tough vowels like *a* and *u*, like being stuck in traffic on a street like Avenida Bolivar, with truck drivers pounding on their horns, taxi drivers banging up on the sidewalks, passing each other at the risk of everyone's life and limb, buses shouldering everyone else out, while motorcycles zip everywhere like so many mosquitos, and then! Then! The fruit truck in front of you suddenly stops and the driver squeezes out and blocks the street, and every horn goes berserk. I mean, crazy—*loco*! Then the *c* is hard and tough, like a *k* sound in *cane* or *clutch*."

"Ahhh," said the whole class, shaking their heads in agreement, "like a chameleon."

"It is ever hiding, ever changing," pursued Jo. "But you can see the clues in the company it keeps: soft like an *s* with *i* and *e*, hard like a *k* with *a* and *o* and the consonants."

Gratified, Jo watched her class of seven dutifully scratch that mystifying information into their notebooks.

Josefina Archer, known to all and sundry as Jo, was 29 years old, a former community organizer before she received God's call to help poor people become something even greater than simply middle class. As in everything she did, she had pursued her early career change with diligence and, after seminary training in Boston both in Spanish and English at the Center for Urban Ministerial Education, she returned to her home town of Richfield, New Jersey, called to pastor a small new Spanish church development at David Brainerd Presbyterian Church of Richfield, or "David B," as the parishioners called it.

Coming back to Richfield after three years away had been quite interesting. Everyone in the Spanish community still regarded Jo as their community organizer, even though they kept correcting themselves to call her *Reverenda* now, but Jo didn't mind, because she found that working in such a helping dimension to her ministry was natural for her. The literacy and second language learning center at David B was a natural gift to Richfield's Hispanic community—an extension of what she had developed when she was still Richfield's Hispanic community organizer. But, now, instead of being in charge, she was just the director of one of its centers. The search for a new organizer was still grinding along, but she treated the interim director of the Hispanic office, a younger woman from Costa Rica, with deference and support. With Jo's center, another on Second Street in a small mission there run by a charismatic and beloved Mexican minister named Mercedes Del Rio, another at the local Richfield State College, another in Richfield State Penitentiary, and a few others at notable places, this program was thriving.

Here at David B, Jo had recruited the clergy couple who pastored the English congregation, Pastors Ron and Toni Bright, to help her. She also attracted an interested parishioner of the Brights—one Lawrence Fennelman, who Jo feared was more interested in her than in the program—and to her delight, her own dad, James Archer, who was semiretired and had a wonderful touch with the students. She had also enlisted her stepmom, Lea, who was always willing to try anything, but she was so brusque and quick to closure that everybody got discouraged. Easy does it works with adult learners.

Well, obviously, *c* was plenty to chew on and ingest for one night, so Jo decided to pause there and see how this had sunk in. "Okay," she swept the room with a challenging glance, "so how sharp do you think you are? Think you can handle a few drills?"

"I think I got it," announced Nilka.

"I don't know if I got it," warned Nilka's mom, who always knitted through the entire session.

"I think *she* got it," chuckled Raul, making the traditional Hispanic gesture of pursing both lips and pointing them in Nilka's direction.

"All right, then, let's see," said Jo. "*C-i-t-y*"—what is it?"

"Kitty," said Nilka's mom hopefully—like downtown Santo Domingo, hhaarrdd!"

"No, Mama," said Nilka. "It is soft—it is with the *i*—the *iiiiii*! You see?" Mama obviously didn't see.

Oh, oh, thought Jo, my illustration overpowered my content—teaching is impossible! "Look, forget, the example," said Jo quickly to the six other puzzled faces confronting her. "Just go with the vowels—hard vowels, soft vowels. Just like Nilka said."

"Bowels?" said Nilka's mother.

"I think we've had enough for tonight," groaned Jo. "We'll pick this up again next week. Oh, and you're all doing so well," she added swiftly. "Don't worry about getting this, right off the bat. It's hard for everybody. But, you're all doing just fine. Just fine! We'll keep at it until everybody's got it."

"Thank you, Profesora Josefina," said Nilka, and everybody joined in. Nilka's mother gathered up her knitting and off they all went as Jo sat back in her chair and puffed out a great sigh.

"How's it going, JoJo?" asked her dad, leaning into the room. "All done for the night?"

"Yes, and done in by the elusive *c*."

Dad chuckled. "Sure, wait until you get them to the sounds without symbols. How they ever got a *th* (he blew a sharp blast of air under his tongue as he rested it on his bottom teeth) out of a *ta* (another blast at the tongue's tip behind his top teeth) and a *haaaa* I'll never know. Something to look forward to. . . ."

Jo groaned. "It was a lot easier back when I was setting up these classes than now when I have to teach them!"

"Yes, that's always the way. But you're so industrious, you'll keep on plugging."

Jo groaned again. "Yeah, that's what's worrying me."

Dad laughed, "Okay, honey, I'm off."

Jo got up, went over and hugged her father. "Thank you, Dad, so much for helping out. I don't know what I'd do without you. You're so busy—this is so sweet of you."

"Honey, there's nothing more important to me than you and your brother and sisters. In whatever and whenever you need me, you know I'm there for you."

"I know, Dad. And I'm here for you too."

"Yes, Jo, you are—you're always there for everybody."

"Hmmummm," cleared a throat at the door. "Miss Archer, may I ask you a question?"

"Of course, Mr. Fennelman. How is that student you are tutoring coming along?"

"Slowly, slowly," said Lawrence, tousling his few front strands of hair and sidling up next to Jo.

"I'll see you later," winked Dad, starting for the door.

"Just a second, Dad," cried Jo in desperation, "You've been teaching for so long, I think you can help us with this question."

Lawrence frowned, as Jo dragged her father back into the room. "Well," said James Archer, eyeing his daughter with a "Thanks a lot!" look. "So, what seems to be the trouble, Lawrence?"

Lawrence fumbled around for something to say, as Jo shuffled up the papers on her desk—now, if she could just make her escape, while Dad had him occupied. A furtive glance, a stealthy stealing along the wall, and Jo slipped out the door and fled. The letter went with her, unnoticed.

2

AT THE SAME TIME Jo was slipping out of the door of her classroom at David B, a world away in the land of Jo's birth—the Dominican Republic—Basil and Starling Heitz were racing out of Puerto Plata as quickly as their rattle trap of an unreturned rental pickup truck could take them. The cause was a "misunderstanding" between them and a prospective investor over some salted iron pyrite in what they had purported to be a vein of gold begging to be mined on some otherwise nearly worthless terrain that they claimed to own in the usually lush farm land of the Cibao region.

Puerto Plata is a lovely, tourist-oriented city on the northern coast of the island of Hispaniola, renowned for its all-inclusive resorts, its golf courses, and its longtime, old-moneyed visitors, all of whom, as a village policy, were protected by the local *policia*. As a consequence, the Heitzes were speeding off into the interior on little Route 5. Their plan: cross the mountains before nightfall, work their way along the border of Haiti, and lose themselves in the peninsula that extended down to the generally undeveloped south, where they would definitely not be known. Here, in what they'd heard were the comfortable little cities of Pedernales and Barahona, they would once again see what fortune would bring.

So far it had not brought them much. They had come to the Dominican Republic after reading about a recent discovery of the gold that had eluded Columbus and his soldiers of fortune so long ago. Of course, they imagined themselves in a plush tropical paradise surrounded by millionaires who would throw money at them. They'd begun in La Romana, a city beloved by tourists as well as humanitarian and church mission groups, but nothing developed. The government years before had hired a Canadian firm to mine the gold and dreams of being 49ers Latin-style evaporated as fast as their meager capital. Puerta Plata beckoned, so they traveled north, but that was disastrous. So here they were at this moment, somewhere west of the mountain village of Platanal, as Route 5 yielded to a precarious winding road, identified only with the number 18, that went up and up and up. Dusk began encroaching upon the mountain fastness like a bad case of disclosure, until both of the erstwhile bunco stock conspirators realized that hiding in the hills was a very poor idea—to say the least. Star was the first to speak.

"What a dump!" she grumbled. "There's like absolutely nothing up here! There's not even like a gas station. There's no restaurants. There's no nothing!"

Basil offered a suggestion. "Shut up!" he growled.

"I will not! If you hadn't oversold him, we would be at the casino right now."

"Me? Me? You were the one talking about gold prices and the government disenchantment with the Canadians and how, if we just offered them four pesos out of every ten, we could clean up!"

"Well, you weren't bringing it home! You knew he had some kind of surveyor set to check it out and some lawyer looking at the documents. What'd you imagine they were gonna find when they checked out our coordinates?"

"Well, how was I to know that old guy was sharper than he looked?"

"You never figure out anything in time. You just push on and on until the whole thing blows up."

Basil glowered at her, but he had no answer to that, and they settled into a grim and completely unsatisfying temporary ceasefire, both licking their recent wounds, which cut a lot deeper than this little common skirmish.

Presently, Star said, "Bo, I'm scared. These roads are so little and there's no lights and there's no guard rails. The sides are falling away and it's a sheer drop over the side. We haveta stop!"

Basil strained into the darkness. "I don't like it either. We got gas—I look ahead—not like you said. But you're right this time. We could run off the side and no one would find us."

The little truck rolled slowly to a halt in the center of what now looked like a tiny path. There was no sound but the wind.

"I can't see anything." Basil opened the door and began feeling his way up the path. He came back almost immediately. "I don't think anybody's gonna come this way tonight. There's no place to stay. We gotta make do."

"I'm hungry."

"Me too."

"Where we gonna sleep?"

"Well," said Basil pointedly, "we could pile the suitcases out on the roadside and stretch out in the truck bed."

"Not on your life," snapped Star. "Not my suitcases! They stay safe in the back. You can stretch out on the ground."

"Right! And get eaten alive by mosquitos."

"Well, what's your plan?"

"We'll just start at dawn."

A night cramped in their little rental with the mosquitos banging against the windows like suicide bombers did little to improve their disposition. Morning entered gently like a blessing. Basil simply woke up, started the truck, and was winding down through little clusters of country houses when Star finally woke.

"Where'd all the shacks come from?" she yawned.

"We're in a valley skirting the mountains," Basil explained.

"Whatever. But I'm starved and I gotta go."

The little wooden structure that served as a store offered them gasoline in little cans and, hanging from small hooks and dangling over the counter, dried, spicy jerky, which they ate ravenously.

Starling almost cried when she saw the accommodations in the shed back behind the store—a hole in the ground, no sink, and a slab of old wood simply leaning in to the entrance to serve as a sort of door, pulled open by a broken piece of rope dangling from a nail. This was the lowest they had ever fallen. Basil shared her sentiment as he gaped mournfully at the broken, filthy porcelain tray in a small, door-less aperture around the far side of the same shed. Neither of them said anything afterwards as they shared a little towelette for cleaning hands that Star had in her purse.

Munching on the rest of the jerky and drinking sweet carbonated bottled drinks that together made their stomachs churn, they were still able to notice that the poor little country villages had begun to multiply. Maybe civilization, as they saw it, wasn't too far away. . . .

The land was arid now, like a wilderness, but makeshift roadside stands had also begun to appear before the little wooden and sheet-metal houses. Beside them sat entire families, selling whatever was in season and watching what came by. Star waved at one little family knot and they broke into big smiles and waved back. Maybe this wasn't going to be so bad, she thought. And she felt almost good about it when they reached the border road at Dajabon and with relief turned south at last.

But the border was another world than the mountains, empty and desolate. Both Star and Basil felt their spirits sinking again. And, as they traveled, the northwestern border villages all matched their mood—depressed little places with empty-eyed people who stared at them as they drove swiftly past—and on the edge of each town cemeteries with all the graves broken open. "This place gives me the creeps," shuddered Starling over and over again as they hurried through town after town. Another stop and the sun was beating upon them as on a voodun drum.

Then about six o'clock in the afternoon, the road left the border and continued winding south, past villages with more encouraging names like "Happy Angel," "Granada" (Star loved that song and began to hum it), and "The Pines." Star's spirits began lifting again. Both of them were feeling as if they were on the brink of some kind of deliverance when suddenly a little city aptly named *Descubierta*—the "Discovery"—hove into sight. This was a lovely little town with an "up and coming" appearance punctuated by motorcycles zipping by like so many new ideas.

Basil paused before the village square and studied the benches replete with lovers lost in their mutual attraction, the tables with old men playing dominos, and, specifically, a mature family threesome sitting next to the road to whom he asked the name of the town in his "get-by" version of Spanish, awkwardly leaning over Star to do so.

The grey-haired man in the center of the trio spread his hands in either direction, smiled, and announced with invitational pride, "*La Descubierta— a gozar.*"

"He wants us to enjoy ourselves!" Star marveled and beamed on them with her hundred-watt smile, calculated as it was to dazzle marks out of their hard-earned reserves, effective up to thirty paces. Nice little town, she was beaming, let's turn it upside down and see what shakes out. But, to the pure, all things are pure, and the trio took her enthusiasm for face value. This was, after all, *Descubierta*—"the Discovery." And they knew there was much to discover.

Gauging a similar response in Basil, so it was probably unnecessary— but, she knew, it never hurts—Star decided to wheedle in her most reasonable and ingratiating tone: "Look, it's after seven o'clock. We put some real miles in today, Bo. This town looks big enough to give us a good meal and a cheap place to stay. Last night was awful—we had to sleep all cramped up. We gotta get a good night's sleep, if we're going to go on tomorrow. Besides, I need a shower—and you definitely need one!"

Basil chuckled. "You're right there, Schweetheart," he replied in his truly miserable Bogart imitation.

"So, let's discover the good life of Descubierta," urged Star.

"Great idea! I think we could enjoy this town," agreed Basil, grinning at Star and then nodding at the patient threesome. "*Un hotel?*"

All three smiled even more broadly, if that were possible, and pointed beyond the other side of the square.

Basil carefully inserted the little truck in among the motorcycles, pulled off an awkward K-turn, and navigated his way back along the road until they had left the central park.

"This is pretty," murmured Star, looking out her window at the far side of the road, where a small waterfall, flowing from the mountains, passed under the street and filled a little valley in which people were wading.

Back on the left, on the next corner just after the park, was the hotel, a small two-story structure with a little restaurant on its ground floor, balconies above them for the front two upper rooms, and yellow and red flowers filling the entrance. A tiny parking area separated the building from the road, and into this Basil squeezed the little truck.

The proprietor, a garrulous and prosperously portly man of middle age, appropriately named Señor Feliz, welcomed them in with an infectious air of contentment. In a mixture of seven-eighths Spanish and one-eighth English, he displayed the wonders of Descubierta before them, as innocently as did Hezekiah show his treasures before the reconnoitering Assyrians. Yes, it was a relatively poor town, but the people were proud of it and hoped someday to complete the construction of the road on the northern outskirts of town. The main attraction was the "little faces" of the Indians. "You must not leave the area until you see the 'little faces,'" he urged them.

So the next morning, bright and early, about the crack of dawn for Basil and Star—that is to say, about eleven o'clock—they headed off on the only lead they presently had: to see the "little faces." When one is out to exploit, no avenue should remain unexplored.

No sooner had they left the comfort of Descubierta, however, than they made an unpleasant discovery. The construction Innkeeper Feliz had assured them was "in process" proved to be a torn-up road with no one either working on it or having worked on it for obviously quite a while. They rattled for a space through broken concrete and clouds of dust thrown up by a huge tractor trailer thundering by them and kicking up stones until Star demanded they turn back. But Basil doggedly bumped "on and on," as she had accurately complained in the mountains. This time, however, he was rewarded by a stretch of recently paved highway and a clear straight-away as a mountain rose up on Basil's side to their left.

"Bo," said Star presently, "there's something happening on my side. I think it's water—I can see it through the trees."

"You mean like a river?"

"Uh, I'm not sure. It's all among the trees. It was like far away at the edge, you know? But now it looks like it's spreading out and getting closer."

Basil tried to strain over her and get a glimpse of what lay beyond the foliage on the right, but it was hard with the occasional bus or tractor trailer that nearly blew them off into the trees as it hammered through.

"I can't see it exactly." He gave up and kept his eyes on the road.

In a few moments, she said, a little worried, "Basil—it's big! I think it might be . . ."

"Wait! Here's the sign," Basil cut her off. "I'm gonna pull over." Basil tucked the truck in a tiny space at the side of the road, barely off the highway, and just at the edge of shrubs and small trees that rapidly spread downward in a sharp decline. He glanced at a huge wooden stairway that zigzagged up the sheer hill on his left, then he peered over past Star toward the right and the water she was indicating. "Wow, it does look like a lot."

They didn't bother to lock the truck, but headed immediately across the highway for the stairway. A huge sign on the left of the first rise of the stairs announced this was the "little faces" national site. A welcome booth was to the right, but it was locked up. No one was around. They started up the wooden staircase and at the first landing paused and leaned on the rail looking back over the road and now over the trees.

"Wow!" said Star.

"Good night!" said Basil.

They were confronting an astonishing sight—a huge body of water stretched in either direction, its far shore, for it had to have one, lost in the distance.

"Wait! We're not in Haiti?" Star cried in a sudden moment of confused panic. "You didn't turn the wrong way and stumble over the border—did you?"

"Of course not!" snapped Basil.

"Well, that looks like the ocean," Star snapped back.

"No, it doesn't! We just stayed in a city called 'Descubierta!' How could they have a city with a Spanish name if we were in Haiti?" he sneered. "It's the lake we saw on the map in the guidebook—what did you do with the book?"

"It's in the truck!"

Basil stared at her in his most commanding manner. Star stared back, unimpressed. Neither moved. Eventually, muttering something Star definitely did not want to hear, Basil lumbered back down the stairs, crossed over to the truck, leaned into the back, and began rummaging around in a pile of assorted odds and ends that either hadn't been worthy of suitcase space or were assigned there in order to be "handy." Somewhere under that mess, he fished out the book, identifiable as much by its battered appearance as by the stamp on it, which read, "Hamilton-Wenham Public Library,

Hamilton, MA 01982," one of Star and Basil's many brief supply stops (in this case with a five-fingered library card) in the wavering trajectory of their uncelebrated flight.

He climbed back up with exaggerated effort, opened the book, and stuck it in her hand. "It's a lake," she admitted, and he was mollified.

Both of them continued their staring, more and more thunderstruck as they tried to form a mental measure of what was before them.

"This is colossal!" Star exclaimed.

"This looks undeveloped!" Basil observed.

"I think our idea might be here somewhere," Star ventured.

"I think so too," mused Basil. "But, we've got to find it. Let's go back to that talky guy at the hotel and see if we can stir up a scam." He started back down the stairs.

"Hold on!" called Star. "What about the faces?"

"Who cares about the faces?" yelled Basil back from the bottom of the stairway. "Come on!"

"I'll tell ya who cares," Star shouted back, "that 'talky guy at the hotel'—that's who!"

"Oh, yeah! You're right! We can't go back if we don't look at those faces he was all worked up about." He clamored back up the staircase. Another zigzag and they were up near the top. The mountainside indented a bit and in the hollow under a small overhang was a series of circles etched into the walls that looked like children's carvings—little round ovals with dots that were obviously meant to be eye sockets with straight or curved lines for mouths. Some looked to them like they were "smiley faces." To the right, at the edge of the cliff, stick figures and more faces on a huge rounded boulder, wedged into the mountainside, showed a commanding view of the sweep of the lake behind it with a small patch of thick trees before the shoreline began.

"How'd they get out there to do that?" Star marveled.

"Yeah, what's it all mean?" wondered Basil. "Some of these look fake, like jokers imitated them, like that one with the ears and the big round circles for hair and the stick arms and hands, but I dunno."

"Why are they just out here?" asked Star. "We haven't seen anything like this in the mountains. How old are they? The people who put them up—what were they trying to say to the lake?"

"Or maybe to people coming in off the lake—maybe a warning," wondered Basil, "but they look friendly enough." He shook his head. "The government's already got these here for free, so the lake is where we should be concentrating. That's got acres and acres of shoreline—beachfront property! There's got to be an angle here."

Whatever the angle was, Star and Basil were getting less help than they expected from the innkeeper back in Descubierta. They kept plying him with questions about the lake: Did anybody own it? Did anybody use it? Who had the rights?

But he kept wanting to talk about the Taino Indians and the little faces and the fact that these simple carvings had been gracing this particular hillside for, maybe, a thousand years.

Finally, Basil broke in. "Look," he said, in his best Spanish. "The Indians are great! The little faces are great! But the lake is great too! We," he indicated Star and himself, "want to do something great with the lake." Not much variety of expression, but he finally had the proprietor's attention.

"You want to buy the lake?"

"Well not the whole thing," explained Basil, "but, you know, some of the beach front—to help somebody set up something . . . like a hotel—wait," he realized he was talking to an innkeeper with whom this idea might compete. "Not a hotel," he corrected himself quickly. "Maybe a park." "Theme park" was beyond him, so he added: "Water park."

Señor Feliz became very serious and suddenly very quiet. He looked at both of them mournfully. "Oh, *Señor, Señora,*" he said, and all but patted their hands in a growing dismay. "You do not know the power of the lake or you would not be talking so. Before you make any plans or invest any money, you must go and see the lake for yourselves."

"But we saw the lake," countered Basil quickly, "from the stairway at the little faces."

"No, no!" said the proprietor. "You saw the size, yes, but you did not see what the lake itself is doing. You must travel now to the south—around the other side of the lake. You must see for yourselves. Here is what you must do. Go now—it is still early—watch for the *desvio.*"

Both of them looked at him blankly. Star opened her little dictionary and asked him to spell it. He did. "It's *detour,*" she said to Basil.

"Yes, *daytuur,*" tried Señor Feliz phonetically. "You watch for that and do not miss it. Take that road and you will come out by the great city of Jimani. After that you must go left down by El Limon. Do not miss either the *daytuur* or the later left turn. If you miss the left at Jimani and you work your way to Mal Paso, you will cross over into Haiti."

Star shuddered. Being xenophobic, she and Basil could not think of Haiti as anything but a mass of spirit-possessed voodooists, thin, with crazed eyes, beating ceaselessly hypnotic rhythms designed to turn all strangers who haplessly stumbled across her borders into zombies. They had both seen far too many horror movies in their youth, and these had helped addle their brains into what they were today.

"I'll write the directions down," said Star nervously.

"Note them on the map," suggested Basil.

The innkeeper produced a pen and made sweeping circles and arrows on the little partial page map in the light-fingered library book that belonged in Massachusetts.

"We won't miss it," said Basil.

"That's because I'll drive," decided Star.

So, with two bottles of water, a couple of grape sodas, and the innkeeper's best wishes, they headed out to discover the power of the waters of the lake. But, little could they know that the real discovery that might change their destiny, bring them fame at last, and even potentially provide a bit of fortune was just beyond the lake and waiting for them later that afternoon.

3

H OME AND SAFE IN her apartment, Jo brewed herself a cup of tea—apple tea tonight, because she needed energy to deal with all the thoughts jostling each other for primacy in her mind. The big bruiser shouldering out everybody else, of course, was Finance, which is probably every minister's mental bully: How am I going to afford everything I want to do for my people? "You can see clearly that you need more money!" it lectured her in its severe tone. "How do you expect to run a ministry on pennies?" As usual Jo had no answer. Her salary was a gracious, but simple, start-up grant from the church—read: Pastors Ron and Toni's tithing off their own salaries because they saw the need and believed in Jo ever since she'd been the local Hispanic community organizer for Richfield, fresh out of Richfield State with a degree in social work and a lot of dreams. After several years, when the dreams of fixing everything had crashed into reality and she had come to realize that change was dependent as much on the internal as the external, she felt the weight of that divine call to help her people become something even more than simply middle class, and Ron and Toni had taken on a new role as mentors. They had been the ones to guide her to Boston's Center of Urban Ministerial Education (known affectionately as CUME). It turned out to be a perfect fit and even gave her an internship at David B, funded, she suspected, again by themselves. They were a couple in their 60s and had swiftly become her role models of how to give yourself to ministry, but she still felt badly that she was drawing so much off their already modest, divided salary as a clergy couple. But she'd joined the great weekend migration of mainly Korean seminarians from Boston to scattered churches in New Jersey and, after three years, naturally segued into a part-time position as the new pastor of the fledgling Spanish congregation of David B. Jo had even attracted a few donors, like, of course, her dad, who also didn't have much, and stepmom, and a steady anonymous donation she feared was coming from Lawrence Fennelman. That was troubling. . . .

But finance was not the only concern demanding her attention. Back in seminary, she had promised herself she was going to equip her congregants with ministry skills, in the same way she had tried to develop the job skills of the people she had served when she was a community organizer. She wanted to teach them to preach and to visit and to minister to people in the hospital. Those she attracted to her services, however, were mostly the same ones who had once depended on her as their advocate and they were mainly interested in learning English to get better jobs than factory work (at which fingers were severely at risk) and domestic dead ends (slaving for the rich folks in nearby towns). Jo was working on grants to fund the center and to buy computers with educational software—which was all doable—but grants took time away from ministry. It was the all too familiar terrain of her old job.

She frowned. The problem was clear: She was turning back into a community organizer without the office or the status or the inside pull. She was more of an outsider now—a sectarian minister, welcomed, of course, but no longer mainstreamed into the social work community. Plus, most of the Spanish community was Roman Catholic and attended Our Lady of the Angels, the big Roman Catholic Church on Center Street. To them, a woman pastor was incomprehensible, and even some of her little flock, she feared, thought of her more as a nun or as their former community organizer back to serve them with a collar now.

Jo put a cinnamon stick into her apple tea—she really needed a lift tonight. Sure, she thought, Mercedes Del Rio, the Pentecostal minister, pulled this off beautifully at the mission down on Second Street, but Pentecostals were now accepted players in the Spanish religious community. Who ever heard of Presbyterians? Jo shook her head. Well, none of this was getting these papers evaluated. Whenever she got into an I'm-not-doing-enough-am-I-really-helping-maybe-someone-else-should-be-here-doing-a-better-job-than-I-am spiral—something that had plagued her even when she was a community organizer—she'd found that, if she buried herself in some small concrete task she had to do, the doubts would get shelved and—miraculously—sometimes somewhere in the process her subconscious (led by the Holy Spirit, of course) would suddenly suggest a solution she hadn't thought of before which would break the whole dilemma open. So, "Time to evaluate the student tests!" she snapped to herself, and mentally told Finance to put a sock in it right now.

Jo downed the tea, poured another cup, stirred it around with the cinnamon stick, and slapped down on the table the English reading assessments that she had done individually that evening, interviewing student by student, while she had the rest of the class paired up and puzzling through a simple assignment, trying to help each other pronounce sentences like "Should I take your dog out for a walk?" "What time would you like dinner, Madam?" "How much does this cost?" "May I have a hamburger?" "Where is the bathroom, please?" "You do remember Thursday is my day off, don't you?" in an accent somewhat recognizably North American. Jo spread the assessments out on the table, wondering whose to look at first. Maybe I'll do Nilka's first, so I can get encouraged, she decided, and shuffled through them for it. That's when she saw the corner of an envelope peeking out from the bottom of the pile.

Jo fished it out. What on earth was this? It was very official looking. Oh, right, this had been on her desk when she'd arrived for class. But, with everybody milling around and asking her questions, and she trying to lay out her lesson across the desk in little piles through which she could move seamlessly along as she made the most of her three-hour class time, she'd forgotten all about it.

What exactly was this? The return address was embossed with an impressive title: *"Dr. Angel Moreno Cueva de Piedra, Licenciado, Abogado, y Notario."* Jo automatically translated it in her mind, "attorney and notary public." She slit it open and read her full name spelled out after the Spanish equivalent of "Dear": *"Estimada Señorita Josefina Anacaona Archer y Mencia."*

Oh, oh, she thought, this doesn't sound good . . . and it wasn't.

"With a heavy heart," she read, "I am writing to you to inform you that your beloved Uncle, Señor Saul Inti Archer, is no longer leading us, but is now communing with Atageira, the Creator of heaven and earth, whom we also call YaYa and with YaYael, God's Son and our Savior.

"Before his departure, since he had no children, he left with me a will, naming you as the heir of his property and along with it his position in the Province of Independencia in the Dominican Republic, which is your birth country.

"Please come immediately to meet with me and his beloved trustees at his home on the beach of Barahona, where you visited and spent many happy hours with him and your family during your growing-up years.

"I know this will come as a shock to you and, perhaps, an inconvenience, but a passing makes its own schedule, and it is imperative that you, as the only living heir, come immediately, or as soon as possible, as there are many serious issues involved that must be thoroughly discussed before you can take control of your inheritance.

"With great respect,

"I am your most humble servant,

"Angel Moreno Cueva de Piedra,

"Licenciado, Abogado, y Notario."

The letter was signed in a tight, neat, hand.

Jo sat back in her chair in shock, holding the letter away from her as if it were itself the cause of this disaster. Her uncle dead, and she not even knowing so she could have run down to see him one last time? His property left entirely to her alone? What about her brother and sisters? They weren't going to take this lightly. And, further, how could she just suddenly pick up and go running off in the middle of all her job responsibilities? Especially her Sunday services? The woman she was visiting in the hospital? The grant she was planning to write? Her weekly class in English, which was a key to her mission and recruitment strategy?

But all those concerns were swept aside as a wave of grief poured over her. This was terrible. She had become increasingly close to her uncle as the years went by. True, he was big and boisterous, and always extremely busy, and oftentimes even absent when she and her family duly visited each year. Usually, though, he had been there to greet them, and then he and her father and mother would leave on some business she did not understand and be gone most of the time. But Jo and her siblings didn't mind. The house on the beach at Barahona was lovely and spacious. It had a pool and a garden and fifty yards away was the Caribbean Sea. The housekeepers were a married couple with several children about the ages of Jo and her brother and sisters, and they were like cousins to them in everything but blood, or so Jo supposed.

As Jo reached her teenage years, she had increasingly resented going, wanting to stay home in Richfield with her friends, but the visits were a family law that brooked no alteration. And that is when she began to notice that, as she was aging into maturity, her uncle, who had always managed to spend individual time with each of the children—going fishing with Ben, who was as wild as Uncle Sol was, taking Daniela shopping, which was Daniela's passion from childhood on, and playing tennis with Ruby, who seemed to be good at everything athletic and approached all of life as a competition to win at all costs—had come to center particularly on Jo, paying her a special attention that her siblings began to resent just a little.

First, he taught Jo how to play chess. Then, he took her for walks through the hills, explaining to her many details about the plants, the livestock, the wild animals, even the insects. He showed her where water was gathered or diverted for irrigation on the mountains. And he told her much lore about the original inhabitants and, particularly, about her ancestors, the Tainos, the people who had come to take possession of the island around a.d. 900–1,000, subsuming all the preceding tribes into their rich culture. For some five hundred years they had lived in peace, visiting each other across the islands in their long, straight canoes that seated eighty rowers and could traverse the waves between Kiskeya, their name for her homeland, "The Mother of All Islands"; Borinken, "Great Land of the Valiant and Noble Lord," but now called Puerto Rico; Xamayca, "the Land of Wood and Water"; Cu-va; and what is now Venezuela and the mainland; and on and on. And he told her a different story of the coming of Columbus and the *conquistadores* than the one she had learned in school: that the Tainos had welcomed the explorers as an answer to their prayers to YaYa for rescue from the invading Caribes, working their way up from South America, island by island, pillaging villages, stealing women, eating the hearts and livers of the men they captured to steal their strength and cunning. How disappointed they were that Columbus's followers had turned out worse marauders than the Caribes, given their superior weaponry. In fact, Uncle Sol had told her the tale so many times that Jo could later repeat most of it back, word for word, to the delight of her laughing siblings.

On Jo's twenty-first birthday, her father had insisted they celebrate this signature event in the Dominican Republic at her uncle's beach house. By then, Jo no longer minded. So many people turned out for it that Jo was shocked. The evening had involved interesting traditional dances and *areitos*, the music of the Amerindians on handmade instruments and, as a crowning event, the bestowing of a beautiful ceremonial dress with long, flowing sleeves on the baffled young woman. Her siblings were all jealous.

Since then, Uncle Sol had always made certain he spent much time with Jo on their yearly visits. He followed her work as a community organizer with great interest, asking her many questions about methodologies and procedures whenever she came. He was deeply interested in her decision to switch over to ministry. He told her he approved (which was surprising to her, since he was her uncle, not her father), but encouraged her to do "YaYael's work" in a way that did not eliminate the skills that she had developed in her social work.

"When YaYael was on earth as Yeshua, Jesus, he did much to share the good news of salvation in a healing manner that fed people and healed their diseases," he counseled her. "You, Josefina, have been gifted by the Great Spirit of YaYa to heal people in body as well as in spirit, and you must do both to fulfill your full ministry. It is a blessed calling and prepares you for greater work to come."

What that "greater work" could possibly be the young minister had no idea. But that was typical of Uncle Sol. In his loud and commanding manner, he always filled his speech with great, sweeping statements of large-sounding import. Everything was big about him. She imagined—and how could she not?—that such a presence would live on and on. For how could someone so—well—so larger than life be gone so completely, so utterly, gone? Certainly, everyone knew he had heart trouble. She knew that too. He was a big man and he was the elder brother to her father. But to be gone so swiftly! Jo began to cry as full grief finally overwhelmed her. For now she was struck with the realization of the extent of her loss as if her mind had meted it out in portions that she could handle, bit by bit. What she had lost in the sudden departure was a lifetime of her uncle's great love and full attention and complete concern. She would never have all this again. Not here on earth. Ever. Jo never broke down—she was too strong—but now she was crying steadily. Even so, she was thinking that, as soon as she could, she would call her father, but before that she must compose herself to be able to talk to him. That was Jo. Always cerebral, but with a passion in her commitments that ran deep.

But her concern for how and when to connect was unnecessary, as suddenly, in startling synchronicity, both the phone on her desk and her cell phone simultaneously began to ring.

4

Sobbing, Jo snatched up her desk phone, at the same time fishing in her purse for her cell phone. It was not her father, but her sister Daniela, who started right in, "Jo! Oh, I'm so glad you're home. Listen, I have a very important party Friday night. Could I borrow *the dress*? It's a masquerade and it's a little long but I could have it taken up temporarily, so it fits and . . ."

Jo groaned, which is not easy to do when one is sobbing, but she managed it. "Daniela, listen . . ."

"What are you—crying? What's the matter, Jo? I won't have them shorten the dress if you're that upset about it. Really, you hardly use it. You don't need to get so worked up about it! All you have to say is no. I can certainly rent some . . ."

"Danny," broke in Jo, "It's Uncle Sol. I've just gotten terrible news—from his lawyer. Danny, he died."

"What?"

"It's true. The lawyer didn't call—he just wrote me a letter—some official thing—it's awful."

"Uncle Sol," said Daniela and paused. "What's going to happen to his beach house?"

"Oh, Danny!" cried Jo.

After they hung up, Jo checked her cell phone call. It had been from her father. Jo punched the number without waiting to access the message. Her father answered on the second ring.

"Jo, I've just gotten terrible news. Did you receive a letter from Uncle Sol's lawyer? I was sent a copy of it, too. If so, have you had a chance to read it yet?"

"I just did, Dad. I was just going to call you."

"I'm so sorry, JoJo. Your mom and I will be right over."

Living in the same town—and it being about midnight, so the usual traffic of the day had dissipated—brought her parents swiftly to her side.

Jo was more composed now, but the ache was still new and her uncle's absence as large in her heart as was Uncle Sol himself and his presence in her life. The three of them sat mourning, huddled together. Her stepmother took hold of her hand. Neither of her parents made any attempt to call her brother or either of her two sisters.

"Do you think we ought to let Ruby and Ben know?" asked Jo once.

"No," said her father, sadly. "Tomorrow is plenty of time to bring them in on it. Ruby will process it swiftly. Ben wasn't home when we left. And you've already told Daniela. She'll certainly let the rest know. You were Uncle Sol's favorite."

"Yes," said Jo. "That was always the case. I could never make head or tail of it. Uncle Sol was so active and—well—dynamic. I don't know why he even noticed me. Ben is more like him—impulsive—always jumping into stuff headfirst. Ruby is the active one of us—he used to do all kinds of sports with her that I was no good at. Daniela's always been the prettiest one of us. I don't even know why he was interested in me."

"He was looking for something, Joey, something your brother and sisters didn't have but only you had," said her stepmother, patting her hand.

Jo looked up in surprise and caught a look passing between her father and her stepmother. "What do you mean?" she asked.

"Oh, oh, well, just, just something special in you that he appreciated," her stepmother faltered and shot a nervous glance at Jo's father.

"He was looking for one of you he could trust his property to is what your mother is trying to say," said her father quickly.

"Yes, that's it," said her stepmother with what sounded to Jo like a nervous chuckle, laced with a kind of relief.

"It's a sizable property," said her father, centering in on the prospect of inheritance.

Jo considered that. "You know, it's an answer to prayer. I've got so many things going here that need money. My salary, you know, is only start-up—it has a three year limit on the present grant. If the Spanish ministry isn't self-sustaining by then I'd have to reapply, and there's no guarantee it would be extended. I suspect that Toni and Ron are funding it at great sacrifice out of their own tithing. I know for a fact that they practice graduated tithing and are giving away something like a third of what they earn—and they don't earn much as it is—on the low end of presbytery salaries. Besides that, I have all these programs I want to do—and stuff I need like new computers and ESL software for the program you've been helping me with, Dad, and . . ." She broke off. Her father was frowning.

"Did I say something wrong?" Jo faltered.

Her parents were looking at each other. Neither of them said anything for a while. Then her father looked at her intently and said simply. "Jo, please don't make any plans about anything yet. Your mother is taking a leave from her work in the coronary care unit and I am dropping everything here. We are both needed there. We have to go immediately to the Dominican Republic—you know—to make arrangements and things. As the younger brother, I'll be considered in charge, and they won't do anything until I come. Give us about three days, then you come. One of us will try to meet you at the airport in Santo Domingo. If we can't, we'll send someone who will identify himself or herself as coming from me. That person will say, 'Baiguanex has sent me for you.' You will know then to go with her or him. They will bring you to Barahona and we will meet you there."

Jo looked at her father with astonishment. But, before she could speak, he added, "And, Jo, you must make certain that you bring the ceremonial dress that your uncle gave you. You must not forget it."

Jo's mouth dropped open.

"It's for the service, dear," said her stepmother swiftly and, to Jo's ear, a little glibly.

"We have to go now, Jo," said her father, standing up. "Use the credit card that we have jointly. Don't go searching unduly for cheaper flights on cheaper days, as I know you always do." He smiled warmly at her. "Sweetie, I'm not telling you to throw away a lot of money, but the most important thing is that you come in three days. Whether anyone comes for you or not is not important. Rent a car and come yourself, if no one meets you. You know the way, for there is only really one road, and you've taken it since you were a child. I am telling you to get there any way you can and at whatever cost it takes. But only go with someone who says what I told you: 'Baiguanex has sent me for you.' Otherwise, come alone. And, Josefina, bring the dress—please don't forget it."

When her father was determined to leave, no force in Richfield or anywhere else could stop this otherwise mild-mannered man, and he was now at the door dragging her stepmother gently but with firm determination by the arm. Just before he left Jo, he paused and said, "Let me pray for you." His prayer, instead of his usual "Dear and Gracious Heavenly Father," was in Taino, an adaptation of Jesus's Lord's Prayer. Jo had come to know it well, since it was now intoned at every family celebration and every gathering of her extended family in the visits to Barahona. Particularly poignant for her this moment was the petition to "Our Father (*Guakia Baba*) [for deliverance from evil] (*Juracan-ua*—bad spirit no; *Maboya-ua*—ghost no, *Jukiyu-jan*—good spirit yes), of God (*Diosa*)." Evil was the worst spiritual bad business— the great cosmic upsetter of all plans and all lives that turned hope to grief and joy to misery. It stopped everything in defiance of good and of progress and it had only one antidote—final grace to match its own finality. And her father called upon that now. When he finished, he embraced Jo and kissed her tenderly and then stepped out. Jo did not try to stop him and ask any of the questions racing through her head because she knew he had to spend the rest of the night securing plane reservations and packing.

But, just before they left, her stepmother stepped back in and said in a low, quick voice, "Jo, you know I love you as if you were my own daughter, and I want you to succeed in everything. Wait a bit, dearest. Before you make any plans to sell, there are some absolutely crucial things you need to know." Her striking eyes pleaded with Jo through her thick glasses. Then she hurriedly kissed her too and left.

Jo simply stood there in the doorway, gaping after them.

5

IF BASIL AND STAR thought the little patch of unfinished road up which they had nipped to see the little faces was a cause of concern in the otherwise well-paved highway north of Descubierta, they were totally unprepared for what lay to the south. They had begun the afternoon's adventure in good enough spirits, remarking how beautiful it all was, as the sight of the lake, now continually in view of the road, filled them both with its promise of a brand-new opportunity about to blossom. That they may have been misreading what that promise was exactly did not occur to them. So, even the poorer little towns to the south, desperately trying to ignore the lake's own ineluctable agenda and carry on business as usual, did not daunt their enthusiasm.

"Nobody's developed this," Basil kept marveling, as Star now guided their little truck up the narrowing road that ran along the lake's western shore. "Honey, I was looking at the map in the guidebook while you were sleeping this morning, and I think we should give Pedernales a miss." He waved down Star's immediate chagrin before it turned into a protest from which he feared there'd be no return. "I know, I know, it's on the Caribbean Sea and all that, but there's a huge mountain range between us and it—look at the map in the book—it's called the *Sierra de Bahoruco*, and I don't see any towns marked on it and no roads going through it, so, if they got 'em, they're worse than what we've been through already. Plus," he added quickly before she could speak, "the only way in is to cross the border into Haiti, and it's a long meandering way back from there."

"Wow," said Star glumly, reaching over to open the glove compartment, where she now stowed the guidebook so it would always be at hand. They'd folded the pages around the map so it fell open at the spot to reveal that Basil was, sadly, absolutely right. As he had calculated, all her fears of Haiti were back into play, so she closed up the book, dropped it into Basil's lap, and kept on driving.

"But, look, Star," he added quickly, now that he'd taken one toy out of her hand, to replace it swiftly with another—a good strategy that he'd often used in a con. "If we take that talky innkeeper's advice and keep going around the lake, I'm sure we can find some more decent-looking towns and figure out an angle for all this. Besides," he laid down his argument's clincher card, "this lake road runs straight to Barahona. That was one of our two targets. It looks huge, and it's right on the beach."

"Okay," said Star to all this, as she too was convinced as much by the little map as by Basil's argument that this underdeveloped area was their only choice if they were going to find a place to hide on the peninsula.

Basil had no idea what the northern shore was like, past the *caritas*, the mountain of little faces, but he suspected it was a lot like this western one: basically barren, relieved only by a few poor villages—but, hopefully, as well, some bigger cities. "Nobody's developed this at all," he murmured over and over again like a mantra, as he looked around pointedly for possibilities. As they drove, he would see an occasional little house between the villages and a few cows or a sheep or a goat with a kid scurrying behind it, making way for them. But, besides several large vehicles barreling by in the Dominican way, missing them by a hairbreadth and making the little truck shake, as the road was narrow, there were few if any cars on the road.

And then Star snapped him out of his reverie, announcing, "There's the detour!"

Basil wrested his eyes away from the lake and realized that the comforts of Descubierta were long gone. The road was deathly white. The detour led into what appeared to be a quarry. The detour itself was no more than a very wide service path, filled with stones. The sides of the path were blanched with a cement-like dust. In fact, the whole area was a desolate plain, broken only by the road construction. No oasis like the lovely little town of Descubierta was anywhere in sight—and to their right, in the distance, a forbidding-looking chain of high mountains rising into the clouds.

"What's that?" asked Star in a querulous voice, slowing the little truck nearly to a stop.

"That's Haiti," Basil said glumly, the map in the little book open in his lap.

She shuddered and started up the road, bumping and sliding along the stones and the ruts.

Basil glanced over at the lake. It looked equally forbidding now. It lay sullen, dissipating into a huge floodplain that had engulfed everything around it. All along its shore was a huge marshland of short swamp grass and the tops of engulfed trees. The water was obviously expanding at what must be a frightening rate. As he gauged it on the map, he noticed something else. "Starling," he cried, "there's another lake just like this, just to our right in Haiti! We're actually going through a little bridge of land between these two lakes. I think they're trying to meet!"

"Can't these countries do anything about this?" Star demanded.

He stared at her. "I think the land is disappearing," he said. He studied the map more closely and then came to another realization. "Star, do you remember when we were up on that 'faces' mountain?"

"Sure, what of it?"

"Did you see an island?"

"No, just water, and plenty of that."

"Well, there's supposed to be an island in the middle of this lake, right next to where we are right now—a place called *Isla Cabritos*."

"Goat Island?"

"Yeah, you see an island?"

Star craned over, slowing the truck to a bumpy halt, and surveyed the great body of water. "No."

"Me neither."

"What are you saying?"

"I think it's gone."

"You mean the land is disappearing?"

"Right—it's submerging."

Star opened her mouth and then closed it again. She started the little truck bumping along the road at a heightened speed, but had to slow it down almost immediately, as they were so jostled about that she was having trouble keeping it straight. "We gotta get outa here," was all she muttered.

The road at times dipped down below the cutaway hill and the mound of whitened dirt, making Basil feel like they were rattling through a valley of concrete, as indeed they were: thousands of small stones on a cement surface. But, always to the left, he could sense the lake, faceless, unfeeling, inexorably sending its water out to claim more and more land. The two lakes were reaching to each other with an underground handclasp only hinted at by this surface expansion. He shuddered. He did not like this lake anymore. Now he feared it.

"A truck!" cried Star, nodding her head forward.

A cloud of white dust shot up in the distance.

"A cow!" yelled Basil, pointing. There on the mound of dirt was a black cow lumbering along the crest. As the white mound beside them tapered off, they saw four more cows grazing on the stiff grass beyond the dust.

The truck rumbled by, and Star waved in delight. Then a motorcycle with two soldiers on it jolted by, and the road turned to the left.

"This looks like a city dump!" grumbled Basil. And, indeed, mounds of garbage replaced the mounds of dust. Some of it was burning, giving off an acrid odor. Cans and food waste and paper and clouds of flies spread for a quarter mile before they came to a perpendicular road with trees and shrubs on the other side.

Star turned left and started up the road, momentarily disoriented, assuming she was on the other side of the lake now and wanting to pick up the shoreline drive.

"Look, a crane," said Basil, pointing to Star's left. A beautiful white crane sat on a small tree limb, regarding them.

"There's one on your right—a brown one," said Star, and Basil turned to see an even larger brown crane in another small tree.

"There are cranes everywhere in these woods. . . ."

"Bo, look at the road ahead," cried Star. She stopped the truck in the middle of the road. What they saw was a panoramic view of what looked like the dissolution of civilization. Twenty yards ahead, the road simply disappeared. No wonder nobody was on this road except for them.

Basil got out and started walking forward. To his right, no more than six feet from the highway they were on, water was among the trees. As he walked the first ten yards, the water came right up to the edge of the road. All the little trees and bushes were standing in water. Two crude little rowboats foundered half submerged in it. Parts of their wooden bottoms were rotted away. Neither had obviously been used for a long time. Basil guessed they had been contraband carriers, smuggling drugs or human cargo in from the foot of the mountains looming to the left. Perhaps here they transferred to trucks. More likely they were just poor little fishing vessels that had succumbed at last to sea worms or simple rot, but positing smuggling was the way his mind worked.

The next ten yards of walking took him to the edge where the road was simply no more. He could not make it out under the surface. Even the trees and shrubs petered out as the lake itself took hold. He glanced behind himself. There was the lonely stretch of road with their little truck and Star's head in the driver's seat twenty yards behind him, watching him intently. And, then, he turned back around. Here was land's end. The road simply immersed and disappeared. Far away was the mountainous shore. He could see nothing on the other side but the foot of the mountain. Whatever the road had connected to was also long gone—and so would be the spot where he was now standing in just a short while. Basil backed up as if it were already happening—which, indeed, it was. The power of the waters. What was it exactly that the innkeeper had said? "You do not know the power of the lake or you would not be talking so."

Basil jogged back quickly to the truck and got in. "The trees are full of cranes," he muttered. "The road is so gone I can't even see it—plus, there's no connection on the other side. It's all gone—completely."

Without a word, Star threw the truck into reverse, backed it up quickly into a jolting K-turn, and barreled up the road. She flew by the detour turnoff and covered the short space to the intersection where this turnoff ended. There a group of young men and boys were cleaning off their motorcycles in an outpour of water that splayed across the road. "Which way?" she grunted.

"Right," said Basil, looking at the map.

Immediately, homes and gas stations and stores began to pop up. Star pulled into the first gas station they saw, for the gas gauge had dropped dangerously low, "bending the needle," as Basil always put it. He got out and eyed the attendant suspiciously. "Fooolll!" he said with the right intonation, and added, "Regulaar!"

"Fooolll 'er up!" smiled the attendant, popping the hose out and, sizing up Basil, he pointed to the meter, clicked it, and said in his approximation of English, "Zaaaro!" pointing with the nozzle at the zeros across the gauge.

Basil nodded and soon parted with the better part of three thousand pesos—about seventy dollars.

"Gas is expensive here," whined Star when he got back in.

"You're telling me!"

"It's all going out, Bo, and nothing's coming in," she warned him as they plunged deeper into the city of Jimani, the last great outpost before Mal Paso and the beautiful inland lake of Haiti, reaching across to Lake Enriquillo like the hands of lovers beneath a table.

"I know, I know," he snapped. "I'm thinking about it. I still think there's something in this lake for us. We just gotta put our heads together. There's an angle to everything that nobody's got a claim on. This is all undeveloped. Well, I can see why, because the lake's taking over everything. Okay, if that's the way it is, that's the way it is, but it's still got an angle. We just got to find it."

But the other side of Jimani did not look like it was going to yield any ideas to either of them. On the contrary, the road led them through a pass and down into a stark, completely undeveloped wilderness. The only sign of the human touch was the flotsam and jetsam of an occasional can or bottle or bit of paper lying here and there at great intervals beside the road or tangled in the low bushes.

Where Jimani had boasted a "Palace of Justice," a concrete and cement works, even some farms, this great plain was desolate, empty except for distant mounds of dirt and little patches of dusty shrubs that stretched far away to hills in the distance.

Behind them loomed the high Haitian mountains. Storms had gathered at their tops as if warning them not to cross over, having enough trouble of their own already to need a Basil or a Star. Happily for Haiti, neither of them was capable of considering it, though they missed a beautiful land and gracious people on the other side, since all they could see was the horror in their own minds. Similarly, all they could see on this side of the mountains was emptiness: the empty road, the empty plains, the empty hills in the distance. Worse yet, the lake was no longer in sight and the road had veered a distance off. In fact, it was so empty that every once in a while now a huge tractor trailer came running down the center of the road like an airplane taking off, using the center line for guidance, and then crowding over to the right lane, whizzing past them, then centering itself once again in the middle of the road. All that lined the highway, besides the bushes and small trees, was a lonely stretch of telephone poles, the only thing connecting the country to itself. When one of these poles sported a wind-battered poster for the election of a prospective president, Basil pointed it out. Then a little house came up by the side of the road in the middle of nothing but scrub on either side. Basil shook his head in wonder. Far off, on a distant mound of dirt he soon saw two men digging with spades. How had they gotten there? Why were they bothering to dig in one of many similar mounds scattered across the empty plain? Why would anyone want to live in such a place? He had no idea.

When the town of Limon—"the Lemon"—came up, it was like a benediction, announcing the end of the desolation. The land was still arid, and the very old and tiny wooden houses that sheltered the people seemed very poorly made from mere scraps of wood. But at least there were people. Then a number of cement houses began to appear around a large National Guard compound. Next to this, in what passed for the center of town, stood a dry little square alive with children playing and graced by the bust of a Taino Indian. The children were climbing up next to it and playing at its base as if clinging to it for protection. A little farther on, they saw a poster of Jesus Christ and a message about deliverance in his grace. The Savior and the Indian seemed connected. Even Star and Basil could feel a healthy exuberance about Limon, perhaps, they thought, because they also noticed an enormous sign announcing a government agricultural project commencing. All in all, despite the dryness of the land, they felt they had come out of the wilderness at last. The terrain was still arid, but they had seen people and they crossed the rest of the great plain, ignored the mountains of Haiti to their right, and then, to Basil's relief, began to glimpse again the great lake in the distance.

Now traffic was picking up somewhat. That is to say, occasionally Star would notice a motorcycle fly by, but Basil had become completely preoccupied with straining in the distance for the shoreline, since the road had diverged quite far from it. By midafternoon, the lake was now completely back in sight. At first it was still some distance away, and then it got gratifyingly closer, and then even closer, and then it began to get uncomfortably close. Suddenly, Star started slowing the little truck down, pulling as far over to the side away from the lake as she could go, but that wasn't very far since at the same time the hills had been encroaching and a sheer wall of rock had begun to hem them in. As she slowly crept ahead, they could see the lake side of the road falling away rapidly to a descending slope beyond which were the rippling waters. At first a few goats and cows and a little wooden house or two and even palm trees would fill the space between the road and the lake, but, as they drove on, they began noticing the road was lowering. Star was glancing at it continually as she drove slowly on. Every few yards it was dipping down, and the space between it and the lake was still narrowing. So she began pausing every few yards. All this time, Basil was staring intently at it.

"Bo!" she said.

"I know!"

There was no doubt about it now. The road was descending to meet the lake. Waters that had been some fifty yards away were now only thirty, then only ten, then lapping up among the trees. Shortly, the lake was beside the road. And then the road dipped down out of sight, and Star came to a sudden halt. The lake had crossed the road and begun to fill the other side, lapping up against the foot of the mountain wall that had been their far-side border. All that either of them could think about was the road submerged to nothing back on the western lakeside above Jimani.

Basil got out once again and surveyed the water over the road. "This is deep," he called back to Star.

Her head was down, and then she leaned out the window and waved the guidebook at him. "Watch out!" she called. "I just noticed they got crocodiles in this lake!"

Basil jumped back. "Crocodiles? They don't have crocodiles in this part of the world!"

"They do here! According to the book, they put 'em in here."

"Geez!" said Basil. "Who would want to put crocodiles in your water?"

"Says they're supposed to be a tourist attraction."

Basil shuddered and peered more closely at the waves.

"Says they're shy," shouted Star.

"Sure! Shy!" Basil picked up a long stick as a tomato truck rattled by, splashing the water around, and spilling several fruit as it bumped back up on the road ahead of him. Basil waited until the stirring subsided, then stuck the stick in and saw it was up several inches. "We shouldn't go into this," he yelled back. "We'll lose our brakes or—worse yet—get stuck."

"I don't wanna get stuck in some crocodile-infested lake."

"Me neither. But what can we do? We can't go back all that distance—and we got nothing to go back for. Lemme drive." He squeezed into the driver's seat, which Star, by this point, was glad to relinquish, and then he grunted as much to himself as to Star, "The other truck made it."

"It was three times our size!" Star pointed out with a nervous gesture.

But Basil just backed up a bit, then rammed his foot on the gas, and barreled ahead, splashing and sliding through the water until their little truck skidded up an incline on the other side.

They both heaved out sighs. Star laughed and patted Basil on the shoulder, and they forged on now with determination, ignoring the heavy trucks that whirled by, splashing through the invasion of the lake until they left it all behind them.

"This might be our future here," mused Basil, "if we can find a partner with some capital."

"Whaddaya mean?" asked Star.

"I'll bet we can buy some of this disappearing property real cheap and sell it to easy marks on the internet. All we got to get is a downpayment and then take off with it. It's not like they didn't get anything for their money. They got exactly what they paid for. It's beachfront property—at least for now. . . ."

"Right!" said Star, catching the vision. "We don't wait for them to come and see it to pay the rest of the payment! In fact—we can't!"

"Exactly!" said Basil. "In the meantime, we can take some pictures, which will look great. Real honest-to-goodness beachfront property. They don't need to know what it's gonna do in a year or two. For now, though, let's keep on going toward Barahona to get the lay of the land. I think we should spend a little time just checking out this huge opportunity."

"And the crocodiles?" asked Star.

"Jungle theme park," grinned Basil. "I'm getting a lot of ideas."

"Yeah," said Star chuckling, "Then it can become completely 'Crocodile World.'"

Basil laughed and they rode on.

Hungry as they were, they felt good. Perhaps the credit for Star and Basil's new positive attitude toward the southern region of Laguna Enriquillo should go to the fact that they now had a handle on a workable scam. That always lifted their spirits.

Perhaps the reason for their lifted hearts was that they had finally begun to leave the lake itself behind and no longer had its terrifying commandeering of the land so uncomfortably in front of them. In other words, their response was proportional: As the lake receded behind them, so did its terror. They were, after all, immediate sort of people. Their final lingering look at the great lake was through a strange portal in a large, grayish white wall of cement, with sidewalls that stopped halfway back, making a three-sided enclosure, but with no rear wall. Its entrance was a large opening with a cross at the top and the result was that it framed a panoramic view of Lake Enriquillo for those who stood before it. Paradise, one might say, through a portal. And this is exactly what Basil did say.

"This is great! Great!" he enthused. "We got to get a picture of this. Welcome to your summer home! Beauty! Boating! Fishing!"

"Crocodiles!" muttered Star, but he ignored her. He had his hands up making squares with his fingers, imaginary lenses through which to capture the best shot of the water.

What he didn't know was that he was standing at the entrance of an unfinished cemetery. The town was hoping as the years went by to afford to complete it.

Another possibility for their positive attitude was the astonishingly lush beauty of the land to the east of the lake. They had been through some beautifully prosperous fields of plenty, but nothing bested the region southeast of the lake. There was a hand at work in these fields that would arrest the attention of anyone. The magic of the land's obvious comestible wealth was working on Star's appetite. In a matter of minutes, she began complaining, "I'm hungry." They had left Descubierta at noon, but without the foresight to pack a lunch.

Basil smirked, however, reached awkwardly into his pockets, and began dropping things into Star's lap.

"What's this?" she demanded.

"Tomatoes. Wipe 'em off. That should hold you until we get to a food chute!"

They rode along, munching the tomatoes that had dropped from heaven, or at least off the tomato truck at the first spillover of the lake, and these allowed them to be a bit picky as several food stands flew by and then they entered a lovely little town named Villa Bahoruco.

"I see a television antenna!" Star exclaimed.

"I smell food!" Basil agreed.

"I wanna stop here!" demanded Star.

"Done!" grunted Basil, and he pulled in by a neat little roadside restaurant out of whose kitchen poured the wonderful smells of *cocina criolla*, traditional Dominican food. Soon they were feasting on rice and beans in a thick warm sauce, chicken grilled in garlic, fresh salad, and—to their delight—*platano maduro*, the sweet banana-like vegetable that was a Dominican staple, good for breakfast, lunch, or supper in all its many guises. This time it was sautéed in cinnamon and honey.

"What a lovely little town," enthused Star.

"It's the best looking one we've seen yet," agreed Basil. "Best" for Basil meant prosperous and, sitting as it did in the midst of great fields of waving green plantain orchards, lined with protecting coconut palms, and filled with mango trees, it was lush and luxurious, particularly after the stark wilderness from which they had just felt themselves delivered.

So, a very contented Basil and Star strolled from the reasonable little restaurant, paused before their truck, and got their bearings from the little guidebook. Now, with full stomachs, they envisioned from the map's promise that the rest of the trip was, indeed, a fairly straight shot to the coast and to the major city (by peninsula standards) of Barahona. More lush greenery spread ahead as far as they could see. And, as they traveled along, their first impression seemed accurate enough. A number of fair little towns and beautiful hills suggested to both of them this was, indeed, a perfect place to set up shop and exploit their idea.

But, just as they were ready to hunker down in Barahona and start to put the scam together, they made another intriguing discovery.

6

THE AFTERNOON WAS GROWING late, but Basil and Star were meandering along slowly now, savoring the fields of sugarcane, corn, plantain, and the orchards of coconut palms, mangos, lemons, and a variety of other delights.

"This is so beautiful," Star repeated over and over again. All the land seemed so spacious and enchanting. A little run of stands perched beside the road with folks who looked a little different than those they had seen previously, and all of them were elderly. No one appeared to be under eighty among them. Still, when Star waved, they would nod and some would flutter a hand back in her direction. Thick trees and bushes surrounded these stalls, which seemed to sit next to tiny footpaths that disappeared back into the overgrowth.

A feeling of contentment suffused them both, not least of which was because of the meal that glowed within.

And then, to their left, they came upon a site that would be of great importance to their lives. A lovely meadow gave way to a beautiful floodplain and both of their mouths dropped open. A different lake, spacious and elegant, bordered by forested mountains on its far side and complete access through wetlands on their side, lay glistening in the slanting afternoon sun.

"Wow!" said Star.

"Double wow!" said Basil. "This is more compact than the big lake."

"And way more beautiful," added Star.

"It is at that."

"And, look, there doesn't seem to be anybody living next to it and it's far off the road. It doesn't look like it's taking over."

"You're right!"

"And, look, Bo, there's some kind of sign."

Basil slowed to a stop, took in the sign, and then, without a word, turned into an empty gravel parking area before a small two-story building, newly painted in a festive light green. "This is an observatory," he said to Star, rather unnecessarily because her grasp of Spanish was better than his.

A woman emerged with a big smile, delighted to receive visitors. This, she announced proudly, was Laguna Cabral Rincon on her side and Laguna Cristobal Rincon on the far side, depending on which side one was on, and, therefore, which side laid claim to it. For short, it was called "Lake Rincon."

To their delight, they learned:

1. It was a government tourist spot, yes, but the land was both publically and privately owned.

2. It allowed fishing and boating, including sightseeing excursions controlled by the local towns.

3. In the morning, flamingos flew up from the lake and flew back in the early evening.

4. It had no crocodiles!

It was stirring information!

To the guide's gracious invitation, they mounted the stairs to the second floor, which turned out to be a barracks for the police who guarded the lake (none of whom were present, to Basil and Star's relief, as they were both allergic to police of any stripe or duty). The barracks provided visitors as well as the guardians with a wide porch that served as an observatory. The guide unlocked the small barracks and retrieved a huge handheld set of binoculars that she offered to them. First Basil then Star focused on the lake—it was breathtaking.

"Who are those people walking?" Star asked, training in on a small knot of women bearing large white bundles on their heads as they picked their way through footpaths in the green wetlands down toward the lakeside.

"The lake is very clean," said the observatory guide. "They are Haitians going to wash their family's clothing in the lake."

"Hot dog!" cried Basil. "It's so clean you can wash clothes in it!"

"This little lake has everything," said Star.

"It does indeed," confirmed the guide.

Back on the tree-lined highway, the Heitzes were no longer marveling at the plantains and palms and mangos and whatall. The dense foliage had now become an annoyance to them.

"We got to get above this all and get a decent view of what we're talking about here. Maybe we can do the scam at the big lake all right, but this one suggests some kind of legitimate tourist business we can horn in on. I don't see anything on this side like an amusement park or a boardwalk or anything. This all just looks like a nature reserve. It's begging to be exploited—I mean—developed."

"Right," said Star. "New jobs for the locals. Lots of tourists. Sort of like Niagara Falls without the falls."

"It's a public service we're offering," said Basil.

Nearby they found what they were seeking. "How about I take the truck up this little mountain a bit and we can look this little lake over before we turn back? This way we don't have to drive all around it."

"That's the ticket," said Star.

Basil turned the truck off the main road and started up the hill. The view promised to be perfect, initially showing a stretch of the shoreline that looked a lot more barren than what they had seen below. But no sooner had they begun to climb when the dense foliage closed everything off. Basil kept ascending up and up, but every time he thought the foliage would break for a better view, the trees and vegetation still obscured it. "Let me look at the map," he grunted, guiding the car to a little level place in a dip in the hill, leaving his foot on the brake, though it hardly seemed necessary since he was in a hollow space with the road rising before and behind them. "Let's see if we've got any other choices for an overview."

"I wonder what's up with the blue line," mused Star, staring out the window at the road, which she noticed now was cut into the side of the mountain like an unwelcome scar.

"I don't see any other choice, but these hills," grumbled Basil. "Maybe we're gonna have to drive around it to get a better look, but that would be a mistake today. It's bright enough now, but once night comes on—oh boy! There are no street lights and we want to be pulling into Barahona by twilight. We still need to find a place to stay. We've got a long way to go. There must be an opening some place in these woods!"

Basil took his foot off the brake, craning around, trying to see if he could get any decent glimpses of the lake between the trees, when an astonishing thing happened. He had put the little truck into neutral to pause and look at the map, but, before he could put it into gear, it suddenly began moving swiftly backwards—speeding rapidly up the incline behind him. "What on earth?" he exclaimed.

"Why are you driving backwards?" demanded Starling.

"I'm not driving backwards!"

"What are you talking about? You're backing up the hill like at sixty miles an hour!"

"I'm not! This truck is doing it on its own."

"Are you crazy?"

"No, watch this—I'll show you what I mean." Basil put on the brakes, drove down the incline to the spot around the blue marking in the road, and put the truck in neutral again. "All right, you see where we are?"

"Yeah, in a little mini-valley between two rises," said Star, peering around.

"All right, watch this!" Basil eased his foot off the brake. The truck began moving backwards. He put on the brake and stopped it. When he released it, it started up the hill again at increasing speed. "Okay, this is weird!" he said.

"What on earth is going on?" cried Star.

"I have no idea," he said, "but we're gonna find out."

"How on earth could a truck, without giving it any gas, take us up a hill backwards?" summed up Star, staring at Basil. "This is mystifying."

"We got to ask somebody when we get to town," concluded Basil.

Now theirs was a whole different attitude than they'd had before. Instead of savoring the countryside, they checked the map, got a gauge on exactly where lay their destination—the city of Barahona—then Basil floored the gas pedal and they went tearing down the road.

La Lista, a town of great interest to tourists, hove into sight. Its specialty was chairs, "manu"-factured from acacia wood in the fullest sense, that is, by hand, by artisans standing in the dirt front yards of homes under lean-tos, ten feet behind the stalls. This town made and displayed rocking chairs, high chairs, tiny children's chair and table sets, great grandparent chairs, primary school chairs, teensy weensy doll house chairs, every imaginable chair, varied and intriguing—but not to Star and Basil, who simply flew by. The "sleeping policemen" (as speed bumps are called in Spanish) had been installed to catch—even demand—the attention of passersby. At each of these many speed bumps, the vendors called from their stands, as they always did, "Look, look, very white, very tan, new and lovely—very, very inexpensive." Their neat little wooden houses testified to how popular their wares were to the gawking tourists they could size up and match to a chair before any of them had even maneuvered over the sleeping policemen, but the little truck bounced over the series of bumps at great risk to all its mechanical parts and tore out of town. Basil and Star were now on a mission.

By the time they reached Barahona, they were starving again, but now the wonderful smells of *cocina criolla* pouring out of the dining room of the hotel and casino combination they swiftly selected was not going to be enough to satiate them. This time they were hungering both physically and mentally. The answer to the mystery of the moving of their truck had to be a simple one, and every puzzle like that had an angle. Somebody here had to know.

Of course, they were right. Everybody knew the remarkable mystery of what caused a stopped vehicle to go backwards up the hill near Lake Rincon. But what Basil and Star could not have known was its puzzle—as immensely intriguing as it was—was not the greatest mystery that they had encountered unwittingly that day. An even deeper mystery lay, of all places, beside the little village of Villa Bahoruco into which they had stumbled for lunch—one so vast it had the potential to dwarf their sorry little schemes with an impact as tumultuous upon their lives as the lawyer's life-changing letter had been to Jo's.

7

J̵O WAS AWAKENED BY both her telephones blaring again. She had had a fitful night and had finally fallen into an exhausted sleep, but the two phones rousted her out of bed. What now?

"Jo!" It was her sister Ruby's commanding voice.

"Just a second, Ruby, someone's also ringing my cell phone."

"It's okay, that's me, too. I rang you on both phones, so I'd make sure I'd get you!"

"Ruby, it's six thirty a.m. Where did you imagine I'd be?"

"I understand from Danny that Uncle Sol is dead, is that right?"

"Yes," said Jo.

"That's too bad. He was a good uncle. I also understand we have an inheritance to check out." That was so Ruby—right to the chase.

"Well," Jo hesitated, "there is an inheritance and a will. Dad asked me to go down for the funeral and the reading."

"I haven't heard from Dad."

"He had to leave in a hurry last night."

"No doubt he wants us all to come. When are we leaving?"

"Well, I was going to call for a reservation today," Jo prevaricated.

"Good," said Ruby. "Include one for each of us."

"Did Dad say we had to fly coach or can we fly first class, since this is an emergency?" said a second voice.

"Is that you, Daniela?" asked Jo, astonished. "Are you on the phone too?"

"Yes, Ruby set it up."

"What is this—a conference call? Ben's not on too, is he?"

"Yup," said her brother.

"What are you doing up at six thirty? You never get up this early, Ben."

"Actually, I haven't been to bed yet," said her brother, "I just got in."

Jo shook her head, though none of them could see it. "Look, I don't know about this. Dad didn't tell me to set up a group excursion."

"It's okay," said Ruby. "He was our uncle too."

"Right," said Ben, "Good old Uncle Sol—and it's our inheritance too."

"Yes," said Daniela, "You don't want to be selfish, Jo, just because Dad was in a hurry and didn't get a chance to call the rest of us."

"Right!" Ben chimed in, "He probably figured you for the organized one of us, and knew you'd call the rest of us as soon as you could."

"Don't make the flight too early, Jo," begged Daniela. "I don't like getting up too early."

"Take us through New York, so we get a direct flight," ordered Ruby. "Don't put us through Miami or San Juan and make us change planes— there's always such a long delay in the airport, and one time when we were young—don't you remember?—there was a storm and we missed the flight and had to stay someplace overnight."

"You know, I'm glad you all called," Jo finally began to rally. "This is such a bad time for me, because I'm so busy. I have to find substitutes for Sunday services and my ESL class and someone to moderate an elders' meeting. I'd really appreciate it if one of you could help me by getting the plane tickets. The only real stipulation is that we have to be in Barahona in three days for the funeral. How we get there would be up to you. This would really help. Can you do it, Ruby?" she ended hopefully.

"I'd love to help you, Jo, but I've got to run. I've got an early practice for the girls' soccer team, so I have to be at work by eight o'clock and I haven't had breakfast yet. Whatever you decide will be fine with me. Bye for now." And she was gone.

"Danny?"

"Ah, Jo, you know I'm no good at this stuff. As it is, I've got to find a substitute for my route. It's not easy finding somebody who's willing to drive a bus full of middle school kids to and then from school on time. It's everything I can do to be on time myself. In fact, I have to start picking them up at seven thirty, which is just a few minutes away."

"I didn't mean this minute, Danny. You have all the rest of the day until two o'clock at your disposal!" Jo waited, but there was no reply. Daniela was also gone.

"Don't ask me," said Ben's voice. "I got to get some sleep. Ruby caught me when I was just getting home, and I'm exhausted."

"Ben," gasped Jo, exasperated. "You don't even have a job!"

"Well, that's not true!" snapped Ben, affronted. "I was working all night."

"At what? You sound like a night watchman!"

"I was working on my system."

"Your system? What—in Atlantic City?"

"Of course, at several casinos. I was tabulating the numbers and working on averages."

"Ben, that's not a job—that's a waste of your life."

"Hey, you sound like Dad now. When I hit the big score, everyone will be sorry they doubted me. But, any rate, Jo, Danny's right. You've got the touch! Whatever you decide will be fine with me too. I'm used to being up at all hours—and I can sleep on the plane. Just give me some lead time, okay? Love ya—bye."

Jo sat staring at the phone. She was alone with her thoughts. And they weren't charitable. It reminded her of their childhood. All her siblings had been so excited when their aunt suggested they adopt an orphan apiece—it had lasted about a week with Ben and Daniela. Ruby had persisted for several months, but when her orphan stopped writing, she stopped too. Only Jo had gone doggedly on year in and year out until recently when Jean-Jacques, her orphan and now her pen pal too, reached age eighteen and went on his own. He'd sent her a nice farewell and thank-you letter. She shook her head, but she was beyond being disappointed. She knew her siblings.

Her day lined up in front of her. Best thing to do first was to shower and get dressed, then have breakfast. Next, she had to call Pastors Ron and Toni and let them know about her emergency. Nilka could actually teach her and her Dad's classes together, with a little guidance, and both Toni and Ron would be there to help her out. They could also handle the high school equivalency part and, as always, make sure the rooms were open and the volunteers all had someone to work with. But helping out with the Sunday services was another story. Not only did they have their own hands full on Sunday, but neither of them had enough Spanish to do a last-minute sermon or a comprehensible job on the rest of the parts. The two other Latino pastors in presbytery were overwhelmed, so no help there for Sunday morning. She could ask Mercedes Del Rio, who ran the Spanish mission in town.

Mercedes was just over on Second Street. Jo had worked with her establishing the very same English as a Second Language classes she was now herself teaching when Jo was still Richfield's Hispanic community organizer. In fact, she and Mercedes had been overlapping classmates in seminary. Mercedes was younger than she was, but actually had gone to seminary before she did and had been in her final year during Jo's first year at the school, so they knew each other from both contexts. Jo admired Mercedes's effectiveness with her people and her example had been one of the reasons Jo herself followed the call to minister when it became undeniably clear that God was calling her. But Mercedes had so much going on herself it was hard to imagine she could cover for Jo as well, and, Jo was well aware, having attended one Sunday herself at the mission, Mercedes's own Sunday services were probably still being held at the same time. In fact, being Pentecostal, for Mercedes and her people, church was pretty much an all-day affair. So, the best bet was to call CUME up in Boston and see if the school could send her one of its Spanish seminarians who did not have a regular commitment—that would work. Next, of course, was get on the net and see if she could locate flights for four now. Dad hadn't said anything about that, but how could he object? Uncle Sol loved them all—and they loved him, each in her or his own way. Grief evokes different coping responses in different people. She had read about that in her pastoral counseling texts, but she had also seen it so often when she was a social worker. Her sisters and brother might be focusing in on the inheritance issue because the pain of the loss was too hard to deal with so soon. She was sure that was it.

But, before she tackled any of these tasks, Jo realized, she needed to pray—to throw herself on the mercy of God. She needed the everlasting arms of comfort, because she was in deep pain herself. She needed God's clarity to help her make the right decisions for what was best for the people whose spiritual growth she was nurturing, and she needed to submit her plans to God so that they would come to fruition, as she had recently read again in Proverbs. And, finally, she dreaded all the delay, expense, and red tape it took to arrange four last minute flights to a surprisingly popular destination. She needed God's help to get them all on a nonstop flight.

God's grace, as always, was with her. Two days later they were winging their way between Newark Liberty Airport and JFK International, scattered all over the plane, perhaps, but everyone accounted for, and then off to the Dominican Republic.

The flight, though nonstop, was four and a half hours. Jo had seen the movie and so gave that a miss. Instead, she worked her way forward from her last row seat across from the bathrooms to see how they were each getting on, only to discover all three of her siblings were fast asleep in their different rows. It was a lot like when they were kids, she thought. Jo, as the oldest, and still the most responsible, ended up as their little auxiliary mother, interpreter, and advocate. Maybe, she reflected, that's why she ended up a social worker. Ben, she figured, probably had the biggest sleep debt of all, no doubt followed by Danny, who was a party girl. Ruby, the athlete, kept early hours, but assistant coaching had a lot of physical demands and though Ruby, as all of them, was still in her twenties—Jo, of course, being about to exit—they all had a good reason to settle in on this red-eye flight. Jo, as mother hen, seeing all her chicks asleep, went back to her own seat and nestled in. All four of them had middle seats and, since most of the rest of the passengers were sacked out as well, it was a peaceful flight.

Thus it was a rested Archer family that woke up when the passengers applauded as the plane taxied down the runway at the international airport of Santo Domingo.

Over the years, Jo had seen a number of changes at this airport. As a very young child, she remembered it mainly as a large empty room where they would wait what seemed to her to be endlessly for their suitcases—not all of which would arrive—even though their little planeload would be the only one going through customs. Everything would be searched and her parents were asked many questions. Those days were long gone. Now the airport was shiny and new. A long corridor filled with wall-sized posters of beautiful palm- and water-filled promises of fun in the sun greeted them. The line for a tourist card for their stepmother, who was Puerto Rican, and now for Ruby, Danny, and Ben, who had all been born in Richfield, had grown longer and longer. Only Jo was Dominican-born and, therefore, holding dual citizenship, since her birth mother was Puerto Rican. Jo alone did not need to buy a tourist card. In addition, several carousels now handled the baggage and one had only to check which of these had theirs. The baggage of two planes each was now doubling up on the carousels, and porters came up and politely asked if their help was needed, having mainly ceased simply grabbing one's suitcases right out of one's hands, tossing them on a cart, and peremptorily hauling them off to customs. *Aduana*, as customs was called, had also been streamlined, and, although baggage claim checks were these days being carefully noted, most North American flight passengers were now waved automatically through.

So, pushing their carts with one suitcase each of no more than fifty pounds (a cruel hardship for Daniela) and two carry-ons, they exited the inner sanctum of passport control and walked the gauntlet of friends and relatives gathered on either side of a long exit ramp—their faces being eagerly searched by hopeful welcomers and then dismissed. Jo and her family made it to the door, but no one stepped up to them and said anything like, "Baiguanex has sent me for you."

"What now?" asked Ben.

"Now, I guess, we rent a car," decided Jo, though hesitating as she carefully surveyed the throng of mainly taxi drivers offering to take them anywhere they wanted to go. Neither her father nor her mother and certainly not an emissary had come for them. Jo was disturbed. Her father normally did what he said he would.

"I'll drive," said Ruby definitively.

In Puerto Rico, the land of their mother's and stepmother's births, a traffic jam is called *el tapón*, the bottleneck. The idea is that all the content of a big bottle is attempting to squeeze out a tiny opening all at once. That is a perfect description of what was happening when, with Ruby at the wheel, they raced from the airport to the capital in the first leg of their journey across the island to Barahona, their destination on the western coast.

Dominicans are a gracious and generous people, friendly and helpful, spending hours sitting together socializing—on their porches, in front of little shops, in gatherings of parked motorcycles at roadside bus stops, really anywhere they can gather. All of this camaraderie, however, evaporates completely when they are installed behind the wheel of any vehicle. The split second lights change—in fact, often several seconds before they do—horns begin to blare. For the countless motorcyclists, every two-lane road is a five-lane road, and four-lane roads are nine-lane roads. Yellow traffic lights for motorcyclists are barely suggestions. Stop signs are decorations. Stoplights will give most motorists pause, after four or five extra SUVs have gone through the red light, so that they now block the cross street, eliciting a cacophony of protest from the completely thwarted and seething oncoming traffic, whose dreams of progress have been maliciously dashed, but taxi drivers will not only turn right on a red light, but occasionally left as well. The sidewalks are, at times for some, access roads, even trucks bumping onto them and heading down them for half a block to take a right turn. And the normal state of any cross street in the capital is for all four entering streets to empty into the center of the crossroads, everyone crowding into each of them so that no one of them can progress until all the cars, trucks, buses, and motorcycles are sliding along each other's sides at glacial speed, no more than a half inch apart, nobody able to break free, and, thus, everyone's horn blaring at once. It was frightening how Coach Ruby took to this state of affairs with complete aplomb.

The dividing line into the metropolis of Santo Domingo proper is a passage over what is called "the floating bridge," an apparently permanent temporary structure only accessed by going the wrong way up a one-way street and then wrenching the wheel awkwardly in a harrowing last-minute U-turn to merge into the proper flow of traffic. Since this is the oldest city in the new world and many of its streets are, therefore, only paved cow paths, a lot of similar, dizzying anomalies present themselves. But Ruby was completely up for it, as she put it. Bouncing over the speed bump in front of the naval academy, Ruby dove into the city traffic with great relish, pumping on the horn like she was beating a conga drum. If every other driver had apoplexy when the front runners were not off the mark like Olympic racers two seconds before the end of a red light, so did Ruby. She matched every young Dominican woman with a cell phone and a large gas-guzzling SUV horn blast for horn blast. Assuming white lines were only indicators this indeed was a road, Ruby was all over the place, passing on the right—along with all the buses careening in every direction—as Ben cheered. Daniela and Jo huddled, strapped up in the back seat, cringing.

Major thoroughfares in the capital are often named for significant dates, and the Twenty-Seventh of February is the main street into and out of the city. It was loaded with clones of Ruby at the wheel.

One might note that the Republic itself is a beautifully lush green nation, and this is not by chance. Rain is frequent, and this day was no exception. As they all shouldered their way together in one great mass of vehicles, no one of which was giving way in any shape or form to any other, the sky suddenly opened up and deluged them with water. Every corner of the Twenty-Seventh of February Boulevard is filled with street vendors, washers throwing sponges on one's windshield and offering to wipe the splash off for a little tip, phone card representatives in colors coordinated with their particular company, fruit hawkers, mop sellers, water higglers, ice cream pushers, bonafide beggars—and, when it rains, suddenly some of these become windshield wiper vendors. Ruby managed not to hit any of them as she splashed through the instant flooding and soldiered on. Almost immediately the rain stopped, and they began working their way to the great circle that led to the country roads, when a red light halted them all momentarily and—splat!—a sponge hit their front windshield.

"Oh, for crying out loud!" snorted Ruby. "The rain just stopped!" Furious, she turned on the windshield wiper, gesticulating at a small dark boy, waving him away from the car. But Jo leaned out the back window and put a small bag of airline peanuts in the boy's hand.

"*Gracias, Señorita,*" he said, delighted, "*¡Dios te bendiga!* God bless you," he added in faltering English. Ripping the bag open on the spot, he stuffed it all in his mouth as Ruby scowled, floored the pedal, and they barreled off in Ruby's great haste to break free of the mass of cars and fly down the main road out of town.

"Ruby," said Jo, from the backseat. "You missed the turn. It's the little side road, remember? That's actually the main road, not the continuation of Veinte Siete de Febrero."

"Oh, rats!" snorted Ruby, screeching to a halt and, with her head out the window and her left arm now gesturing wildly at drivers swerving around her, she backed all the way up to the turnoff and insinuated them all onto the right road while horns blared, Jo groaned, Daniela screamed, and Ben grinned and hung on tightly. This took them over a bridge and into a new world. The industries that lined the city limits soon gave way to numerous tiny fruit stands which gathered as plentifully as fruit flies on a pineapple, some no more than buckets filled to the brim, harbingers of the countryside and the great orchards to come.

As the first glimpse of high distant mountains began to appear, Jo felt a sharp emotive pain shoot through her heart. Her memory filled with her many long mountain walks with Uncle Sol. She could hear his voice, see him stop to point out a particular flower, a significant medicinal herb, a scurrying iguana.

"Oh, look, beautiful pots," cried Daniela. "Can we stop and buy some?" Jo snapped back to see that the fruit stands had yielded to pottery stalls of all sizes and shapes, including eight-foot-high fountains made entirely of pottery, displayed with gushing water before large and impressive roadside shops and warehouses.

"No!" snapped Ruby, racing along on a now clear and fast road.

As in the city, where nearly no one receives a ticket without an actual accident, no matter how flagrant a violation the driving atrocity they are in the process of committing appears to be, here too the police simply lounged next to their motorcycles as drivers flew by like contenders at LeMans.

Jo noticed a culvert at the side of the road whizzing by, no doubt a run-off ditch for the frequent rains, but on the white cement at every crossover, someone had painted the words *Ya Cristo Viene*, "Christ comes soon." With Ruby's driving, Jo speculated, that might be sooner for all of them than any of them had expected. A road sign above them also announced the small town of *Semana Santa* or "Holy Week," which was certainly appropriate, and, even at their accelerated speed, Jo found the air suddenly filling with a sweet scent not unlike the incense at a high church service.

"Smell the cane!" murmured Ben, inhaling theatrically. Large fields of sugarcane were stretching now on both sides of the road.

But Ruby simply jetted through the expanding, panoramic countryside, flying by the little knot of uniformed children who emerged from the cane fields and waited patiently for a bus, racing by a knot of uniformed highway workers cutting back the overgrowth from the side of the road with machetes, and zipping by a lone walker with a black T-shirt that sported the puzzling inscription, "I hunt the Jabber wok." That seems appropriate to our present quest, thought Jo. And she remembered her Uncle had told her that Route 2, which their highway had now become, followed the very route the Taino Indians had taken to escape Spanish oppression as they fled to the sanctuary of the region where Jo and her family were now heading.

"Look at that!" cried Ben, and Jo's attention was once more diverted, this time to a truck with an open flatbed in which was crammed an entire baseball team, bats propped up against the sides, gloves in each lap, all uniformed and ready to play. Passing them, on a motorcycle, whizzed an entire family: father driving with a child in his lap, two middle-sized children wedged between him and mother, who carried a baby on her back in a tight sling. What a different world this was from Richfield, Jo mused, where nearly everyone who shared the road with them, including Ruby, would be by now ticketed or jailed for driving to endanger. But, as another motorcycle with a father and son sped by, the father awkwardly cuddling his son, his left arm stretched around behind his boy's body like a safety belt, she realized it was not so different at all. Maybe it was like the Wild West, at least on its roads, but it was a land full of love.

Finally, deep in the countryside, Ruby was forced to stop. A huge highway construction project had snarled traffic up as a great dump truck was slowly backing a load of stone into the quarried-out space that would no doubt be two new lanes. Out of nowhere, for there were no buildings in sight, cashew vendors, with the cash crop of this part of the country, were pushing bottles stuffed with cashews in through their windows. "A free gift," they were offering in Spanish and then in English. "You like. Trust me."

"Never buy anything on the street that doesn't come in a skin you can peel," father had lectured them over and over, so all of them said, "*No gracias, no gracias*," and, to the most persistent, waved an index finger back and forth, the island's universal symbol for "No means no!"

Twenty minutes of "no" to the world's most patient and vigorous vendors, at least in Jo's mind, finally ended with the bus in front revving up and nearly asphyxiating the four of them. But they were on their way again, and no one complained, even though the construction site had barely disappeared in their rearview when they were halted again, bumping slowly over the sleeping policemen of *Escondido*, literally "The Hidden"—an appropriate name, if there every was one, Jo thought, for a little town in the middle of nowhere.

"When we get to Bani, can we stop?" asked Daniela suddenly. "I need to get out and stretch."

"At the Sirena, right?" asked Ben, smirking. *Sirena*, the Siren, is the large department store at the very edge of town.

"Of course," said Daniela. "You can get sodas, and I'll just take a quick look at the reasonable styles for right now in the Republic—the stuff I brought along is sooo old! I bought it last year!"

"How about it, Jo?" asked Ben, craning around from the front seat.

"It's okay with me; we're making good time."

Ben checked down what he considered the pecking order, "How about it, Rube?"

"Whatever," snapped Ruby.

Bani is a full-fledged mini-city, a little town that grew and grew. It is not exactly on the main road, but—¡no problema!—its town council one year simply put up a one-way only sign on the main highway and rerouted everybody through the center of town. The "welcome committee," so as to say, was a fleet of motorcyclists asking all tourists if they needed a guide, and both Ruby and Jo had to convince them out their two respective windows that they were no strangers and knew their way around. All anyone needed to do was follow the flow of traffic, though, with countless motorcycles darting everywhere like flies on a picnic, this was easier imagined than accomplished.

Daniela was glued to the window, which she'd closed to discourage vendors, and her practiced eye sorted through the high-tech computer shops next to the paint stores, the open market, and the cafeterias and bars, searching for clothing shops that were a little higher class than the thrift store, the open-air clothing market, and even an assorted pile on a divider attended by two young men at a cross street who were holding up various articles of clothing for display according to who was driving each car stopped at the light.

"Oh, there's a place," cried Daniela, pointing to a little boutique with mannequins with big rears proudly displayed in the store windows.

Ruby glanced over. "You're so skinny, three of you could fit in one of those pants! Besides, the deal was Sirena and power drinks." Ruby drove on.

Finally, the big yellow warehouse-like structure that was Sirena came up on their right. Across the street, Jo noticed a little *colmado*, a tiny traditional market with cans of food, fresh fruits, and even a sign for aspirin and other pharmaceutical products. Sirena, of course, also had a complete supermarket, making up what appeared to be half of its megastore. But the *colmado* was still here. The old and the new surviving directly across the street from each other, she mused. It was such a symbol of the nation itself: the oldest one in the new world, with one foot in the future and one foot in the past.

They walked back to their van, Ruby downing her power drink, Jo with a small mango juice, Daniela sipping from a soda, and Ben with a beer— "Just one," he assured Jo and Ruby. Jo looked for the mountains beyond the fence. Again, two worlds: The fence encased the buildings, but the hills stood sentinel beyond.

The day was growing late on the far mountains, which were misting over, and even the near foothills were gathering shadows. They had traveled a lot that day—from Richfield on an airport shuttle to Newark, from Newark a hopover to New York, from New York a great bound to Hispaniola, and now from the airport through the capital, the countryside, and nearly onto the threshold of the entrance to the province of Independencia, the legendary refuge of the great Taino nation and to the seat of Barahona, the end of their journey.

Just on the other side of the cement works on the outskirts of Bani, Ben spied some cabañas, the lovely but thoroughly disreputable little "hotel motels" rented by the hour. "If it gets late, we can always stay in one of these," he offered.

"Never," said all three women at once.

Ben chuckled. "I wasn't serious."

"They have to hose 'em down after every guest!" growled Ruby.

"I was only kidding!"

The land beyond the cement works was becoming very dry. The air was filling up with the whirring of insects and cactus had appeared among the bushes and sandy soil.

The little roadside settlements were now mainly made of scrap metal and concrete. Ruby was racing along, passing cement trucks, when a huge tractor trailer came up on the left directly in her way. Ruby gunned the motor and charged head-on. Daniela shrieked as the truck flicked its lights at them and then Ruby slid seamlessly in front of the latest lumbering cement mixer and barreled on. Ben laughed and Jo shook her head.

By the time they got to Cruce de Ocoa, the land had become more fertile. Now it was all looking familiar to Jo. Huge plantain orchards lined with coconut palms and mango trees made a beautiful setting for stalls of skillfully hand-carved mortar and pestle combinations, hundreds of them of every size: some as large as a person, some as tiny as a druggist's tool. Daniela didn't bother to ask if they could stop.

The hills were closing in now and the terrain itself was changing every few miles, as if it could not make up its mind what it wanted to be. Here were green plantations and then hillsides of cactus and scrub grass and bushes. Then a large green valley announced the borders of Hatillo, hemmed in by small mountains to the right and to the left. And, at last the Caribbean Sea became visible. Now everyone was aware that they were nearing their second home.

Goats came running in and out of the scrub bushes, and Ruby was doing her best to avoid hitting the little kids scurrying after their mothers, oblivious of the rocketing death on the road.

The picturesque orchards of La Famosa foods whizzed by like a video, as did little municipalities like Charcao, nestled in among the fruit-filled mango and plantain fields. Together, they were like an advertisement, announcing that this was indeed a land of plenty.

Now Ruby had to slow down, because trucks bearing fruits and vegetables began tearing or lumbering down the highway, depending on their size, bringing this wealth to the bigger cities. When Este Bonia presented itself, Jo was delighted to see that the flowers still lined the fields: orange, purple, and white. It was a prelude to the magnificent entrance to Azua, the historic home of the Tainos. The name was a mistake by the Spaniards. The Indians in their long canoes coordinated their rowing with the chant "A-zu-a!" and the *conquistadores* mistook this for the settlement's name. The Tainos did not bother to correct them. These oppressors knew too much already. And, if thinking the rowing chant that could synchronize eighty or even a hundred and twenty rowers from the mainland of what would become Venezuela across the sea to *Kiskeya* was the name of their little settlement, so be it.

Love for this land of her birth, rich in personal and collective memories, filled Jo's heart as Ruby drove them through the red, purple, yellow, and pink flowers that heralded their advent into Azua, the ancient seat of the nation. Here was the neglected burial site of the great Enrique, the Taino warrior who had rescued his people with a cunning mastery of battle strategy that ultimately forced the invaders from Spain to sue for peace. Retreating before the heavily armed soldiers sent to capture him, he led them up into the mountains where their horses stumbled and their armor roasted them from the merciless heat of the sun. Then, when they were panting for water and their swords and spears had grown to be great weights in their hands, Enrique's warriors simply rained arrows down among their enemies. The hapless survivors threw down their arms, but instead of the slaughter routinely practiced by these enemy invaders, Enrique simply had his warriors round up the Spanish, relieve them of their weapons, and then he produced a Bible, requiring those who wanted to continue to live to swear upon it at peril of their souls before the one living God, the Great Spirit, and the Just Son of God, *Jesucristo*, who rules the earth and calls all to account, that they would never again kill or even strike a Taino. The oath included endless hellfire as the penalty promised to the Great Triune God, who had formed each of them and determined their fate. Useless to the governor for a goon squad now, the soldiers were soldiers no longer: the fear of God was in them. Finally, no one wanted to go and fight this deeply respected, ferocious but merciful liberator. The war was over, and the Taino nation survived.

Jo had stopped many times at the little church that Doña Mencia, Enrique's grieving wife, had erected at his grave a year after the peace treaty was signed and Enrique himself died. It was a monument in ruins. No one cared for it. The Tainos knew Enrique was not there, just his bones, as the bones of all those killed by the cruelty of the invaders or the diseases they had brought filled the hills of the province. Still, Jo's uncle brought her there to pray in thanksgiving to the great God who had given their people such leaders and they mourned the site together, the old man and the little girl who had now become his heir.

Much like Bani, the road to Azua was also deflected through the center of the city. But here a huge chemical factory polluted the air with an acrid, pungent odor that clung to the car long after the streets thickened with pleasant, small hotels with dining rooms, baby shops, hardware stores, and fast-food chicken and fruit stands that filled the rows of connected shops, as they had in Bani. So much history, thought Jo, but so little seen to the incoming eye. This was progress, she thought. And she mused, and not for the first time as she traveled this road, that progress is temporal, but all that remained, down through the ages, was the earth and its produce, the gift of the Creator, displayed so lavishly in the spacious valley that graced the passage into the peninsula.

After the turnoff to the town of Vicente Nobile, just before the peninsula commenced, the terrain began to transition back to semi-desert. The people filled the small and sandy front yards of their homes with flowers, little fruit trees, stalls of huge stalks of plaintain and mountains of ripe mangos in season to create a link, Jo always felt, between the spacious valley and the coming of the great orchards, ringed with coconut palms that heralded the peninsula itself. Towns and little villages came swiftly now, beginning with Jaquimeyes, one after another. By Palo Alto, in the well-watered entrance to the peninsula, vast fields of sugarcane rippled in the waves of trade winds blowing in off the Bay of Neiba, which the road would soon meet at Barahona, the point where it touched the Caribbean Sea.

Jo always felt a strange stirring within her when she crossed the little river, the Río Yaque del Sur, which marked to her mind the transition from the mainland proper to the land of the Tainos. The name of the river itself was a Taino word. The river began far away in the union of a number of tributaries that trickled down from the mountains of the interior. These little rivelets merged gently, almost unnoticed, as they wended their way to the valleys. Then, gathering strength in sheer numbers, they became together a commanding river that flowed for miles, irrigating and thereby enlivening all the land drinking thirstily from it, until it reached the peninsula, finally siphoned off all along its trajectory to become once more a steady stream that emptied at last into the sea. To Jo, it was so representative of her own people, the Tainos, a gentle tribe that gathered up the peoples who preceded them into a populous nation that filled the islands. Their strength was depleted, first by the Caribes, and then the *conquistadores*, until they became a small nation that emptied itself into all the nations of the sea of humanity, enriching everyone it touched with its knowledge of medicinal herbs, its preparation of foods, and its language that described each of its true treasures, the yuca, guayaba, guánabana—Taino names all—and with them all the rest of the banquet that created today's *cocina criolla*. The Tainos also

bequeathed their heroes to the island's history, like the incomparable Enrique and his magnificent aunt Queen Anacoana, the stateswoman and Jo's
direct ancestor, and all the rest of the wealth that is Taino lore and art and
history, embedded in the culture of the country.

As the family arrived at last at the impressive entrance to Barahona itself,
Jo took the great welcome sign that spanned the road as a personal invitation.
This time, however, the welcome would have to remain for her alone. If she
walked in the hills, it would be alone. She was entering an empty house. Her
house now. But what that meant she began to fear. Her father's and then her
stepmother's cryptic words came back to her. What "responsibilities" did they
mean exactly? Why did she have to bring the ceremonial dress? Why should
she not sell the house? What more was involved? Suddenly, what lay before
seemed larger to her than she had thought. And she was absolutely right—
right beyond anything she ever could have imagined.

8

"YOU MEAN TO TELL me there's a load of magnetic rock so big under this particular little hill that it can pull a huge truck or car backwards up a mountain?" demanded Basil.

"That is exactly what I am telling you, *Señor.*"

"That's amazing!" said Star.

"It is unique," said the desk clerk at the hotel with a casino that they had selected, because, as Basil put it, "You don't find a gold mine in a pig sty." "I know of no place else in the entire world that has such a thing," the clerk ruled with an interesting mix of helpfulness and haughtiness. Star sized him up: This was not a garrulous bonhomie kind of guy like Señor Feliz back in Descubierta, but he knew his stuff and was willing to play the host to the guests, even if they were tourists—a breed of people which he obviously did not personally care for, simply because they rarely respected such treasures of his homeland of which he was so proud.

So Star decided to respond appropriately, "Nowhere else?" she mused.

"And how come there's no sign?" asked Basil.

"There was a sign once and a restaurant announcing the Polo Magnetico, but they fell into disuse. Everyone knows that it is there. We take small children to it to amuse them, but that is the extent of it."

"It's like the eighth wonder of the world!" exclaimed Star. "I've never seen anything like it."

"Nor will you," said the desk clerk, and he turned away to answer a call on the hotel phone, for he had had drummed into him the universal reasoning of all innkeepers: these people have already paid; perhaps this is yet another customer who needs a place to stay.

Up in their well-appointed new room, Basil was already at work. "Magnetic World!" he tried, looking at Star.

She glared back at him with an eye more critical than he had wished. "Bo, it's on a hill. A hill with a steep incline with neither side usable. A hill on a public highway. You think they're gonna let you set up shop on a hillside road?"

Even he could not deny she was right. "What a missed opportunity," he said glumly.

But Star was thinking. "Not necessarily. I'm getting an idea."

Basil grabbed hold of the tail of his fleeting hope. "Whatcha got, honey?"

"I'm thinking about some jewelry I saw a couple of years ago."

"Jewelry?"

"Yeah. Something about magnetic hemma-something. It was like ankle bracelets or something. I can't remember it exactly. But, it claimed to have some kind of healthy stuff radiating out of it—you know, like healing properties. I don't remember exactly, but it was claiming it was good for headaches and hypertension, and I don't know what all."

"Wow, you're thinking about some kind of snake oil sales thing," enthused Basil, getting into the swing of things. "But, wait a second," he paused. "How exactly are we gonna mine this stuff? Remember, it's under a public road on the side of a steep hill. . . ."

"Who says we're gonna mine it? We can buy metal bracelets or pendants or earrings wholesale from anywhere and tell the suckers we got 'em from the hill."

"That's right, we could! So, what are you thinking, set up a little shop nearby and sell 'em? You don't think the locals would see through this?"

"Right now, I'm just thinking," said Star. "We gotta find the angle to it."

"That's my girl!" said Basil, proudly.

That encouragement was all she needed. The next morning at a supermarket in town, standing next to the magazine rack at the checkout where they had bought a meager amount of lunch supplies (and surreptitiously slipped a few other items into their pockets or big tote bag), it suddenly came to her almost completely full blown.

She was glancing at a woman's magazine while she waited for the checker, who was leisurely servicing a friend buying a basketload of baby items, when she flipped a page and discovered a horoscope in the back. Automatically, she searched for Virgo and translated that "something big was about to happen to you, so keep your eyes open."

"Horoscopes, new agey stuff—magnetic jewelry!" she cried, and then, "I got it!" The two women looked at her and then the clerk picked up her speed checking out the baby food jars. Basil, who was standing there holding some ham and cheese and bread and sodas and wondering if there was still enough room for one of these to disappear in his pants pocket, leaped an inch into the air and almost dropped everything.

"You got what?"

"The angle!"

"Wow! Really?"

"You bet!"

Out on a bench at the local central park, as they sat with the food between them, awkwardly brushing off flies while trying to cram some ham and cheese into little white rolls, she unfolded the plan before him. "Something new-agey," she said.

"New-agey?"

"Yup."

"That's not a little passé?"

"Nope."

"You sure?"

"They got it in the women's magazines, so it's still hot enough."

"Okay," said Basil, knowing this was turf he did not ordinarily trek. "So, what's the angle? How's it work?"

"We find a cheap little place somewhere nearby we can renovate."

"We got to have a partner for that, because you know we're broke," cautioned Basil.

"Of course," said Star. "That goes without saying. Some place people can stay. The angle is the healing power of the pole—see?"

"It's got healing power?"

"It does now!"

"Oh, right!"

"Then we come up with a name and a slogan."

"Like the 'magnetites?'"

Star glared at him. "No!"

"Okay," said Basil, "the Magnetic Healers, uhh, the Healers of no— no—something to do with the pole . . ."

"The Polarians!" cried Star.

"The Polarians! Oh, that's good! That's really good!" said Basil, gazing at her proudly. "I really, really like it."

"Make it like a quasi-religion."

"Yeah, yeah—like people could orient their lives around it."

"Or with it!"

"Of course! We could come up with a slogan like 'May the Pole orient you!'"

They both broke up with laughter.

"This is great!" said Basil. "These kinds of religions are popping up all the time. You can't lose. It's better than a real estate scam—it's like a heavenly real estate thing. Who's to say if you're right or wrong? I mean, look at all those motivational speakers. What sounds like a load of positive thinking proverbs gets a new twist and suddenly they're speaking at convention centers and making money hand over fist. We could even write a book: *How the Pole Oriented My Life*, by Basil and Star Heitz."

"Who needs a book? You commit yourself to too much in a book. It takes too long to write. You use our real names? Do you remember how many people are looking for us?"

"Right, no book."

"What we need is some capital."

"That's right and to develop the angle."

"But above all," said Star, "we got to find a sponsor."

And that was the moment Ismael Balenzuela, scion of ancient Spain, rose from a first-class seat on an Iberian Airlines flight from Madrid to Santo Domingo and strode regally down the ramp to customs. This was, in fact, his first time in *La Republica Dominicana*, but absolutely no one watching him would have guessed. As he entered, he sized up the tourist card situation and was among the first in line. He signaled to a porter and had his bags—first-class bags so they came out at once—picked up and carted to customs. He bantered lightly with the female checking his tags, smiled with a self-confident air at the gentleman at the checking booth, and paused at the first set of rental car booths. Within an hour, with a marked map, he was on the road.

Delighted to see an announcement for Valenzuela gasoline just outside of Santo Domingo, he counted it as a sign of inevitable progress as well as an omen: the natural world and its dead denizens fueling the world of today and tomorrow that Man (he always used the exclusive term) had created.

As he drove, he gazed with a proprietorial air at everything around him. It was poor, yes, he expected that. But something was stirring deep within him. Some kind of inherited memory, he decided. He had learned about the Tainos and how they were all exterminated by his ancestors, though he laid as much blame on the Italian Cristóbol Colón as upon the soldiers and adventuring third sons, as he was himself. Offered only a place—even if it was a vice presidency—in the family business, while his elder brothers were made president and chief executive officer respectively, he preferred to take a job with another, non-family-based development firm of worldwide resorts—one in which he could prove his worth and rise to the top. The assignment was Barahona and its environs on the western shore of *La Republica Dominicana* in the Caribbean. The company already was involved in the machinations going on in the Bahia de las Aguilas, and the other stiffly competitive struggles to develop the tip of the peninsula of Enriquillo and, to hedge its bets, it decided to put up something earlier at the entrance to the peninsula. Ismael's job was to find the locale and set up an all-inclusive resort that would bring in the money to finance the other beach developments. How hard could this be? Confidence he had in fistfuls, born, as he was, with the sense of entitlement that comes with an ancient, moneyed family that saw itself as the heir of the great *conquistadores*.

All through the little towns in his several-hour trek to the west, he could not help feeling like a conqueror himself. He had resources at his disposal, a company that believed in him, and the heritage that, to his mind, made all the difference. He noted all the Taino names on the map and in the towns and knew that, by these same culpable ancestors, they had been exterminated and replaced by Africans. It was a shame, of course, but, he defended his forbearers by noting to himself that there is a price to progress—the weak must yield to the strong. It is the way of the natural world.

This was the confidence that he brought into Barahona and, after driving up and down, surveying the available establishments in town, to the very hotel and casino where the Heitzes were staying. He was, one might reason, a lot like a hornet diving into a spider's web.

Basil and Star, lounging in the comfortable reception area, took his measure as he strode in. "Let's spring for supper in the restaurant," whispered Basil.

"Okay, but we've got to watch the spending," warned Star.

"I think we got a live one here."

That night, Star, sitting next to the maître d's stand in the restaurant, beamed her smile at Balenzuela as he stepped into the room and swept his gaze around.

He spotted her, of course—how could he miss her? Balenzuela grinned back.

"Oh, good, another American!" she greeted him warmly.

"Actually, Madam, I am Spanish from Spain," he replied in perfect English.

"Oh, I love Spain," she cooed. "What a wonderful country. Please, we would be so honored if you would join us. My name is Star. This is my— uh—my brother, Basil."

Basil's eyes flicked at her for an instant, and then he rose courteously. "Yes, dear Star's brother, Basil. At your service."

"I am Ismael Rodrigo Balenzuela Cordoba from Cadiz in España."

"We are so honored to share a table with you."

"Thank you." He sat down and a waiter set a place for him.

"Here on business, no doubt?" said Basil easily. "You are a man of obvious determination."

Balanzuela swelled a bit and thought to himself that these are obviously people of great discernment. "Yes," he said, "I am here on a development mission."

"How wonderful," said Star. "So are we."

"You are?"

"Yes, we are. And what do you wish to develop?"

"A resort here in Barahona."

"Ah," said Basil, "a beautiful little city."

"And you?" said Balenzuela courteously.

"Our work is of a more spiritual nature. We are here for the magnetic pole."

"The magnetic pole? What is that?"

"It is the eighth wonder of the world," Star assured him. "But no one here values it. We represent a new and deeply spiritual movement. We call ourselves the Polarians, after the mighty pole."

"And what does the pole do?" asked Ismael Balenzuela, intrigued by this charming couple.

"Let us tell you all about it," said Basil, warming up. "You see, when Columbus and his"—he paused a moment, studying Balenzuela intently, and then continued glibly—"his liberators came to this lovely land, seeking a new world of opportunity, they did not know that they were actually drawn here by a magnetic mountain, a pole as powerful as the North and South Pole. For us, it is the center of the universe."

"Really?"

"Oh, yes," said Star, melting him with her eyes and nearly taking his hand. "You see the pole is powerful. It can literally move metal! One can stop one's car and the magnetism will pull it backward up a hill and over into the valley below. You see, the mountain and the valley form two counterpoints—two poles, one active, one passive. This is the kind of reconciliation we are seeking in Polarism—to adjust the natural magnetism of our lives into a harmonious synchronicity ordered by the natural pull of the earth."

"Yes," tag-teamed Basil. "Just as the north and south poles orient the natural polarities of our world, the magnetic pole in Hispaniola orients the spiritual polarities that we possess within ourselves. The magnetic mountain takes the vehicles which are our lives and pulls them to its own rhythm."

A waiter cleared his throat deferentially at Balenzuela's elbow and asked if they were ready to order. Balenzuela glanced at the menu and looked up instantly. "Sea Bass," he said, definitively.

Both Star and Basil went for salads, the cheapest things on the menu.

There was a pause and then Balenzuela looked at them loftily. "I am very sorry, but I have to be honest. This sounds to me like a load of rubbish."

Both Basil and Star froze and stared back at him intensely, and then Star took a gamble. "Of course, it is," she said. "But this is the kind of thing that pays—and pays big with the right customers. No one at all has cashed in on this. And we mean to do so."

"And we're looking for a partner," added Basil.

There was a moment of crackling silence, and then Ismael Balenzuela laughed heartily. "And if anybody can pull this off and sell this nonsense to the spiritually confused, I think you two can."

"Are you in?" asked Star.

"I'm interested. But, if I'm putting up the money, I'm not talking about 50/50."

"We're not greedy," said Basil.

"But, we're not stupid," said Star. "If we're taking the risks, we need a decent cut."

"Like what?"

"60-40," hazarded Basil.

"80-20," said Balenzuela.

"Meet in the middle," said Star, "70-30."

"What is the outlay?"

"We need a place to bring folks to. A lot like a retreat center. Anywhere around the area will do."

"I think I can do that, but it's going to need advertising. Don't these kind of things need a book to push them?" asked Balenzuela.

"I told you," said Basil to Star and turned to Balenzuela, confiding, "I've already been drawing one up in my head: *The Dynamics of Polarism*, I'm thinking of calling it, but more a booklet than a book. Something we can bang out pretty fast and then distribute far and cheaply. We could make some kind of perk that every pilgrim to the magnetic pole receives the right to wear a small magnetic pin and to distribute copies of our 'bible,' which, of course, they buy from us at discount to them, but a good markup for us, and give away or resell at a profit. It makes them feel special, like a very spiritual state to be in."

"I can see it would be," smirked Balenzuela. "You know," he mused, "we could charter a cruise ship wherever the idea took hold and bring it here to Barahona."

"Sure," said Star, "devotees would begin feeling more 'polarized' the minute they got off the ship."

All three of them laughed uproariously.

"Do you imagine they'd think it's a good thing to be polarized?" chuckled Balenzuela.

"Well," said Basil, wiping his eyes, "Nobody wants to be 'depolarized' do they? It's like being lost."

"Yes," jumped in Star. "Unlike most religions, we wouldn't have a concept of sin and salvation, doncha see? Just polarization and depolarization. And all sorts of aids to help people get polarized."

"Look," said Basil, "We're not idiots. We realize explaining it to someone means they could steal the idea and do it all themselves, but we've got the inspiration and the experience and the skills to pull this off."

"I can see you do," said Balenzuela. "I confess that did cross my mind, but it would cause problems with my company back home. This, however, if it were worked carefully would be an investment. With the right presentation, it would fly, or I could simply do it myself with my own money, but, if I invested, I would have to know it would really work."

"Listen," said Basil, "I envision a fine line of magnetic products people can place under their beds or in the boardrooms of companies to draw people into harmony with a leader's vision. In fact, we could bang out another book, *Winning through Personal Magnetism*, about how to use it in business. . . ."

"Or in one's personal life, like one's love life," said Star. "Oh, that's good. I really like that."

"Are you really brother and sister?" asked Balenzuela.

"No," said Basil.

"I thought not."

"So, are you in?" asked Star.

"I'm in," said the daring, and also routinely quick to closure, heir of the *conquistadores*.

"You won't regret this. It's perfectly legal. We deliver what we promise," said Basil.

"So, what's the next step?"

"We need a dupe."

"A dupe?"

"Yes, someone legitimate that we can sell on the idea and have them round up all their friends for us."

"Ah, I see you really have done this before."

"Many times," said Basil, "but, I have to tell you, this is the best one yet."

"So, where do we find this 'dupe'?"

"Tonight, we'll go shopping in the casino."

"Isn't it a little early to start?" asked Balenzuela. "We don't have a center, any booklets, or magnetic bric-a-brac. We don't really have anything yet."

"It's never too early to find a dupe," said Star.

9

THE "BEACH HOUSE" OF Saul Inti Archer, or Uncle Sol, as his nieces and nephew called him, because they said he was so "big and bright" (and it was also the Spanish translation of his Taino name, *Inti*) was hardly a shack on the sand. It was a palatial two-story compound more reminiscent of a small hotel than of a getaway bungalow. The ground floor had a large dining room and living room that opened into each other to create a great room into which guests were welcomed through the main entrance. A bedroom for visiting dignitaries was hidden by a large mahogany door off the dining room toward the front of the house. It had its own private bathroom, and this is where James and Lea Archer stayed when they visited. A bathroom just to the right of the dining room served all three of these rooms, as well as the kitchen, which was as large as the dining room space and opened from the left into the combined public entertaining area. While visitors may have been puzzled at first why its kitchen was in the front rather than the back of the house, the observant noted that a porch in the left-hand corner had access to the kitchen alone, making a favorite place for meals to be served out in the air. Its access to the kitchen also served as its service entrance, thereby neatly sealing off the two back rooms that were not accessible from that porch. In that way, the house had front public rooms, but back private rooms. The very back corner of the house had become Uncle Sol's own private bedroom as his heart condition worsened and he was no longer permitted by his doctor to use the stairs. The final room of the first floor was his private office. A personal porch that allowed him to enjoy the breeze of the trade winds and his own private view of the sea was also sealed off from the great porch to its right that spread all the way around the dining room and living room until it reached the front door, ensuring him that he could entertain many guests while his private space was protected.

The second floor was the home away from home that Jo and her siblings knew well, with its three bedrooms with two bathrooms: one for the three girls and the other for the lone boy. Ben always grumbled that his bedroom in the front of the house had no sea view. But Ruby snapped, "You have your own private bath and balcony. All three of us have to share our bathroom, and it's no fun just sitting on our balcony, looking at the ocean, while Danny is dawdling and primping when it's my turn to spruce up!"

In the very front of the property, tending the gate that was the main access behind the large wall that sealed the entire compound in, was a large cabaña for the family that served Uncle Sol as his cooks, housekeepers, drivers, gardeners, gatekeepers, and administrators who oversaw the entire property, its maintenance and repair. They were completely devoted to "Don Inti." The home he had built for them was very comfortable. They had their own porch and their own little version of a dining and living room combination. Their kitchen was in the back of the cabaña facing the main kitchen so they could cook in whichever one they wished, depending on whether guests were present. The laundry room to the left of their kitchen comprised the rest of the cabaña's back area and served both houses. Three bedrooms and baths off a common hallway made a private space for the parents and their children to live. They loved the home that Uncle Sol had himself designed for them. To the left of the cabaña they had their own small herb and vegetable garden, and the fruit trees, spread around the whole property, served them with coconuts and other edibles that survived in a shoreline climate.

All in all, *Las Olas del Sol*, "The Waves of the Sun," was a sanctuary well beloved by all who came to find warmth and encouragement there.

As Jo and her family stopped their car before the great metal gate, she felt so bereft. This was the first time she had ever come to "Las Olas" without her uncle's warm welcome—and not even her parents were with her. She and the children were now on their own.

Ruby idled the rental car and blared the horn. They heard no immediate sound, so she leaned on it, as Danny covered her ears, Ben grinned, and she only stopped when Jo cried out, "Rube, that's enough!"

"I can go bang on the gate," Ben offered.

"Wait," said Jo. "They're very old now. We need to show a little patience."

"Maybe they're not here," snapped Ruby. Her hand was hovering above the horn.

"They are always here," replied Jo. And then a scraping sound began. First, a quivering of the metal gate, then the screeching of movement as the gate slowly, painfully lurched open, infinitesimally space by space, until a grey-haired man wedged his body in between it and the wall frame and walked it open enough to allow Ruby to edge in the car.

They drove inside and everybody but Ruby piled out.

"Don Ramón," said Jo and threw her arms around him.

"¡Querida!" he murmured, and hugged her to him as if she were his own daughter. "Such a sad time. I am so, so sorry for your loss—for all of our loss. Your uncle was a guiding light for us. Already we miss him so."

"I was thinking as we drove up," said Jo, "'Las Olas del Sol,' it is so much a part of him—it will be so different without him."

"Yes, as if the sun were eclipsed from the sky. All of us feel it here, but a 'sun' will shine again. It always has." And then he added something that Jo would think about later—again and again. "And, Josefina, you are here now to bring back that light." Then, he paused and looked to the others who were standing awkwardly at the car, a bit nonplussed by this display of emotion. "Ah, you are welcome all! We did not know that you would come."

"Of course, we'd come," snapped Ruby, leaning out the driver's window. "He was our uncle, too!"

"Naturally, naturally," soothed the older man. "We should never have thought otherwise. Always, you are—all of you—welcome. You are family." And they were mollified.

He looked them over. "Every time, more beautiful, Daniela—you are like the daylily in the garden, lovely from morning to night!" Daniela simpered.

"Ben, you are the strong cane stalk, capable of so much."

"Yeah, I got a system that might make us all rich!" agreed Ben and looked like he was about to embark on explaining it before Ruby's commanding voice sunk that idea. "Where shall I put the car?"

"Ah, Ruby—the rose—even your thorns are useful! Please, put it in your uncle's own slot. Do you know it?"

"Of course," shot back Ruby and prepared to barrel off.

"Wait for us!" cried Daniela." I can't walk in these heels."

"Yeah," added Ben. "I'm beat after the trip."

Don Ramón paused and looked to Jo.

"I'm fine," said Jo quickly. "You three go ahead. I want to stop and see Doña Lucia—and maybe if either of the boys are home—Tamaya is married, isn't she?"

"Yes, yes," said Don Ramón, delighted.

"And she has a baby," recalled Jo.

"She does indeed. And thank you so much for the lovely gift and sweet card that you sent. It was so thoughtful of you and it helped very much."

"It was from all of us," Jo faltered, "Danny, Ben, Ruby."

"Of course, of course," agreed Don Ramón, diplomatically, "And now you must see my wife, who is eagerly waiting to greet you."

"How is Doña Lucia?"

"She is well, Josefina. She is over in the main house. She has so much to supervise in the preparation for the dignitaries—we both do. They will be coming from all the tribal centers—Borinken, Nueva York, Kuva. They will be coming soon—the delegates for the 'passing and passing on' celebration. You are ready, *Querida*?"

Jo looked at him baffled. "Ready for what?"

"You have spoken to Señor Cueva de Piedra?"

"The lawyer? No. I received a letter from him, but we didn't speak. In fact, we've just arrived. We came here right from the airport. Dad and Mom said they would meet us or send someone, but they didn't. I'm worried about them. Are they all right?"

"Yes, of course. YaYa has not heaped sorrow upon sorrow. They are safe, but something has happened—not to them directly—but they have gone to the mountain."

"The mountain?" said Jo.

"Yes."

"Don Ramón, all of my life, when I've come here since I was a little girl, my parents and Uncle Sol would leave us and go to the mountain. They would be there while we stayed with you and your children here. I've always been puzzled by it—why to 'the mountain'? Uncle Sol would take me out onto the mountains to walk and talk, but—is that what they would do for a month? Walk and talk on the mountains?"

"No, Josefina. You are very wise. That is not exactly what they would do."

"So, what would they do on the mountain?"

"Nothing."

"Nothing?"

"No, what they would do was *in* the mountain."

Jo stared at him. She realized her mouth had dropped open. "*In* the mountain. What on earth does that mean?"

Don Ramón smiled and said, "Josefina, you have much to learn in the next several days."

"What is *the mountain*?" she demanded.

"It is your inheritance."

"*My* inheritance? You mean, along with the beach house I am inheriting a mountain?"

"No, your inheritance *is* the mountain."

"What? What about Las Olas del Sol? We are not inheriting this property?"

"No."

"Oh, it's going to our dad."

"No."

"Who is inheriting this?"

"No one."

"I'm confused. I thought I was Uncle Sol's heir."

"And that you are, my dear."

"Wasn't this his house?"

"It was his home."

"His home, but not his house?"

"That is correct."

"Who owns the house?"

"The Tribe."

Ruby, Danny, and Ben are not going to like this, thought Jo. And so much for my plans to sell the beach house and finance the learning center and the rest of what I'm planning to do in Richfield. "I see," said Jo, though she really didn't see at all. "So, someone else will be staying here, then."

"No, my dear one, this will now be your home."

"*My* home!"

"Yes, of course."

"Wait a minute!" cried Jo. "I'm not moving to the Dominican Republic—I have a life—I have my ministry in New Jersey. I can't come here!"

"Josefina, you really must talk with the lawyer. He will explain everything."

Jo's head was reeling. "I want to talk with my father," she insisted.

"And so you shall. Let us go up to the house. Your brother and sisters are no doubt waiting for you."

"And also—no doubt—getting in the way of Doña Lucia."

Don Ramón smiled, "As you say."

This was indeed the case, as Jo knew it would be. Ben was sitting in the kitchen when they arrived, eating from the various pastries the chefs were preparing. Ruby was barking orders to several patient helpers who had been moving furniture, and they listened to her deferentially as if she actually knew where everything should be. Daniela was among the missing. Jo guessed shrewdly Danny was up in the bathroom gauging the damage that the trip had caused her hair and her makeup. After that, she would be laying out the new beach attire she had bought in their one obligatory stop on the way.

When Jo finally rounded up her three siblings, they were none too pleased that they would not be staying at the beach house.

Jo tried to lay it out for them. "Many important people are coming from every tribal center to honor Uncle Sol. They must talk with each other and plan the celebrations and meetings and what they have to do."

"Well, we're important," huffed Ruby. "We are the *heirs* after all!"

Jo decided to let that lie for now. "We have the best of accomodations. We will be staying next door at Los Diamantes del Mar Hotel." Well, that changed everything, as Jo knew it would.

"Oh, that's great," enthused Ruby. "I love Los Diamantes."

"Yes, the proprietor, who is a staunch friend of all of us, is always gracious and willing to serve you," said Don Ramón.

"I'm for Los Diamantes!" agreed Daniela.

"I, for one, would rather stay at the Bravado Beach Hotel. I love Los Diamantes, of course—who doesn't—" started Ben, "but . . ."

Jo shot a glance at Ruby.

"No, you don't!" ruled Ruby in her most definitive coach-makes-the-rules style. "All you want to do is belly up to the gaming tables there. You're staying with us so I can keep an eye on you!"

"Hey, Rube, you're not my mom."

"Mom isn't here. I'm the stand-in!"

"You're younger than me!"

"Yes, but a whole lot smarter—and I'm not broke."

"But, I got a system I got to try out . . ."

"I'll go with you some night," offered Daniela to try to bring back peace.

Ruby shot her a withering glance.

"Let's get back to business," said Jo. "We can sort this out later. Right now we need to see how we can be helpful around here. There's a lot to do."

"If we're moving, I've got to go over to reserve our rooms," contended Ruby.

"Me, too, I'll go with you," agreed Danny.

"Don't look at me. I'm not the organized one," grumbled Ben, still miffed at being thwarted from camping out twenty-four hours a day at the Bravado Beach casino.

"Fine," said Jo, resigned as always. "You all go ahead. I'll be there later. I can walk over."

As the three piled out to the car, Don Ramón Romero leaned toward Jo and confided, "It's just as well, Josefina. For you will be staying here."

10

The next night, Basil and Star Heitz stood at the entrance to the casino of the Bravado Beach Resort, surveying the layout through the glass.

"Let's go shopping," said Basil, pushing the revolving door open for Star to enter. His manners were always gentlemanly in public. You never knew who was watching.

Both of them glanced around the entire room, taking in the present population with practiced eyes, and then centered on Daniela, standing beside Ben, as he played blackjack with fierce abandon. Ben had wasted no time in pursuing his goal. As promised, Daniela had tagged along. This was the first time they had ever seen this part of the city.

Through all the years as children they had been in Barahona, they had mainly stayed in the beach house, frolicking on the long, isolated stretch of beach, playing among the rocky promenades that loomed above it, strolling through the town, discovering. Being children, they could not enter the casino alone as they were underage and their parents had forbidden them to go there. As young adults, their visits to Barahona had become less and less frequent, since their parents had only insisted that Jo visit Uncle Sol. Only every three years were all of them urged very strongly to visit him.

Of course, no one called the Barahona beach "Bravado Beach." The residents of the small city suspected the hotel had simply invented the name to try to horn in on the reputation of the far more successful and il-lustrious Bavaro beach resorts on the eastern shore of the country. Admit-tedly, no one yet had confused them, as far as the hotel administration was aware, but you never knew. Tourists were not that bright. Daniela herself had always wanted to check out the Bravado because the name of the hotel had intrigued her. The beach, she was disappointed to see, was no more lovely than all the beautiful beach that stretched along the coast of Bara-hona, and the casino was like every other casino she had ever seen, though these, of course, were few. Daniela didn't like casinos. They were dark and closed in, so she couldn't be seen, and, besides, she didn't understand most of the games. Her money always disappeared quickly. She knew she wasn't clever like Ben, although she noticed his money disappeared as well. Perhaps not so rapidly, but just as irresistibly. This one was like the others. Security guards were everywhere—watching you as you entered—watching you at every game—watching you as you left. Ben breezed right by them, but Daniela found them unnerving, and she crept by, hesitating. Daniela was a social creature and this was all so antisocial. There were no windows, no clocks, just individuals, each of them a tiny island of desperation in a sea of neon-lit darkness.

She and Ben had paused for a moment after they'd entered. They had found themselves emptied into the far right corner of the casino through the same revolving door from the hotel through which Basil and Star would soon come. Daniela didn't realize it, but the door was wired to stop at the press of a button at any table if a dealer or a guard suspected anything amiss. It was a lot like entering a prison, though this one very plush. It had about the same number of security guards in proportion to inmates. To their left was a cashier's booth. Ahead were the games.

"Let's go check out what they've got," urged Ben.

Daniela tagged along.

In front of them was a roulette table. It was automatic.

"Uh huh!" noted Ben.

To its left were slot machines and at the beginning of the line an automatic bingo table. Just beyond it were three blackjack tables presided over by the same number of hard-looking females who flipped each previous card with the edge of the next card.

"Oka-a-ayyy," murmured Ben.

As the centerpiece of the room, standing in state, was a large, ornate, hand-spun roulette wheel. A half dozen people crouched over it as a slick-looking woman called the numbers.

"Hmmm," mused Ben.

To its right, to complete the center, were two smaller roulette tables and then the rest of the gaming space was devoted to slot machines. One row had nautical names—"Blackbeard's Treasure Chest" with a laughing Pirate generously opening his cache of booty toward all and sundry, "Pirate's Mate" with an image of a scantily clad buccaneer-ess smiling invitingly, and many others of that ilk. The next row was themed to the ancient Near East: "Pharoah's Daughter"—she was lounging seductively beneath a grape vine, "Rose of the Nile," "Potipher's Wife," all obviously sharing with the "Pirate's Mate" the same clothier. The third row was devoted to food—"Hot Tamale Sauce" and "Diablo Peppers"—suggesting to Daniela a bad case of indigestion. At two of these machines in the food-oriented row, "Hot Cha Enchiladas" and "Joltin' Ginger Snaps," a woman was losing twice as fast, playing two slot machines at the same time—each with one hand.

"Figures," observed Ben.

To complete the room, on a raised platform next to the cashier's table and running the entire distance of the right-hand wall until it broke off before a small service entrance, was a bar with a dozen tables scattered in front of it.

"This whole place gives me the creeps," shuddered Daniela.

"Let's try the blackjack," said Ben. "The rest of this is all suckers' games."

"What do you mean?"

"I mean," said Ben, "you never see anybody leaving these machines with a smile on their face, and the same goes for the roulette."

"You mean they're rigged?" asked Daniela, shocked.

"Oh, no, no," Ben countered quickly. "The houses are honest enough. It's just that they have so many extra chances to win—so many unclaimed numbers and unmatched slot combinations."

"I thought you came here to win," wondered Daniela.

"It's not about winning," explained Ben. "It's about how the staff treats you. Whether you have a good time—you're treated well enough. The house always ends up winning. Only a loser plays these games of chance. Only the skill games are worthwhile."

"I like roulette," nearly whimpered Daniela.

"You would," sneered Ben. "Lemme show you how it's done. Come on." He stalked over toward the blackjack tables, pulling her by the hand, as one would a child.

All of this Basil and Star were taking in intently. They couldn't hear the actual interchanges, of course, but they were watching the facial expressions, the postures: who was talking and who was responding. Star, particularly, was sizing up Daniela—her short but tastefully in-style dark designer dress (a really expensive investment she had actually saved up to buy), her high quality amber jewelry, and her habitually lost girlish look—and said, "I think I'll go and befriend that little lamb."

"Lose something at roulette before you head over so you don't attract attention," cautioned Basil.

"Of course," said Star.

While Basil ensconced himself at the bar, she strolled over to the nearer roulette table, played the number seventeen, then waited a bit, pretending to study the table while she watched Daniela and Ben with a well-honed peripheral vision. When Ben seemed absorbed enough in losing at blackjack, she played seventeen again, clucked her disgust, and then, mumbling audibly about trying something else, for the benefit of any guard who might be listening, she wandered over to the blackjack table, sidling up to Daniela. "I've been losing at roulette," Star confided. "How's your husband doing?"

"He's not my husband, he's my brother. He's losing," explained Daniela, adding, "He's got a system."

Star smiled her most confiding smile. "All men do." She paused a moment, gauging how deeply Ben was involved. He was obviously in plenty deep. "You gamble yourself?"

"Heavens, no," exclaimed Daniela. "I hate to lose."

"So do I. I think I've dropped enough for today. Losing gets boring. I'm going to go get a *piña colada*. You want me to bring you something?"

"No," said Daniela, "but thanks just the same. I'm really bored too. I think I'll come over with you."

"That would be nice." Star smiled again, radiantly. "I'll treat you to one."

"Thank you so much," said Daniela. "Ben," she ventured, "I'm going to go get a drink." It took three times before she could capture his attention enough to hear him mutter, "Whatever!"

Off she went to the bar with Star.

"Oh, here's my husband," said Star, perfectly feigning surprise. "Bo, dear, this is a new friend I'm just making. Oh, what is your name, honey?"

"I'm Danny. It's short for Daniela."

"What a lovely name," said Star. "My nickname is 'Peep.'"

"Oh, that's cute," said Daniela, "Bo and Peep."

"Yes, that's what all our friends call us."

"My friends call me Danny."

Star smiled, sizing her up correctly to herself as "some great displays, but not much inventory in that boutique." What she said, however, was, "And so, Danny, what brings you down here to the wrong side of the Dominican Republic? I would have thought a snazzy young jet-setter like you would be dancing the night away up at Punta Cana with the rest of the beautiful folks."

Daniela giggled. "I've come here a lot because my uncle lives—lived— nearby. He just died and we're come down to check out our inheritance."

An inheritance, do tell? thought Star. "Well, that sounds exciting, dear."

"I guess. Not really, but it is a nice place."

"Oh, it's a house?"

"Well, more like a mansion. It's a big two-story beach house up the road just around Los Diamantes del Mar Hotel."

This is too easy, thought Star. Next, she'll be giving me her bank account numbers. "Oh, my," Star enthused. "That's wonderful. Now you'll have your own place to stay whenever you come here."

"Oh no," said Daniela quickly. "We don't want to keep it—we want to sell it."

Bingo! "We?" queried Star.

"My brother and two sisters."

Hmmm, a four way split. The brother was the wastrel throwing his money away at the table. If the sisters were anything like she was. . . . "Well, this is very exciting, Danny. It's good to have money when you're young. You can enjoy it then, when you are still new at life, before you move on to deeper things."

Daniela looked at her, puzzled. "What do you mean?"

"Oh, you know, the things that really count. The deeper meaning of life."

"What deeper meaning?"

"Why, dear, haven't you noticed that people seem so disoriented. I mean, people all around us. No offense, dear, but, well, like your dear brother. So absorbed in that game that he doesn't even have time for you, but what's the point?"

"You're telling me!" cried Daniela. "He keeps saying he's got some kind of stupid system to win at cards and stuff, but he's always losing. When he gets his part of the inheritance, he's going to fritter it all away at blackjack!"

Not if we can help it. "I know, I know, sweetie." Star took her hand. "But, honestly, I have to confess that we were the same way—weren't we Bo?—before we got oriented."

"Yes, yes," Basil hung his head. "It's true. I'm not blaming anybody who's still caught in the wasted pursuits of life. There, but for the Pole, we would still be too."

"The Pole, what Pole?" asked Daniela. Was this about some Polish guy—some motivational speaker people were all watching on the net or something?

"Why, the Magnetic Pole!" said Basil with the awe with which one would describe the discovery of a brand new tax shelter. "You've heard of the Pole, no doubt, a woman as well informed as you appear to be—and as obviously spiritually sensitive?"

"Well, no," said Daniela. "Honestly, I haven't. But," she added quickly to preserve the high opinion they obviously held of her, "I'd like to."

You will, you will, thought Star, saying aloud in her most charitable tone, "Don't blame yourself, Danny. It's the best kept secret on the island. It's on all the maps, but no one pays it any attention. Right now, it's just a mark in the road, but the fact is that it's the secret to all human orientation. You see what I mean of course."

"Sure," agreed Daniela.

Of course you don't, you little actress, thought Star, but said, "Well, good. It just so happens that this evening, Bo and I are holding a very small and select 'orienting service.'" She stopped and checked her watch ostentatiously. "Why, Bo, how the time flies. Did you see what time it is?"

"No, dear, let me check." Basil flipped back the sleeve of his elegant guayabera shirt to display an elegant, if lower-priced, Rolex watch, once the possession of a gullible real estate agent who unwittingly took it off to wash his hands in a washroom in Newark, New Jersey, and never saw it again. "Why, Peep, my dear, you're right. Look at the time! It's nearing the sacred hour."

"There's a 'sacred hour?'" asked Daniela.

"There is indeed," Basil assured her.

"What's that?"

"Eleven eleven," he said confidently. It was ten thirty-five.

"Eleven minutes after eleven o'clock at night is sacred?" asked Daniela.

"It is, Danny, and in the morning too."

"Why is it sacred?" Daniela was out of her depth, but struggling to surface in all this deluge of information.

Basil swelled himself up in his best southern politician style, and, while keeping his voice down, intoned, "Because that is the symbol of the great orienting poles."

"What are the poles?"

"You know the poles, dear," confided Star, "the North Pole and the South Pole. These are at the ends of our world and all that we do and say and live are done within their guiding confines. And right near the center of our globe is the sacred Magnetic Pole, the one nearby here in this sacred land."

"This land is sacred?" Daniela was astonished. To her it was just the vacation spot she was accustomed to visiting every summer since she was a child.

"This island, known to us as Hispaniola," lectured Basil, "was once called *Quisqueya*. It was sacred to the original inhabitants. Its name means 'the Mother of All Islands.'" And he carefully sounded out the ancient island name with Qs, not Ks, repeating it twice and emphasizing the Qs.

Star looked at him proudly. The five minutes she had insisted on him reading in the guidebook was paying off handsomely. Now, if he just didn't overdo it. . . .

"I knew that," said Daniela.

Now it was Star's turn to be astonished. She really didn't think this little pigeon knew anything.

"I've come here all my life . . ." started Danny, about to give her own lecture.

Quickly, Star headed her off. "How fascinating, dear. But, now we are nearing 11:11 and we must hurry to the beach so we don't miss out on our orienting service."

"I've got to go to the bathroom first," worried Daniela.

"Of course, dear, we'll wait for you, but do hurry," urged Star. "It's over there." Star always reconnoitered the lavatories whenever she entered any public place. One never knew when one needed to duck into a nearby women's room to avoid someone—especially a powder room with a window that opened on a back alley.

"Quick," said Basil, as soon as Daniela left, "I gotta call Balenzuela. Get him on the beach—pronto!"

Ismael picked up the call immediately, "Yes, what is it?"

"We got a live one! Can you be down at the beach, right outside the casino by eleven o'clock?"

"That's pretty good on the 11:11, Bo," said Star, when he'd hung up.

"Yeah, we're certainly making this up as we go along."

"Well, you're going to have to come up with a fourth pole to fill out the bill."

"True, but otherwise we would have been stuck waiting until one o'clock, and I don't know if this sparrow's got the attention span to last two hours."

"You're probably right there."

Basil looked at her with expectancy. "Star, you came up with this scam. You got any more ideas?"

Star paused a moment. "Well, we gotta keep it on theme. How about the orienting pole within each of us?"

"Good enough. Especially for this peacock. We're good to go."

When Daniela returned hurrying, her new friends had taken on a deeper tone of sanctimoniousness.

"Will your brother be all right," asked Star, appearing to be concerned. And then, "Would he like to come with us?"

"Him? Naw! He's good for the night."

"Come then."

They stepped out into a bright star-covered night. Waves gently played along the shore, driven by the moon and the trade winds.

"I always think Barahona is so beautiful," said Daniela.

"No prettier place," said Basil.

"And the perfect place to orient," said Star, "don't you agree?"

Of course, Daniela did.

"Oh, look," said Star. "Here is a deeply spiritual friend we have known for many, many years. He has come with us on our pilgrimage to the pole. Let me introduce you to a friend. He is Spanish, from Spain. This is Daniela."

"A pleasure to know—you," said Daniela. She felt a little disconcerted because her new friend, "Peep," had neglected to tell her his name and she was too embarrassed to ask. But Balenzuela put her immediately at her ease by a heavy application of his most courtly manners.

"The pleasure is mine, dear lady. Any evening I have the delight to meet someone as deeply spiritual as my friends and graced with such beauty as well is a night I am doubly rewarded."

Daniela felt warm all over and blushed. "Thank you," she said.

"You know, friends," Balenzuela continued, still holding Daniela's hand as he turned to Basil and Star, "I know you won't believe this, but I have been feeling 'disoriented' all day."

"It's the place," said Basil smoothly, "and, of course, the proximity of the pole. It always pulls at us until we orient."

"How true, how true," agreed Balenzuela.

"Let's all assume the sacred position," suggested Star and, turning towards Daniela's expected confusion, said, "Have you ever done yoga, dear?"

"Yes," Daniela brightened.

"It's similar," said Star glibly, "but not so directionless. We are not simply involved with the self, but with something greater. We are looking to the poles. Here, let me show you how to adapt it." She sat down on the sand, speaking as much to Basil and Balenzuela as to Daniela. Lithe and young, Daniela followed her with the grace of a ballet dancer, while Balenzuela, and particularly Basil, lumbered into an approximation of what Star was doing. "Danny, see yoga as one step in the path to enlightenment," continued Star, keeping Daniela's attention focused on her so the other two could straighten out.

Balenzuela was smirking, but a frown from Basil cleared the signs off his face.

"Just so, my dear, just so," murmured Basil.

And then Star began herself to intone in a low and compelling voice, "All people are disoriented sheep. All of our lives we search for balance. May the Pole orient you!"

"May the Pole orient you!" replied Basil and Balenzuela just a half step behind him.

"Daniela," continued Star, her voice deepening with what suggested a profound and vast solemnity, "May the Pole orient *you*!"

"May the Pole orient *you*!" imitated Daniela with great sincerity.

Balenzuela smiled over at Basil.

"Heiress," Basil mouthed without sound.

Balenzuela's smile grew even brighter.

"Do you see how I am sitting?" Star asked shifting easily in the same voice to instructions. "I have one arm pointing north toward the North Pole. The other arm is pointing south toward the South Pole. My body is oriented to the Magnetic Pole. I, myself, am the fourth Pole—the Pole to be oriented."

"I am the fourth pole," murmured Daniela.

"Now you can know the truth," confided Star, almost trance-like. "This island is the first stop Columbus made on his voyage of discovery. Do you know why it was first?"

Daniela waited breathlessly, holding her position as exactly as she could.

"It is because he was drawn here—by the Magnetic Pole!"

Balenzuela almost fell over backwards howling. It was all he could do to keep it muffled in. These people were good, he thought to himself, really, really good!

Basil, long in practice at keeping a straight face while his beloved put out one outrageous fable after another, simply nodded, murmuring, "Yes, yes, how true, how true."

"For us, the Magnetic Pole is not just the center of our world. It is the center of our universe. The Sun to our Earths. It is where all nature meets. The adjusting conduit for all of the natural magnetism of our lives, melding it into one harmonious synchronicity—ordered within us by the natural poles of the earth. The polarities within each of us are reconciled! May the Pole orient you!"

"May the Pole orient you!" said all three in perfect response.

All the while, Star was putting this line out to snag this fish completely, she was wondering, how am I going to cut it off? She opened her eyes and sent a deeply meaningful glance toward Basil. He'd seen it before and was ready for it.

"We are Bo and Peep," he intoned. "Our mission is to the lost sheep who are wandering about without guidance to direction. We present to them a Pole, a sacred lodestar to orient their path—and their lives!"

Star suppressed a smile. Good ol' Bo.

"Tonight, as we have passed the sacred hour that symbolizes the orienting poles, and in deference to our new friend, sister, and devotée, I won't ask you all to join me and sing our great hymn of praise to the pole, 'O Great Magnetic Pole that Orients our Lives.' I will simply sing the first verse to close our sacred session." And then in a deep rich voice Basil sang softly, but loudly enough for anyone listening in to be attracted:

"O great Magnetic Pole that orients our lives,

when all direction's lost, cut by sorrow's knives,
O keep us now from wandering like he who only strives,
to know the peace you give us, as you orient our lives."
"Amen," said Daniela.

And then, with Star leading once more, they all said in unison, "Let the Pole orient you!" Then they hugged each other individually and altogether.

Through Daniela's mind seemed to race a dozen thoughts at once. In this one moment she felt her inferiority disappearing. This was it! What she had needed all her life was not to be smarter or more devout or more accomplished—what she needed was orientation. That was all. There was nothing wrong with her. She wasn't just a pretty face who feared age with the trauma of a sports star. Her life wouldn't be over when lines began to appear and the deep richness of her hair had to be replaced with that from a bottle. Look at Peep and Bo, she thought. Obviously in their forties, but vibrant and alive. They thought nothing of age. Nothing of money. Nothing of anything but the rich spiritual peace that came from being oriented with the universe at last. Now, she herself, Danny—no not Danny, but Daniela—a new maturer Daniela—could look straight into the eyes of the decisive Ruby, the daring and adventurous Benjamin—why, she gasped, she could even look face to face at the spiritual Josefina and even be more spiritually attuned to the universe than was her sister: the all so venerated "Reverenda" Jo. Oh, it was rich. Rich!

"Dear, one more thing I have to warn you," Star said leaning toward her, her face full of concern. "You are wearing amber."

"Yes," faltered Daniela. "Is that bad?"

"Well, no, not exactly, but the problem is that amber has a great magnetic quality. Oh, it doesn't affect the masses who are disoriented, but, now that you are beginning on the path to true enlightenment, it could be a serious drawback for you. You see, the magnetism of common things can conflict with the sacred magnetism of the Magnetic Pole. Things like amber can pull you back."

"I don't want that," said Daniela, startled and concerned. "What should I do?"

"I can take them for you, so you won't be tempted," said Star kindly.

"Oh, thank you. Here, here," cried Daniela, hurriedly taking the amber earrings out of her ears. "You are doing so much for me. Is there anything I can do for you?"

"Oh, no, dear, we Polarians—for that is what we call ourselves—never ask for money. You saw no collection plate at our brief orienting service, did you?"

Daniela shook her head.

"Eventually, as you deepen in the truth, you may want to share something to help our mission enlighten others, but always remember—and tell everyone who asks—it is a joint mission. We are all in this together."

"Together," agreed Basil.

"Yes, yes, together—always," added Ismael Balenzuela.

As Daniela walked back into the casino, she felt warm and found and oriented altogether. Ben simply waved her away. Los Diamantes del Mar Hotel was not so far away she could not take a taxi or even walk if she wanted to think. It was a beautiful night. It might take her a half hour, but she had so much to think about. One thing she was agreed upon with herself: She would not tell Jo or Ruby anything about this. She would keep this discovery and this secret strictly to herself. What Daniela did not notice, however, as she walked slowly home, was that she had not gotten her promised *piña colada*.

"Nice earrings," said Basil approvingly, as he and Star and Ismael went laughing back to their rooms.

"Yes, I thought they'd go great with my green dress," explained Star.

11

ALL NIGHT LONG, Jo was restless and her dreams were troubled. She woke up feeling cramped and queasy. She felt like she expended all her effort just to get out of bed. Her head felt sleep-drugged, her chest constricted, her arms and legs heavy. She managed to drag herself to the window and peered between the heavy curtains out across the water of the bay of Neiba, toward the stately white walls of Martin Garcia Point, where she saw the sunrise struggling with an equally difficult effort to free itself from a ponderously heavy cloud cover. She knew how it felt.

"Uhhh," she groaned and told the dawn, "I feel terrible."

The last several days had been so hectic. The stark interruption of sorrow and sudden travel piled itself on an already overwrought schedule of overcommitments. It added poundage to the already thick tonnage of launching her fledgling ministry to immigrants who needed so much to survive in the swift, urban, East Coast northern American society that demanded they hit the pavement at a run to keep up. All of this had begun factoring itself in with her new but now central spiritual dimension that had become the mediator for what she chose to do—determining to what she could say yes, as usual, and to what she now had to say no—all to baffled, uncomprehending stares. It had finally overwhelmed her. All this redefining of her role to people she had already served before, Jo wondered, maybe this was all a mistake?

She groaned again and leaned wearily on the window sill. How could she reinvent herself when the redefinition was only somewhat clear to her? Small wonder it was thoroughly murky or completely missed by most of those with whom she had already forged a relationship. She was their community organizer, returned to them, in their eyes, as a "nun" now—a kind of one-stop spiritual and social shopping that streamlined the meeting of their many needs of enculturation.

Jo groaned again. Two years of pending doubt came pouring down on her like a sullen rain, soaking her resolve, leaving her self-image totally bedraggled. *I guess it's because I'm here,* she thought, *back on safe ground in my childhood retreat. Here, where I've always felt safe, where I have to explain nothing about the way I look or the things we value or the weight of our heritage that always marked us off from the kids among whom we grew up in Richfield.* Multicultural enough to avoid out-and-out prejudice, still the mix in her adopted hometown of Richfield had invited cliques and marginalization. "Where are you from?" some of them had asked when she was very young. "Where's that?"

Then the tsunami of Dominican immigrants had swept across the state and the *Republica* had become familiar and even notorious in some spots. But even among the Dominicans, Jo and her siblings had been marked off as *indios.* Each of the siblings had sought to close the gap of heritage in her or his own way. Ruby had become a sports star—driven, excelling, hard, directed. Daniela had her beauty, and it got her into parties and into school plays—always in decorative, nonspeaking parts. She was not the football queen—her personality was not strong enough—but she was a member of the court—a "lady in waiting." And that term had summed up her life so far. Danny as well summarized herself as a "looker," and so she played that through high school like a trump card. But now that was over, and junior college had not worked out. She ended up driving a school bus to the disregard of a cruel new generation to whom she looked old and out of date. No wonder she dreaded aging, Jo thought—and not for the first time. *What else does Danny have—and what have I ever done to help her find more in herself?* And then Ben—his trump cards were devastatingly exacting.

Sick and helpless before pent-up feelings she could no longer hold at bay, Jo staggered off to the bathroom. The reckoning she had been holding off for two years followed inexorably and banged on the door of her heart like a summons server. This time she had no escape into her daily routine. "I've got to work this through," she muttered to herself. "I've been putting this off too long. I've got to face the inevitable. What on earth am I doing? This whole job change, the way things are working out with the family, this is all a mess." She felt like the summons had been shoved under the bathroom door and "Inadequate" was stamped on it as the charge. "It's all worse because I'm sick," she cried.

Three days in the Dominican Republic with its different water—all bottled now because you could not drink anything from the tap—its own current flus of the week that everyone was passing around and sharing communally, its specific subtropical mosquitos and microbes that formed a welcoming committee with the attention of a Bravado casino dealer sensing new amateur blood, usually meant the next three days were given over to *té criolla* and the mandatory proximity of a network of lavatories wherever one had to go. This time, however, she had not even made it through twenty-four hours. "I must have brought this with me," she lamented, "or I must be getting old." Thirty was looming like a watchful security guard outside a Barahona bank, looking her over intently. Reckoning was now like a financial counselor, shuffling through her personal accounts with a jaundiced eye and challenging, "Are you putting anything in reserve from this decade you just spent in overactivity? Have you got anything at all to show for it? Remember, energy is like income; it's not inexhaustible. . . ."

"Uhhhhhhh," Jo groaned and stumbled from the bathroom to the bed. "I'm not ready to do anything, but sleep." And that's what she did.

About eleven a.m.—nearing the witching hour of the Polarians, on tap twice daily whenever they needed it, and which, at this point, Jo, providentially, knew nothing about—Doña Lucia decided it was more than time to go up and see how her new guest was faring.

She peered in and said, softly, "Josefina, are you up?"

"Uhhhhh," groaned Jo.

Doña Lucia opened the curtains wide, letting in the light, and took in the situation at a glance. "Do you want some *té criolla* this morning, Jo?"

"No," murmured Jo, "but I think I need it."

"I'll be back," said Doña Lucia. "You rest."

Down in the kitchen, Lucia Romero took a dozen cherries out of the freezer, broke off two, and put the rest back in. Next to them, in another plastic bag, she retrieved a chunk of passion fruit, the seeds still in it, and then a medium-sized onion from which she cut a quarter on the cutting board on the counter. From the cabinet came a stick of cinnamon, and then she went out the back door to a tree over by the compound wall, picked off a green lemon, brought it back inside, and sliced it twice so that the four quarters were half separated, but still joined. All these she washed down with bottled water, then added enough to cover them in a small pot, placed a lid on it, and put them on to boil. When the mixture was bubbling away, she turned the range down and let it boil at close to simmer for about six minutes, then turned off the gas and let the concoction stand for ten more minutes. At the end of the time, she strained the liquid out through a metal colander, discarded the pulp, put in a tablespoon of brown sugar, and filled a mug with the pungent juice. This she presented to Jo, who sat up, drained it with a grimace, thanked her in muffled tones, and went back to sleep. Doña Lucia kissed her on the head and tiptoed out.

About midafternoon, Jo finally marshaled herself together and stumbled downstairs. She slogged her way to the back porch and eased into a rocking chair. "Uhhhh," groaned Jo.

Don Ramón, alerted that Josefina was finally among those present by a text message from Doña Lucia—since they both considered it undignified to shout from the main house across to the bungalow—found Jo slumped in her chair and sat down beside her. "Can you handle some breakfast, *Querida*?" he asked gently.

"I don't think so, but thank you, Don Ramón."

"My wife has already fixed you up with some *té criolla*, I assume?"

"She has indeed," murmured Jo.

"It will work wonders for you."

"I'm banking on it."

"The old ways are always the best ways," said Don Ramón Romero. "That's why they are still with us, because, in so many cases, they are best."

Jo had heard that adage times without number from this gentle couple who had practically reared her and her siblings each summer when their parents and Uncle Saul were gone, so she merely nodded. No reply was necessary.

"I'm sorry you are not well, Josefina. The lawyer was coming in from Villa Bahoruco to meet with you today."

Jo turned bleary, bedraggled eyes toward her surrogate "uncle." "Don't let the cracks in this earthen vessel deter you," she murmured, waving her weary hand down the length of queasiness that was today's Jo in the flesh. "Rallying is what I do best. I need to know what happened to my parents for peace of mind. Without that, I can't get better."

"Yes, that *is* you, Jo. But you don't want to overdo it."

"It is a family failing."

Don Ramón smiled, "It runs down the generations, but I really think you should rest today. Tomorrow is soon enough, and you will hear much. I promise it will be a lot for you to process. My wife is even now making you some chicken soup," he added reassuringly.

"What would I do without you both?"

Don Ramón beamed.

"What would Uncle Sol have done without you both? You have been so wonderful to our family—I can't imagine life here without you and Doña Lucia. In fact, I don't want to. . . ." She sent her gratitude to him with what would have been a dazzling smile, if she could have mustered it.

"It is our mission in life," said Don Ramón softly.

She thought he was joking.

"I'm sorry," said Jo in what was going to have to pass for hasty on this morning. "I have to use the bathroom again."

"Of course," he said, rising. "After that, go back to bed and sleep a little longer. Lucia will have some nice chicken broth ready when you awaken."

"Bless you," said Jo and staggered off. This was the best advice she could have received, and Jo was a lifelong connoisseur of good advice.

The day passed with applications of chicken soup, sweetened gelatin, steady glasses of bottled water, and one more steaming mug of *criolla* tea, and then Jo slept all night long. Her sleep debt, she mused, as she drifted off, must rival that of Ben's blackjack losses at Atlantic City—and then she was gone.

The next morning, Jo realized she was on the mend: not there yet completely, but definitely on the way.

Doña Lucia was delighted to see her up already when she peeked in. "Ah, the wonders of *té criolla,*" she smiled.

"Yes, and God's grace and your good care."

"Amén, amén."

"Do you think you are up to meeting with the lawyer today, *Querida,* or would you want one more day to rest?" asked Don Ramón, when she came downstairs at a steadier gait.

"Do I go there, or does he come here?" asked Jo, before answering.

"Wisely said," chuckled Doña Lucia.

"He will come here," Don Ramón assured her.

"Then, yes, I think I can talk for a bit—understanding my present limitations. . . ."

"At my age, that is always understood," smiled Don Ramón.

The three of them sat rocking on the porch while they waited, talking over desultory family topics. Jo caught up on the progress of each of their children, and they both asked many questions about the development of her ministry, whether she continued using the things she had learned in community organizing (to which she had answered, "Of course, they are very much overlapping in many areas"), exactly what she did as a minister, and how her two callings meshed and differed. Suddenly, in the midst of this, Don Ramón received a cell phone call. He glanced at it and then sat up quickly and said, "Excuse me, Josefina, I must take this one—it is important to our meeting today." He stepped off the porch and moved a brief distance away so as not to disturb Jo and his wife as they continued to chat, but they heard his voice take on a tone of reproach and a note of urgency before he closed his phone and walked back to them, frowning.

"Bad news?" asked Jo, immediately concerned.

"Somewhat," he said. "Not terrible news, but somewhat disturbing."

Doña Lucia simply gazed at him, waiting.

"Ricky finds he cannot come today."

"He cannot come?" Lucia asked, astonished. "And why not?"

"He cannot work it into his schedule."

"Cannot work it in?"

"That's what he says." They passed a look between themselves that made Jo pause and begin to rise. "If you both would like to talk. . . ."

They hesitated.

"I really need to make yet one more stop inside," Jo assured them.

"I'll make you more tea later, Josefina," said Doña Lucia.

Jo grimaced, said thank you, and left. *Té criolla* is admittedly an acquired taste that few acquire, but it does—indeed—work wonders.

When she returned, they picked up the inquiry into her activities as if nothing had intervened. Their questions were intelligent, detailed, probing. Jo knew they loved her as one of their own children—she had known them, after all, since infancy—really since birth—but this was closer to an examination. But, what of that? she thought. Who cares this much about me to want to know about the details of my life besides my parents and these dear people, my extended "family"? So she answered everything they asked until a phone call from the lawyer heralded his impending advent and then a second announced he was now arriving.

"I think I can walk you down to the gate," Jo offered. "I'm feeling better, really."

Don Ramón smiled. Jo was hardly up to helping him push back the heavy gate in her present condition. "No need, *Querida*," he assured her. "Our youngest son, Ernesto, has come to help us today. He will be staying on to assist me when the delegates arrive for the reunion."

"Someday we will have to get that gate mechanized," exclaimed Jo. "I don't know why it wasn't done years ago."

Both Doña Lucia and Don Ramón simply smiled.

"Some of the new ways are good, too," said Jo.

"Of course," Don Ramón assured her. "We do have cell phones, you notice."

Licenciado Angel Moreno Cueva de Piedra was a man Jo knew by sight, but had never really gotten to know. He came on business from time to time to talk with Uncle Sol and her father when she was here on vacation, but, since that never concerned her, they had never really spoken. He was a quiet man, gentle, and dignified, as were so many who visited Las Olas. He was somewhere in his middle age, sharing the same warm skin tone as she, her siblings, her parents, and the Romeros: lighter than Dominicans, but with a rich creamy olive complexion. Jo herself was tall and slim to normal with lovely long dark hair, a beautiful smile, and warm, encouraging eyes. She was not Daniela, of course, she had often told herself, with the features and figure of a model, or aquiline and all muscle and drive like Ruby with her short hair and flashing eyes and set chin, or sensual and promising a hint of future weight like Ben, but now altogether endearing with his expressive eyebrows, engaging, boyish smirk, pleasantly rounding face, and framed with the same smooth skin they all possessed. She was just Jo, the eldest, the one who stood in the back behind the sports star and the dashing gambler and the dazzling beauty and tried to take care of them all in her own humble way. Her siblings exhibited the best of their Taino heritage, her stepmom Lea had exclaimed over and over again, winning the young children's hearts—both her own and Ben's—with her praise, while Lea's simple—and, in that, profound—loving kindness won Jo's love.

The lawyer, on the other hand, was a small man—very small by their standards, some five foot or so—not over five foot two. He looked nondescript. He was very deferential, greeting Doña Lucia and Don Ramón with a cordial, almost old-world formality. He bowed to Jo, asking her not to rise or prepare to go anywhere because he could spread his papers on his briefcase and answer all of her questions as he was able to do so. He sat in a straight wooden chair that Don Ramón dragged over for him, scudded forward, and opened his briefcase to reveal a neat little portable desk top with an upright back in which was strapped pen, paper, and documents, all secured in with soft brown bands. Jo suspected this was the standard way he dealt with documents when he ranged about the countryside, visiting his clients. He even shifted a little around so that Jo would not be staring into a brown wall behind which he would be obscured.

"I have all these documents on computer as well," he assured them, nodding to the computer bag he had sitting by his chair. "We could look onto the screen, but I thought you might all want to have your own copies to examine, so I printed out copies of the will for everyone. He paused and looked around. "Señor Asenao is here already?"

"No," said Don Ramón.

"He is on his way then?"

"No, I'm afraid he's not coming."

"Not coming? He is not coming?" The lawyer's mouth dropped open. "How is it that he is not coming? Did he say?"

"Just that he was too busy."

"Too busy?"

Jo looked from one to the other. She saw Doña Lucia shake her head. All of them appeared deeply disturbed.

"This is not right."

"No, it's not," said Doña Lucia.

Jo just sat and waited. She was not Ruby, full of demands, wanting explanations on the spot—and those snappy, as well!

"Should we go on?" asked the lawyer.

"Yes," said Doña Lucia, "we must."

Don Ramón nodded in agreement.

The lawyer paused, said, "Well," and then "well," again, and became very serious. He hunched his shoulders and nodded to Jo, deeply deferentially, with the air of one who is dreading the answer he fears he will receive. "May I ask, please, did *he* meet you at the airport in Santo Domingo?" It was clear by his intonation the "he" was in reference to their missing guest.

"No one met us," said Jo, "and we did wonder about that." And then she added, as her first attempt to clear up some of the mystery of that whole fiasco, "No one did. And my father—you know my father, of course?"

The lawyer nodded an obvious, unspoken assent.

"Well, he gave me a message about picking us up himself or sending someone who would say, 'Baiguanex has sent me for you.' You must know that is my father's Taino name. But, no one came saying that or anything else. So we rented a car—on my credit card, I might add—and we drove here. Are we speaking of the one who was supposed to meet us? He must be *very* busy, indeed, neither to come as promised nor meet with us today. Is his presence so imperative that he must be here for us to meet? And, who is he exactly? Do I know him?" Jo looked again from one to another, searching all their faces. But they were all impassive now as only the heirs of the First Nations can be impassive.

"Not imperative," said Don Ramón, "but his presence would have been very helpful."

"And," added Doña Lucia, "well mannered."

"Yes, both," agreed Don Ramón.

"His assistance is going to be necessary for you to see your inheritance," said the lawyer carefully. "It will be very difficult without his cooperation."

"Not impossible," said Doña Lucia.

"No, not impossible, of course," agreed the lawyer, "but very inconvenient."

"Inconvenient?" echoed Jo. "What is this 'mountain' you spoke of Don Ramón? Something on his property—is that it?"

"No, no, Josefina. He is simply a guardian."

"A guardian?"

"Yes," said Doña Lucia, "one of many, but very important. He should be cooperating with us. This is very disturbing."

"I'm sorry," said Jo, "but I'm not making head or tail of all this. I have an inheritance, but it is not here. It is elsewhere. I have lost an uncle, but I have heard nothing about his funeral. I have two parents who are missing, but they are somewhere, though not here. Honestly, I am a bit sick today and perhaps my patience is not where it should be, but I'm feeling a bit like my sister Ruby. I would like to know—with all due respect, and I mean that sincerely—what on earth is this all about?"

Whether they would have answered her or not Jo often wondered afterward. But none of them had a chance if they had been so disposed, because at the very moment she had ceased putting her questions to them, a young man hurried around the side of the house, dashed up to them deferentially, and paused, waiting to speak. Jo recognized Ernesto, the Romeros' youngest child.

"What is it, son?" asked Don Ramón in surprise.

But, before the young man could reply, around the same corner strode a tall, and somewhat imposing man just over Jo's age, dressed in a gray sports jacket and black designer slacks. He had wavy black hair and a broad smile. He surveyed the entire back yard with approval, spending a moment gazing at the sea and what he could see of the beach behind the back fence. "Very nice," he murmured in Castilian Spanish. "Yes, very nice indeed." He framed his hands as if he were setting up a camera shot, swept them across the vista, and then with a satisfied grin turned toward the porch, and nodded at the gathering there, who were staring back at him, baffled. Then he turned around and spoke to someone just out of sight, "I'd like to see the house now."

To Jo's shock, around the corner came her sister Daniela and her brother Ben, obviously, eagerly awaiting some sort of response and then directions from him.

"Right this way," said Daniela and began mounting the steps at the far end of the porch.

12

WHAT WAS NOW A "public awakening," so as to say, for Jo and the private gathering on the porch at Las Olas had actually begun at the Bravado Beach Hotel early that morning.

Star and Basil had dawned in a state of excitement laced with caution. "We've got a couple of live ones here, but we gotta be careful," warned Star—the first words out of her mouth as she stretched and popped her eyes open.

"Yeah," agreed Basil, peering out through the beach hotel's mahogany-stained windows at another perfect Caribbean day. "This guy Ismael is all full of himself. He acts like he owns the whole place already. Five centuries ago he woulda been lethal."

"He might be now, if we cross him," yawned Star, propping herself up.

"Right, I can see that. He could also do us in and grab the whole shebang out from under us."

"Yeah, he's like one of those mechanical bulls they got. It's a wild ride, if you don't get bumped off."

"Don't use terms like 'bumped off,'" Basil shuddered.

"Well, how do you like this one, then?" asked Star as she swung her legs out of bed. "This fire's hot, we better strike!"

"Exactly," said Basil. "We gotta get a move on and get this guy looking at beachfront possibilities today around that Lake Rincon. As soon as you get dressed, let's call his room and get a field trip going."

"Right—that's the ticket!"

But ringing Ismael Balenzuela's room proved as fruitless as banging on his door, which they did next. Neither did a third degree on the front desk clerks turn up anything helpful. "No, Señor Balenzuela did not leave or leave a key while I was on duty," was all the first clerk could offer. "Perhaps the night staff would know, but they have all gone to their homes." The other clerk just shook her head "yes."

Basil scowled and looked to Star for answers, "Now what?"

"What," of course, was already in progress at Las Olas del Sol. "Dawn" for Basil and Star was hardly "dawn" for anybody else except Ben, and long before eleven o'clock Balenzuela had risen up, spruced up, breakfasted up, geared up, and glinted up, and had already shot off his first sally of the day, a broadside of charm fired just up the beach at Los Diamantes del Mar Hotel, a dazzling fireworks display targeted to wow Daniela and anyone else that might be of value. Ruby, however, was out running eight miles of deserted beach and Ben was still sacked out, so Danny got it all full force.

"Lovely lady," he had begun, when he recognized her on a lounge chair next to the pool, already stretched out in a chic bikini, working on her tan. "I could not let a day slip away before I found you again. You made such an impression on me last night." His teeth glistened in the early morning sun.

"How did you find me?" puzzled Daniela, squinting at him sideways behind her large, round, designer sunglasses.

"I called every hotel in the area."

"You did? Every hotel—just to find me?"

"Yes, every one until I found you." She took off her sunglasses to get a better look, and he gazed deeply, soulfully into her beautiful, empty eyes. With the help of the night staff, he had limited the choice down to three and Los Diamantes del Mar, right near Las Olas, was the best choice and his first call, but no need to mention that finding her was quite effortless.

Daniela stirred, reached behind herself and tied her bikini top and sat up, displaying all her beauty like a return salute from the shoreline.

The galleon of Balenzuela's ambition hove in closer to her battlements. "May I take you to breakfast?" he hazarded.

"I don't eat breakfast," said Daniela, swinging her long, sleek legs over the side of the lounge chair.

"But, perhaps, a morning juice?" He felt like he was talking to a child and he sensed it was definitely too early to suggest a *piña colada*, which she would probably only sip for hours, wasting an enormous amount of time.

"That would be nice," said Daniela.

"Then it's done," and his smile was like the sending forth of a small troop carrier, now landing on her beachhead. The invasion had begun. "May I get it for you," he offered courteously in full European manners mode.

Danny smiled, delighted. "Oh, would you?"

"Of course, dear lady," he assured her, his campaign now in full battle mode. "No, need for you to leave the comfort of your chair. After my quest to find you, it is a privilege to serve you." He nodded deferentially and strode off toward the hotel porch.

Danny simpered. He was sooooo attractive, she thought. With his wavy black hair, his dashing eyes, his courtly style, but so sure of himself. He looked to her like money, power, an ancient and deeply respected lineage—and all of this was true. By the time he came back, Danny had already envisioned herself resplendent on his arm in a black and white photo in one of those European magazines you could not read for the strange language, but thumbed through for the pictures of the celebrities at their dazzling parties.

Danny sipped the bright morning coalition of orange, pineapple, and passion fruit punch, guaranteed to put a sparkle in any brain, and the bright explosion of electrolytes in her system sparkled in her eyes.

Whether this cannon shot from Danny's ramparts made a dent on his decks, Ismael Balenzuela was unaware. His was a simple, primal nature: target the objective, move in to range, fire away, and take the flag. If he suffered any wounds of the heart, it would be long before he did roll call for casualties. Right now he was ready for another broadside, while he had Danny sipping the juice and giving him what passed for her full attention.

"Last night you were telling us a fascinating story about your inheritance here on the beach. I am a developer, sent from Spain to find such properties and help the owners realize riches beyond their dreams. What a joy it would be for me to help someone as lovely as you." He paused to gauge the effect.

Danny kept on sipping and looked at him steadily, drinking him in along with her fruit punch.

Let's go to phase two, thought Ismael. "If you would be so gracious as to take me to see this property, I will tell you what can be done—and how you can turn it into much money. Really quite a great deal of money. Thousands even. . . ." he paused.

"Okay," said Daniela, still sipping her punch.

"Ah . . . would now be a good time?" He paused. She was simply concentrating on the punch. There was a pause and he wasn't certain if she was even listening to him until she finished the drink, sucking up the last few drops noisily through her straw.

Then she said, simply, "Sure."

"Do you mean yes? Now would be a good time to go and see it?"

"Sure."

"Well, can we go then?"

"Okay, I'll go get dressed. My brother's asleep. My sister is out running, so she won't be back for a while. My other sister is staying at the house." Danny wrinkled her nose in a pout.

Balenzuela factored this all in: two more sisters beside the wastrel brother he'd learned about last night.

"Please do," he said, "though it would be a pity to hide such beauty," he added in what he considered a gallant remark.

Danny tittered a little laugh. "It's okay. I'll have shorts." And she strolled back toward the hotel like a model on a runway.

Ismael puffed out a huge breath of air and sat down on the lounge chair. As he watched her go, he thought of an observation Star had made when Daniela had left the night before: "Great for a poster cover, but there are a couple of guests missing in that conference."

But, when Daniela had primped and dressed herself and combed her beautiful flowing hair to her approval, she banged on Ben's door incessantly until she had roused him up.

"What?" he growled peevishly through the closed door.

"Get up!" Danny ordered. "We got the guy here from last night and he's talking about giving us thousands of dollars for the house."

Suddenly, Ben was up and he cracked open the door, "What was that?"

"I need you. I met a guy who works for some company that might make us an offer for the house. Maybe we can all go home with checks." She did not add: we can all go home in case nothing works out between me and this good looking prospect. If something does, I'll stay here.

"Money, huh? Good work, Sis. I'll throw something on and be right out."

"Hurry up. I'll wait for you here down the hall. This guy is pushy and he might have me off to the house before you get out here."

"Gotcha! Okay, I'm movin'." And Ben shut the door and she could hear water running inside. Danny went back to her room and sat on the bed, leaving her door open. Presently, she heard Ben's voice calling her.

"Let's go," he said.

Ismael Balenzuela was shocked to see Danny return with Ben in tow. Well, he thought, I'm going to have to deal with them all later anyway. Maybe, if I like the place, I can just take them all out to eat and deal with them all at once. That would work. Then I can get in touch with the company and see what my limit is. I'll have to find out what the place has been assessed at and then make a low offer and see how low I can keep it. I need a lawyer already. This is moving right along.

By the time Daniela and Ben had crossed the short space to the pool, Balenzuela had all these thoughts in line. He noticed she was wearing shorts, just as she had promised. He grinned. Vanity was certainly the key to this one, he assured himself. He didn't realize that, though Danny was certainly aware of her attractiveness and used it regularly as her tool to get by; hers had mainly been a statement of fact. Daniela always wore shorts when she was on the beach at Las Olas. She had done so since she was a little girl. Shorts was beach attire. Danny had a sixth sense for the right attire in the right setting.

Balenzuela welcomed them both with great cordiality. "Thank you so much for conducting me to this lovely homestead of yours. I treat family homes with great respect. It is a privilege for me to see it."

"Yeah, that's fine," said Ben, shaking his hand. "We wanta dump the place, but," he suddenly backtracked, "I mean, it's a great place and all—really valuable and stuff—but we live in the States and can't get down here much. . . ." He broke off.

"I understand, of course, of course," smoothed over Balenzuela. "All of us young move on. It's the way of the world, the natural rhythms of life."

"Yeah, that's it," said Ben, gratefully.

"We'll take you there, it's just down the beach," said Daniela.

"Thank you," said Balenzuela, proffering a hand to indicate she should go ahead. And he added unnecessarily, "Lead on, Lovely Lady." Oh, oh, he thought, I'd better tone that down. I don't want to do an overkill.

The short walk to Las Olas was dominated by Ismael's expanding observations to Danny and Ben on the suitability of the beach and of the location. But, of course, he cautioned them, it will need much work—much, much work to be suitable for sophisticated tourists. And that will take much, much money for development. So that will cut into the amount that can be paid to the heirs. But, of course, heirs can also become investors and triple their earnings, if they are enterprising enough. And on and on he went until they were at the great sliding door that let one into the mini-paradise that was Las Olas.

Ramón and Lucia's son Ernesto was delighted to see Daniela (whom he also secretly admired) and Ben (with whom he'd had such wild days of fun) and he welcomed them and their guest in—and then could hardly keep ahead of them as Ismael immediately took charge and propelled them all in a fast gait to the house.

And, that's when Ismael Balenzuela first met Jo, Don Ramón, Doña Lucia, and his first stymie. As one man snapped a briefcase closed, a second began to rise, a young woman started with chagrin, a dignified, elderly woman stood up and stopped Daniela with a gesture and, indicating several empty rocking chairs, said, "Welcome, please sit down and join us. I have some freshly made *pasteles* of the countryside and *chinola* nectar."

Ismael found himself sitting down in a rocking chair, thoroughly charmed by this gracious hostess.

"Now, what's this about, young man?" she asked, as she set a *pastele* before him and poured him some nectar.

13

Tʜᴇ ᴍᴏᴍᴇɴᴛ ᴡʜᴇɴ ᴏɴᴇ's feelings turn from chagrin to complete mortification is sometimes difficult to pinpoint exactly. For Jo, however, it came clearly when Daniela suddenly let go.

From the moment she and Ben had sat down with this strange man at Doña Lucia's invitation, Jo sensed trouble. She watched her sister and her brother warily: the way they sat forward and tight-lipped in their chairs, neither rocking, both concentrating on the guest they had brought. He was fairly young, early 30s, Jo guessed. Dressed in designer fashion, pricey casual elegance, an expensive white shirt over grey pants and matching grey Roman sandals, he was obviously at ease—a veteran of whatever kind of encounter was coming, she guessed. At the moment, he was smiling warmly at all and sundry, and no sooner had he taken his chair than he began to speak.

"Thank you so much for such a warm welcome. To whom do I have the honor to address?"

"I am Lucia," remarked his hostess.

"Ramón," grunted her husband, despite his normal, gentle air of equanimity, looking at this interloper as if he were some cockroach that had scurried across the porch and into the *pasteles*. What an impossible meeting this had been to organize, his frustrated gaze was announcing—one thing after another!

"I'm Jo," said Jo, simply, studying him carefully.

"Cueva de Piedra," said the little man and he added, "a lawyer."

"Ah, this is indeed a happy meeting. I need a good lawyer. Perhaps, we can talk soon? But, first, let me introduce myself." Ismael paused for a moment and beamed on the gathering, dramatically taking each individually into his confidence. This took a moment as his eyes engaged each of them in turn, sending out a message of complete candor and good will. Then, he announced with a flourish. "I am Ismael Balenzuela. I am the representative of the Encomienda Development Corporation—the EDC, or E-corp, as we affectionately call it. Ours is an ancient and respected properties development company—we are multinational in scope. I have been sent here to this wonderful country to locate and develop properties for E-corp into resorts, at first, and then also businesses, upscale homes, and whatever your lovely nation needs to serve its progress. Ours is a wide vision. Our specialty at E-corp is assisting more fledging nations to catch up with the contemporary world. Our specialty is underdeveloped nations." He paused to let that sink in. Then he sailed on. "Believe me, dear friends, we are much more than simply real estate agents: E-corp is a wish-pursuer and dream-fulfiller. Our focus is people, not simply property. We want everyone to win and our joy is to help owners like you realize riches beyond your dreams." He paused to gauge the effect.

Apoplexy would have been a nearly accurate description of the reaction of this particular gathering. But this is not what Ismael saw. What he saw was impassiveness, the impassiveness that people of the First Nation adopt when they confront the outrageous.

He took it for confusion. "I know this must sound sudden and quite shocking to you all. But, really, if you think about it, it's not. This lovely lady," he indicated Daniela, "has told me of your recent loss. I am devastated, too. So deeply sorry. She tells me that this property is the inheritance of the heirs who live in the great United States and do not want to be encumbered with it. This is where E-corp can be so helpful to all of you. As you know, the connection between Spain and this Republic is a deep and ancient one. We first discovered this lovely island centuries ago and helped this side of it become the great nation that it is today. The ancestors of E-corp, the great liberators, saw its potential immediately and set about helping the natives realize its full potential."

If Balenzuela had suddenly rose and slapped each of his hosts individually and soundly in their faces, he could not have made a more serious social blunder. Don Ramón's mouth dropped open. But, before he could speak, Balenzuela launched into his pitch.

"I can see potential here—great potential that perhaps you have not even dreamed could be. There are possibilities—great possibilities. Do you know what I see?" His gaze took them all in confidence as he unfolded the future before them. "I see not simply a house—but a resort. A beach full of laughing children, frolicking on the sand. Families playing together in the surf, making your happy home a home for many—a home away from home. And for you—for all of you—I see both a legacy you pass on to the wider world family as well as quite a great deal of money." He winked at them all. "Thousands for each of you."

He was just about to use the same ploy he had used on Daniela and Ben and inform the new sister specifically, and remind the two siblings he already knew, that "All of us young move on. It's the way of the world, the natural rhythms of life." And he was about to caution the elderly that to realize this development "will need much work—much, much work to be suitable for sophisticated tourists. And that will take much, much money for development. So that will cut into the amount that can be paid to the heirs. But, of course, heirs can also become investors and triple their earnings, if they are enterprising enough," and on and on, when he became aware that another player had entered the scene.

Up onto the porch stomped a severe looking young woman who had apparently heard his latest sally. She launched right into the conversation in clear attack mode. "What's going on here?" she demanded. "Who are you? And what do *you* want?"

"Welcome, Ruby," said Doña Lucia with complete calm. "This is Señor Balenzuela, a new friend of your sister and brother." She gestured Ruby to pull up another of the rocking chairs scattered across the huge porch. "Please sit down and join us. I have made some *pasteles* and we have *chinola* nectar. I was just about to explain to this distinguished gentleman that the house is in a trust. It cannot be sold. It is itself the property of a corporation for which we are caretakers and, as such, it cannot be put up for sale. But," she continued, regarding Balenzuela with a cordial smile that she mustered up from the depths of her emotional reserves, "we can be very helpful to you. We do indeed have a real estate connection nearby. Her name is Aña and she is deeply involved in the new developments in the most active part of our country's real estate market in Bahia de las Aguilas. No doubt you've heard of it? Well, she was in from the beginning and can help advise you of the best of all the options—and get you a fair price as well."

It was now Balenzuela's turn to have his mouth drop open.

"And I can help you make your connection with her," spoke up lawyer de Piedra.

"Oh, thank you, thank you so very much," said the suddenly flexible Ismael.

And that was the moment, Danny let go. "What? What?" she screamed. "What did you just say? A trust? What are you talking about? This is our inheritance! This is from our uncle, left to us—the heirs. You're both the caretakers! That's all you've ever been! How dare you take away our inheritance?"

"Danny!" cried Jo.

"You stay out of this! All my life, you've been pushing me around! Uncle Sol preferred you—everybody knows that! And now you're staying at the house and we've been farmed out. Even if it is to our favorite place. Me and Ben, we're being pushed out—you're getting everything! You're gonna leave us nothing—well I won't have it! Ben won't have it!" She looked wildly around for her newly arrived sister. "Ruby?"

"Leave me out of this," shot back Ruby. "I trust Uncle Ramon and Aunt Lucia. You need to calm down, Danny."

"I won't! I won't! I found something—something important! You just all want your selfish share. Well, I want to do something more important with my money and with this place and you won't take that away from me. It's bigger than you and bigger than all of us here. I found the orienting truth of life and I'll not have that taken away from me!" Daniela was up and stamping her feet.

Doña Lucia rose—the only one who could approach her in this state. "Little one," she said so gently. "No one wants to take anything away from you. All of your life we have loved you as our own. We want you to have dreams too and to reach them. And we want you," and she turned to take in the other siblings, "and all of you to find your destiny and to be happy."

But, Danny stepped back and pushed her away. "Well, I'm not happy—and Señor Balenzuela is not happy. We'll get our own lawyer and we'll see about this. If you're not going to be with us, Ruby," she said, turning imperiously toward her sister, "then you'll be against us." It was an ultimatum.

"Don't be ridiculous," snapped Ruby. "I'm on everybody's side—whatever that is—or whatever they are."

"What?"

"You've got to figure things out, first. You've got to get the whole picture before you can start laying down the law—or bringing it in."

"I've had enough of all of you! Ben?"

"Me too." He was on his feet.

"Señor Balenzuela, let's go—we can all sort this out with our own lawyer."

"If it's all the same to you, lovely lady," said Ismael, still as courteous as ever, "I think I'd like to stay for a bit and get the details from your dear family about this new contact that can tell me about some of the properties in Bahia de las Aguilas, if you wouldn't mind, dear lady."

Daniela gaped at him. Then without another word she stormed off the porch, Ben in tow. Very shortly afterwards they could hear her screaming at Ernesto at the gate, then its hurried clanking, and then silence.

14

"WHAT ON EARTH WAS that all about?" asked Ruby, taking a big bite out of the *pastele* Doña Lucia had laid before her. She swept her gaze around for clarification and centered in on Balenzuela.

He could see this pretty, little one was going to be a handful, so he armed himself with his most ingratiatingly cordial smile and launched carefully into his patent speech. He had just begun with "All of us young move on. It's the way of the world, the natural rhythms of life"—the message he had wanted to get to her when Ruby first arrived—when she snapped, "Yeah, yeah, but, if you don't mind, can you cut to the chase?"

"The chase?"

"Yeah, who are you with and why are you here?"

"Ruby," said Jo, with disapproval.

"Yeah, yeah—with all due respect and all that—I know. I know."

But Balenzuela was unperturbed at this rudeness and not to be deterred. He'd won over tough ones before. There was always a skeptic in the crowd. Sometimes they turned out to be his best allies. What was that expression these Americans used? Money talks? Sometimes it talked most powerfully through the ones he'd won over. So, he focused his full attention on Ruby, getting her completely in his sights and gave her the stripped-down version to suit her style. "I'm with E-corp," he said.

"What's that?"

"A development company. Specifically, the Encomienda Development Corporation—the EDC, or E-corp, we call it. It's an ancient and respected properties development company—it's multinational in scope."

"Uh, huh," said Ruby, taking this all in in the split second a hummingbird needs to snag nectar. "Development is good."

"It is, indeed," agreed Balenzuela, proceeding with the scaled-down version: "I develop properties for E-corp into resorts, but we're also looking to do businesses, upscale homes." Ruby nodded. This was working. So, he added simply: "My name is Ismael Balenzuela." He left off the flourish.

"You want to make an offer on the house?" summed up Ruby, putting it all together.

"I would have been very much interested to do so."

"Would have been?" She picked up the nuance. "What's the catch?"

"These dear folks tell me there is an encumbrance."

"There is?" Ruby looked at Doña Lucia and Don Ramón. "What's that?"

"This house is in a trust," said the little man. Ruby had a vague feeling she had seen him before.

"Excuse me. You are . . . ?"

"Angel Moreno Cueva de Piedra. I am your Uncle Sol's lawyer."

"The one who sent the letter."

"Yes, about his passing."

"Okay, I'll get to you later. I've been wondering about that—and the funeral and all."

Cueva de Piedra nodded at her deferentially. Whether he took offense at her brusque tone, he did not indicate.

"So, what's this about a trust?" She made her demand to Don Ramón and Doña Lucia. "We've never heard about this before. What's up with that?"

Doña Lucia looked pointedly at Ismael Balenzuela. "It's complicated," she said.

But Ruby was not to be deterred. "Well, is there an inheritance or not?"

"There may be," said Don Ramón.

"The letter said there was."

"Yes," said the little lawyer.

"Well, is there or isn't there?"

"That depends," said Doña Lucia.

"On what," pursued Ruby.

"On your sister."

"My sister? You mean it depends on Danny?" Ruby was shocked.

"No," said Doña Lucia. "It depends on Josefina."

"On Jo? How on Jo?"

"Whether she accepts it, or not?"

"What is 'it'?" asked Ruby. "And why does it depend on Jo and not on all of us?"

"The letter was sent," explained the lawyer carefully, "just to your sister Josefina. It simply concerned her. You are all welcomed back to your homeland, of course, and to your family here, but the inheritance would be hers primarily."

"Primarily?"

"Specifically," clarified the lawyer.

Ismael Balenzuela swiveled his eyes around toward Jo like the sights on two cannons. "Well," he said softly to himself. "Well, well. . . ."

"And what is this 'inheritance'—if it's not the house?" demanded Ruby.

"It's the mountain," said Don Ramón simply.

"The mountain? What mountain? And who needs a mountain," snapped Ruby.

"A mountain is good. That could be developed," offered Balenzuela. He was ignored.

"But, it's a mountain that comes with responsibilities," explained Doña Lucia. "Your sister may not want to accept these."

"What responsibilities?" demanded Ruby.

"Those," said Doña Lucia, "are not ours to say."

"Well, then whose are they?" Ruby turned to Jo. "You need to know that before you get yourself into something deep. We all know how busy you are saving the world!"

Jo winced at that description. She'd have to sort that out later. What kind of message was she actually sending out in her ministry? It wasn't her job to save the world. That was God's. Was that what people thought of her? What she said, however, was more mundane and immediate: "I was about to ask about the responsibilities myself before everyone arrived. But I'm wondering if this is the place and the time to do that." She glanced toward Balenzuela.

"Well put," said the lawyer, beginning to rise. "I was just thinking that myself. Perhaps you would like to spend some time with your 'uncle' and 'aunt' and sort some of that out. In the meantime," he smiled his deferential smile at Ismael, disarming him for the moment, "I can bring Señor Balenzuela to my office and give him Señora Aña's address and information."

"Yes, yes, the real estate agent. That would be very helpful," beamed Balenzuela, storing the information that Jo was the one to center on if he was to snag this property secretly as well—since nothing about "a trust" was about to veer him away from such a beautiful and strategic prospect right on the very beach he sought to develop. And, he grinned within himself, this was exactly the kind of location for what might prove to be an even bigger financial payoff for himself. This was the perfect center in which to base that hare-brained scheme of the con couple (as he had come to summarize Basil and Star in his thinking). Theirs was just the kind of off-kilter venture that ended up making millions. And he would even attempt to smooth things over with that mercurial wildcard of a sister, Daniela. Flashing through his mind was a quick plan of attack.

Jo was obviously steady and thoughtful. If he was going to get the property, he had to exploit her doubts—whatever they were—so she would or could want to accept it, depending on what worked better for him. For that, he would befriend her, become her counselor, the shoulder to lean on, and he could wheedle it away from her by simply, collegially, convincing her that the hassle wasn't worth it. Ruby was a tough nut, for certain, but a quick buck looked like the way to crack her resolve. She also obviously cared about her sister, so he would play on that sympathy by enlisting her as an ally. The responsibility would be far too much—she had already hinted at that. That's what he would exploit, and together they would turn Josefina's head.

Daniela, of course, was still useful. She was a great potential attraction for the magnetic pole scheme. Astoundingly, she was a believer. And one already deeply committed. That was obvious by her reactions today. Balenzuela was shocked. How could anybody be so dumb? But, he had himself this very morning looked into those beautiful, empty eyes and had seen the vacuum that yawned where her self-regard should have been. How could this woman be so astonishingly beautiful and yet think so little of herself? It made no sense of all. He himself knew he was handsome, and he used that information to full advantage as he made his deals. And he had seen her display her beauty before him. But, that had obviously not been enough. Chalk it up, he thought, to the competition with two sisters with superior intellect—one thoughtful, one decisive. Well, the lure of "orientation" had obviously satisfied her longing and, as that wise scoundrel Starling had so wisely put it, Daniela would, indeed, look great on a "poster." A young woman this devoted and this attractive could bring hordes into the scam. And, shortly, it would not be a scam anymore, but a chic movement. Who is to tell what orients one?

He paused a moment in his thinking to check the present situation, but the lawyer was still engaged in conducting a kind of courteous departure "ceremony" of his own with his hosts and the two sisters, shaking hands and murmuring compliments and gracious words, so Balenzuela relapsed into his scheming. Still, he mused, there was one troubling aspect to this all: Seriously, how could anybody besides the gullible believe that a bunch of magnets—under the ground or on your wrist—have the potential to orient anybody? But, it's true enough that people had been falling for that kind of nonsense for years with crystals and what have you, so why not magnets? And even that had been done before. Nobody he had ever heard of had been arrested for fraud for this kind of thing, so why should they be? Danny was definitely part of their ticket to success here—their mascot, so as to say. Ben, of course—and Balenzuela actually frowned, but no one noticed, since they were absorbed in whispering among themselves—well, Ben was actually quite a liability. He was the true wild card in play, but he didn't have to be part of the scheme proper. Simply siphon him some chump change from time to time and send him off to the casino and he was out of the way, as long as he didn't get himself in too deep.

The lawyer had now turned toward him, apologizing for the delay, but Balenzuela was completely satisfied with having had the moment's pause for lining up his whole strategy and assured him it was all fine. But he added he had wanted to apologize for his boorish intrusion and say goodbye to Jo and Ruby—specifically meaning, without, of course, saying, that he wanted to throw out the connecting lines to snare them for a future go-round. But he noticed they had stepped inside with Doña Lucia and Don Ramón, so he detached himself momentarily from the little lawyer and had to content himself with calling politely from the threshold of the door.

"Thank you so much for such a delightful time," he said, copying the deferential tone of the little lawyer. "I am so sorry to have barged in on all of you so unannounced and so discourteously. I was simply following the lead of my new friends, Daniela and Ben. I had no idea a conference was in process. I am so very sorry and I hope I did not disrupt it too badly."

Don Ramón stepped out, leaving the two younger women with his wife, and assured Balenzuela that, if any lack of courtesy had taken place, the fault was theirs; that the *señor* had been a perfect gentleman; that the problem was within their own family; that this had been an awkward time to receive visitors; that normally they were all very hospitable; that even today they were so honored to have made his acquaintance and that now he was in the best of hands with Señor Cueva de Piedra, who could help him realize his employment tasks. At that Don Ramón courteously took his leave.

While all this was going on, the conversation inside the kitchen was going hot and heavy between Ruby and Doña Lucia, while Jo looked on from a chair, wondering if this was all going to give her a setback in health. It was clearly to her a case of irresistible force and immovable object.

Ismael Balenzuela had no sooner left the porch with Angel Moreno Cueva de Piedra than Ruby let her voice rise: "But who does it all depend on whether Jo gets her inheritance or not? That's what I want to know! Who? Who?"

"The chiefs, and your sister, herself" is all that Doña Lucia would say.

15

Star and Basil wasted a frantic morning, fretting and calling Ismael Balenzuela's room every fifteen minutes.

"I don't like this! I don't like this!" Basil kept muttering, until Star wanted to strangle him.

"Cut it out!" she finally snapped. "You're driving me nuts!"

"So where is he? Where *is* he? We're supposed to be partners in this thing? He's supposed to be going with us to check out the pole. And he's no place here. I've got a really bad feeling about this. I think he's leaving us behind. . . ."

"Maybe," Star admitted, "So, just in case, we gotta be smart too and play our options."

"What options? He's the only egg in our chicken!" fumed Basil.

"Yeah, well the only thing to do then is change birds," ruled Star, picking up his metaphor and extending it.

But it was just a cliché to Basil, so he couldn't follow her flight: "Whattaya mean?" he asked her, dumbfounded.

She clucked in disgust. "The only thing to do is go after the chick! That's our only other lead. And," she said with just a trace of smugness scattered within her alarm, "I got her number the other night."

"That's right! You did! Way to go!" Basil beamed on Star with delight and then a realization hit him like someone had instantly wrung his neck. "Ahhhggg," he gasped and squawked with sudden insight. "Hey! Hey! Heyyy! I'll bet that's what *he* did! HE CALLED HER UP!" And he flung both his arms up in dismay.

"You bet he did," snapped Star. "And that's what we shoulda done the first time we couldn't get hold of him in his room. We've got to head all this off, or he's gonna carry off that little chickadee and gobble up her inheritance and you and I will be left with nothin' but chicken feed!" And then, being as extra punitive as she was, she added, as much in disgust with herself as with

Basil at this turn of events, "It's just that you're such a bird-brain at times, I can't think straight. With you running around like a chicken with its . . ."

"Hey," Basil cut her off with instant umbrage, "What are you crowing about? You were flying around just as willy-nilly as I was! So don't start going after me with the hatchet!"

"All right! All right!" Star had to chop this conversation off—or there would be more waste, waste, WASTE! So she quickly admitted, "Okay, you're right for once. We've both been bird-brains for sure, but now we've got to settle down. We've got to get off our perches and get out into the yard ourselves! I'll call her up right now."

Basil instantly pecked at this grain of hope. "Right! Do it!" And so she did.

Secretly, of course, neither of them thought it was a Grade-A idea. Both figured Balenzuela had plucked her off hours before, but to Star and Basil's astonishment and delight, Daniela answered on the first ring. Her voice sounded strange.

"Is something wrong, honey?" asked Star, and got an earful. Starling cupped her hand over the phone and whispered to Basil, "She's as frustrated as we are."

"That's good," murmured Basil, somewhat mollified, since everyone knows what misery likes, and Basil was chief among these with all the schemes that had blown up on him on a depressingly regular basis over the years.

"He did, sugar? No, really? Oh, that's awful. Oh, I'm so sorry for you," Star was cooing into the phone. "Well, we won't desert you. Yes, you can *always* count on that! Of course, we can get together. Of course, we can help you get oriented again. . . ." Star rolled her eyes at Basil. "Now? Of course, now is a wonderful time. We are always there for you. Would you like us to go to you, or do you want to come here to see us? Come here? No, wait, I'll tell you what: Why should you have to go out in the stressed state you're in? We'll come to you, honey. See it as a house call. Yes, that's right. Now, where exactly are you and how do we get there?" Star began jotting down directions.

When she hung up, after another round of assurances, she leveled her eyes at Basil. "He was there all right. He went around with her and her loser brother to the house she's supposed to be inheriting and they ran into a brick wall."

"What are you talking about," snapped the startled Basil. "What do you mean 'supposed to be inheriting'?"

"I don't know yet exactly," said Star, "but it seems the older sister is trying to cut out the other three!"

"That's terrible," cried Basil, mustering up the inordinate degree of righteous indignation that only a con man who for one moment is innocent of a particular wrongdoing can display. "Cutting out her own sister? Who would do a thing like that? And, besides, if that inheritance belongs to anybody, it belongs to us! I mean," he backtracked suddenly, as he realized how that sounded, "I mean to say, to us as helpers of this poor unfortunate girl—and, naturally, to all the heirs, as well."

"Naturally," agreed Star, smirking. These attacks of conscience in Basil were so cute, she thought, as long as they didn't get in the way of success.

"Let's go check out the lay of the land," she ordered.

"Right!" said Basil, catching up the truck keys. Action, thought Starling, was what he did best.

While all this was going on, Ismael Balenzuela had followed Angel Moreno Cueva de Piedra through a panoply of little villages. As soon as their two-car caravan had left the city of Barahona, they also began passing along a lovely little lake. He realized that this must be the one that con couple had been telling him about. He would definitely have to check this out more thoroughly. It had wonderful possibilities. He also reasoned that this must mean their silly scam of a magnetic pole was nearby. Maybe he should ask this small lawyer about it when they reached his office . . . but then, he thought, maybe not. Better to stay a silent partner in all this just in case this end of it blew up. He also realized he felt badly about the way things had worked out with Daniela. He certainly didn't want to alienate anybody. He had determined to patch things up with her, but, even so, maybe he could have played his hand a little more carefully back at the house. Maybe he should have left with her to help her save face and contacted the others later. But, no, that wouldn't have been good, either. He did right, he assured himself. They were proving to be closer to his goal than she was, so he had to prioritize currying their favor. Besides, this Daniela, or Danny as they called her, was an emotional kind of woman, and he could always win her back with his charm. It was the other two—the reflective and decisive ones—that he had to worry about.

As he thought and drove, town after town slipped by, each one of them displaying their wares, each one having a different product or produce to sell. And each one had a speed bump to negotiate where sellers, and window washers, and begging children lurked and crowded around his car every time he had to slow down. Children of the "sleeping policeman," he muttered to himself—but you couldn't blame them. Everybody had to get by. He tried the radio, but every station he could get out here was either someone jabbering away or that music they called *romantico*, which he dismissed as "soap operas set to tunes." Ismael Balenzuela's was not a romantic soul. So, he was delighted when some fast *merengue* suddenly came on. It suited his style and his mood—get this done quick!

And that was the attitude he adopted at the lawyer's house, when he finally sat ensconced in the small cement home and office building in the neat little town of Villa Bahoruco, not to be confused, he was cautioned by the precise little lawyer, with the region of Bahoruco that lay to the north. Ismael Balenzuela agreed he would make a note of that, as he dismissed this information from his mind. No time for pleasantries, he wanted to indicate—now it was time to get down to business.

"Thank you so much for agreeing to work with me," he opened, hoping he could establish from the start a strictly employer-employee relationship.

The little lawyer nodded and waited.

"As you can imagine, I am very grateful to be able to make a new contact and explore some new options, but, I must confess, I am still deeply disappointed not to have a chance at that lovely large beach house back in Barahona. It exactly fit my picture of what I need, and I find it hard to imagine that I will be able to find another place as perfect as is that one."

The lawyer nodded again.

"Is it really true that I have no chance—no chance at all to purchase that one?"

"I am afraid that is true."

"No matter *how much* I offer?"

"The matter is complicated and really out of our hands."

"In whose hands is it then?" pursued Balenzuela.

"The hands of others," the lawyer replied.

"Now, you're not going to be secretive with me, are you?" Balenzuela spoke with just a hint of disapproval, since he gauged this lawyer was a gentle touch. Maybe that would be enough to pry this thing open. The lawyer hung his head, but nothing more was immediately forthcoming.

So Ismael tried the outsider-who-wanted-so-much-to-belong ploy, since the lawyer was also evidently the familial type, judging by his solicitous behavior toward each of the various factions during the recent blowup. "I really didn't understand all that information that was flying around in that rather stressful scene at the house."

"Of course, of course," said Cueva de Piedra, sadly. "That was really rather unfortunate that you were exposed to that. They are all good children, really, though not children any longer, but adults," he admitted. "They simply don't understand, but they will, they will."

"I don't understand either," pursued Balenzuela. "Can you enlighten me somewhat, since I still hold out hope that I can make an offer?"

"But that would be futile, *Señor*."

"But, I can try. . . ."

"I really would not recommend it. But, well, I suppose you can try. But," he added, shaking his head as if it gave him personal pain, "I really hold out no hope for success for you or for anyone else."

"There's someone else?"

"There is always someone else."

"Isn't that true!" admitted Ismael Balenzuela, seasoned already in business, young though he was. "And who is that someone else? You know you can tell me, since you are now my lawyer."

"It's really pointless, since he will not be successful either."

"Still, I'd like to know."

"You're wasting your time," counseled the lawyer, almost pleading with him.

"It's my time," said Ismael Balenzuela a bit more firmly, "and I'd like to know." This was not going anywhere.

And then, at his frown, the lawyer gave him a morsel. "It's a mayor of one of the nearby towns."

"A mayor? He wants it too?" This was certainly problematic. Once politicians get involved, things become impossible. "Why? Why does he want it? He must own several homes—he's a mayor. . . ."

"I really don't know, and that's the truth. He really does have far more than he needs as it is. Just as you say. His town is very rich."

"Which town is it?"

"It's called Villa Riqueza and it is appropriately named. The town is the wealthiest in our area for its size."

"Maybe I should look into that one to consider building a resort," tried Balenzuela, watching the lawyer closely.

"I suppose you could do that," said Cueva de Piedra slowly. "They have the resources."

Ismael Balenzuela did not like this cautious approach at all. Was this man going to work for him or not? But, of course, there was still his lead in the Bahia district. He did not want to blow that off.

"All right, I'll check that out, but please put my mind at rest. Why can't I buy the beach house in Barahona?"

This one is very persistent, thought Angel Moreno Cueva de Piedra. He is not going to let anything go without a struggle. I must proceed very carefully. "The house belongs to a corporation, you might say," he finally admitted.

"A corporation? You mean like a business?"

"I mean like a people group."

"A people group? You mean like gypsies or something?"

"Yes, something like that. But, it's a people group here in the Dominican Republic."

"Oh, I see. And who are Don Ramón and Doña Lucia exactly? They are very distinguished people, I can tell. Much more dignified than I would expect simply caretakers to be."

"Yes, that is true. They are leaders in the people group and the executors of the house. The deed is in the name of the people group and they are assigned to pass it on to the next candidate delegated by the group to steward it. That is really all I am at liberty to tell you, you must understand."

"The older sister, Josefina," concluded Balenzuela aloud.

The lawyer simply nodded.

"But, only if she fulfills some provisions the group has set for her," recalled Balenzuela.

"You are very perceptive," observed Cueva de Piedra.

"You have to be in my business to survive," explained Balenzuela.

"Yes, in both our businesses," pointed out the lawyer.

Ismael Balenzuela nodded back. "That is true." He paused and then added, "So, now please tell me about the real estate agent in Bahai."

Cueva de Piedra relaxed and grew more expansive. He had entered on safe ground, Balenzuela concluded, as he himself thought, maybe I'll go to Villa Riqueza and see that town and meet the mayor. I might find something interesting to my benefit there. But I don't think I'll mention it here. Let me find out what I can on this other lead since this little lawyer is now so suddenly full of information. He picked up what the lawyer was saying: "She is not actually a real estate agent full time. That is her part-time work."

Ismael Balenzuela frowned. He wanted full commitment from his workers, not another conflicted contact. He had enough of that with this present lawyer!

Cueva de Piedra noted the change cross his client's face and hastened to add by way of explanation, "It is a tent-making job for her."

"She makes tents too?" cried Balenzuela, astounded. "A real estate agent? She doesn't deal with houses?" What on earth was this all about?

"No, that is just an expression. She is the area director of Christian World Service, an organization that does humanitarian work in *La Republica*. The term 'tent-making' means that, since much of that work is volunteer, she finances herself by doing real estate on the side. She is very shrewd and very good at it."

Ismael Balenzuela relaxed again. "'Shrewd' and 'good at it' are both very good," he smiled. And then a thought came to him. "Would she happen to be a member of this 'people group' as well?"

The lawyer paused for a moment, thought about it, and then admitted, "Yes, she is."

"Well, that's fine. Of course, it makes no difference to me," Ismael Balenzuela assured him. But his mind was racing through a myriad of possibilities. Maybe this one, selling real estate and all, would be more amenable to cajoling the "people group" into parting with the beach house property. In the meantime, he thought, as soon as I wrap up here, I am off to this Villa Riqueza to get a second opinion on all this—and maybe I can uncover the key information my so-called personal lawyer is not about to divulge. But what he said was, "Thank you so much. And now may I have the contact information, so I can see what she has to offer?"

The lawyer was all cordiality as he fished in his files for it, little knowing Ismael Balenzuela was now speculating to himself: I wonder if I could get someone trustworthy to burgle this place and get all the inside information I'm sure it holds? Because this man is holding out on me. . . .

16

J
O SLUMPED BACK IN a chair, exhausted. The sudden explosion of Daniela, the departure of the lawyer in the center of what was already a tense meeting to which she had dragged herself in hopes she would finally get news on the whereabouts of her parents—and with it the resulting loss of the opportunity to dig finally to the bottom of what all this was about—the intrusion instead of Ismael Balenzuela, bringing with him a whole new set of problems to complicate her relationship with this house, her real inheritance, the resentment of her sisters and brother—all of it together—heaped in upon her sudden illness had taken quite a toll on her. What a day this was becoming! How on earth could she handle all this?

What she wanted most of all, she realized, was to crawl back into bed. That was the sensible way to proceed. But, at the same time, she could see clearly it was not the most expeditious. No, the most efficient way to satisfy all these questions and get a line on how to deal most effectively with all this trouble was to dig down to the root of it all. And where would she find that root? Well, one obvious place that appeared to her was to explore the last contact she had had with her father. And that meant to center upon an interview with the missing factor in all this mystery—the no-show emissary.

As she had heard the account of his rudeness unfold, she began to realize that she knew this emissary, this Ricky from childhood—a curt boy, older than she by three years or so, and therefore uninterested in this younger child behind his age. Yes, she recalled, he was a curt boy who had now obviously grown up to be a rude man. But, rude or not, he knew the secret of her inheritance and perhaps what had happened to her parents. Whatever he knew, she meant to find it out. After all, she had been trained as a social worker and had, in her few years, taken on local authorities back in Richfield when it was necessary on behalf of her people. If she could handle New Jersey politicians, how tough could a far distant cousin of hers be?

How tough she found out very shortly, as she confronted him at his home in Villa Barohuco, when she drove the rental car there the next morning and surprised him "in his lair," as she put it to herself. He was not in any way glad to see her.

"So, you've come without call ahead or invitation?" he sneered by way of greeting.

"Yes."

"How did you know how to find me?"

"Don Ramón and Doña Lucia."

"They let you come alone?" he sneered.

"Their only hesitation was whether my present health was up to it. That was all." Looking him over, Jo nearly congratulated herself for having the insight not to bring Ruby along. His greeting would have been the end of the interview. Ruby with her featherweight trigger would have lit into him like a bullet in a driveby and that would have gained nothing. Jo paused a moment and then asked quietly, "May I come in?"

The effect was far stronger than she expected. This was the soft answer—obviously not what he had expected. He had come out to fight and he appeared momentarily non-plussed. "Uh, hmmm, well," he fumbled, "Yes, I suppose so," and he cracked the door open such a small bit behind him and stepped somewhat aside. She squeezed in, thinking, maybe it's a good thing I'm so thin and gangly.

His home was a neat little cement structure in the traditional style. It was one story and flat, but larger than it appeared from the outside. Every piece of furniture in his front room appeared to be acacia wood. Termite-resistant, she noted mentally, but not as heavy as the mahogany that comprised the beach house. It was all surprisingly neat. Not what one would expect from a young man living alone. There was a scarcity and a precision here that belied her memory of this Ricky as a child. He had struck her as a mercurial individual, but not in the same way that her sister Daniela was mercurial. He was very intelligent and decisive, as she recalled. And when he made up his mind, it was unchangeable. She remembered him being buffeted about by other boys, always at the center of some fight and always being warned by his elders to settle down. She wasn't certain how much of that advice he had taken to heart. So, she decided to keep the soft tone that turns away wrath. After all, it had gotten her through his door. So, "thank you," is what she said simply in her low, soft voice.

"I suppose you want something to drink," he said grudgingly.

"That would be nice, thank you."

"Do you know what *chinola* juice is?" he asked her.

It was an insult and she took it that way, but decided it was not in her interest to respond accordingly. "I've been living on it for the last few days—that and *té criolla.*"

"Hah, can't take the water, huh?" His voice had the sound of triumph in it.

"It's not that at all," Jo explained still softly. "The water is all bottled. It's that I came suddenly and I brought the exhaustion with me. I am working hard in my calling."

"You work?" he asked.

"Of course, don't you?"

"Well, yes, but that's different."

"How so?"

"Well, I mean, I have responsibilities—to the Tribe."

"And I to God, and, yes," she added, "I recall that. You head up the communications that network us all together."

"You know that?" he asked incredulously, his eyes enlarging as he looked at her, astonished.

He had beautiful eyes, she noted, deep, rich brown eyes that shone with health and vigor. In fact, as she took him in, she saw he was tall, stately, well-proportioned and—to her own astonishment—he was handsome. She hadn't remembered that. Just an unpleasant, pugnacious boy. And now he was a rude, pugnacious—but surprisingly handsome—unpleasant man. She longed momentarily to put a smile on his face. But right now she was too tired to make the effort and she was on a personal mission and would not be veered from it.

"May I sit down?" she asked.

"Oh, yes, of course," he said with what might have sounded like a tinge—perhaps, a shade—of self-incrimination for his lack of courtesy? Maybe? But probably not, she concluded, as she sat down in a well-made acacia rocking chair, a product of the countryside. No reason to project something onto him that was not there, just because he had beautiful eyes. What was happening to her? she wondered. She must still be a lot sicker than she thought. Maybe she should have let Ruby in on her plans and brought her along. She would have "made short work of this guy and brought him down a few pegs," as Ruby would always describe her battles with so many people she met.

"Well," said her host. "You're here now. Why is that? What is the purpose of your visit?"

She almost said, "Well, I see diplomacy is not among your skill set," but what she said was, "I am concerned about my parents. I thought you might know where they are."

"And you don't?" he countered.

"If I did, would I be here?"

"Are you sure that's the only reason you've come?"

"Why else would I come?"

"You tell me."

"If you know nothing," said Jo, getting up, "then my time can be used better. I am sorry I've disturbed you." And she headed toward the door.

"Wait," he said.

"Why?" she asked, as she put her hand on the latch.

"We have something to discuss."

"If it's not about my parents, it can wait." And she opened the door.

"Your parents are safe," he said.

"You know this for a fact?" asked Jo.

"Yes."

"Why did you not tell me when I first asked?"

"I don't know you."

"You know me, Enrique Asenao, generally known as Ricky. I saw you at every gathering and celebration I attended when we were growing up. You were at the funeral of my mother. At every celebration, you would hang around with your friends—Tomás and the other boys. You had no time for me then. I have no time for you now. I want to know what happened to my parents. If you won't help me, I'll find someone who will."

"Well," he sneered, "aren't we the little *hurona*."

"Look," she replied finally with the firmness that her social work training and experience had provided her. "Whatever your problem is—it's yours. Not mine. You were supposed to meet us at the airport. You were 'too busy,' I was told. My father told me he had entrusted you to meet us and tell us whatever it was we needed to know. You failed in that mission. You appear to me as someone who lets his lack of personal skills and his own emotional agenda get in the way of his efficiency. I have no time and interest in dealing with someone like this. I have goals, and I will reach them, with you or over you—it makes no difference to me. Do you understand me?"

Ricky stopped and became very still and stared at her. And then he said the last thing she expected to fall from his lips. "I'm sorry. I have not treated you correctly. Please forgive me."

Jo looked steadily and carefully at him for any hint of mockery or of deceit, but she could not find either. He appeared to be completely sincere.

"Thank you," she replied simply and then, "Can you help me with any information at all? I have to tell you I'm very worried about my father and mother."

"I understand," he said more gently than she could imagine he could say anything. "I am conflicted, you are right. I didn't meet you because I didn't want to see you."

"Why is that?"

"For a number of personal reasons."

"You hardly know me."

"That's true," he admitted, "But, you see, I have to be honest. I don't approve of you."

"You don't 'approve of me?' That's mystifying to me. Why would you need to 'approve' of me?"

"All the leaders need to do so."

"What? In order to tell me the whereabouts of my parents—you have to approve of me? Do you know how insane that sounds?" demanded Jo.

"I told you your parents are safe."

"But you haven't told me where they are."

"That's because something happened when they arrived here and they had to flee for refuge. They found it. They told me that they were safe and to tell you personally that, but they gave me no other details."

"And you failed to do that until this moment?"

"I wouldn't say I 'failed,' exactly."

"What would you call it then? Erred? Blundered? Shirked?"

"No! I'd call it protecting the interests of the people I care about."

"Well, that sounds like nonsense to me. They're my parents, not yours. Why would you withhold such information when it didn't take much imagination to know that I and my brother and sisters would be worried about them? And you"—she added with a touch of sarcasm that she could not keep out of her voice—"the director of tribal communications?"

"It's just because I am as you say that I monitor what I share, and I have to be careful because information now is a dangerous commodity."

"I can see that!" said Jo. "Nobody wants to tell us anything. Not even Don Ramón or Doña Lucia, who practically reared us when we lived for the summers here. How complicated can it be?"

"Extremely complicated," Ricky said. "And only to be dispensed by those who have the authority to tell."

Jo gave out a great sigh of exasperation.

"I can tell you this, however," Ricky said. "There is great evil present—in the mountains, in the towns. No one is trustworthy—even in the Tribe. Especially now that we have lost our *cacique*—," and then by way of explanation, "our chief . . ."

"I know what the term means," snapped Jo, sounding to herself more like Ruby every minute—a place she did not normally want to go, but there are moments. . . . "I'm not interested in anything but the wellbeing of my parents," she confirmed. "That's what I care about now."

"And that's the problem—that's the very problem," cried Ricky. "You don't care—how could you?" And he looked at her accusingly.

Jo stared back, unmoved. "What on earth are you talking about?"

"I'm talking about the people—the Tribe—you don't care about them."

"Of course, I care about them. I am Taino descent on both sides. The Tribe is my tribe. The people are my people. I am the niece of the *cacique*, whom I loved dearly and mourn daily. How can you say I don't care about my family?"

"You are a minister in New Jersey, I am told," and he said it with distaste.

"Yes, and before that a social worker—a community organizer, to be exact, so what?"

"Well, how can any Taino believe in Christianity after the devastation its marauders did to us?"

"What's this—a history lesson? Well, you should know that the great Enrique, for whom you're named, had no problem believing in it—and worshiping the one true God by name—and saying his rosary as he walked guard around the perimeter of his camp—and forcing his enemies to swear on the Bible never to attack another Taino on point of hellfire! You know all this—or should know it!"

"Well, yes," he said grudgingly. "I'll admit you are right. But look at Columbus—he and his marauders destroyed our people."

"Columbus, as you should know," lectured Jo, as if he were one of her pupils—and a wayward one at that—"was well-intentioned but weak. And he was conflicted—he tried to serve God and gold. Yeshua had warned us that can't be done. Columbus should have known better! Besides, "she added, "he had to recruit his men from the prisons—nobody else would come to this so-called new world, and that wasn't helped by all the idiotic things that ignorant fool Amerigo Vespucci wrote about our beautiful homeland. These weren't real Christians with whom Columbus was saddled. They were criminals. The whole enterprise was poorly set up, dismally peopled, and doomed to failure from the start. It had nothing to do with the real good news of Yeshua—whom we know as YaYael—it was nothing but bad news from the beginning. And it's the reason we have all the tensions today across the Americas—north and south." She was preaching now, "It set a legacy of violence and oppression and the demonic delusion of 'manifest destiny' from which we have yet to free ourselves. There's no division between the north of America, the southern America, and these islands, when it comes to the legacy of oppression. We're all the heirs of a fallen inheritance."

"You sound like you delivered that speech before!" observed Ricky.

"Nearly daily," Jo assured him, "Everybody says the same stupid things. Nobody seems to have thought through anything. You're not the exception you imagine yourself to be."

"Well," grunted Ricky, "you're a lot stronger and more definitive than I imagined you would be."

"And what did you imagine?"

"Some rich kid from America, looking for a quick buck out of our misfortune in losing our *cacique*, and wanting to cash in and clear out as quickly as possible."

Jo gasped. That hit home more accurately than she really wanted to admit. She fell silent for a moment. She had to think that over. After all, she *had* actually planned to sell Uncle Sol's beach house and use the money for her ministry back in Richfield. She hadn't really considered its impact on the people here anymore than had Danny, or Ben, or even Ruby. She had to admit, he did have a point. She looked at him and saw he was watching her closely. She didn't like lying, but, she realized, something else was going on here and that sensation warned her to proceed carefully. Something was at stake that she did not understand. She had to know more before she could reply with any adequacy. Rushing to respond was not her usual mode of proceeding, anyway. Everything always turned out to be so nuanced. So there was no reason to lie, but there was no reason to divulge all of what she thought either. Nobody else was doing that. Why should she? So what she said was, "I see your point. I can see why you thought what you did. However, you must know that Las Olas del Sol is not my inheritance. It belongs to the Tribe. I can't sell it. It is in a trust and I have no desire to challenge that trust. I have spent many happy hours in that house and it is filled with memories of my uncle. With his departure, the glory, as the Bible would have put it, is gone. It's just a house to me, but I can see it is the seat of the tribal chief of our people. It must always remain for the people, and I would myself yield it to the next *cacique*, even if it were my inheritance, for to take it away would be wrong."

"I'm surprised to hear you say that," said Ricky in what was obviously genuine amazement.

Jo looked at him, puzzled. "Why would you say that?"

"Well, you of all people."

"What do you mean, 'You of all people'?"

"They haven't told you?" asked Ricky with even greater surprise.

"Told me what?"

He paused and became impassive in the native way.

"I'm at sea in all this," cried Jo. "Everywhere I turn is innuendo and secrecy. I'm really fed up." And then she let herself go, "I've lost my beloved uncle, which gives me great grief. But do I see his body so I can mourn over it? No. What are they afraid of? I am, as you say, a minister. Do you think I will faint at the sight of death? I preside over funerals. The ministry is all about death and life and," she added, "resurrection." If he didn't believe in it, that was his problem! "And," she continued, her voice rising, "I'm worried about my parents. I want to see for myself that they are all right. I want to hug my father and kiss my stepmother and I won't rest until I do. And—in a very, very lesser matter to me right now—I am told I may be saddled with a mountain. What on earth is that all about? Nobody tells me. Why would I want a 'mountain?' I could tell you, I want to go home. But this is my home! This is the land of my birth. My sisters and brother were born in America— but not I. I am a citizen of both countries because my stepmother is from Puerto Rico and had me naturalized when I was a child, but my heart extends to both countries. My homeland embraces both."

"And so it should," said Ricky slowly, "if you are actually given the task ahead."

Jo simply stared at him, dumbfounded.

"I have no idea what that's supposed to mean," she said, still exasperated.

"I'm sorry," said Ricky, with what sounded like it could be genuine sentiment. "I do feel a pull to tell you all you want to know—well, maybe not all, because I don't know all. I can guess some of it, but I may not be right. But," he drew back a bit, "you have to understand that I am a man under authority. I have some authority myself, but there is greater authority over me. I am subject to the tribal council and I cannot say what I am not authorized to reveal. It is the way we live and I cannot discard it or go against it."

"I'd like to say I understand," said Jo more humbly now, "and, in a way, I do. I respect authority. But, you have to understand, I am not in the power structure, so I do not feel that I have the same responsibility as you do. As far as I am concerned, I will pursue the truth until I find out what it is—no matter what effort it takes me. I have enough of the same genes as my sister Ruby to persist to whatever extent I need to to find out what I want to know."

"I actually do remember her," smiled Ricky. "She can be a spitfire."

"She can, indeed," said Jo.

"And I think you can be very persistent too."

"Bank on it," Jo assured him.

"I still have doubts you could do the job better than I, but I do need to think this over more carefully. There is much more to you than I had surmised. That was my mistake," and then he stopped and what looked like a great realization suddenly widened his eyes, as he murmured, "but, not Sol's obviously."

"What job are you talking about?" asked Jo.

"For that you must go to the mountain," said Ricky.

"To the mountain? What on earth for?"

"Well, you see, that I cannot tell you."

"You have no authority."

"Exactly."

"I get that part—so who has it?"

"Well," Ricky thought that over, "I think the answer is back in Las Olas del Sol with Don Ramón and Doña Lucia."

"Why with them?"

"Well, they are the trustees."

"But the beach house is not involved. I told you that!" Jo had, a momentary urge to strangle him—beautiful eyes and all!

"Well, I mean, of course, your 'uncle' and 'aunt' and the visitors who are coming."

"Who's coming?" asked Jo, nearly at the complete end of her patience.

Ricky looked at her with disbelief. "Why the *caciques*, of course—representatives from everywhere: Puerto Rico, Nueva York, Cuba. It is the great gathering of the clans." And then he added something that totally shocked her. It was the last question she expected to fall from his lips. What he asked was: "Just in the remote case it actually happens, did you bring 'the dress'?"

17

VILLA RIQUEZA WAS EVERYTHING the lawyer Angel Moreno Cueva de Piedra intimated it would be. The entrance to the city was graced by vast orchards of plantains, oranges, lemons, standing as if they were troops at attention, guarding the city against need or want. Towering high among them, stately palm trees reared up like sentinels. Ismael Balenzuela had the odd feeling he was being watched, as if everything around him were on guard. Fields of plenty, he murmured to himself, as he gazed around, amazed.

The city itself offered no contradiction to his first impression. Homes were upscale and ornate. Some, of course, were more modest, but every one had a satellite dish, and even the smallest, traditional-style home had fruit trees in the front yard, a receiver on the roof, and a large color television playing away to no one that could be glimpsed through an open window. Ismael doubted anyone here bothered to lock their doors.

In the center of town reposed a stately cement building in the old Spanish style. The *alcalde*, the mayor, he was informed, would be in to a developer who proffered a card from Spain and, within twenty minutes, the mayor received his visitor with expresso and pleasantries.

His honor Nicolás de Odnavo was all about cordiality, but Ismael Balenzuela had the same impression he had had when he was entering the city: the strange sensation that he was being examined carefully like some new species of lizard. The mayor seemed to be determining whether he bit, stung, or simply would be useful in ridding the *hacienda* of flies.

Unperturbed, Balenzuela sketched his plans for developing area property before the mayor and was gratified to see the mayor smile and relax like anyone who holds complete power over an area.

"Yes," his honor admitted, "I do oversee the entire municipal region, so you are very wise to seek my counsel in any course you want to initiate for your company."

So, Ismael Balenzuela talked about Lake Rincon and the possibility of developing this magnificent site and the area about it. (But, of course, he did not mention the magnetic pole.) The mayor sat back, smiling and amused, though his eyes continued to watch his visitor warily. But, when Ismael came to the beach house, suddenly everything changed. The mayor sat forward. "You have seen Las Olas del Sol in Barahona?" he asked. "They let you inside?"

"Well, no, not inside, per se," confessed Balenzuela.

"I would think not," observed the mayor.

"And why is that?" asked Ismael Balenzuela. "I understand that it is under the ownership of a 'people group.' Is that correct?"

"It is, indeed," said the mayor, "and more than most people realize."

"And what is this 'people group' exactly?" pursued Balenzuela.

"You don't know?" asked the mayor.

"No, I don't exactly. Do you know?"

"Of course," said the mayor.

"Will you tell me?"

"Why should I?"

"Is it that much of a secret?"

"How would it be in my benefit to distribute information?"

Ah, thought Ismael Balenzuela, now we are getting to the core of things, how Villa Riqueza becomes '*riqueza.*' "I very much want to cooperate with you—and to direct my company to do so," he assured the mayor. "How could we proceed if we did not work closely with the local authorities? That would be very foolish. It's bad business sense."

The mayor nodded but said nothing.

And then Ismael Balenzuela hazarded a bold move. "I understand you yourself wanted to make an offer on that beach house. . . ."

The mayor recoiled back and the smile faded. "Well," he said, "you seem to be well informed on some matters."

"It is my business to be informed," said Balenzuela.

"Make certain the information you seek is not detrimental to your plans," said the mayor.

"That is part of my business too," Balenzuela agreed carefully. "I am only interested in benefitting those for whom I work and with whom I work. That is good business. And," he added quickly, "I want very much to work with you."

"And you want to benefit yourself," the mayor added, watching him closely for his reaction.

"Of course!" Balenzuela assured him.

"Yes, well, see that you keep that attitude, young man. We'll draw up a contract to that effect," said the mayor.

"Thank you," said Ismael, though he was not feeling very grateful. A contract would certainly complicate matters, he realized, because it would weigh any outcomes in whatever direction the mayor wanted them to go. He had to see if he could neutralize this development. "I have a lawyer," he offered hopefully. "He can draw up a contract with no extra work for you. . . ."

The mayor looked at him like a judge at a truant child. "You have a lawyer? Already?" he asked peevishly, as if announcing: "Well, I can see you are going to be a bother."

"Yes, of course," said Balenzuela quickly. What a locked-down town this one must be. This mayor was close to paranoid. "It's good business sense," he bleated.

The mayor gave a snort. "And who is your lawyer?" he demanded.

"A man named Cueva de Piedra, who has an office in Villa Bahoruco," said Ismael nearly in dismay. This was not going well at all.

Mayor Nicolás de Odnavo actually barked out a short laugh. "Why am I not surprised?"

Ismael Balenzuela stared at him blankly.

"I suppose," said the mayor, in what sounded like a nasty tone, "the good people at the beach house in Barahona recommended him to you?"

"Why, yes," faltered Ismael. "He was there when I arrived to see the house and was very cordial and helpful."

"Yes, he would be," said the mayor. "He is very helpful."

"Did I make a mistake?"

"That remains to be seen." The mayor paused and thought this over. Then he changed his tone, "But not necessarily. It may actually be useful to us."

The "us" encouraged Balenzuela a bit. Maybe this wasn't going as badly as he thought it was. "So, you think I should keep him?"

"Yes, of course, you should—for now."

"What do you think I need to do, or to know for now?" Balenzuela asked like a schoolchild trying to spell it all out right.

The mayor sat back and regarded him for a long moment. Then he seemed to make up his mind about something, for he said. "Yes, I think we can work together Señor Balenzuela. Only, you must understand, I know this area and its people and, particularly, its nuances, much better than you do."

"That goes without saying," agreed Balenzuela.

"You, in fact, I would hazard to observe—and, naturally, as respectfully as I can, you understand—well, you know nothing. Is that correct?"

"Hmmm," replied Ismael, thinking that one through but inevitably coming to the same conclusion, "Well, how could you not know it better? You are the mayor of a rich town."

"The richest town in the area and the most successful by far. And do you know why?"

"Because you are good at what you do?"

"Well, that, of course," confessed the mayor. "But it is because I grew up here and I know it and its people and its dynamics intimately. How could a stranger—no matter how astute," he added diplomatically—"know an area and its people as well as a native does—humble though I may be? For I am just a simple citizen myself."

Ismael Balenzuela stared at him. "A simple citizen" was hardly the regard in which the mayor so obviously held himself and which was coming across so blatantly, but, he said, "Yes, yes, but, at the same time, you are clearly a man standing out among his people with the God-given ability to lead them. What you have done here is admirable, Your Honor, and I am deeply honored and grateful to have the privilege to be mentored by such a man in this matter." Ismael knew he could heap it on with the best, when the situation so demanded.

The mayor obviously knew these were all *pamplinas*—empty praises in the traditional Spanish style—but it sounded like the right note to him and he realized he couldn't help feeling himself swell up with a bit of pride. Even though it was probably all just diplomacy, there might be a spark of grudging admiration in it, and this he would nurture in this young prospect. At the same time, he told himself firmly, he would have to watch this one. He wasn't as callow a youth as he appeared to be. Wrong choices are always part of being a stranger. How could they not be? But this young man knew how to handle himself in a tight situation, and much of the mayor's aggressiveness had been designed to ascertain how this one would react under pressure, if the mayor himself decided he was one with whom it was worth the trouble to work.

So, the mayor chose to help the relationship along. "I will tell you one thing, at this point," he offered, like a *pastele* he was laying before his guest, a kind of gesture to show that he could, indeed, be very helpful to this hopeful developer's progress, if the young man showed himself to be sufficiently cooperative.

Ismael Balenzuela looked to him expectantly.

"And that is that you are, indeed, wasting your time pursuing the beach house at Barahona."

"The lawyer said the same," admitted Balenzuela. "But I don't know why that is."

"Of course, you don't," agreed the mayor. "But now I will tell you why." He paused and Ismael Balenzuela said nothing, but kept the emotion of expectancy on his face. It was finally working.

Yes, thought the mayor to himself. This is the right attitude, if we are to get along. And then he gave his morsel to his new lapdog. "It is because the one who holds the property holds great power in this area. The property is symbolic of that power."

"So," said Ismael Balenzuela, "that is why you made your offer. Not because you wanted another beachfront holding. It is because you are a man who knows the power of a symbol."

"Yes, I do, and I mean to have it," said the mayor. "And I will brook no interference from anyone in this quest." And he gazed meaningfully at Balenzuela.

"There are many beautiful sites in this area," said his guest very carefully, "any one of which would make a beautiful resort."

"Yes, there are," said the mayor. "And many of these can be made available to the right man: the man who understands how things should go."

"I am that man," replied Ismael Balenzuela, as sincerely as he could muster up sincerity in the midst of such a disturbing conversation.

"Yes," said the mayor, watching him closely, "I believe you are."

"May I ask one more question?" asked Ismael Balenzuela.

The mayor looked annoyed, but said with faux cordiality, "Of course, you may, but, you must understand, you are prying into delicate local matters, and some answers I may not feel free to give out until we know each other much better."

"Oh, it's not that kind of question," Ismael raced to assure him.

"Well, what is it then?"

"My lawyer, Cueva de Piedra, recommended to me a real estate agent named Aña Behechio. Is this a good recommendation? Should I go with her as I look for properties?"

"My, my," said the mayor, sitting back and smiling. "Yes, you really do get around, don't you?"

"What do you mean?"

"By all means, go with her. I can see you may be more useful to me than I imagined."

Ismael Balenzuela stared back at him, uncertain that he liked the way that sounded.

But the older man simply nodded at him with what appeared to be approaching genuine affection and said, "You are in very good hands, my son, very good hands indeed." And he almost appeared to be rubbing his own hands in delight, as Mayor Nicolás de Odnavo then asked Ismael Balenzuela for all his contact information and, after a few assurances and parting pleasantries, ushered the puzzled young developer out the door.

18

Jo's mind was in a complete turmoil as she left Ricky's little house. He did not see her to the door. He was obviously conflicted, but so was she—that, and mystified. She paused with her hand on the gate. She went to the car, but simply stood next to it. Then she opened its door and sat inside, but did not start it. Instead, she prayed, leaning her head on the steering wheel, laying it all before her Great Heavenly Parent. "*Guakia Baba,*" she began with the traditional Taino "Our Father," and then "*nabori daca Diosa*" ("a servant of God am I"). And then, some in Taino, some in Spanish, some in English, she laid before her Creator her confusion; her anxiety for the safety, and her yearning for the presence, of her parents; her stress, and her concern over the wellbeing of her siblings; and the most disturbing and monstrous fear that she was going to be asked to do something that would change her life's direction in the most irretrievable way. "You are the God of all wisdom," she prayed. "You know the beginning and the end. You are the Revealer of all secrets. The prayer for wisdom is the prayer you always answer. I pray that prayer now. May your Great Spirit impart to me the insights I need to understand these secrets and in all to do your will. *Amén, Jan-jan catu* (So be it)."

As she sat back up, a single compelling thought took shape it her mind and filled her with peace. She must go and see the lawyer Angel Moreno Cueva de Piedra. And she must see him now. She felt herself completely fill with the conviction that all her answers lay in the mountain. And he was the one who knew its secret and its connection to her. She snatched up the leather purse that she kept with her always, normally slung over her shoulder, but now waiting beside her on the car seat, and fished out his card. "Villa Bahoruco," she read. "Why he's right here in this town," she exclaimed and then added, "Thank You, YaYa!"

At nearly the same moment Jo was bowing in her little rental car in Villa Bahoruco, praying to God, the only Lord of land and water (*Guami-ke-ni*), Ismael Balenzuela was hunched in his quite larger SUV at a left angle from her position, up on the other side of the steadily receding shoreline of Lake Enriquillo. He was also deeply disturbed, but he wasn't praying. He was plotting within himself.

I've got to be really careful with this one, he thought over and over again. This man could easily destroy everything—everything! Words of the mayor kept echoing in his thoughts, specifically: "I can see you may be more useful to me than I imagined." What did that mean? Did Ismael actually want to be "useful" to this mayor? What kinds of demands did this man mean to make on him? And what would happen to him if he refused? Failure, of course. But, there had been a hint of something more. Was it muted malevolence that he had detected, especially when the mayor accused him of "prying into delicate local matters?" That's exactly what he had said: "You are prying into delicate local matters." This man was taking all this very personally. Ismael felt like he had been caught planning to poach on the mayor's game reserves and had been dragged before him, rather than having come to see him on his own initiative. Now that he was thinking it over, Ismael felt a shuddering chill cross his shoulders. This locked-down town was a fiefdom—obviously. This mayor seemed to consider everything his own property!

Another thing he had said: "I will brook no interference from anyone." The words were imperious enough, but it was the way he had said it: as if this were grounds for capital punishment. Ismael shook his head. I can't let my imagination run away with me. After all, what can he do to me? He mulled that over for a minute. Honestly, he didn't know. He was a stranger in what he considered to be a half-civilized land, compared to Spain, with which he compared everywhere in the world. I could disappear and no one would know where I had gone. I must proceed very, very carefully, with this one, he counseled himself. This Nicolás de Odnavo is too strong and too self-assured. I really don't want to find out what would happen to me if I crossed him or any of his desires for gain. And, suddenly, Ismael Balenzuela felt a great desire to leave Villa Riqueza. He would explore carefully his other option: the real estate agent named Aña. And he would try to have as little to do with this Mayor Nicolás de Odnavo as he could.

So, obeying all of what he guessed would be the local traffic laws in regard to speed and other matters of motivation and vehicular etiquette; he carefully navigated his large car steadily out of town. But even as he nurtured his resolve, he realized that he would never really be able to keep it. All of his roads would invariably lead back to Villa Riqueza. It was in macrocosm what the mayor described the beach house in Barahona to be in microcosm—a seat and symbol of power.

While all this was going on with Ismael and to Jo, Star and Basil were sitting on the sand of the Bravado Beach Hotel with Daniela Archer, sunning.

Star had on enough sunblock to keep out all solar influence and, over her watchful eyes, enormously large sunglasses, so no one could see what she was watching. She was seated on a lounge chair with Basil on one side and Danny on the other, feeling a lot like a big game hunter, replete with bearer boy and tethered goat. She was content.

Basil was already beginning to burn on his nose and shoulders, but waiting patiently as Star did her magic.

Daniela was tucked into a string bikini, the kind that put the law to the test by exposing two extra cheeks with only a suggestion of fabric between them. It would not have served her in Ocean Grove on the New Jersey shore, but this was not New Jersey. She had a matching yellow, sleeveless wrap to put over it when she went inside the hotel proper, and Star managed to scud up her chair so as to block Basil's view of Danny luxuriously stretched out on her lounge chair. No need to confuse matters for him, she reasoned.

"Well, dear," she was assuring Daniela. "You are clearly the victim of a great injustice."

"That's what I think," murmured Danny, half asleep in the sun, her own sunblock clutched drowsily in her hand, yet being leisurely applied every half hour with startling regularity.

Basil intoned, "So wrong, so cruel," like a scorched Greek Chorus.

"But, you know, dear," Star assured her. "We can do something about this."

"We can?"

"Absolutely. We can check into the inheritance laws of the country. You know they may be different from those back in the States."

"Do you think so?"

"It's certainly worth checking." Star, of course, had already begun checking and so far had discovered—thanks to the hotel's pay-by-hour computer room—that, no matter what any will said, property went automatically in division to legal spouse and children. Gaining that information had stretched her Spanish to the limit, but the payoff was worth it. She had already ferreted out of Danny that Uncle Sol had never married and, therefore, had no spouse or children. And, since Daniela's father was his only living sibling, the property could very well go to him and all the children and not be able to be designated only to one. And, as she had assured Basil, what Danny received was as good as in their hands. So far it had been an extremely delightful and profitable day information-wise, and Star was happy and content. How gullible can a person be? she wondered to herself, and thanked her "lucky stars."

And this is where Ismael Balenzuela found them when he came sliding onto the beach in search of them in his slippery patent leather shoes, his wide white trousers, his open white designer shirt, and white panama hat, making him look, for all the world, like a hero in a silent movie. He took in the scene with mixed emotions. He gasped when he saw the resplendent Daniela, but as much for her proximity to the proprietorial Star as to the display of her undeniable charms. He readily took in Star's quizzical and mutely hostile look. Oh, oh. He was supposed to have done something with them—what was it? Oh, go and see their silly magnetic pole. He had forgotten. Basil, he took in and dismissed, but he did note that the man was badly in need of more sunblock and would pay the price of his neglect later. Ismael decided on all cordiality. "Dear friends," went his opening sally. "I am so sorry, so very, very sorry, that I was called away suddenly on business. Company matters, you understand. I wanted to leave you a message, but it was such a rush. And I hurried back as quickly as I could so that we could go on with our plans together. I hope you were not inconvenienced." He paused to see the effect.

Star regarded him with a fish eye, which, of course, he could not see behind her sunglasses, but said, in order to maintain appearances, "Of course, dear Ismael. We know how busy you are on business matters. We were simply all waiting here for you, enjoying the surf and the sand." And she nodded her head slightly toward Danny, saying in a single gesture: and we weren't wasting our time. We got the pigeon and we're keeping her here next to us. No reason to upset her, but we'll work this out later. We've all got to get some kind of workable game plan so we don't waste any more time. We're broke, see? So we've got to get something on, a.s.a.p.! All that packed into a look and a gesture, but Ismael Balenzuela understood most of it fully and exactly as she intended it.

"I'm here now," he said soothingly. "Let me put on my swim trunks and we'll chat a bit, and then I'll take all of you to lunch. How would that be?"

Basil brightened up completely and Star nodded and let a small smile play on her lips.

Well, that worked, thought Ismael, as he knew it would.

He was back quickly and the only one of the four to go into the water. He was a strong swimmer and cut sleekly across the waves, conveniently placing himself so Danny could have a front-on view of him bobbing about without having to turn her head. She did take him in and watched him from behind her own great sunglasses as he strode in from the water, shaking the drops from his curly hair. She noted with approval and a little bit of excitement his manly, slightly hairy chest, his rippling pectoral and shoulder muscles, and the flexing of his biceps and triceps, invigorated by the sea.

Whatever works, Ismael thought, as he fired his bring-it-home smile at Danny.

That evening, supper was full and jovial at the hotel restaurant. Basil and Star had obviously been scrimping and they nearly shoved it in with both hands. Danny picked at her food, but downed the *piña colada* Balenzuela urged on her with his cordial, "You've never had one? All these years you've been coming to this wonderful country? Well, tonight we'll rectify that!"

"I don't really drink," she warned him. "It's bad for the complexion."

But then another one followed.

Ismael began wondering what effect the rum might have on her, but she seemed to like it and winning her regard and affection was a crucial part of the plan.

Just how much effect it had on her he was to discover very shortly.

By the time the evening's entertainment was about to begin at quarter of ten that evening, Daniela had put away quite a number of *piña coladas* and, as Star put it, their guest was "feeling no pain."

Daniela was laughing and talking much more loudly than usual. She was still dressed in her yellow wrap over her tiny bikini and she had fished out of her purse a pair of pendant earrings so big it looked like she was hung on them, rather than vice versa. But, as with everything she chose to wear, they worked. She had also left her big sunglasses on in the bright lights of the open-air pavilion where the show took place each night and she stood out like a shooting star—a yellow blaze of activity that caught the attention of the entertainers who were out working the crowd before the evening's presentation began.

On the agenda before every song and dance performance in many all-inclusive hotels is what is called euphemistically the "icebreaker." What it amounts to is members of the staff cajoling unsuspecting tourists up onto the stage and humiliating them in public for the amusement of everyone wise enough not to mount those fateful steps.

To spot Danny and get her onto the stage was the work of a moment. She practically flew up there for this evening's "icebreaker": the Ms. Bravado Contest. This added a seventh to the six poor souls from around the world who stood uncomfortably against the back curtain as if in a police lineup: two waifs from France in short little blue and black sundresses; a voluptuous, medically enhanced thirty-something from Argentina who stopped all Latin male hearts in the pavilion; a couple of college girls from the United States who couldn't say no and "thought it might be fun"; a seasoned,

I've-been-here-before Dominican woman who was obviously bound to win as the local choice; and the inebriated Danny, lurching toward a chair in center stage in order to lean on it.

The contest started calmly and innocently enough with a merengue and bachata competition that eliminated the two college girls by lack of audience approval. Danny, to the amazement of Ismael, Star, and Basil, suddenly righted herself and did an impressive set of Dominican dance steps, beaming her dazzling smile on the audience.

The Argentine heart-stopper was out on the next set of deep bending exercises, getting down and waving her new assets around, but having trouble getting them all back up to the hooting of the audience.

Now came the standard oldies rock 'n' roll strutting to an atavistic Bill Haley tune and out went the French, and it was down to Danny and the Dominican incumbent. The audience had been cheering and clapping for them both equally, Danny having identified herself at the introductions as Dominican, not American, for this evening, so it was now a hometown contest.

As everyone knew it would be, the final slot was given over to *reguetón*, driving Latin rap, in general, and, particularly, to the booty call specifically. By this time, Danny was sweating all over from the dancing and so she flung off her wrap. To the astonishment of the audience, she was now dancing solely in nothing but the string bikini. The audience leaped to its feet. Danny and her Dominican opponent spun around at the musical cue, almost in sync, with their backs to the audience. The control room pumped up the volume of the musical beat. It and the cheering were now deafening, practically at the level of pain. Balenzuela snatched his paper napkin out from under his drink, tore it in two, and stuffed the two halves in his ears. Star was staring at Basil; Basil was fixed on the stage. The audience went delirious as Danny and the Dominican woman shook their backsides in every conceivable direction. Basil began gasping for breath, holding his sides, and practically falling on the ground, shaking with great gales of laughter.

The contest thundered down to the wire. People were shouting either name. The master of ceremonies was running back and forth, indicating with a pointed finger down toward one head, to a tumultuous roar, then the other to equal pandemonium.

Suddenly, Daniela stopped shaking and froze stock-still. Her eyes glazed over, then seemed to roll back into her head. She turned around, facing the audience and half crumpled forward, leaning way over. And then she regurgitated all over the front stairs up to the stage.

The audience gasped and gaped as Danny collapsed back and slowly slumped down onto the stage, passed out.

The staff simply handed the complementary bottle of alcohol that was the winner's prize to the panting and staring Dominican woman, as Star and Basil rushed forward toward Danny and Ismael hurried off to his room.

Hours later, Daniela slowly came to. Her head felt like a tour bus was parked on it. Her eyes ached and she had trouble focusing. Slowly, her sister Ruby came into view.

"Where—where am I?" Danny managed.

"Back at the hotel," snapped Ruby.

"Which—which hotel?"

"Los Diamantes, of course! Your 'new friends'—you know who I mean? —the ones who sound like they escaped from a 1930s movie?"

Daniella nodded and winced.

"Yeah, those! They called us and I had to go and get the rental car from Uncle Sol's and haul you back here." Ruby said it with a snort and Daniela winced again and held her head.

"I don't remember too much," said Danny feebly, trying but failing to sit up.

"Well, you will," said Ruby curtly. "There were plenty of cell phones there last night, and some of those little personal movie cameras too, and your antics have gone viral. Your little escapade is all over the net!"

19

IF ANGEL MORENO CUEVA de Piedra was surprised to see Jo standing at his door, he did not show it. "Please come in," was all he said, and stepped back with a deferent flourish of his hand, indicating he would be deeply honored if she would condescend to enter.

"Thank you," said Jo, noting the closed-circuit camera mounted above the outside door and surmising this is why the lawyer himself and not his assistant had come to greet her.

If Ricky's reception had been the depth of boorishness, Lawyer Cueva de Piedra's was the height of courtesy, as she expected. But, she doubted she was going to pry much more information out of this one than she had out of the other, despite the disparity of styles. At the same time, Jo felt she had been led here as a result of her prayer and she had brought with her the crowbar of her determination. So, she was prepared to pry like a safecracker. She didn't care how guarded or protected he kept his own counsel. She meant to crack open the storage bin of his resolve. If the skill of her questions didn't work, of course, there was the dynamite of action, as every community organizer knows. She could create a strike force out of her siblings, throwing a few garbage cans around—and making a nuisance of themselves—as she went after the strongbox of secrets with whomever would break it open for her. Whatever it took. But, right now, what it took was following the wayward path of a courteous conversation, so she embarked on that.

"How are you feeling?" asked the lawyer with what looked like genuine concern and affection. "The last time I saw you, you were quite ill."

"Yes, and thank you so much for asking. I think it was a combination of payment due for overwork at home, the ramifications of a sleepless flight—I can never sleep on planes—and a harrowing journey—my sister Ruby was driving!—and, of course, all the change. But, I guess what exacerbated it all and pushed the effectiveness of my immune system aside was not finding my parents or being able to bring closure by proper grieving for my beloved uncle." All this she delivered in the correct Spanish style, choosing the vocabulary carefully for its politeness and formality.

The little lawyer obviously approved and nodded with his deferential style. "So glad you are obviously recovered now. Won't you have something to drink?"

And now, thought Jo, the mandatory pause for refreshments: either espresso calculated to jump-start a zombie, or *chinola* juice to follow up the recent applications of *té criolla*. She was putting her bet on the juice, since this man appeared genuinely concerned about her wellbeing. "How kind you are to offer," she said.

"Would *chinola* juice be suitable?" he asked.

Bingo! She thought. I'm on the wavelength. "How nice that would be. Thank you so much for your kindness." She waited as his office assistant, whom he introduced as Octavia Belgrada, an angular and efficient-appearing young woman, a head taller than he, bustled about in the latter part of the house and returned with a little tray with napkins and a large glass of orange-colored passion fruit juice on a leather coaster.

Then the assistant left the room and closed the door behind her. Both Jo and the lawyer glanced automatically at the large monitoring screen in the bookcase behind him and saw Octavia seat herself at her own desk and continue to work at her computer.

"Please excuse the lack of ice," he apologized. "Octavia is a new worker. She keeps insisting on using filtered rather than bottled water for ice and I know this would not be the best thing for you just now."

"How kind you are to think of that," she answered and took an expected sip of the juice, to indicate that she trusted his concern for her welfare completely and did not feel she had to check with him whether the juice had been made with bottled water. The juice really did feel refreshing, and it triggered one thought she had not realized before. Ricky, despite his acerbic temperament, had thoughtfully not included ice in the same drink he had served her just hours before. He hadn't couched it in the pleasantries she was now receiving, but he had been attentive to her health just the same.

The lawyer looked at her expectantly. The amenities were over. "How can I be of service to you?" he asked.

Jo thought a moment and then decided to hit him with a big shot—pull rank and fire off the Big Gun. "I was led here," she said, "by the Great Spirit."

"Indeed?" said the lawyer.

"Yes. I went this morning to speak with Enrique Asenao."

"Well," said the lawyer, with genuine surprise, and then again, "Well . . ." He was calculating. And then he asked: "How did you know to whom to go?"

"All of you—yourself, Don Ramón, Doña Lucia—kept referring to a 'Ricky' when we were speaking at Las Olas del Sol. It did not take much imagination for me to figure out it would be the Ricky who is our director of communications. It stood to reason."

"Of course, of course," agreed the lawyer, shaking his head yes. "He is really a very fine young man. He takes his duties to the Tribe very seriously, but at times he is a difficult person with whom to deal."

"I am glad to hear that difficulty is confined to 'at times,'" Jo grinned. And though Angel Moreno Cueva de Piedra seemed incapable, given the barrier of his courtesy, to break out in an actual laugh, he did allow a slight—but, of course, at the same time cordial and deferential—smile to suggest itself on his lips.

"You see," said Jo, following up her opening gambit, "I did learn some information of value to me from Ricky. I learned my parents are safe and the answer to their whereabouts and to this whole, convoluted inheritance matter lies at a 'mountain.' I do not recall ever visiting a specific mountain in my youth as I roamed the Sierra del Bahoruco with Uncle Sol. What I mean and what I am saying," she repeated for emphasis, watching the lawyer steadily to underscore that emphasis, "is that I walked with him over many mountains, but none of them was ever highlighted as specifically special or above the rest in importance. And he never indicated one of them would one day be my mountain. And beyond that," and she played her trump card, "how can someone own a mountain in a public forest? It makes no sense!"

"No," agreed the lawyer, "You are absolutely right. The mountain to which Ricky and all of us are referring is not in the national reserve. It is different." He paused, measuring his words out carefully in his mind, and then he said. "It's not really so much of a mountain as a hill. Everyone who lives and farms on it is a member of the Tribe. The Tribe itself holds title to it, as it does to much of the land in that area. No one goes there without a specific reason."

"I was told often of the secret compound which is the heart of the tribal community: of the homes and the farms and the refineries," pursued Jo, "These are different than the mountain?"

"The compound? Well, they are related," he said carefully.

"But, now, the mountain somehow figures into my life—but I am not allowed to visit it or see it—and yet it may hold the answer to the whereabouts of my parents. You must see how frustrating all this is to me!"

"Of course," agreed the lawyer and spread his hands out toward her, as if to say in a gesture: but what can I do?

Jo thought to herself, you can give me another key piece to this exasperating puzzle. So she said, "You understand I am a person of action. I have been a community organizer and am now a minister of the gospel of Jesus Christ—Yeshua—YaYael—son of YaYa." She paused again, watching him carefully. This was a conversation, she told herself, in measures, being meted out like artifacts being loaned for display from an archive. So she added to show her sincerity and her caution, indicating, if these were tribal secrets, she was responsible enough to keep them, "And I make no move without consulting YaYa. So, when I left Ricky's home, I paused to consult the Great Spirit and was led here." That was all she had, so she stopped. If this appeal to the leading of no one less than God's Holy Spirit didn't work, her arsenal was empty.

The lawyer nodded slowly. And, then, like a miser, painstakingly opening his tightly locked wallet, he parceled out his words in a slow, low, measured voice, "No one can tell you the way to go to the mountain, be-cause, my dear friend, you are being watched." It was the clinking of coins into her hand.

"Watched! You mean I am being monitored by the Tribe?" she de-manded, thinking of Ricky's inane statement that he had to approve of her.

"Oh, no," hurried the lawyer, gesturing with his hand to speak softly, "Not the Tribe. That may come—and perhaps it is being done now by some, but that is not what I mean at all."

"Well, then by whom?" asked Jo more softly.

"There is a presence here," whispered the lawyer carefully, "A great evil that extends across the region. It is hidden and lethal and it is opposed to the wellbeing of our tribe, yes, but—even greater—to the wellbeing of our very nation. It keeps itself largely hidden and is driven by those who hold great power in the area. Their network is everywhere. Few, even among us, can be completely trusted. That they know of your presence must be accepted as inevitable. This is why all of us must be so careful."

"My presence?" gasped Jo. "Who cares about my presence? Whether I am here or in the States or anywhere—I am of no significance." She paused a moment and reflected. "Wait!" she said, suddenly. "Does it have to do with the inheritance?"

"Well, the inheritance in this case is sort of an afterthought. . . ."

"What are you saying?"

"Well, of course, it has to do with keeping the whereabouts of the mountain a secret. How can one hide a mountain? It is just one of many, many mountains that are in or about or before or within the simple foothills of the great Sierra de Bahoruco. How can one identify one mountain in a range this vast that it extends over most of the region of Independencia? But, if that could be done, the result would be devastating." He paused and with eyes widened in concern he assured her, "Devastating on many, many levels. The Tribe would be in serious jeopardy." "And," he added, "so would be the entire western region."

"All this for a mountain?" scoffed Jo, gently. "Why is one mountain, or foothill in this case, perhaps, more valuable than any other? What is this mountain, a symbol?"

"No," said the lawyer. "That's not it."

"That's not it? Then what? It is, after all, my inheritance you say, but I am not told where it is because I am being watched by someone. All right, I can accept that for now, for the safety of the Tribe. But you also tell me it is not of symbolic value, so, to me, I begin wondering, why should I care about a mountain or a foothill? You already told me that the Tribe holds title to it. It is then in a kind of trust. And, to assure its safety, everyone who lives upon it is a trusted tribal member. Then it is safe enough, and yet you and everyone with whom I speak is worried about it. What is it about the mountain that makes it so important? What's on it exactly?"

"There is nothing on it of value or significance, besides the herds and the farms," said the lawyer, watching her face carefully.

"Then what?" said Jo, narrowing her own eyes so that what he saw, she hoped, was implacable determination to learn the reason for the demand for caution. And then it came.

"It is not what is *on* the mountain," he said in a hushed tone, "it is what is *in* the mountain. And that is everything I can tell you and really much more than I should." He was whispering so softly now, confidentially—no, nearly conspiratorially—that she had to strain to hear him. He was literally glancing about toward the monitor and the little windows of his office. It was probably theatrical in intent, Jo figured, but it got the point across.

"So, for this everyone lives a life of caution?"

The lawyer suddenly stepped around from behind his desk and took her hand, which shocked Jo. He was so locked into the old traditional courtly style that the idea he would touch her was astounding. He leaned in and whispered, leaning over his desk so he could speak directly into her right ear, so she leaned her own head downwards to save him the effort. "All of this is tied together." His tone was urgent but still hushed. "*This* is why your parents fled. People have died for less. You must not know too much about it until things are settled. If a process goes as many of us believe it should, then you will know all. But, until then," and he punctuated his words as best as he could while still whispering, "you must—for your own wellbeing—remain like a tourist. That is the only way we can be assured of your safety."

"Ahhh." Jo looked at him with consternation. "And, as are my parents, I am in jeopardy too?"

"You would be, if you knew the location of the mountain and could lead them there."

"What am I to do?" pleaded Jo. "I am determined to find my parents."

"You must wait."

"For what?"

"The gathering of the *caciques*." And that was all he would say.

20

DANIELA SAT BEFORE RUBY'S traveling computer and watched the clearest and most graphic of the videos over and over again. She could not believe her eyes. She remembered vaguely being on stage and people cheering, but no really specific moments. She winced each time she watched the final segment: her near nakedness, the degrading gyrations in her drunken lurching, the hooting and jeering of the crowd. Early on, she had begun to cry. Now there were no tears left. Ruby was out running. Ben she guessed was at the casino, broke now but just watching others. Jo was gone somewhere. She was utterly alone.

The image she had of herself was shattered. She was not that stupid; she knew this was now with her forever. She would never be free of what she had done. Her father and mother might see it. Her eventual children might see it! It existed forever on the internet. She would never be rid of this disgrace.

Daniela found some more tears and let them go. But nothing helped. She turned the computer off and looked at her tear-stained reflection in the dark screen. She was all obscured. She was a shadow. That was all she'd ever been, really.

And then she made a resolve. She would turn this into something that changed her life. She'd been Danny the party girl. She would be Danny no longer. She was a woman now. From now on, she swore to herself, she would be Daniela, the better for it all. She would change her life. She would orient herself. And she would become an orientor of others.

After all, Ruby guided her college students into maturity through sports, and Jo mentored her parishioners into deeper spiritual maturity. Why couldn't she, Daniela, become the great orientor of the disoriented?

The profoundly spiritual Star and Basil could become her mentors, she reasoned. They could teach her the way of orientation and she could become a teacher of others.

She had been wasting her life driving a school bus. She had never been able to control the children anyway. And it was so hard always being on time—keeping on the route schedule. She had almost been fired a half dozen times, but the work was so difficult few others wanted to do it or succeeded at it. She worked with mainly mothers who had a built-in authority that Daniela envied, but could not emulate.

But now things would be different. Now she herself would leave the conveying of pupils and become, instead, their enlightener: a teacher, herself. No one would ever associate the woman she would become with this foolish girl she had been lamenting on the all-seeing screen.

"I promise myself this," she said aloud, solemnly. She dried her eyes, rose up carefully and, since she was still a bit shaky, guided herself along the edges of the furniture in quest of a cold shower. When she felt she had washed off all of the previous night, she dressed as modestly as her wardrobe allowed, went downstairs, still gliding along the railing, and ordered a meal of vegetables and fruits. Then she sat on the porch for a long spell, watching the waves of the Caribbean Sea roll out the old sand and debris and roll in the new waters of change.

It was a pensive Daniela that Ruby found when she returned.

"What? Are you still hung over?" Ruby demanded, clattering up the steps.

"No," said Daniela. "I'm fine now."

"Good."

"I mean, I'm really fine now."

"Fine," said Ruby. "I'm going to go take a shower."

"May the Pole orient you," called Daniela after her. But Ruby was already gone.

Alone again, Daniela decided it was time now to think her behavior through very carefully, starting with the previous night. I need to discover what is really driving me, she thought. I've never done that. But I need to now, because I've got to know—how did I fall so far as to make such a *bobo*—such a fool of myself? She realized she was slipping in and out of Spanish and English. Maybe it is because I am here and I've dropped my guard. It's true, I got caught up in the excitement—caught up in the expectations of the crowd. But, then, no, that wasn't it exactly. She shook her head and winced. "OOOHHH," she moaned. It was the rum. That was it. It's true, she thought, Ruby's right. I'm hung over because I was drunk. And, how many times have I laughed at others who did stupid things when they were drunk? And how many times have I warned myself that too much drinking makes one do things in public one never imagined one would do?

Into her mind flooded the memory of her friend Barbie lurching onto a table, trying to dance at a bar they'd been in back in Richfield. Everyone at the table leaped back and a woman screamed because she thought Barbie was going to plummet off head first. The bartender and the bouncer had to coax her off the table, explaining they couldn't afford the lawsuit if she got hurt. They'd asked both of them to leave and not to return. Daniela was ashamed, but Barbie was just laughing and laughing about it all. "Are you the designated driver?" they had asked Daniela. And she'd said she guessed she was, although they had not come together. And then Barbie had thrown up all over the front seat and floor of the car. And it wasn't even Daniela's. She had borrowed it for the night from her sister Jo. Danny had had to have it fumigated, it reeked so much. Well, she realized with a sickening feeling, seeing herself in the exact place of Barbie, whom she had come to despise, that's what she herself had done last night. She was no better. In fact, she was worse off, because Barbie had not been photographed or videoed and you could not see her cavorting about and the disgusted reactions of those whose night she was ruining plastered all over the internet. And Daniela felt her eyes well up again and several tears trickle down her face.

She wanted so much to be respected like Jo was and Ruby was. She wasn't just a pretty face. Sure, she had modeled a little when she was a teenager and at twenty. Mainly brassieres and other lingerie, and didn't want to be thought of that way by all who knew her, so she'd quit. The money wasn't worth it. No one would respect her the way she wanted by just seeing her smiling in a bra.

And how many times had she reminded herself not to drink? And how faithfully she had followed that advice—and stayed out of so many jams because of it. Barbie had finally gotten herself pregnant by some guy she had met in another bar and had ended up a single mother, so sorry about not dealing with her drinking when she should have, and stuck now with a child she really hadn't wanted, but couldn't give up no matter what was best for it. Her little girl was now in a foster home, but Barbie kept visiting and countermanding and undermining the authority of the foster parents. The girl was so confused she was out of control. Daniela realized, I could easily have ended up in the same place last night if I had been in any other company. Some man might have picked me up and who knows what would have happened to me? I can't remember most of what happened, as it is. And she thanked God for her new friends. But, she wondered, how many of those *piña coladas* had she put away anyway? And what was the result? This time she didn't shake her head—at least not physically. See? She told herself. See? She was learning. She could change. She would change!

But all those cell phone videos up on YouTube spreading her momentary indiscretion all over the world of the net! Literally, they had been the work of a minute. In sixty seconds of display and sixty seconds investment in downloading, her lapse had gone viral and that—as they say—was that. For all she knew, all her friends at home had seen it and tweeted it. Text messages may have shot around like fireworks on the fourth of July. It was all naughty enough to be exciting, because she was beautiful, and she was noisy enough to attract attention. And worst of all, she had done it in front of Bo and Peep and their friend from Spain, people she had wanted to impress with her spirituality and her intelligence.

Daniela began to cry again. Would anyone ever let her change? Had she annulled that possibility? It was bitter—bitter. She would always look like such a plaything. She hadn't asked for her beauty. It was a gift, but she was squandering it. Maybe she wasn't as smart as Jo or Ruby, but she had a brain and she had aspirations. She wanted to be so much more, she told herself, and this orienting at the Magnetic Pole—so new, so exciting, so trendy—this might have been it. But now, who could take her seriously? Bo and Peep had to be ashamed of her. And that Ismael from Spain! Why, she realized with a sudden shock, he had been the one plying her with drinks. Maybe it was his fault? But, no—she would have shaken that thought away if she could have shaken her head without pain; it wasn't his fault. She had no doubt been demanding the drinks. And all her life she had gotten what she wanted when she was out and in a party mood; her looks assured her of that. She couldn't blame anybody else. He wasn't up on the stage. She was. She had gone along with it all. Nobody had forced her to do anything.

So, now her reputation was all shot to blazes. All that up until now being so careful? All that not allowing herself to be drunk, rejecting illegal drugs entirely, even carefully watching the effect of food on her complexion and her waistline, her smooth freedom from age? All that care to present a lovely face and personality to the world? All that care was down the toilet! She had vomited on stage—the climax of every video—some enhanced with effects to get her mouth up close to watch her projectile heaving on to the steps and then cutting to the audience to watch them howling—some in laughter and some in dismay—and all after waving herself around like a five-buck hooker. And Daniela began crying so hard that she shut her eyes.

And then a hand took hers. She wiped a sleeve across her face and looked into the sympathetic eyes of Peep herself. "Oh, dear, how are you today?" said her voice softly. It was really her!

"You're here?" Daniela gasped.

"Of course, dear Danny. We brought you home last night."

"And had to walk back," grumbled Basil, who was standing behind her. Star kicked him on the shin out of sight with her heel, and he grunted and sat down heavily on the porch rubbing it. But Daniela took no notice.

"I'm so ashamed," cried Daniela, still consumed entirely with her self-inflicted misfortune.

"You're still disoriented, dear," said Star glibly. She patted Daniela's hand. "It happens."

"Why didn't you stop me?" pleaded Daniela.

"We tried to," lied Basil. "But you were having such a good time. . . ."

"And, you know, dear, our faith is all about freedom," said Star, making it up as she went along. "You are the measure of what is good for you and what is not. Sometimes, one has to discover the positive from the negative for oneself."

Basil paused in rubbing his shin. Star was so good on her feet. He had to give her that. "It's like negative and positive images in art," he intoned, drawing on a scam they had once done, selling forgeries of middle-level living artists as the real thing, until one of the painters got wind of it and called in the cops.

Daniela gaped at him.

Tone it down, buster, said Star's glare.

"What I mean," backtracked Basil, "is that one sees the positive when one rejects the negative."

"Just what I've been telling you, dear," said Starling, shooting him her seal of approval with her wink. Simply using my words is always the best policy she was lecturing by her look.

Basil nodded to them both and responded, "All people do such foolish things before they are completely oriented. It stands to reason. So, don't blame yourself. Everyone is in that cellblock before they are freed."

"Oh, you mean I haven't blown my chance to be a Polarian?" asked Danny with a note of hope so pathetic that even Star's heart might have melted, had it been capable of it.

"Of course not! All of us—even Bo and I—have done things we regret."

Basil's mouth dropped open and he sent her a warning glare, but she cruised on.

"These things give real substance to our testimony of delivery," she explained. "We use our failings as our strengths!"

"What do you mean?" asked Daniela, sitting forward.

"Why, it's easy to see that you regret your actions. So, yesterday you may have been the party girl who danced and fell, but today you are beginning to become oriented. You are now turning into a sober, mature woman whose life is being salvaged!"

"You're ready to give everything to the Pole," offered Basil, hopefully.

Oh, oh, thought Star. He's about to overdo it—as always. "What Bo means," she said quickly, "is that all of your thoughts, all of your energy, all of your heart's desires are ready to be sacrificed to the quest to orient others. Let those who have fallen like you into disappointing lives gain the true oriented lives that they always dreamed they could have."

"Let the Pole orient you," intoned Basil, like a benediction.

"Let the Pole orient you!" cried Daniela and reached over and hugged Star. Star smiled—Daniela was in the bag! They had their mascot. The idea to exploit Daniela's beauty had been a no-brainer to all three of them. Her lovely face gracing all Polarian product lines, her seductive gaze luring readers from the cover of the book they would slap together, her lovely, soft, little-girlish voice speaking over the internet, reading a script they would write, inviting the hordes of marks to come to their retreat center to be oriented. They would make her a kind of New Age icon, like the good old '70s and '80s—when so many made so much off so many more—and the best part was they would do it entirely on her own money, too, if they could finagle enough away from the other heirs. Danny herself, reasoned Star, would all but throw it at them. They had their bait for her: cleaning up her image from last night. And they had their bait for others in Danny and her allures. Now, all they needed was to ready their trap.

"Why don't you come back with us to the Bravado Beach Hotel?" urged Star.

"Oh, I can't! I can't! I can't face everybody since last night." Daniela's eyes widened in horror and she began to cry again.

"But that's exactly what you must do," explained Star. "You go and face your failing and triumph over it!"

"Like falling off a bike—or off a horse," offered Basil for support. "You have to get back on immediately. That's a rule!"

"It is?"

"Of course!" Basil and Star said simultaneously.

Daniela faltered. "I don't know . . . ."

"We'll be beside you every step of the way," Star assured her.

"You might actually be a celebrity," grinned Basil.

"What?"

"He's kidding, dear," snapped Star. "What he means is that by today most people have already checked out of the hotel."

"They have?"

"Certainly," said Star. "It's a hotel. Nobody stays long. Besides, it's a new day. Nobody will even notice you."

"Just stay behind those sunglasses," agreed Basil.

"But I had them on last night," whined Daniela. "I saw them in the videos."

"Don't worry," persisted Star, taking it down a few pegs to communicate to the fragment that was her view of Daniela's intellect. "You aren't dressed like you were last night."

I'll say! said Basil to himself, but not out loud. What he said out loud was: "No one will recognize you in the modest clothes you have today."

"They won't?"

"Of course not," Star assured her as she gently pulled Daniela to her feet. "And don't forget, dear. We'll be beside you every step of the way."

"I don't know. . . ."

"Danny," said Star in her entrepreneurial tone.

"Daniela," corrected Danny. "I'm Daniela now. It's the new mature me."

"Of course," said Star easily. "The new you on the way to orientation."

"That's it!"

"Well, Daniela, I want you to look into the distance, over the ocean." Star said it with a flourish.

Basil caught the gleam in his beloved's eye and thought to himself, oh boy, here it comes. This ought to be good!

"It's the Caribbean Sea, actually," murmured Daniela.

"Right!" said Star. "I want you to gaze out over this sea of possibilities. Think big thoughts. Let your mind race across the globe. Around the world! I want you to think of the masses!"

The masses of marks, grinned Basil to himself.

"All these poor unfortunates drudging through lives of miserable disorientation. And now, I want you to think of what we—you!—have to offer them. Meaning, redemption—orientation!"

"Orientation," breathed Daniela.

"We have a world to right," said Star, her eyes shining.

"A world to right!" repeated Basil, leaning in closely.

"A world to right—and a campaign to plan. Let's go do it!" ordered Starling, and, keeping her grip on Daniela's arm, she walked her down the stairs. "To destiny," she said.

"To destiny!" cried out Daniela.

To the best scam we've ever had, smiled Basil as smugly to himself as he had ever done.

21

As soon as Jo left Ricky, he watched her go by past his window and then turned to walk to the kitchen. But before he could do anything, he was called back by another knock on his door. He frowned and tossed it open, assuming she was back again for something or other. Instead, his childhood friend Tomás, short, square, solid, pushed past him into the house.

"What have you got to eat?" demanded Tomás, "I'm starving."

"Pork, in the refrigerator. There's some *casabe* in the bread box. I have some plantain . . ."

"What kind?"

"It's *mangu*. I made it for breakfast."

"You still got any onions on it?"

"Of course! What's mashed *platano* without *cebolla*?"

"Good!"

"I thought you were someone else."

"Yeah, Jo Archer." Tomás began rummaging about in Ricky's refrigerator. "You've got some *toyota* here too."

"It's from last night. Help yourself. How did you know she was here?"

"She's out in her car now."

"Just sitting there and thinking?"

"I don't know," said Tomás, his mouth full of cassava bread from the bread box as a prelude for greater foraging. "She's got her head down on the steering wheel."

"Humph! Maybe she's crying!" snorted Ricky.

"I don't think so. She looked pretty composed when she came out. I was watching the house till she left. I don't want anybody to know that I was here."

"Why? Where have you been?"

"In the mountains, in the valleys, I've been tracking where the carbon thieves have been. There's destruction in spaces all across the unguarded border. We need to act, and we need to act now!"

"We can't move before the new *cacique* is chosen," said Ricky quietly.

"Yeah, that's what everybody says!" grunted Tomás.

"The forest is vast. We can wait and do things in a coordinated order."

"You sound like the old chiefs," sneered Tomás. "When you were young, you would not have hesitated."

"'Wisdom comes with living. . .'"

"You hurl proverbs at me, while our trees are being decimated? Well, there are others who feel as I do. And, you, Enrique," he tried to shame his reluctant friend, "named for the great *cacique!*"

Ricky was unperturbed. "Yes, and what did he do? He took his time to know his enemy and lay his plans. And when he struck, he struck decisively."

"Well, I think time for planning is too short. I'm taking whoever will go with me to the trouble spots and we will rid our land of at least some of these *contrabandistas.*"

"You speak like you were still a child!" snapped Ricky. "You think these marauders work alone? There are forces—internal agents—that are making this possible. They are killing forest rangers. How are they doing that? The army is in the mountains now. Why can they not find them? There is so much more to this than any of us knows, including you! We have to learn the true faces of our enemies—and then, like Enrique, we can strike at them all!"

"Well, while you do your research, some of us are convinced we must act. I'm going back to the mountain with my men. We'll save what trees we can. If anybody gets hurt, that's their problem. You can ferret out the rest of what's going on."

Ricky looked at him and his voice softened. "Go with caution, my friend."

"I'm armed," said Tomás.

"You don't know what you are fighting," warned Ricky. "You think you are going to face a few Haitian businessmen, sneaking across the border to drag a few trees into the river to burn on the other side where two trucks are waiting with burlap sacks? Is that it? Well, I think there is so much more to all this. I think these thieves are being allowed to come. I think they may be supported. I think you may find yourselves outmaneuvered, outgunned, and out of luck."

"Well," said Tomás, "we'll see."

Ricky could see and he could understand how resolute Tomás had become. He knew about resolve. And he knew how serious the decimation of the forest had become. Every one of the Tribe knew.

"All right, but, first, take this." He took a hammer off a peg on a back wall and pried up two floorboards in the kitchen, uncovering the bare ground beneath them. Underneath in oilskin sheathes were two Humboldt Drilling Protector rifles, each one with three barrels. Ricky handed him one, warning, "Don't use it unless you absolutely have to. Remember, it's a strictly defensive model, effective for any emergency. If you have to use it, then shoot over their heads. Don't aim at anyone. Don't maim or kill anybody. I'm holding you to this."

"Soooo, this is why you don't have a cement floor," observed Tomás, smirking, all but ignoring Ricky's words of caution.

"Yes, and I came by these dearly. You take one and bring it back to me, both of you, in one piece."

Tomás took the gun and, as he did, he snarled as much to himself as to Ricky, "You'd think my dad with all his money could have given me something as good as this! In fact, he should have sent some of that bodyguard of his that he keeps parading around in Villa Riqueza to help us out, but he's so wrapped up in his showpiece of a town, I have to raise my own funds and find my own soldiers. It's not right! Nobody helps me but you, Ricky. You won't come with me, will you?"

"I can't. I've got my hands full here with you know who!" And he jerked his head toward the street where Jo presumably still sat in her car. "But, be careful, my friend, and heed what I say."

Tomás shook his head, disgusted at his friend's priorities, tucked the sheathed rifle under his arm, and, without another word, stalked out.

22

Aʟʟ ᴛʜʀᴏᴜɢʜ ᴛʜᴇ ᴅʀɪᴠᴇ, Jo prayed and puzzled over all the information she had pried loose first from Ricky and then the lawyer. And, by the time she arrived home at Las Olas del Sol, she had pieced it all together. She did not like the picture that was resulting.

She greeted Ernesto quietly at the gate, asking him one brief question, "Have any guests arrived yet?"

"No, Josefina, not yet," he answered. "But we are expecting them momentarily."

"Thank you Ernesto," she said, relieved she would have a few hours alone to confirm her fears.

As she stepped onto the porch and into the house, Doña Lucia looked up to greet her, paused as she saw her face, and then picked up her cell phone from the table next to her and called Don Ramón to come at once. Jo waited silently. The two women stood there, thoughtfully regarding each other. When Don Ramón arrived, Lucia put her hand on his arm. "It is time," she said softly.

Ramón searched Jo's face and then nodded. "Yes," he said.

Jo, in turn, searched both their faces and, then, without a greeting, said sadly, "Has all this secrecy been a test? I need to know."

"All your life has been a test," said Doña Lucia.

"And my parents. They are part of this?"

"No," said Don Ramón, "your parents came upon something they were not meant to see—something deeply evil. They barely escaped with their lives. But they knew where to flee for refuge and they are now in complete safety. You need not worry about them at all."

"And I?"

"You are not in immediate danger, *Querida*."

"Perhaps not physical danger, but something I fear even more. I believe you want to change my life—radically!" complained Jo.

"Not really change it at all, Josefina," replied Lucia, "but fulfill it. This was your uncle's choice. He carefully considered all the options and concluded you were the one sent by YaYa for the task—the only one truly qualified to perform it."

"I am a minister of the Gospel of Jesus Christ," said Jo, her voice rising with a touch of indignation. "It is a calling you and all must take as seriously as I do. I cannot walk away from it."

"*Querida*—beloved one," said Don Ramón, "you are not walking away from God or God's calling. You were destined to fulfill that calling. For this time and this place, before the foundations of the world, you were created by YaYa, chosen by YaYael, gifted by the Great Spirit. All your life has been a preparation for this one, great calling. It has always been your destiny. We see that now. Inti knew it before any of us did. He discerned it as he talked with you since childhood, as he walked with you in the hills, as he taught you the woodcraft, the traditions, the soul life of the People. He has been preparing you for it all your life."

"You want me to be *cacica* of the Western land," said Jo, spelling it out. She sounded more like she was making an accusation than an observation.

Doña Lucia paused and looked at her with pride mixed with pity. "Josefina, you alone are Inti's choice. He was our *cacique*. His was the authority to choose his own successor. He carefully chose. He chose you."

"Why me, when so many others have so much more to offer? They live here. They know the land. They know the people. . . ."

"You are speaking about Ricky," surmised Lucia sagely.

"Well, for one. Yes."

"He is very competent; it is true. He does his work with diligence, but he cannot be *cacique*. He lacks the personal skills. You, of all people, should readily see that. The chieftain must be a diplomat, steady and thoughtful in making decisions, not hasty to act. He cannot be that. He is also in direct succession from Enrique on only one side of his family. We must analyze the direct descendants of the great Enrique on both sides first before we choose from other descendants in his family."

"My father, then?"

Ramón and Lucia glanced at each other. Ramón nodded at Lucia. She turned back to Jo. "Josefina, your father is a great man. All of us love him and honor him. He will not accept."

"He 'will not'? Why is that?"

"He knows his gifting."

"What do you mean?"

"In a way, he is exactly the opposite of Ricky. He is kind and encouraging and sensitive. He is the ambassador of the Tribe. But his kindness—he is aware himself—is his snare. He cannot make the hard decisions that will rule against others. It is not in his nature to do so. He is too wise to ask to be *cacique* and would not be confirmed if he did. You see, the tribal council must confirm."

"And the guests?" asked Jo.

"They advise," answered Don Ramón. "Each clan and confederation is independent—each ruled by a hereditary or selected chieftain. Ours, you understand, is a true democracy with selected local rule. But you know this already. The *cacique* or *cacica* is chosen by representatives elevated by the tribe. It is something like a mayor, but not exactly, though it has elements. It is also rather like a selectman in some of your local governmental systems."

"Not in Richfield, but in other parts of the States. Yes, I know that," said Jo.

"Or better still a governor," continued Don Ramón. And then watching her reaction carefully, he added, "But a governor who is chosen for life."

That set off the explosion he was anticipating.

"But what will I tell my parishioners?" objected Jo. "I have barely begun to serve them. They are still dependent on me. I have yet to train them sufficiently so they can take rule themselves. And what will I tell the presbytery and the clergy couple that have given so much to support me?" She paused and then spoke slowly, "I cannot just simply walk away," and she punctuated each word. "I made a commitment and I must honor it."

"You can tell them it is your destiny," said Doña Lucia, taking her hand. "Sit with me," she said and drew her to the porch.

"You can also tell them it is provisional," called the always practical Ramón after them. "You will be interim for a time as acting *cacica* until the council and the people are convinced you can serve them with skill and wisdom—that you are truly heaven's choice."

"But am I heaven's choice—or just Uncle Sol's?" pleaded Jo.

"This is why you brought the dress," added Doña Lucia, as if this evidence was a concluding argument.

"The ceremonial dress," said Jo, ruefully. "But I was asked to bring it. It was not on my own accord."

"It is much more than a 'ceremonial dress.'" Doña Lucia raised her eyebrows. "You have had it for many years. Did you not know it is the raiment of a queen of our tribe? That you are named for our greatest queen?"

"Anacoana. Well, yes . . . I have her name," admitted Jo.

"Yes, of course. You are Josefina Anacoana Archer. Your very names are the names of royalty. Josefina from the great Joseph of the Bible who ruled one land and brought two nations together to save his people. Anacoana, our greatest queen, Enrique's aunt, tribal mother of the Xaragua region, sister to the *cacique* of Xaragua Bohechio, and ruler after his death. Your birth mother, you know, was a direct descendent of Anacoana, from whom you are named."

"I know that," said Jo, with a sinking feeling, as all this history piled up upon her. She knew it all, of course, but it had been little more than academic for her in her youth. Now it had suddenly become much more than that.

"I did not know what the dress was—exactly," she murmured, but Doña Lucia raced on.

"Your mother was being cultivated to become a *cacica* in Borinken, as we call it—Puerto Rico, as they call it now. Did you know that?"

"No. No one ever mentioned that to me," said Jo, surprised.

"Your mother was a great woman and a great leader. Raquel was very gifted. Her death was unexpected—untimely as they say. You, Josefina, have her gifting."

"And Archer," said Jo, "the name the descendants of Enrique adopted. I suppose that figures in as well?"

"Yes," explained Doña Lucia, "to show their aim is true."

"This is a lot to take in," sighed Jo, and sat back in the chair and closed her eyes.

"You can't be completely surprised by this," suggested Don Ramón, catching the tail end of the conversation, as he came onto the porch and sat down in the chair on Jo's other side.

"No," said Jo, opening her eyes, "And that's the problem. I guess I always felt it, but I never wanted to admit it, for who am I to rule anybody?"

"Far more than you give yourself credit for, Josefina," Don Ramón assured her. "All of us know that. Your Uncle Sol knew that."

"Well," said Jo, shaking her head, "that remains to be seen."

23

S TAR HAD BEEN RIGHT! Right all along! She had said nobody would laugh at Daniela or come on to her or even recognize her—and that's exactly the way it was. The hotel bar was dishing up *piña coladas,* rich with rum, just like they hadn't been anybody's downfall the previous night; families were splashing in the Caribbean Sea, tossing colorful plastic balls to their children, so they could continually send the young ones back to the edge of the beach from the water in watchful camaraderie; along the shoreline, a fresh new batch of nubile teenage tourists in bikinis stretched on lounge chairs scattered on the sand, sunning; while in the casino the staff wiped off the rails and gaming wheels, chatting easily with each other, as a few lost souls, like winter moths, flitting about the still-closed tables, lingered in the twilight vale of approach/avoidance until those tables opened and regrettably hasty, impulsive ideas could be swiftly formalized into bad memories. Each of them would be leisurely swatted in turn. Daniela could see clearly it was all just business as usual.

"I want to bring Ben," she told Star and Basil, before she was willing to head up with them to their room.

They glanced at each other, but they had to look open, so Star managed to inject a measure of enthusiasm into her tone as she patted her victim's hand, "Sure, Danny—uh, Daniela. Glad to have him along." Underfoot, he would be a nuisance, she reasoned, but eventually they would need to include him and his share of the inheritance anyway, so why not now?

"I think he's in the casino," guessed Daniela.

Duh! thought Star. But, "Perhaps, you're right, dear," is what she said.

"Would you like to go see?" Basil asked Daniela, trying to be Mister Helpful.

"Let's all go," said Star, quickly. There was no way she was letting this pigeon out of her clutches. Daniela, as she fancied herself this week, had the attention span of a parakeet. Especially, Star was hanging on tight because she didn't know where Balenzuela (that poacher!) was. As usual, circumstances were threatening to turn out as she always dreaded they would, blowing up on them just as a scheme was getting underway. How did they know whether their so-called confederate hadn't already made a move to take it out of their hands? Basil was far too trusting!

To all appearances, it was exactly as she feared.

Basil gasped as they entered the casino, still basically empty, since it didn't open until noon. Star, too, drew in her breath sharply, stopped, and stared. Leaning against a slot machine was the wastrel, chatting in a familiar manner with—of all people—the living confirmation of her fears! Ismael Balenzuela lounged beside him—a drink in both their hands—and she didn't have to guess whose patronage at the always-open bar supplied those! She knew it! She knew it! She knew it! Star set her teeth. It's hard for most to turn a grimace into a smile of delight, but Starling hoped she'd managed it by the time they reached the row of slot machines. This one doesn't miss a trick, she told herself with chagrin mixed with grudging approval. Well, it's a standoff. He's got the wild card, but we've got the queen of hearts.

"Good morning, dear friend," she cooed, as their little entourage entered like a wary safari onto the sacred escarpment—gingerly but cautiously.

'Hi, Ben,' said Daniela.

"Hey, Danny," said Ben, nodding without enthusiasm.

"I'm Daniela now," she corrected him.

"What do you mean? As opposed to what? Jane?"

"No, I mean, this is the new serious me."

"Oh," Ben's eyes narrowed and then widened a bit with surmise. He'd overheard people laughing at the bar about the night before. It had not been hard to guess who the beautiful drunken tourist was. But he only said, "I see. Whatever."

"Ben," opened Star, deciding to enlist herself and Basil into whatever cause Ismael was preaching and coopt as much of it as possible by the ploy of apparent inclusion, "We—all of us—want you to be part of us." And, smiling her most inviting smile, she indicated Balenzuela, who smirked back at her. Then she paused for Ben's response, hoping to assess the extent of any damage Balenzuela might have made to their plans, if he was attempting to divert Ben's share of the inheritance into some competing scheme he might be conjuring up. Ben, of course, provided the response she should have expected.

"Huh?"

"What, my beloved wife is trying to say," Basil picked it up in his man to man tone, "is that we represent something significant and we could use a solid, young, energetic, and far-seeing fellow like you."

Ben regarded him with narrow eyes. "What's in it for me?"

"A substantial payoff," replied Star, not missing a beat. From spiritual doyenne to flim-flam entrepreneur had become with practice as easy for her as changing from sunglasses to dealer's specs. Versatility was her watchword.

"Ben has just been explaining his system to me," winked Balenzuela.

Daniela groaned.

"Whatever," said Ben, frowning at her. And then, undeterred, he turned to Star, the live wire here, he figured, and asked, "What's up?"

"Do you remember the other night when your dear sister went with us to the beach to the service of orientation?" asked Basil before she could answer, still playing the sincere seeker card.

"Oh, that magnetic crap—whoops!—sorry," said Ben. After all, they might really believe this garbage.

Balenzuela began to chuckle, but then caught himself as he glanced at Daniela and reshaped his features as swiftly as he could into what he hoped was a sober look, masking it all with a manufactured fit of coughing. "Choked on the olive," he gasped, coughing a few more designer coughs. Star just shook her head, nudging Daniela and slightly nodding toward Ben.

"Ben, I want you to come with us. This is important to me," Daniela pleaded.

"Whatever," said Ben. "I've got no money left I want to risk, and this dump isn't even open yet. I need to test my system a little more anyway," he added as an afterthought. "I don't want to invest any more cash into it until I do that."

That's because you're probably completely broke, Basil smirked to himself. But what he said was, "Sounds wise to me. Good ideas take a while to mature."

Ben looked at him suspiciously, but Basil had mastered the art of the straight face.

"Please come to our room, where we can share an important idea in privacy that may solve all of our money worries," invited Star in her lower-toned conspiratorial voice.

The straight-faced Basil treated himself to another internal smirk. He recognized this voice as the one she used when she was oiling a trap.

"Whatever," said Ben.

Daniela led the way.

Star and Basil had taken a more commodious room than they would have, had the credit card been theirs, but, as they figured, the octogenarian from whom they'd lifted it hadn't perceived its absence yet. So, only Basil had to sit on the bed. There was a small ottoman and two comfortable acacia wood chairs, but no rockers. Ben plopped himself on the floor, yielding the hassock to Balenzuela. Star and Daniela appropriated the chairs.

Star took control immediately. "I can fully empathize with your reluctance, Ben—may I call you Ben?"

"Sure, wha-"

Star raced on before he could repeat his utility word. It was driving her nuts. "Ben, you may not believe this, but Bo—that's my husband—and I were fully as skeptical as you when we learned from a true believer about the powers of the pole."

"Which are?" Ben asked, as clearly unconvinced as she knew he was.

"Healing powers!" breathed his sister.

"Oh, right. . . ."

"You see," said Basil, warming up for his stint. "We humans are not only basically comprised of water, but we are metallic too."

Everyone looked at him.

"That's why there are so many metals in the vitamins we take daily— like magnesium and, uh, calcium . . . uh . . ."

Star rushed in to his rescue, "Iron."

"Yes, iron," he agreed, relieved. "That's a big one." Calcium had just kind of slipped out. He didn't actually know whether it was a metal or not. But no harm done. This nitwit probably didn't know either.

Everyone looked at Ben for confirmation.

Ben yawned. It was the large, weary sigh of someone who had stayed up until all hours.

Better bring it to a close before this dope flops his head down on the floor and conks out, Star decided. "So, we want to bring this message of healing to the people," she announced.

"We calculate it is not only worthwhile," agreed Balenzuela, and, then, having taken Ben's measure in their earlier conversation, he dropped his hook into Ben's pool, "but we can also see there is a substantial amount of profit to be split among us."

"But why do you want us?" asked Ben, surprisingly coming back to life, swimming around it but not biting yet. "We haven't got any money," he confessed. "Danny's broke all the time and so am I."

"Daniela," his sister corrected him.

But you will, was the silent, simultaneous response of all three of the ad-hoc Polarian party. But none of them said anything aloud, since it was also their immediate conviction that now was definitely not the time to mention any hint of inheritance. Star and Basil, particularly, knew from experience that this was the moment that most scams blew up—when a fish was circling the bait—because that's when reluctance was at its height. Balenzuela was smart enough to guess it. Daniela looked at them helplessly.

So, Star leaned forward and captured Ben's full attention as she explained with utterly faux sincerity: "Ben, as I know you do, we find your sister refreshing. She is a new, excited face who is discovering the benefits of polar magnetism. We—all of us—believe that she would be a wonderful ambassador for our mission. We want her to work with us to be the face of polar restoration," she smiled warmly at the relieved Daniela, who glowed back, "but," Star added, "as my perceptive husband Bo observed earlier, we also perceive that you would provide a wonderful contribution as well."

Basil gave a start. Watch it! his narrowed eyes cautioned her. Words like "contribution" are deal breakers.

But Ben was now regarding Daniela with a critical eye. "Well, Danny's the looker in the family, no doubt about that," he admitted. "You really think she could put this across to the suckers?" His doubt was certainly understandable, Star thought. He knew this dim bulb best.

"Daniela," said Daniela.

"Absolutely," Ismael assured him. "Dan—uh—Daniela brings with her everything she needs: charm, beauty, sincerity." Everyone but Daniela could see what was missing from the list.

"So what do you want with me?" Ben still looked at Star. "Are you planning a men's line or something?"

Maybe if we marketed it to the losers at Atlantic City, thought Star. But, "No, not at this point," she said, pleasantly. "Daniela thought you had a good business head and could help us with that end." Not that we'd ever let you get your dissipating mitts on a single cent, she promised herself.

"Well, yes, I'm clever at business," Ben puffed himself, sitting up straighter. "Just my system alone is going to make me millions one of these days—millions." He nodded his head for emphasis and looked around.

"So what this involves, first of all," said Ismael quickly to keep him off that beaten route, "is rounding up some key contacts. You seem to know your way around here."

"We grew up here, partly," Ben assured him. "I know lots of folks."

"Well, there you go!" interjected Star, to keep the two men from taking over and botching it all up. "The best thing is to start with family." Mentally, she was now grabbing hold of his fin and racing him right into the bait on the principle: Get them involved, give them a sense of ownership, and they're all yours. She leaned even farther toward Ben and beamed her warmest familial smile fully on him, "I think Danny—Daniela, that is—told us you have a couple of sisters? Maybe they'd want to join in?"

"Jo and Ruby? I doubt it. . . ."

"Well, we should at least give them a chance. Perhaps, if you asked them. . . ."

"Hmmm, well, maybe. . . ."

"Sure, if you asked them both, you know they would come," said Daniela. "They probably wouldn't come if I asked them."

"Yeah, probably not."

"Will you do it, then, Ben? For me? I came to the casino with you when you asked me to."

"All right. All right!" grumbled Ben.

"Do you have a cell phone?" asked Balenzuela.

"Uh, not with me right now. . . ."

Probably hocked it, if you can do that here, mused Ismael. "Here, you may borrow mine," he said generously.

"Uh, okay. I guess I can call them now."

Ruby snapped onto the telephone line immediately. "Where are you?" she demanded.

"I'm at the Bravado with Danny."

"Might have known."

"Rube, we need you here right now."

"What, are you out of money again?"

"Yeah, but that's not why I'm calling."

"No?" Ruby's voice was loud and everyone could hear the disbelief in it.

"Actually, I'm not," said Ben, like Basil, adopting the righteous indignation that only someone who is normally guilty and now, for one instance, was not, can summon up. Ruby had heard it before.

"Okay, okay, so what do you want?"

"Actually, I'm onto something here that might help you and me and Danny from being cut out of the inheritance money."

"Daniela," said Daniela, but everyone ignored her.

"How's that?" Ruby's tone was understandably cautious, thought Star.

"Well, you know those new friends of Danny's?"

Daniela frowned and, basically, gave it up for the moment, settling for just whispering to herself, "Daniela."

"Yeah, I met them the night Danny puked all over the stage."

Daniela winced. "I'm going to use the bathroom," she said and left the room.

"Well, they are actually land developers. One of them's been sent here from some big company in Spain and they want the beach house. They think they might be able to help us get it and sell it to them."

"Naw," said Ruby. "Uncle Sol's place is in a trust. Jo explained it all to me. The actual inheritance is some mountain somewhere."

"That's not a sure thing," said Ben. "This guy from Spain has been explaining to me that they've been checking out the inheritance laws here, and stuff passes automatically to the heirs. Jo can't cut us out."

"Really?"

"It's the law."

"Jo isn't going to like this."

"Well, we don't want to cut Jo out. But, we don't want her to cut us out either! Besides, you just said nobody can sell it from what she thinks, and that means none of us gets anything, so this is good for her too."

"Are you sure?"

"Absolutely, like I just said, right now even Jo doesn't get anything from the house either. She can live in it for some reason, but that's it." Speculation had become certitude, noticed Star, musing. Maybe this guy can sell this scam to the "suckers" as he puts it. If he can sell it to his own family, he can sell it to anybody.

Ben raced on, "You know, Ruby, Jo wants to go back to New Jersey and do her church stuff. She doesn't want to live here anymore than any of us do. And all of us can sure use the money."

"That's true."

"So anyway, they want you both to come over so they can lay it all out for us."

"Now?"

"Well, yeah—just a second. . . ." Balenzuela was waving at him. Ben put his hand over the phone. "What?"

"Tell her I want to invite everybody to lunch at the restaurant, especially her and your other sister—everybody," said Ismael. You've got to speculate to accumulate, he told himself. That was the right motto for this enterprise.

"Somebody wants to treat Jo and me for lunch?" interjected Ruby, having picked up Ismael's voice and its offer.

"Yeah, me and Danny too."

"Hmmm, well, I've got nothing to do. I can't speak for Jo."

"Can you go next door and see if she's there and if she'll come?"

"Sure, I don't want to sit around here and watch these Latin soaps."

"Yeah, some woman hanging on to some guy's leg as he's dragging her across the room on his way out the door?"

"Exactly."

Well, thought Star, Basil, and Ismael simultaneously, they must have that scene in every installment! All three of them had tried surfing the flat-screen television channels in their Bravado rooms over the last several days.

"Do you think she'll come?" asked Ismael as soon as Ben hung up.

"Who—Jo?"

"Yes."

"Sure," he answered with a smirk. "She's always worried about me."

"This could get to be quite an expensive little proposition," Balenzuela warned Star and Basil, turning towards them. "I mean, it's so worthwhile and all," he added, for Daniela's benefit, as she came back into the room. "What I mean to say is, I believe it will make a great contribution to humanity." He looked at Ben, who was grinning sardonically. "But, since this is a sideline to what I'm actually here to do, I can't let this get out of hand. We must concentrate on moving swiftly to some sort of effective plan of action."

"Sure," said Ben, elbowing into what might become a private conversation and eventually leave him out. "We need a steady source of income for this."

"Well," said Star, including him in. "We were hoping to rent, or, better yet, buy a location and set up a center connected to the magnetic pole. You know about that, of course, but Ismael here has never seen it."

"Sure," agreed Ben. "Everybody ought to see it. It's a fun thing that you take kids to. Danny and I used to be brought there from time to time when we were kids. You remember Danny?"

"Daniela," she tried again.

"There used to be a restaurant nearby that was named for the pole, but that closed years ago. See, there's nothing there. It's just a blue mark or something on the ground and you get pulled up backwards in your car. It's fun, but there's really nothing else to it. It's just a space with a mark. I don't think there's much on the sides of the road. One side's got the mountain and the other one is just a narrow strip of the down side, as I remember. I don't think you could build anything much there. What do you have in mind?"

"That's why we wanted to see about the beach house," offered Basil.

"Sure," said Ben. "Makes sense. But that might be problematic."

"I want to tie it in with Lake Rincon," parried Ismael.

"Whew!" Ben whistled. "That's a beautiful little lake. Way not as scary as Enriquillo. I've often thought of developing it myself," he lied, eyeing them all, trying to look like a player.

They all let that go.

"It's going to take a lot of money," speculated Ben. "So, how much have you got back in Spain to back this up?"

"A lot less than you all imagine," said Balenzuela, looking pointedly at Starling and Basil. "I'm on a budget. This 'Magnetic Pole' thing, if the truth be told, is coming out of my own pocket. I'm not loaded and I can't put that much into it. It has to start paying off right away."

"If I get my inheritance, I can help," offered Daniela, glancing around at all of them with wide eyes.

Bingo! thought Star, Basil, and Ismael.

But Ben glowered at her. "You're barely going to pay off your credit cards with what you get out of this—if you get anything."

Daniela clammed up and looked down.

"Man!" he laughed. "What you'd need is the Rosary of Enrique, or something like that, to finance something this big!"

"The what?" asked Basil and Star simultaneously.

"The Rosary of Enrique. You haven't heard of it?"

"It's a legend," said Daniela.

"Yeah, probably," admitted Ben.

"Tell us about it," requested Ismael Balenzuela, leaning forward with obvious interest.

"Well, like Danny says, it's probably a legend, but it's a persistent one. You know who Enrique was?"

"An Indian chief?" hazarded Ismael.

"Well, yeah, but more like *the* Taino chief. The word for him is actually a *cacique*. And calling him an 'Indian' is, of course, a mistake. You guys in Spain were looking for a route to the East Indies. You know your history on this?"

"Sure," said Ismael, "kind of."

"Well, it was drummed into us."

"I'll say!" confirmed Daniela.

"See, Columbus and his criminals—oh, sorry—I mean the *conquistadores.* . . . But, you know, the only guys Columbus could get to come with him he had to get from the prisons, because everybody thought they were gonna fall off the end of the world—or something. . . ."

"It's okay, I'm not offended," said Ismael.

"Anyway, they were looking for a new route to the East Indies that wasn't so hard to navigate, so Columbus, who'd read up on his Greek history—you know they knew the world was round back then? Yeah? Well, he decided to go the other way and stumbled on us. That was pretty much it. Anyway, they did a whole lot of bad stuff, because they were looking for gold and couldn't find any. Actually, they didn't find any until recently and the Canadians had to pull that off."

Star and Basil sat back and shuddered. That little salted mine scam had nearly put them in jail. It was still too recent to get involved in this conversation.

"And the Rosary?" prompted Balenzuela.

"Oh, yeah, well, see there was this priest who noticed that killing off the Tainos was like stupid and vile and he liked us and was nice to us and he and some other priests befriended us, and when the marauders killed parents, the priests like took in the kids and took care of them and stuff. And one of those kids turned out to be a brilliant general."

"Ah, so that's who Enrique was," said Ismael Balenzuela, putting it all together. "The lake must be named for him."

"Yeah, like that and a lot of stuff. There are towns and stuff out there named for him. See, this whole area is a peninsula," lectured Ben. "He got done in by this greedy jerk who was given our land. The invaders were chopping up our land and parceling the chunks out as plantations. And this like useless younger son, who didn't inherit or go into the church or anything"—

Sort of like you, thought all three of his audience.

"—well, he was like working the Tainos hard on his plantation and periodically sending them off to a mine he had, where they weren't finding any gold. And one day he raped this young guy's wife. See, Enrique had been like his straw boss. And so he—I mean Enrique—went to complain to the governor. But the governor was a jerk too and he and everybody just laughed it off and threatened to have Enrique whipped—can you imagine? So, he just went underground. You know, like 'Yes, Massa!' and 'No Massa!'—they actually got a name for this. . . ." Ben puzzled for a moment. "Ooof, I can't remember it."

"Quashie," said Daniela. Everybody looked at her astonished. She saw it in their faces. "I know stuff too," she pouted. Star reached over and patted her hand.

"Anyway," said Ben, commandeering the floor again. "Enrique laid his plans carefully and one day he and his work party left for the mines and didn't come back." Ben looked around. He had them rapt, so he paused and said, "I'm getting thirsty. Do you have anything to drink?'

"Soda," said Star, definitively. "It's in the little refrigerator."

Ismael swiveled around, opened it up, and passed 7-Ups and Cokes to Ben first and then to Star and Danny. He and Basil had to do without, to Basil's dismay, but, to Ismael, it was another investment.

There was a sudden knock on the door, and Star and Basil glanced at each other, nervously.

"Housekeeping," said a thickly accented woman's voice.

"Can you come back later—please?" called Star.

"Hokay!"

"Please, go on," she said to Ben. "This is very interesting."

"And the Rosary? Why is it so valuable that it would solve our money worries?" asked Balenzuela.

"I'm getting to that," said Ben. "Anyway, this young guy, Enriquillo, they were calling him this nickname. . . ."

"Like the name of the lake," urged Balenzuela.

"Yeah, right. Well, he was like a brilliant strategist. So why he wasn't coming back is that he was fortifying the mountains of the peninsula. So like the planation owner gets all worked up—you know, he's got this sense of entitlement being from Spain and all—no offense."

Balenzuela didn't say anything.

"Well, so, he has the governor send this small force out to get Enrique and like the Tainos under Enrique's leadership beat 'em all up. But it was more than that. Enrique did all this brilliant kind of stuff. He like led 'em up in the mountains and the climb was so hard because they had on all this armor and they got real hot and they didn't bring any water and they were like falling off their horses. And then their horses collapsed and they started dragging their big swords around and then they were ripping off their armor and the swords were trailing on the ground. We, of course, had been watching them, so, we just started potting a few of them with our arrows and the rest of them immediately gave up."

"So, you Tainos killed them all?" asked Balenzuela, figuring that's what he would have done.

"No, and that's the thing! That's what makes Enrique so brilliant!"

"So what *did* he do?" pursued Basil, fascinated.

"Why, he comes out with a Bible and makes them an offer they can't refuse."

"Like the Mafia?" asked Basil unnecessarily.

"Like God's Mafia," said Ben. "He told them he could either shoot them all down now—and they look around and see there's all these sharpshooters' bows in the trees and behind the rocks all trained on them—or on pain of going straight to hell—skippin' Atlanta and purgatory, if you know what I mean, and blazing away forever in the eternal barbeque—well, they could all swear on the Bible that they would never fight a Taino again. Guess what choice they all made?"

"A no-brainer," agreed Basil.

"You're not kidding," said Ben.

"That's where we got our name from," said Daniela, suddenly.

"What?" asked Balenzuela, turning toward her.

"Archer. That's our last name. 'Because our aim is true.' That's what everybody told us when we were growing up. See, we're all descended directly from Enrique himself. Me and Ben and the others. That's why Jo's getting the house, I think. It was our uncle who owned it—or at least lived there. That's why it's our inheritance. See?"

They certainly did see. Oh boy, thought Star, direct heirs. "Just you all?"

"Yup!" said Ben.

"And the Rosary?" prompted Balenzuela.

"Oh, yeah, right. Well, anyway, Enrique had really taken this all to heart. He had become this really, really devout Christian. Like our sister Jo is and our pop and stepmom and all. Well, all of us really," he added, slightly ashamed. "But I mean, he like acted on it. And he used to circle his camp saying the Rosary. People came to believe the Rosary itself had great spiritual power given to it by God to protect the Tainos, because the fact of the matter is we basically slaughtered the soldiers when we felt like it and hardly lost anybody. Pretty soon everybody who could escape from the overlords was making their way to the peninsula. And, if they could get there safely, they were all set. Enrique's army was getting bigger and bigger and bigger. The governor sent out some more expeditionary forces and some pretty big army detachments, but they all came back without any weapons and with the fear of hell in every one of them. No matter what the governor threatened them with, none of them would fight again. They had to send them all back to Spain—they were useless as soldiers. So, finally, the overlords had to sue for peace, you know? And Enrique was real choosy. He turned down the first several offers and didn't even show up for some of them. Finally, they had to give him a good deal for his followers and they made him a 'Don,' that's like a noble," Ben added for Star and Basil's benefit. "And then, can you believe it? After everything was set, he died like a year later. Everybody figures his job was done and God just took him home to heaven. His wife built a church in his honor and he's buried there, but it's just in ruins today—over in Azua."

"Really? Why is that?" asked Basil, shocked.

"We don't put much stock in 'funerals or generals,' like the Rastafarians say."

"But a church? You'd think you'd keep that up."

"Naw, we've got churches in each of the centers, see? But they're like Taino church buildings. Now Azua—that's an interesting story—it was named for a mistake the Spanish made—no offense. But, see, when the Tainos from Venezuela used to row over in those eighty-person canoes, they used to have this rowing chant 'ah-suu-ahh' to keep rhythm and the *conquistadores* were so dumb they thought it was the name of the settlement, see? And—"

"And where's the Rosary now?" interjected Ismael. It was hard to keep this blowfish on the topic.

"It's a legend," said Daniela.

"Well, no, not exactly," corrected Ben. "I think it's real enough. And really valuable. Some say it was buried with Enrique, but most say it's not that at all. We keep it hidden for when we need real spiritual power. And, if that's the case, it's like our secret weapon, you know?"

"It must be very valuable," exclaimed Star.

"It must be very powerful," breathed Balenzuela.

Both their eyes were shining with lust.

24

THE SEA: SO VAST, so calming. What was it about the sea that always spoke to Jo's troubled heart? So many times in her early youth she had trekked the rocky shoreline of Las Olas del Sol, as alone as she was today. Winds off the water always seemed to lift her, the murmuring of the waves to assure her, the shimmering on the water to symbolize a comforting promise through bright afternoons into peaceful nights. It was a sign to her of the generous hand of the God who adorns the flowers of the field, captured in the sun's reflections, undulating like gold shavings borne on the wind, floating to her on the water.

The Caribbean Sea was the constant in a landscape of altering modalities. The movement of the sea was continuous, but it always returned to its primal state. This is how it sustained all the life within it. The storms were on the surface, but beneath it was the ever-present calm of complete reliance on Providence. How she longed for such assurance in her own life—she had always longed for it. And how she loved the sea! This was the foil to land and life, for on land and in life change was not always temporal and restoration not always inevitable, as it was with the sea. Too often, as she feared now, life on land would alter and a new configuration would take permanent shape. A mountain would thrust up from a seismic explosion and block out the sun from that moment on—forever. Suddenly, it was a factor in everyone's reality. There was no tearing it down.

"All your life has been a test," Doña Lucia had said to her.

"I am a minister of the Gospel of Jesus Christ," Jo had replied.

"You are not walking away from God or God's calling. You were destined to fulfill that calling. For this time and this place, before the foundations of the world, you were created by YaYa, chosen by YaYael, gifted by the Great Spirit. All your life has been a preparation for this one, great calling. It has always been your destiny."

Their gentle voices sounded over and over in her head. Here was a mountain! No, she realized, this was *the* mountain—the one she had always feared would thrust up into her life, altering her landscape forever. All her life she had felt the tremors, now she had experienced the earthquake.

"This was your uncle's choice. He carefully considered all the options and concluded you were the one sent by YaYa for the task—the only one truly qualified to perform it."

How she had basked in Uncle Sol's attentions! Enjoying the excitement, as the earth was slowly rumbling. "We see now. Inti knew it before any of us did. He discerned it as he talked with you since childhood, as he walked with you in the hills, as he taught you the woodcraft, the traditions, the soul life of the People. He has been preparing you for it all your life."

She had been chosen out from among her family—but chosen, she realized now, as a kind of sacrifice. How well she had put it when she recoiled against this volcanic mountain: "something I fear even more. I believe you want to change my life—radically!" There would never be the opportunity to traverse this sierra and find the other side. There were no mountain passes here, despite their assurances.

"Not really change your life at all, Josefina," Doña Lucia had tried to calm and assure her, "but fulfill it."

But this was neither the calmness nor the assurance the sea represented. For in the sea everything would be restored—but this was like the land. Here everything would change and there would be no returning. Her life, her calling, her plans for her people in Richfield: these would all end. "You want me to be *cacica* of the Western land!"

And all the pieces locking so completely in place: "Josefina, you alone are Inti's choice. He was our *cacique*. His was the authority to choose his own successor. He carefully chose. He chose you." He chose you. He chose you! He chose you!!

Jo shook her head. "Oh, God" she prayed. "Why me? Am I not doing enough for *you* in Richfield? Why give me that calling and then take it away for another?" But, all she heard in her mind were the persistent voices, gentle, of course, but drowning out every other sound: "We must analyze the direct descendants of the great Enrique first before we choose from other descendants in his family." "A governor who is chosen for life." "You can tell them it is your destiny." "Did you not know it is the raiment of a queen of our tribe? That you are named for our greatest queen?" "Your mother was being cultivated to become a *cacica* in Borinken, as we call it—Puerto Rico, as they call it now. Did you know that?" "Your mother was a great woman and a great leader. Raquel was very gifted. Her death was unexpected—untimely as they say. You, Josefina, have her gifting."

"You are Josefina Anacoana Archer. Your very names are the names of royalty. Josefina from the great Joseph of the Bible who ruled one land and brought two nations together to save his people. Anacoana, our greatest queen, Enrique's great aunt, tribal mother of the Xaragua region, sister to the *cacique* of Xaragua Bohechio, and ruler after his death. Your birth mother, you know, was a direct descendent of Anacoana, from whom you are named." "And Archer to show your aim is true."

"But am I heaven's choice—or just Uncle Sol's?" And what was her choice? Did she even have a choice? Sea or land? Jo began to cry. She felt it all crushing in on her, destroying everything she had planned in that seismic eruption of order and the inevitable landslide of change.

And this is the state Ruby found her in as she dashed up the beach from Los Diamantes del Mar Hotel, took her in quickly, and snapped, "What's the matter with you? Danny and Ben need us over at the Bravado. I think we need to go, I don't know what they've got themselves into. You need a tissue or something?"

"Oh, Ruby," said Jo. "This is all too much for me. . . ."

"Yeah? Well, you can tell me later. Right now, we've got to go."

"I can't go now!" Jo frowned at her. Ruby could be so unfeeling.

"Look, Sis. Ben is in trouble." Ruby was clearly irritated. "You're the only one who can make any dent on him. And," she added almost accusingly, "do you know what Danny was up to last night?"

"No," said Jo, pulling herself out of her own pit, though dreading to peer into Daniela's.

"Yeah, I'll bet you don't! Take a look at YouTube!"

"What do you mean?"

"Danny's quite the celebrity! Come on, we'll drive over. Gimme the keys."

The entire entourage was waiting for Jo and Ruby in the lobby. Jo looked immediately at Ben, but he looked chipper enough and grinned back at her ingratiatingly. Daniela was wearing sunglasses, but Jo noted she was looking away and didn't seem to want to meet her eyes.

The same man who had strode up on the porch at Las Olas del Sol, acting so proprietorial, stood up the moment he saw her, stepping forward. Jo took two steps involuntarily backwards. But, he was very deferential in his manner now. "Dear ladies, so good of you to come and be my guests," he murmured.

Jo was immediately on her guard.

Ruby simply nodded at him. "You want to take us to lunch?" she clarified.

"I do indeed."

"Why?" demanded Ruby.

"We want to get to know you both."

"Why?"

A smiling woman in her forties, well dressed, no doubt to be attractive to men—and dyed blond, Jo noted—stepped forward and beamed on them both. "My name is Peep," she said, looking as if she were threatening to hug them both in a motherly embrace, but, thankfully, restraining herself.

Jo and Ruby simply gazed at her, waiting.

"You must be Jo and Ruby," said a large, smiling man, stepping to the woman's side. They were all amassing around them. "I am Bo," he announced, somewhat pompously. "This," he added with a flourish, "is Señor Balenzuela. From Spain!" He was obviously impressed himself, or at least wanted to convey importance, Jo noted to herself.

"Ismael, please," said the other man to them, maintaining the deference.

Jo smiled wanly, nodded, and simply waited. So did Ruby. They were both Taino, after all, thought Starling, and impassive is what Indians did. These were going to be tougher sells than were their brother and sister. Maybe they had enculturated less. Star glanced nervously at Basil. This whole deal could be easily lost right now if he overdid it. "Bo, dear," she said. "Let Señor Balenzuela welcome our new guests." A quick narrowing of her eyes seemed to Jo to add an unspoken "Shut up, for now." The large man subsided immediately.

"I want to take everyone to lunch," spoke up Ismael, deciding honesty was probably going to be the best policy, but, an honesty tempered, of course. "If you will do me the honor of accepting my invitation," he added humbly, "I would be ever so grateful."

Jo hesitated. "I believe our aunt and uncle already pointed you in the best possible direction for your search for available property to develop. . . ."

Oh oh. Time to temper. "Yes, and for that I am so grateful," Balenzuela interjected swiftly. "It's partly out of gratitude that I want to express my appreciation by offering this luncheon."

"That works for me," said Ruby. "I'm starved."

Jo still hesitated.

"Come on, Jo," cajoled Ben. "Nobody's going to poison you."

"It's not about the property," lied Star easily. "There's a whole exciting idea we were sharing with your brother and sister and they were the ones who wanted to include you in the opportunity."

"That's right," said Daniela, addressing Ruby and still avoiding Jo's eyes. "It's important to me."

"Fine," said Ruby, impatiently. "Where are we going to eat—here or somewhere else?"

"This is a very fine restaurant," said Star, who knew the danger of letting easy marks out into the wide-open spaces where anything can happen. Keep them contained was her motto, so she could work fast. There is no better friend than a controlled environment. "And there are luncheon specials," she enthused. "And really quite reasonable," she added, obviously for the benefit of Balenzuela.

"Yes, this is fine," he consented.

"Good, thank you," said Star.

Everyone looked at Jo.

"All right," said Jo, still hesitant. She gazed carefully around at each of them, studying them. There was too much obvious agreement here. She felt every guarding fence she possessed raising up in her mind.

"Let's go," ordered Ruby, striding off toward the restaurant. Basil caught up with her and graciously opened the door. Ruby nodded, grinned, and went in.

Star moved to one side of Jo and Ismael to the other. Jo felt like she was about to be mugged, but neither of them spoke. Basil had paused, after his courtesy to Ruby, but Ismael nodded him on and gallantly held the door for the two women. This was well orchestrated, thought Jo. Daniela and Ben trailed behind. "A table for seven," Balenzuela ordered the maître d'. Jo regarded him carefully, thinking about his tone. Entitlement, she decided. Hmmmm.

"Please," he said, holding a chair back for Jo. But now, Jo thought, he seemed so humble, not at all like the man who had mounted the porch at Las Olas del Sol—or even the one who ordered the table from the maître d'.

Basil held the chair for Ruby, who plopped herself in it and scudded it forward on her own power, and then he drew back a chair for the waiting Star. They were very polite, thought Jo, though it seemed to her like a studied rather than a natural politeness. Then Jo caught herself. That was certainly harsh. She began to wonder: Am I being *too* harsh? I should at least give them a chance. They have been nothing but courteous and intending to be generous so far. What is it about them that's giving me such a negative reaction? Is it just the incident at Las Olas? But how could they know? This could be driven by Ben and Danny and their quest to get some money out of all this. Jo concentrated for a moment on Balenzuela. What is this man really like and what exactly does he want? Ismael noticed her look and smiled warmly back at her. Jo, embarrassed, averted her eyes. She picked up the menu hurriedly.

Ben, taking all this courtesy in, fumbled a chair back for Daniela, who, obviously nonplussed, smiled brightly and insinuated herself into it with her usual grace.

"Well, isn't this nice," said Star in her cozy tone.

"Yeah, thanks," grunted Ruby, perusing the menu.

I'll let you know, Jo thought to herself, conflicted, as she protected her feelings behind the menu.

"Anything you would like to order. . . ." offered Ismael Balenzuela. "Some wine, waiter!"

"Not for me," said Ruby. "I'm in training."

"No, thank you," said Jo.

"I'll have some," said Daniela.

Ruby glared at her. "Better stick to juice today," she warned.

Daniela looked down. "Maybe . . . maybe you're right. I'll take orange juice, please."

"I'll have a beer," said Ben. Then he called over to the waiter, "¡*Cerveza, por favor*!" just in case anybody had an inkling to interfere with him as Ruby had with Daniela.

But Ruby, pointing at the menu, cried out, "Look at this! ¡*Arroz con pollo*! They never have that here—only in Puerto Rico. That's what I'm getting." She snapped her menu shut and surveyed the rest of the table, her eyes flashing a kind of challenge. "You all set?" she demanded.

"I'll have a salad," said Daniela, meekly.

"What's this *arroz*—what was it you said?" asked Basil.

"Chicken and rice," confided Ben, before Ruby had a chance to reply.

"Isn't every meal here chicken and rice?" asked Basil blandly.

Star groaned.

"It's a style," explained Ben. "Sure, chicken's a staple—so's rice. But every place has got a different way to do it. Puerto Rico, Costa Rica, Mexico . . ."

"I know about Mexican rice and chicken," agreed Basil.

"I'll have a salad like you, dear," said Star, closing her menu and smiling with camaraderie at Daniela. Just a couple of girls, sacrificing for their figures. Daniela smiled back.

"I'll take ribs," said Ben, "with some hot sauce and *tostones*—that's fried plantain," he added for Basil's benefit. "You'll like them; they're like chips. And how about some cassava bread for the table? Give you the whole experience?"

"Sure! And I'll take the same as you," said Basil. We're pals, he was communicating, copying Star's move on Daniela.

"May I have the filet mignon?" asked Balenzuela. "Rare please."

Everybody looked at him, astonished, but he ignored them all and concentrated on Jo. "Would you like the same?"

Jo hesitated.

"I don't want to splurge alone," Ismael urged her.

"All right," said Jo and let herself grin at him, beginning to relax. "But, please make mine medium to medium rare," she told the waiter. "It's been a tough day."

"It has indeed," said Ismael Balenzuela.

"You're having difficulties securing appropriate properties?" asked Jo to be polite.

Balenzuela had seated himself next to Jo and now he leaned toward her so he could monopolize her attention. "I have to confess," he confided to her. "Things have been much more difficult for me than I imagined they would be. It's not that there's no land. There are vast tracks of it! But owners are hard to find, deeds are ancient and," he paused and said pointedly to her, "so many are in trusts."

Jo simply nodded back.

"But," he added quickly, "I am so very grateful that you gave me a lead with your aunt. A connected real estate agent is just what I need."

"You've called her then?" asked Jo.

"The next thing on my agenda," he answered glibly.

Jo took this in and mulled it over for a moment. "And what is the present thing?" she asked.

"The present thing?" he echoed, warily.

"On your agenda." She wondered if he was stalling for time.

"Well," he said, "that's what Ben and Danny here wanted us to discuss with you."

"Daniela," corrected Daniela.

"I'm listening," said Jo and then, turning to Ruby who was punching up messages on her cell phone, she said, "Ruby, may we have your full attention for a moment?"

Ruby looked up.

"Señor Balenzuela wants to tell us the reason we've been invited to lunch."

"Ismael, please," Balenzuela coaxed her.

"Ismael," she conceded.

"Shoot," said Ruby, snapping off her phone.

"It has to do with a vision," began Ismael, sweeping in everyone else at the table. Even Ben stopped giving Basil pointers about Dominican cuisine on which he had grown quite expansive.

"Fate has put the seven of us together," Ismael became infused with a kind of piety (Ruby smirked to herself) by the sound of it mainly reserved for Mafia-financed chapels. "I came to this beautiful and ancient land with no more thought than to extend my company's holdings—to the benefit of all, of course!"

"Of course," agreed Star and Basil simultaneously—like a Greek chorus.

"But then I ran into these dear folks," he indicated Star and Basil with a wave of his hand, "and my vision expanded."

Everyone waited for the revelation.

He paused and then said, as if announcing the cure for all the ills of the world, "I discovered Polarism."

"What?" asked Ruby. "You discovered what?"

"The powers of the Pole."

"You met somebody from Poland?" Ruby was baffled. "Here in the Dominican Republic?"

"No, Rube," scoffed Ben. "He's talking about the Magnetic Pole."

"You mean the load of iron—or whatever—next to Lake Rincon that pulls the cars up backwards—that pole?"

"Right."

"What about it?"

It was more than time for Star to dive in. "Excuse me, but I don't think you dear folks have any idea of the treasure you have here—hidden away as it is from the rest of the world. It's more than just an oddity. We believe the Pole has the power to take our lives—just as it does our vehicles—and pull them to its own rhythm."

"Whoof!" snorted Ruby.

"We want to open that blessing to the world," Star raced on. "We want to see the Magnetic Pole receive the honor it was always meant to have. We want to invite in pilgrims to the Pole. They'll find healing and orientation here."

"They want to do this up big," interjected Daniela, unable to restrain herself any longer. "They want to make up pins that everybody who's done a pilgrimage to the Pole will have the right to wear. Small magnetic designer pins. And they're even going to distribute copies of their own 'bible.'"

Jo started like she'd been slapped. "Wait a second!" she cried.

"Oh, no dear, it's not a 'Bible,'" Starling immediately corrected, trying desperately to do some damage control on the cusp of Jo's strong reaction. "It's just a manual, dear," she said directly to Jo. "God forbid anyone should take this for a religion!"

"It's not?" asked Daniela, faltering. "I thought that orientation was . . ."

"It's neutral, just a health thing really," Star's commanding voice cruised like an ocean liner right over Daniela's rowboat of thought. Daniela felt herself spinning directionless in the wake of Star's forward thrust.

"It's to be called *The Dynamics of Polarism*," announced Basil, trying to be helpful.

Starling glanced around exasperated. Was everyone against her? "Look," she said desperately to Jo, "it's totally focused on the healing powers of magnetism. That's an old and respected form of organic healing, alternative medicine. It's very popular in the United States."

"Like healing with crystals?" asked Ruby, trying to negotiate this bizarre turn in the conversation.

"Exactly, like that," agreed Star, seizing on this comparison like an extra, succumbing rapidly to quicksand, grasping on a branch in an old jungle movie. "We want to reveal to people how the Magnetic Pole can give you success in business, achieving your life's goals, and succeeding in your personal relationships through reorientation."

"They're on to something," Ben assured Jo.

"Yes, and it will be good for local business too," Ismael Balenzuela hurriedly agreed. "Think of all the tourists who will come in off the nearby coast. It will be an economic boom for the area. These towns are small and some—not all of course," he added, thinking of Villa Riqueza, "are impoverished. This will help them all." He paused for a moment, but couldn't actually think of any town he had seen in the area that actually looked impoverished, but, tag-teaming, Star dove in, jumping back onto the mat to give her version of a body slam.

"Yes," she said, pulling out all she had. "We're thinking cruise ships. Excusions! We could charter a cruise ship and bring it right here to Barahona!"

"Why, they'd feel more polarized the minute they step off the ship!" concurred Basil, shaking his head for emphasis.

"You can count on that!" scoffed Ruby under her breath.

Jo was glancing from one to the other as they spoke and noticing now that all of them were concentrating entirely on her. She suddenly had the odd and completely unnerving sensation that she had been thrown into a horror movie and the entire table had suddenly revealed itself to be peopled by zombies. Only Ruby was not staring at her.

"Let me get this straight!" ordered Ruby, like she was going over a complex new play being suggested by an overly-helpful parent of one of her team's members. "You're talking about the Magnetic Pole, right?"

"Exactly, dear!" declared Star with a smile so broad that Jo wondered if it hurt her face.

"And," said Ruby, taking it apart to examine it, "by 'orientation by the Pole' you're talking about healing for humans—am I getting this right?"

"Exactly right!" Basil tried to echo Star. Big as he was, he pictured himself the anchor rower in a regatta, dedicated to take his team home first by twenty strokes. He was obviously not expecting to hear the referee's whistle, but then . . .

"Okay," said Ruby, "oriented by a magnetic pole works on cars. It's for metal. It would work for humans if you were a cyborg—or more likely a robot!"

Star's smile froze.

In what had become for her consistent predictability, Ruby was producing the equivalent of "one more unhappy parent"—which is why, despite her phenomenal athletic prowess and expertise, she would probably remain an assistant coach and never a head coach year after year.

There was a moment of stunned silence.

Basil was about to launch into the same speech he had used to try to convince Ben earlier that same day up in the hotel room, when Daniela spoke up. "Magnetic bracelets have been popular for years," she announced directly to Ruby with a tone so authoritative that it shocked everyone. "I bought them and, when you were younger, so did you, Ruby. You had an ankle bracelet. It had little metal beads alternating with squares. It was very pretty. It was soft metal. You told me it improved your energy, got the circulation going so you could run and kick faster, and you also told me it kept you safe from injury!"

Anyone else might have dropped her head in embarrassment, but Ruby just stared back at her thinking. Then she said, "You're right, Danny! I did buy one back in middle school. I can't believe you remembered that. But, that's true. I did think all that back then." She simply stopped and let that hang in the air.

"Daniela," said Daniela.

And then Jo spoke. "You speak about being 'polarized' . . ."

"Yes," said Star, eagerly.

"Usually that term is a pejorative one," continued Jo, thoughtfully. "It means being marginalized—pulling people apart from one another. . . ."

Star broke in, "Yes, but we mean to change all that!"

"So this is a good thing?" asked Jo. "To be polarized?"

"Yes, of course," explained Star, glibly, "you don't want to be depolarized do you? That's like being lost."

Basil beamed at her. She was so good when she got going on objections. There was no one alive, he told himself, who could shovel the bull with such a straight face as his beloved. Even Ismael Balenzuela was impressed with Star's bald-faced instant innovations.

"Ah," murmured Jo, obviously thinking it over.

"Unlike a true religion," Star went on, eyeing her, "we don't have a concept of sin or salvation—just polarization and depolarization."

"I see," said Jo, "and that's why you're developing aids to assist people getting 'polarized,' as you put it."

"That's it exactly," Star assured her. "We're planning to develop a wide range of magnetic products you can place under your bed or in your boardroom to draw people to your own harmonizing vision."

"Like we're going to say in our upcoming book: *Winning through Personal Magnetism!*" Basil announced.

"I see," said Jo.

"And, dear," Star moved in for the kill, "we don't want to hoard this gift or this opportunity. We've found such kindred spirits in your brother, Ben, and your sister Danny—uh, Daniela—that we want to share it with them and," had she been closer, she would have reached out and patted Jo's hand, "we want to share it with you."

Jo stared at her and nodded.

Star, taking it for a sign, moved to suggested action, the next vital stage. "Jo—may I call you Jo? I feel like we're almost family now. Will you come with us to the Magnetic Pole and see it all with new eyes? Behold it as you've never beheld it before—through our vision?"

"A vision of faith," murmured Daniela, her eyes wide with wonder and purpose.

"Will you come with us, please?" urged Star again. "And share our vision with us—and with the world?"

Suddenly, she stopped, leaving the air pregnant and pulsing. Everyone could feel it profoundly and paused expectantly, while Star concentrated completely on radiating toward Jo the most polished version of sincerity in her whole arsenal of emotions. This was it!

And then, "No, thank you," said Jo.

"Not this Tuesday!" muttered Ruby.

Star's mouth dropped open. She had just been about to congratulate herself on what a great job she had done and look toward Basil for more plaudits! "Why not?" she faltered.

"I have the Holy Spirit to orient me," said Jo in a voice so authentically sincere that Ismael Balenzuela himself felt a tinge of something that caught him suddenly at his heart. What was it? he mused. It felt like shame. . . .

Then Ruby took back the floor. "Listen," she said, "I don't want to spit on your papayas, but the fact is," and she spoke directly to Daniela, "the ankle bracelet I had when I was twelve was kid stuff. Nothing replaces hard training! Athletes have all kinds of superstitions. My girls have tons of silly ideas. Some of them don't want to wash their shorts if we're having a winning season. I make the team manager break into the lockers and toss them all in the suds. Some of these kids get dismayed, but I tell them that all they're going to get from that is the crud and then they won't play. Wearing a hunk of metal around your ankle isn't going to make you fast or strong or anything. In fact, if you get a cheap one, the chafing can irritate you if you try to wear it in practice. I'm not impressed with this stuff myself, but," she added, looking around and centering in on Ismael Balenzuela, and nodding the side of her head toward Ben, "I think you're both right. You're on to something that's going to do some good business. There are plenty of people out there who do believe in this stuff. I think they would crowd in down here and spend all kinds of money and go home feeling fulfilled and—who knows?—it might actually help them. You feel good about yourself and you will be more confident in business, more attractive to others, more 'oriented,' as you say, just because you have a better self-image. And that's not a bad thing."

"So, are you in?" asked Ben.

"I'll have to think about it," said Ruby.

"What about you, Jo?" Ben turned to her and looked her directly in the eyes. Everybody stared at her.

"No," said Jo. "Definitely not." She turned to Starling. "Despite your—I'm sure—sincere expression that you do not intend this to be a religion, it is clearly a substitute for one. People who are finding themselves in something like magnets or crystals or self-focused meditation or whatever are not finding themselves in God's Spirit. Whatever help it may give them—and I won't argue that it wouldn't help them—it might—but it would still not provide them with any ultimate help. You see, it focuses only on the present, but we are much more than that. We are temporal and eternal beings and, therefore, whatever solution we seek for the 'disorientation'—as you call it—that we have inherited from our plight of being born into a fallen world has got to include both. Including only one is not enough."

"You're preaching now!" scoffed Ben.

"Maybe so," admitted Jo, smiling, ruefully, "but you know what I'm saying is true. If we're just focused on the eternal, then we're just selfish. We don't care about anyone else. If we just focus on the temporal, then we don't ultimately care about ourselves—our eternal destiny—and we're not grateful to the One who created us and wants to share now and eternity with us."

"Well, I think you're selfish!" suddenly spit out Danny with a vehemence that startled Jo and everyone. Star stared at her with an absolute astonishment she could not keep off her face. This pigeon had revealed a hawk.

Jo stopped short and stared at Daniela.

"You're hogging everything for yourself! Peep just told you this is not a religion, what's your problem? You're always saying no to everything. All you do at home is work in that stupid church of yours. You wouldn't even lend me that stupid dress of yours when I promised to take care of it. Now down here you want to take everything. Me and Ben and even Ruby here aren't going to get anything! You're so selfish, you're going to hog it all! You'll probably sell Las Olas and use it all for your stupid church and all those maids and factory workers you're always carting around and helping. You don't do anything for your own family. You don't care about us!"

"Get hold of yourself," snapped Ruby. "This is all crap, Danny. Jo does plenty of stuff for you—what do you ever do for her?—or anyone but yourself!"

"Daniela!" thundered Daniela. "Call me Daniela! I've said it a hundred times! Nobody takes me seriously. Well, that's going to change! I like these people and I believe in Polarism! And," her voice was so fierce that even Ben scudded his chair back a bit away from her since they were all sitting so closely together, "I'll have my inheritance—if I have to sue you for it! And, if we decide we want Las Olas del Sol for our center—I'll sue whoever I have to for it, too!"

And that was the moment the food arrived.

Three waiters were instantly flourishing about, placing steaming plates and bowls of Dominican delicacies, bringing an air into the proceedings that made it feel like the old theater of the absurd to Jo. Star was staring at Daniela open-mouthed. Ben looked very abashed and uncomfortable, which was definitely a refreshing break from his unusual brazenness. Daniela's lip was quivering and she looked like she might burst into tears. Ismael Balenzuela had drawn back in his chair and was looking speculatively at Star and Basil. Only Basil was smiling at the waiters and poking at his food. "Let's eat," he said, being the survivor of so many aborted scheme disasters that he could remain calm. "We can sort this out later—on a full stomach. It's always best to eat."

Star smiled wanly at him.

"Daniela," said Jo, in her low, soft voice, "I'm so sorry you feel this way. I had no idea. Would you come with me and we can talk this over—just you and I?"

"No!" Daniela slapped it away. "I'm going to eat my salad." She poked her fork into it, but did not eat anything.

"I'm for eating," said Ruby, and then to the others, "Sorry about this family tiff. We're brother and sisters—we fight from time to time—sorry we got you all into it. Would you pass the hot sauce, please, Ben?"

"Sure, Rube. Danny, pass this over," and he proffered the little sauce jar at her.

"Daniela!" she shouted and suddenly burst into tears. Then she pushed herself back violently from the table and ran toward the bathrooms.

Jo pushed back her chair and started to rise when Ruby caught her arm.

"Let her go," said Ruby. "She needs a minute without you smothering her. Eat your steak—how often do you get filet mignon?"

25

"I FEEL WE OWE you an apology," said Jo directly to Ismael Balenzuela.

"No, no," he began to murmur, a bit disconcerted at Daniela's blowup and hasty departure.

"Yes, we do," pursued Jo. "All of us. This was completely uncalled for." She turned to Star and Basil and regarded them with obvious regret. "You have all been so gracious to us."

Basil looked at her hopefully. "Does this mean you'll reconsider our invitation?" he asked eagerly.

Jo shook her head sadly. "I'm so sorry. I don't feel in good conscience I can join your enterprise myself. I am disturbed by the pseudo-spiritual dimensions of it, though others in my family may see no conflict at all."

"Like those yoga sessions in church buildings?" offered Basil, happily.

Jo winced.

This time, Ismael Balenzuela came to the rescue. "It is enough," he said, matching her mood, "that you heard us out. And, for that, I, for one, am very grateful. I understand that not every opportunity works for everybody."

Jo smiled with gratitude at him and expressed it openly. "Thank you," she said.

Balenzuela sensed this was a moment to bide his time. He picked his way carefully along. "Your sister is a lovely woman," he hesitated and then chose a tentative, "but she is a little high strung."

"I'll say!" said Ruby, through a mouthful of *arroz con pollo*. She swallowed and paused to observe: "Danny's got a lot going for her in the looks department, but she's kind of lagged behind in the race to maturity."

Ben guffawed.

Jo shook her head. "I think this all means a lot more to her than I guessed. It's also been a very trying time for us all." Then she offered to complete her explanation: "We were all very close to our uncle."

"And don't forget mom and dad disappearing," chimed in Ben, not looking particularly concerned. "Did you ever find out what happened to them?"

Jo shot him a glance full of caution and suddenly all three siblings became passive and inscrutable—even Ben.

Ismael Balenzuela noticed it immediately and chalked it into his memory for future contemplation. This Jo was the center of power. One look from her and they all went Taino. The lines of communication were instantly cut. Ben was not in their pocket as fully as they thought. He was still connected to Jo in a way Ismael did not understand. That was worth noting before they invested anything into him rather than simply used him. The first might not be such a wise idea. Daniela, however, was a different matter entirely. She, he felt certain, was breaking free. What Ruby was choosing to call a lack of maturity might be fledging independence. She might be their real ingress into all their plans for the area. It was still completely a matter of business to him. The Taino endorsement might be crucial—or at least their forbearance. What he could not afford was their opposition, since he could not yet calculate the extent of their power in the area, but he surmised it might be extensive and without their good favor he could not proceed. His real estate agent, his lawyer, the property he so much wanted, were all connected to them. These were, for all purposes, tribal lands.

Balenzuela needed something to counterbalance all this power. He thought of the mayor of Villa Riqueza. He certainly appeared to be a might within himself. A separate city-state, so as to say. But this mayor was so unnerving. From one conversation, Ismael was already connected to him so that he felt a not-so-subtle pressure to report each of his movements to the mayor. That was crazy! Yet, crazy or not, clearly, he sensed, the end result of that connection, if that's all he could secure, would be either a measured success—measured out, that is, by the mayor himself— or something catastrophic. How deeply the abyss ran between these two eventualities he had not yet sounded. The mayor of Villa Riqueza was like electricity—he could arc that gap and empower transactions that would complete Ismael's mission. But this live wire might also electrocute him, if Ismael was not careful in how he chose to plug in.

The present meal, of course, had become a stilted disaster area as far as moving their projects forward. Ruby was hunched down over her plate, quietly pushing her favorite meal in with more cautious, slower bites. Ben was sipping his beer, engrossed completely in the fading suds. Jo just sat silently before her food in deep contemplation. Daniela had not returned. Basil was noisily shoving *cassava* wafers in his mouth, heaping them full of tangy salsa, obviously waiting for someone to start the next excursion into damage control. In the meantime, he was provisioning up for whatever followed. Star had the look of a long-time homeowner, dismally surveying the wreck of her house and land while the floodwaters settled rankly on everything she had tried to build. For the moment, she was speechless. If anything was going to happen to start some recovery, Ismael was going to have to initiate it. So he brought in his first rescue effort and launched a rowboat full of suggestions to see if he could discover any secure land.

"Look," he said as gently as he could to Jo, "I feel so bad that we got your family involved in our plans. We think our ideas are a good thing and helpful to this area. Good business for all. And I still think they'll be useful for your brother, Ben." And then he made a daring move, stepping out of the boat and taking his chance there was some sort of footing in this morass. "It would be better for him, I think. We think," he indicated his confederates, Star and Basil, to keep them all together in Jo's mind, "than investing his great energy and his considerable intelligence in trying to best the casino."

Jo looked up. Ruby stopped eating. The air went electric. And everyone, even Basil, pausing with an incredibly high pile of salsa teetering on a very small fragment of *cassava* as it entered the cavern of his mouth, stopped in freeze frame, looking intently at Ben.

Ben's head snapped up, he put his beer down, glanced all around and then began to laugh uproariously. The tension was broken and everyone but Jo joined in, Basil sputtering and gagging into the napkin Star immediately shoved into his hand.

Star came back to life. "This is a big gamble," she agreed, and nodded at Ben, "the biggest in your life." She turned to Jo, who was now nodding herself and even smiling wanly at them all with—was that hope? So Star jumped out of her boat too and swam toward her with, "So, Ben, dear, would you please stay away from the casino?" She was looking, however, at Jo not Ben.

"Okay," said Ben. "I guess this is risky enough—for sure!"

"Thank you," said Jo, looking from one to another. "You have my undying gratitude."

Now that was worth it! Ismael Balenzuela said to himself and started calculating again. He still was not exactly sure what power Jo held. But he could sense it was more than he imagined. Perhaps, it was potential enough eventually to counterbalance that of the mayor of Villa Riqueza. When he finally understood it and could at least enlist it in some way, he might be able to protect himself—even play both sides against each other if he needed to do so. Ben, even more so than Daniela, might actually be the key he was holding to unlock Jo and her compatriots' good graces. He—and even his "Polarians"—might very well be back in business.

Having found his footing, Ismael decided to build his reconstructed shelter on this patch of dry ground.

"You know," he confided. "I was quite wild in my own youth." He smiled broadly at them all, letting a look of regret play ruefully upon his face. "I wasted my teens and twenties," he exaggerated, "mainly at drinking and playing polo." Why polo? he wondered later. He hardly ever played polo, but it was the only thing he could think of on the spot (perhaps, he decided later, because the Magnetic Pole was on his mind).

"And," he confessed, projecting such sincerity, "I only got serious myself three years ago at twenty-nine. That's why I like Ben here so much. We can identify." He beamed a flow of goodwill at the wastrel himself, donning a guise of charitable camaraderie designed to warm all hearts. Then he raced on to keep the floor. "I am, as you might have guessed, from an old, connected, aristocratic family." He paused and looked around expansively. He had them now. Even Jo, he noticed, had begun to cut tiny morsels of cold steak and put them one by one in her mouth. So he took a gamble based on something he had learned back in college in a debating class whose skills had served him well in business ever since—anticipate your opponent's argument. "I suppose," he let the rueful smile expand, "all of you might actually disapprove of us three—Peep, Bo, and myself." He waved down any opposition to his statement, though none was forthcoming. "I suppose you would see me simply as the heir of the *conquistadores*. Yes, and you would probably be right. What can I say?" He spread his hands in supplication, moving his empty plate back to give himself more room to build his bridge to their shores.

"I am their heir, there is no denying it. My ancestors came exploring, with what was for the world of then new technology, new ways, and, yes, bearing a price for progress. But the result was much more than any of them could have imagined. They were all filled with a lust for gold, for profit. I admit it! And they were driven by the ever-human failing to think that the way of the natural world is for the weak to give way and yield to the strong. Perhaps you fear that I have come to raise the same kind of havoc among you and, once again, leave your world a poorer place. But, I tell you sincerely, from the bottom of my heart, such a fear is unfounded."

He paused and deepened his look of regret. But, then, he let his face brighten, displaying a hope so certain that it made it nearly shine, as he explained, "But, you must all remember, and never forget, that the great Las Casas—the priest who championed the Tainos, your ancestors, was also my ancestor—the ancestor of my people, that is, though some of us, of course, may have believed in what you who are North Americans once called Manifest Destiny. You see? I know my history too," and he paused and nodded at Jo, Ruby, and even Ben.

"Yes," he assured them, "we learned about the conquest of the New World back in school, too, just as you did. Though," he conceded, "perhaps the story was told differently by our families. But, still, it was more fairly presented to us than any of you probably imagine. It was not just told as a tale of glory, of how my ancestors—the liberationists, as they considered themselves—came to this benighted country and opened up its possibilities since the residents had done nothing to help it progress. No, that was not the only story we heard in Spain. There is a great standing pool of Marxist professors in our universities, and they tell us different tales than our grand-parents often did. We children—we heirs—know that the truth probably lies between each extreme."

Everyone was looking at him intently, but Jo, he was gratified to see, was still eating slowly but steadily as she studied his face. She seemed to him to be considering all he was saying. So he placed the final bricks in his bridge. "We can't redo the past. I know that. We all know that." He waved his hand around, as if beckoning all of them up onto his completed bridge of reconciliation. "But, together, we can change the way we make our futures. I am here for business. Yes, you know that already. But I assure you from the bottom of my heart I am not a *conquistador*, not a conqueror. I don't want to steal anything from anyone. I want to work for everyone's benefit."

Then he laid out his plan blandly. "I have been very open that I am here for my company to find property we can develop to bring tourists. And that means money for my employers, yes, of course it does. I would be a fool or a charlatan to deny that. And that would make me dishonest. Something none of us three want to be!" and he looked pointedly at Star and Basil. Basil had the grace to look down, but Star stared brazenly back, a smile playing at the corners of her mouth.

A dramatic pause and then Ismael Balenzuela continued his tour of the bridge: "But this time it is not money we rip out of your country. No, it is money we bring into it that you would not already have. This time," he emphasized, "in today's enlightened world—it means tourist money brought to you by ship, not taken away by ships. Tourist money brought to you by planes. It means for the people jobs—and not just domestic po-sitions, though there will be those. It means opportunities for high staff managerial positions. I am talking about a sharing of the wealth—for all. This is something I have already been promising to all of you—consistently. It is something my company has been doing all over the world. Why should this lovely island and its wonderful people not share in the global boom of wealth? And, there is more!" He was sounding now like a game show host. But it was working—at least on Star and Basil and Ben.

"Since I met these good folks," he swept his hand again toward the now broadly grinning Basil and Star, "my interest has been captured by their vision for an alternative healing spa enterprise. It would be a sideline for me, of course, not involving my company. Just a private investment. It's just us, for now, those you see before you, and," he added smiling at Ben, "your brother and sister who want to share our vision." Then he added for Jo's sake, "Please believe me. I'm not here to plunder anyone." He shook his head with an emphatic gesture of "yes" and then he stopped and watched for the reply he hoped was forthcoming. And in this last expressed hope, at least, he was authentically sincere—despite the history he had fabricated on the spot.

"I can hear you're not here to plunder," said Jo, thinking it all over. And then she said the first thing that gave the three conspirators any hope at all: "I may not agree with the spiritual aspect of your enterprise, but I always thought the Magnetic Pole is a marvel of God's creation. You know, you could swing a deal with the Bravado Beach Hotel. This is the kind of tourist-oriented idea I think they would love." She paused, then conceded, smiling self-consciously, "I know that it's always better when you own your own place and I haven't been much help on that. I understand why you wanted something that is not in my power to give you—Las Olas del Sol. But, you understand, you could always build eventually around Lake Rincon, which is far better situated to all your plans. It could dovetail them together, your company's enterprise and your private spa. And it is nearer the Pole itself for excursions. You know already that I can't personally endorse what you are all doing, but I will not oppose it either, on the strength of what you say. Aunt Aña will help you find your properties and I can ask her, as well, to put a good word in with the Bravado, if you wish me to do so. They know her—everyone does. And she is highly regarded by all."

"She's a kind of muckity muck up in the north," agreed Ben, jovially.

Jo winced.

Ruby took offense, so thoroughly, she put down her fork. "Aunt Aña's in line to be the *cacica* of the north western lands, Ben! Don't disrespect her!"

"Oh, sorry," said Ben and murmured, "touchy touchy," under his breath.

"And Jo here is in line to be the chief of the whole south western lands, unless I miss my guess!" continued Ruby, definitely, setting them all straight.

The whole group gasped.

"Oh, Ruby!" pleaded Jo.

"Whoops! Did I let the iguana out of the sack too soon?"

Jo just shook her head. "Nothing's definite," she corrected her.

"Yeah, right," scoffed Ben. "But, who else but you, Jo? It's got to be one of us."

"No, it's not," said Jo. "Who told you that?"

"It stands to reason—and, let's face it, you're the best qualified."

"I think that's enough of this. This is family business and just boring to our guests."

None of them looked bored at all. Every one of them was calculating.

Jo's plate was empty now and she nodded at them all. "This was so gracious of you," she repeated her earlier phrasing, then added, "I for one am so grateful to you for your kindness. I am sorry to eat and run, but, you might say, my business 'plate' is also very full today." She smiled her strained, wan smile at Ismael Balenzuela.

He immediately sprang to his feet. "Thank you so much for fitting us in today."

Basil and even Ben lumbered to their feet as well. Star also stood up. Only Ruby remained seated.

"Are you coming, Ruby?" asked Jo.

"Naw," said Ruby, picking up the menu, which the waiter had left conspicuously tucked between the salt and pepper shakers and the oil and vinegar cruets in the center of the table. "You take the car, Jo. I can always jog back. I've still got my running gear on from before I found you on the beach. You've got to do all kinds of 'family business' that doesn't involve me, and, if the meal's still on, I'd like to check out the desserts. I know, I know," she waved her hand deprecatingly, "I'm usually storming against all sweets and all that 'minute on the lips, lifetime on the hips' stuff, but they've got some great fruit and sherbet here. . . ." And she looked up at Ismael, hopefully

"Absolutely," he jumped right in. "I'd like to try some myself. All this wonderful food is new to me. Let me just walk your sister to the door."

"No need," said Jo. "You have my assurance of whatever cooperation I feel it is within my good conscience to give you. Please stay with your guests." And she smiled—a less anemic smile this time—and left.

"I think I'd better go find, Daniela," said Star, as soon as Jo had gone. "You won't mind if I go, will you?"

"Not at all," said Ismael, in hearty agreement.

"Bo?" she said.

"I think Ben and I could use a beer at the bar," said Basil.

Star frowned. "Don't drink too much, dear," she said, and her glare warned: We can't afford it!

"Lead on!" said Ben, already on his feet and ready to follow Basil to any bar he chose, inside or out on the grounds.

Ismael sat back down and looked to Ruby. "What would you suggest?" he asked in a very relaxed and friendly way.

"I remember the compote is great," she said, passing the menu over to him.

He waved it away. "If you recommend it, I'm for it."

She smiled and actually giggled a little, for one flash of a second, sounding a lot like Daniela. But Ismael Balenzuela was not deceived. These two sisters were a world apart. This one was much stronger and could be quite definitive. He had noted how she had stood up to Jo, simply dismissing her suggestion to leave—and Jo had accepted it without question. In fact, he reflected, as he sat smiling at her, she had expressed her opinion all through the meal. She was the first to demand to know why they had been invited to lunch. The one to move the luncheon along by asking where they would be eating and the one to lead the way into the restaurant. She also was the first to order, to refuse the wine, to order Daniela not to drink anything alcoholic—an order Daniela simply accepted, also without question—in fact, Ruby was the one to first begin the questioning of the validity of Polarism and to raise objections to it hardly any of them could answer. When Daniela started her tirade, Ruby had remained calm, answering Danny's objections by defending Josefina. And when Daniela stormed out, Ruby had restrained Jo from following. There was no doubt, Ismael realized, that this girl was smart—no doubt of that—and she was listened to—even by her older sister Josefina, who was clearly the leader.

But, unlike Daniela, who was still in a chrysalis stage, Ruby was already clearly independent in her thinking. He could use an ally like this on his side. And, as he looked at her, he realized something else. She was also quite attractive. He hadn't noticed that before, because she was always in the shadow of her beautiful sister. By herself, however, she was very pretty. Her face was really quite cute. Her eyes were sparkling and full of life—like fresh ground ginger—with a snap. And her body was the tight, trained body of an athlete, a lot like a dancer's. Suddenly, he snapped back, realizing Ruby was simply sitting there, watching him, a bemused smile on her face.

"Oh, I'm sorry," he stammered.

"What are you thinking about?" she asked, but not unkindly. "You seem miles away."

"I guess this was all a lot to take in," he admitted and she laughed.

"But what I was thinking of is how nice it is to be here alone with you."

"Oh come on!" scoffed Ruby.

"I'm serious."

"Tcch!" she hissed, "Eat your compote. You'll like it."

He did indeed like it.

"You have good taste," he complimented her. "I only regret I didn't try the *arroz con pollo*."

"Why? You didn't like the filet mignon?"

"Oh, no! It was very good. But, like I said, this compote is good. I also think a lot of what you said was very wise."

"What do you mean?"

"I mean, I don't believe in this Magnetic Pole nonsense any more than you do."

"Then why get involved?" demanded Ruby, grinning at him.

"Because it's good business and that's what I'm trying to do."

"The younger son trying to make his fortune in the world?" Ruby surmised.

"Something like that," admitted Ismael.

They finished the last of their compote.

"Where will you go now?" he asked.

"I don't know," said Ruby. "I have the rest of the day free. Do you want to walk with me?"

"That would be nice. But I need to stop up to my room first and get my sunglasses. This sun is way too bright for me."

"I'll go with you," said Ruby.

His room was on the third floor and she insisted they take the stairs to work off the dessert. Ruby took them two at a time, which he found very impressive, judging by her small stature. She was the smallest of the four siblings.

When they arrived at the door of his room, they paused. He began to say he'd be right back, when Ruby, looking at it, suddenly seemed to have a thought.

"Are you sleeping with my sister?" she demanded.

"What?" He started, flabbergasted.

"Daniela. Are you sleeping with her?"

"No, of course not!" replied Ismael, shocked at this turn of the conversation.

"Why not?" asked Ruby, eyeing him. "She's beautiful, isn't she?"

"Yes," he admitted, "she is that. One of the most beautiful women I've ever seen."

"Did you know she is a virgin?"

"No, I didn't know that."

"Well, she is. There's more to Danny than anybody would guess. She looks stupid, but she's not. She won't sleep with anybody until they marry her. Everybody misjudges her. But, I don't."

"Well, I probably shouldn't either," admitted Ismael Balenzuela. "But I never entertained the idea of trying to seduce her."

"I'm surprised at that," grinned Ruby. "Lots of men have tried. No one successfully. And," she added, looking him up and down, "despite what you said at lunch, I think you are a *conquistador* and a most dangerous one."

"What do you mean?"

"Oh, you're very handsome and very sure of yourself and women find that irresistible."

"Do you?"

"The jury's still out on that one," grinned Ruby.

"Well," said Ismael, looking down into her pretty, smiling, sardonic face, "I'm not interested in your sister because she is driven by her emotions. I couldn't live with that. Anybody not driven by reason is too unpredictable and no one can make plans with them."

"And yet," said Ruby, "you want her as part of your enterprise."

"Part of *our* Magnetic Pole enterprise," corrected Balenzuela. "Her greatest assets are her grace and her beauty. Daniela, as the face of the spa and the product line and the whole enterprise, would draw people from all over the world. Women would love to be her—men would love to be with her. She is an achievement in herself. This isn't all just raw talent. I can see that clearly. As you say, your sister is not as stupid as she sometimes acts. She has obviously polished her deportment; she moves with great grace and style."

"She was a model and studied acting, but couldn't remember her lines," explained Ruby.

"She also has an unerring sense of style."

"That's innate."

"But, she would drive me crazy," concluded Ismael. "And once you get intimate with someone, you are making a connection you had better consider beforehand, because you can't break it easily afterwards."

"That was my point," said Ruby and then added, "Look, it's hot. How about we forget walking and go swimming. I can swim in what I have" and she displayed her sleek, designer running outfit that clung to her lithe body like a second skin. "Did you bring any trunks?"

Ismael Balenzuela took her all in, sweeping his eyes down the lovely length of her and then he did something on impulse that would change the course of his whole direction. He murmured, "I have a better idea," and, reaching out to her, gathered her up in both his arms, lifted her up to his height, enfolded her against himself in a full body hug, and kissed her deeply.

At first, Ruby went stiff in shock and then, suddenly, she melted in his arms, like the winter's snow on the mountaintops of Constanza in the growing warmth of the Caribbean summer's sun.

26

THE CELL PHONE RANG while Ricky Asenao was driving between his home in Villa Bahoruco and Las Olas del Sol, where he had been summoned by Don Ramón, a summons he could not ignore. He glanced at the number, then jerked the steering wheel hard to the left, narrowly missing a horn-blaring oncoming truck as he swung into the wide parking area of the observation station at Lake Rincon, screeching to a halt, the gravel popping and spitting out beneath his tires.

"Tomás!"

"It's bad," said the voice of his friend without a greeting. "Much worse than we had imagined."

"What did you find?" asked Ricky.

"Clearings, tracts of land. Burned right there. Hauled through paths slashed through the forest and burned to carbon on the spot!"

"Did you see anyone?"

"Yes, and that's the worst part. There were only five of us, counting myself. I'd brought Rafael and his cousin Pablo and Sergio, of course, and I also brought Letty."

"Yes, good choices. And she knows her woodcraft."

"Yes, she does—and it's the main reason we learned anything, because we went deep this time, out past Boca Cachon on that dirt road—you know—that leads to Tierra Nueva and ends at Las Lajas? There we left the jeeps and went through the woods until we came upon a large group of them."

"Them?"

"The contraband runners."

"You saw them?"

"Yes!"

"You were right on the border!"

"We were—on the far side of the mountain, above Lake Saumatre, near the border."

"There's nothing there at all but dry woods," observed Ricky, thinking it over. "We have no one living there and I think the only town on the Haitian side is some ten kilometers to the north—Comillon, I believe, but I'd have to check a map."

"That's right. It's a desolate area. No one goes there but sheep herders and no one else would go there normally."

"There are no roads," said Ricky, "only cow paths."

"There *were* no roads, but what's happening is that these *contrabandistas* are slashing down the green trees, hauling them into thirty foot circles, piling up makeshift kilns, piling on mud for natural ovens, and then igniting them and burning them down to carbon. They shovel the carbon into sacks and cart the sacks across the border in transport trucks. How they're getting in is they're making a road of the residue. They've destroyed everything on their side and have now come encroaching truck-length by truck-length into ours. If they keep this up, we'll have a slash-and-burn swath all across the highland between the far western border of Lake Enriquillo on our side and Lake Saumatre and the highlands on theirs."

"Why, this is part of our own district Independencia!" exclaimed Ricky.

"It certainly is! Maybe it's a part nobody goes to, but we better start paying attention to it—fortifying it or doing something, because if these trees are doing anything to hold off the two lakes from one another and these *contrabandistas* keep slashing them down, eventually the whole lowland at the bottom will fill in with runoff water."

Ricky was silent, thinking of exactly what the implications of that were. And then he cried out, "It's the city of Jimani! That's what's in danger!"

"My thought exactly," agreed Tomás. "Jimani and all its surrounding towns—Mal Paso, first. Then the city itself. Then Ola Perla, Arroyo Blanco—maybe even Piedra Blanca—every habitation along the isthmus between the two lakes will submerge. If this is not stopped, it could even take the northern shore towns as well—La Descubierta, Postrer Rio, Los Rios, Clavillena—all washed away."

"There'll be no border!" cried Ricky.

"That's right! Nothing but the two lakes, finally becoming one."

"How much devastation are we talking about?"

"Not much yet that we could see, but sufficient to show real invasion—and, if it keeps up, the lakes are already doing their part trying to reach each other. . . ."

"That's a lot of people at risk in those towns," Ricky calculated. "And many of them are our people."

"Yes, but I haven't told you the worst part."

"There's a part worse than what you told me?" exclaimed Ricky.

"Oh, yes! They're not alone!"

"What do you mean 'not alone'?"

"These are not just contraband runners!"

"No?"

"No, they've got some kind of an army there, guarding them."

"An army? What do you mean an army?"

"I mean, we saw soldiers in uniform, armed with two or three military transport trucks hidden far off the dirt road in these makeshift swaths from the devastation I've been telling you about that's making their new clandestine road through the center of the forest. Nobody could see them from the air. There's not a lot of them, but there's enough! We counted about fifty soldiers guarding the entire thieving operation."

"Is this the Haitian army?" demanded Ricky.

"No, not at all! And that's the thing! I haven't seen these uniforms before. It's got Haitians sure, but it's also got Dominicans—and what looks like North Americans. Letty heard some talking and it sounded to her like Dutch or German. What it looks like to us is a mercenary army recruited from the dregs of all around the world."

"Well," said Ricky. "One thing's certain. Haitian *contrabandistas* couldn't afford any army. They're dirt-poor normally. How old do the trucks they're hauling the carbon in look to you?"

"Not as old as we'd expect, Ricky. This is a more sophisticated operation than any of us imagined. We're not just talking about a small band of Haitian opportunists sneaking across the border and gathering up a few twigs for the home fires to cook fish from the lake—if there's any left! We're talking about solid transport trucks—maybe a half dozen of them—and a gang of maybe fifty lumberjacks. We saw one detachment led by this large, enormously strong-looking woman who was leading them all in a work chant, something like 'What do we want? What do we want?' And then the workers would chop away and yell, 'All the wood free and no Dominicans anywhere! No Dominicans anywhere!' And they'd all laugh and shout to each other and haul the living trees to their burning site and burn them up boldly to make their carbon and, at the same time, extend their road."

"This is terrible," said Ricky, shaking his head, but Tomás could not see the gesture.

"And the worst part is the soldiers," concluded Tomás. "We couldn't get too close, because they are all armed. And I'm not talking about lackadaisical guys armed with cheap surplus guns like you see in our Dominican guards, slouching around outside, leaning against the walls of banks and restaurants, chatting leisurely with each other, with the barrels of their rifles stuck in the ground. I'm talking about real military precision. Semiautomatic assault weapons! Vigilant guards! A real militia. If we'd engaged them, we'd all have been killed. Easily!"

"Somebody's behind this," said Ricky.

"Somebody on *our* side must be behind this!" agreed Tomás. "Because there were far more Dominicans and North Americans and Germans or whatever they were and soldiers of all kinds than there were Haitians— though there were those, as well. Contraband runners don't have the kind of money to hire a mercenary militia!"

"No, they don't. You're right! We need to start looking around on our side to see who's benefitting from this."

"Our thought exactly."

"Can you get home safe?"

"I think so. The only reason why we have all this is because Letty and Sergio went in by themselves. The rest of us stayed back about a half a kilometer. We would have just lumbered around snapping brush and drawing fire. We might as well have brought a loudspeaker and mounted it on our jeeps!"

"You say they have all-terrain military vehicles?"

"That's exactly what I said. They would have run us all down before we could have gotten away."

"This is really bad."

"Extremely bad, but Letty was able to shoot a number of pictures with a telescopic lens."

"Yes, she's like a little bird herself."

"Yes, flitting from tree to tree, and Sergio slithers along the ground like a lizard, so they crept in silently, reconnoitered as best they could, and then melted back into the bush. We were all in camouflage anyway and we had left our jeeps about six kilometers away near the woods directly outside of Las Lajas at a farmhouse there and slipped the rest of the way through the forest—pretty much following the goatherders' paths."

"Did the helicopter reports we gathered help you decide where to go?" Ricky asked.

"Yes and, believe it or not, as we crossed over the mountain, we could follow the scent of smoke and the sound of the saws in the distance, though visibility is low. It wasn't hard. They are hardly hiding anything."

"They're getting bolder," observed Ricky.

"Yes, that," agreed Tomás, "and the fact that they've dug up a small army from somewhere for protection now."

"And we'll find out where!" said Ricky.

"Yes, we will!" Tomás assented. "Whatever it takes. And wherever it leads." And, with that promise, he hung up leaving Ricky deep in troubled thought.

27

ON THE SHORT DRIVE back to Las Olas del Sol, Jo was turning the developments of the luncheon over in her mind. Where was her duty exactly? She was realizing that she was a lot more invested in what was going on here in Barahona with Daniela and Ben's connecting up with Ismael Balenzuela and the Polarians than she had imagined. The thought was striking her that, personally, she was even more connected to all of this than she was to her ministry to those she was serving so diligently back home in Richfield. And for that matter—and, at this revelation, Jo slowed her car down unconsciously to a crawl—was Richfield really "back home?" Where was "home" for her exactly? Doña Lucia had insisted that "home" was here, the land of her birth. Jo herself had been operating on the understanding that "home" was Richfield, the place of her calling to serve God. Now, she was wondering, is "home" wherever her family found itself connecting? She thought of Daniela's violent reaction. This was a development she had certainly not expected. Where was home now for her sister?

Jo slipped deeper into self-reflection, and the cars, piling up impatiently behind her, pounded their horns with exasperation, several trying desperately to pass her—two at a time! Finally, pulling off the main highway onto the gravel road that led to Las Olas, Jo did not even notice the roaring of engines and screeching of tires and brakes as they barreled by, each vying for the lead, as she was suddenly consumed by yet another realization. Señor Balenzuela had expressed his regret that he had brought division to her family. Was that exactly what had happened? Or was a division already there? Jo had to admit to herself, she was now so wrapped up in the fate descending upon her personally that she had lost track completely with what was happening to her siblings.

"Lord, what am I going to do about all of this?" she prayed. "This is all turning into a phenomenal mess!"

As her car bumped down the path of scattered stones to the exit where she normally had to pause to bang on the metal gate, blow her horn, or get out and ring the bell to gain entrance to Las Olas, she was in for another shock that snapped her back to the here and now. The gate had certainly been as secure as always when she and Ruby had driven out earlier, but now she found it standing wide open. She could never remember such a thing! This sliding metal wall was always closed and bolted, day and night. But, now it was completely open and no one was in attendance. What on earth was going on here? She drove her car in, looking toward the cottage to the left, but no one was there. Not Don Ramón, not even Ernesto. But she did spot a strange car in one of the private parking places. Ah, she realized, the first guest must have come. The arrival of the rest must be impending. Was she ready for this? Did she have a choice?

Jo parked and, steeling herself up, walked slowly to the back porch. Sure enough, from inside the house poured out a bubbling voice she recognized. Mara! she thought to herself, and felt a wave of relief.

The second she entered, a smiling woman of young middle age in a sea-blue dress cried out, "Here she is!" and hurried over and embraced Jo. Jo felt so comforted in the warm hug that she wanted to stay in it. "I am so glad to see you," Jo murmured.

"And I you, Josefina! Big doings! Big doings! I had to come over early to find you and see if I could help."

"The *Cacica* of the Collanos is always welcomed in our home," smiled Doña Lucia and nodded to Jo for confirmation.

"She is indeed!" cried Jo, and couldn't resist hugging her once more. "I can't tell you how glad I am to see you, Mara. How was your trip?"

"Oh, the ferry was fine. It's a long and slow ride across the Mona Passage from Puerto Rico, but it gives me a chance to catch up on my email—did you know the ferry has wifi now? There are always so many details. I need a day and a night just to answer this week's email—and all the rest of the tweets and check the website—it never ends! And, of course, I have a few things to bring up at the meeting, so I have to think those through. I had to pretty much jump off and into the rental car. No matter how carefully I set that up before I come, it's always a complicated mess whenever I get here!"

Jo shook her head emphatically yes. "Time stands still when you arrive at the Dominican car rentals!"

"Doesn't it just?" laughed Mara. And then, having disengaged herself, and looking steadily into Jo's eyes, she reached out and took Jo's hand. "Of course, I'm here to help. I can move furniture around with the best of them, but I'm really here to see you, Josefina."

"Thank you so much."

"They've told you what's up?"

"Not in so many words, but I've guessed it."

"Of course," said Mara, "how could you not? All your life you have been prepared to lead. But, it's still overwhelming."

"Yes," agreed Jo and added, "and that's the thing!"

Mara shook her head and smiled knowingly. "Doña Lucia has been filling me in. You have other duties now."

"I do."

"You are an ordained minister, if I remember correctly."

"You do indeed," said Jo. "I have a parish in New Jersey and a little fellowship of immigrants that I care for."

"The cure of souls," agreed Mara. "Yes, I understand."

"It is difficult for me simply to uproot."

"Uprooting is what you did to go to *Los Estados Unidos*," Doña Lucia reminded Jo.

"Yes," laughed Jo, "I feel like a potted palm being moved from here to there and back here again."

They all laughed.

"An apt description," chuckled Mara. "But it's all connected."

"How do you mean?" asked Jo.

"It is one God who gifts and calls and so lifts us up and moves us around, like transplanting us now and again in God's garden. 'The earth is the Lord's and the fullness thereof.'"

"Amen," said Doña Lucia.

"Right," said Jo. "It's where in the 'fullness' I'm supposed to be that's troubling me."

"Go sit on the porch," urged Doña Lucia. "We have plenty of help here to move the furniture. And," she added, grinning ironically, "your sister hasn't arrived yet to boss everyone around, like she knows where everything belongs, so that we have to move it quietly to the right place when she is off giving orders in another room!"

At that, they all laughed uproariously.

"Bless her heart!" Doña Lucia wiped her eyes. Ruby was well known from past meetings' preparations.

"No need to worry about that," Jo confided. "I left her mulling over the dessert menu at the Bravado Beach Hotel."

"The dessert menu!" exclaimed Mara. "I would not have believed such a thing possible, if you had not told me yourself. It is many a time she has lectured me on the evils of *postre*! This is a strange day, indeed."

"Isn't it just," Jo reflected.

"Come, we will talk!" *Cacica* Mara had adopted her official tone, a pleasant combination of pleading and command that always got results. "We are just in Doña Lucia's way now. We can either cook, or clean, or move furniture, or go onto the porch and counsel together, but I doubt if we can stay here, blocking the entrance, completely in everyone's way."

"Amen!" smiled Doña Lucia again and whisked them out with a benedictional wave of her hand.

The late afternoon sun poured in off the water in a steady breeze that was like a benediction itself. Of all the people with whom Josefina Archer might have counseled at this particular moment, if she could not have her father, then *Cacica* Mara Luz Bayamancoel Collas, hereditary chief of the Yukayeke Collano Taino Tribe in the Central Mountains of Puerto Rico, would have been her exact choice. About fifteen years older than was Jo, Mara had ascended to her status at the age of thirty, nearly a replication of Jo's own current age of twenty-nine.

Mara traced her ascendance to Bayamancoel, a legendary ancestral patriarch who, the tales insisted, helped YaYa in the very creation itself. But Mara astutely reinterpreted the legend as meaning he had led his people of the Collano region of the Andes across the vast mountains and down to the sea, then over that sea to Borinken, where they had found a new home in the central mountains of what was to become known as Puerto Rico. And, during those centuries of change, the new people Bayamancoel had created from the Collanos had grown into the thriving community they were today, thanks to a succession of wise and gifted leaders, among whom was this worthy heir herself. Jo had always looked up to Mara as an older sister, a heroine. When Mara ascended to lead her people, Jo admired the deft skill with which she did it. From their valley in the central mountains, the Yukayeke Collano Taino Tribe ran several very successful businesses that were able together to support the entire community, not least of which was a museum and traditional ballpark that was a tourist favorite. Its hotel accommodations were three star, very comfortable, and family oriented. Their kitchen was legendary in itself. They had a business in leather goods that were exported all around the island and, Jo had heard, popular all over the world.

While Jo's own calling to lead had been quietly distilled into her subconscious, Mara knew from childhood she would someday be chief and, being of a serious nature and not even frivolous as a child, Mara had consciously prepared herself for her destiny. Her father, the *cacique*, had no other children? Well, what of it? Neither he nor she—nor their tribe, for that matter—worried about that. Everyone was satisfied—in fact, delighted—with Mara. And she was satisfied with herself as chief.

Jo watched her, striding so confidently, so easily sure of her own authority, as Mara led them both to the porch. If Jo had not been so humble in nature and had not trained herself to resist any spirit of envy from the moment she had embraced her faith and, as a result of it, eventually her calling to serve in the ministry, she would have certainly envied Mara for her assurance. Assurance about anything was something with which Jo knew she constantly struggled.

Mara eased down into the rocking chair and took a deep breath of the sea air, blowing in off the Caribbean. "Ahhhh," she breathed deeply, "We have the blessing of the mountain breezes, but there is something about the sea."

Jo stood for a moment, looking at what she had come to regard as "the rocking chair of fate"—because it was in this same chair on the second day here she had begun to discover the full implications for her of Uncle Sol's passing. Here we go again, she thought, and settled in once more for the next go-round!

Mara simply breathed deeply, smiling, closing her eyes, then stretching luxuriously, not in a hurry about anything.

So Jo said once again, "Thank you for coming," and waited.

"I had to come, Josefina," said Mara finally. "I had an inkling this was going to come down hard on you."

"You're very perceptive," confessed Jo. "Yesterday I was dead set against it. Today? Well, today I am not so certain."

"That's good. It is a big responsibility. No, that's not it exactly." Mara looked off again into the distance across the rocky beach and out over the ocean. "I believe," she mused, "this is the best place for us to have a discussion. It is such a wide perspective here—and this—well, this is such a vast responsibility."

Jo gazed out over the ocean herself. "I started today doing just the same thing: standing on the beach, thinking over and over about all of it—and I mean, *all* of it. There is so much to it all for me and the implications for my life."

"I know it was so different for me," Mara confessed. "I thought of my calling lightly as a child," she confessed. "It was something I did not question."

"I wish I had your certitude."

"Well, it is really all I have ever known. There was only me. No other children came. I was the hereditary chief in training. No one ever questioned that. So, I didn't either. I always felt such confidence, because everyone else from my father on down was confident already. This was all I ever knew." She paused and they sat silently together. Then, after a space, Mara spoke again. "When I ascended to guide the *Cacicazgo*—the whole territory over which I was to be chief—I came to realize very swiftly that all of my preparation—right to the age of thirty—was actually not enough. Not enough at all. It was increasingly overwhelming. That certainly challenged my smug confidence, I'll tell you!"

"So what did you do?" asked Jo, leaning closer.

"I prayed to YaYael!"

"Well, that was a good move!"

"It was the only move! I had majored in business in college and helped out in the leather works when I was going through school, and I hung out with my dad and all the tribal council, but, when I realized I had to guide the decisions myself, it was certainly a 'whole 'nother set of *platanos* to fry,' as our chief cook in our restaurant in the Misty Peaks likes to say."

"And what did YaYael through YaYa's Great Spirit tell you?" pursued Jo.

"That I couldn't do it all myself. That was plain enough! That I had to diversify the power, if this was going to work. My father had taught me so much and he had explained that, but I never really heard it until I got desperate. It was very early on. He had just died and I was grieving—deeply—but we needed a chief, so I stepped in, as you will tomorrow night, and then it all came down on me. So, I prayed one night on the mountain—all night. I just poured it out and, finally, I fell asleep. And such dreams I had! And in the morning, when I woke up—there on the mountain, feeling like my hammock was the embrace of the everlasting arms, one thought was clearly impressed into my mind."

"What was that," urged Jo. "Please, tell me what that thought was."

"That I was inadequate!"

"That was it?"

"That was it."

"All that preparation—your whole life worth? And what you discovered was that you couldn't do it?"

"Exactly!"

"You must have been crushed!" cried Jo with great empathy.

"Are you kidding?" exclaimed Mara. "Not at all! Josefina, you're missing the point. I was so relieved! You can't imagine how peaceful and grateful I felt!"

"What?"

"All my life, I thought it was all up to me. That's fine when you are a child and feeling all affirmed. But, when you're an adult and suddenly have to do it—deliver on all that self-confidence—and you realize you aren't capable of doing everything—that nobody has the skill sets to do everything— then you either toss it all in and leave or you learn how to share your power and your responsibility. God's Great Spirit told me to share. And a big, big burden went off me. There, on the mountain, in the bright light of the most beautiful dawning I had ever seen. I thanked God and I made my decision and I found the peace that passes all understanding."

Jo breathed out a great sigh. "Because you learned to share," she mused.

"Yes, so I thanked YaYa and came right down and that very day began to find the best people to head up each task and I mentored them if they needed it and stepped back when they didn't, and, working closely with the wise leaders on my tribal council, I invited the best of the best in each area of responsibility to lead with me. And, when we had no one in the present tribe to take a key task, we advertised to other *cacicazgos* and interviewed candidates across the island. It took a while to get it right and it takes great effort to keep it right. I am the chief administrator. Keeping the staff happy and productive is what I do."

"I see."

"Josefina, dear little sister, that was the only answer for me. Find the best people, equip them with what they need to do the job you assign them, and step back. Don't micromanage them. I have a business degree, you know."

"Honestly, I envy that. I majored in social work."

"That was a fine choice, too."

"So, what did your business degree tell you?"

"Well, the way I read it was this: The duty of workers is to do everything in their power to complete their job in a satisfactory manner and—and this is important—make their boss look good."

Jo laughed.

"And," Mara continued, "the task of the boss is to do everything in her power to make the workers as happy as they can be. Ensure the best working conditions, keep the raises coming, care about them, their spouses, their children, their extended families. Work for legislation that supports them. See to their physical and their spiritual needs. That's what's overwhelming. No employees who are good will shirk, or steal, or undermine, if they know you care about them. They will want to do good to please you and they will take pride and ownership in their work."

"Treat them as you want them to be," mused Jo.

"What's that?"

"Oh, it's almost a mantra that I used to apply when I was a community organizer. You treat a person as you want that person to become and she or he becomes that."

"Yes, that's what I'm talking about. That is what YaYael, Yeshua, Jesus did, isn't it? He made vacillating Peter aspire to be a rock. He loved the intellectual John and took him into his inner circle, so that same John could return that love by becoming the one not only to care tenderly for Jesus's own mother, but could also use his intellect to open the great secrets his Lord had shared with him in the most philosphical of the gospels. Why," declared Mara, warming up to her topic, "Jesus even offered to the rich young ruler a vision of what he could be—one of the greatest philanthropists the world had ever seen, dispensing first his own wealth and then, when that was expended, spreading out all the wealth of heaven. And Jesus built his teaching all on his own caring example." Suddenly, she broke off with a slightly self-deprecating laugh. "But now I am lecturing the lecturer. Who am I to preach to the preacher?"

"The woman who knows," declared Jo. "That's who! Believe me, I can use all your good advice you want to share. In fact, all the good advice I can get from everyone."

"You see? That's the right attitude to adopt!" And Mara smiled warmly at Jo. "So, what I say to you, little sister, is use all your skills from school and work. Use all your gifts from God. Don't worry about how inadequate you feel you are. You don't need a degree in business—you just need people who have such degrees to work with you. You see? Your social work degree is perfect preparation. What could be better? Once you have faced the truth of your own shortcomings and devised a game plan to supplement what you are missing to serve your people well, a true *cacica* has no time in the schedule for any further doubt. You are too busy now. You are done with that. So, depend on your tribal council, work closely with the leaders you identify, mentor the young ones, elevate the best, and redirect the rest. Keep an eye on everything. Surround yourself with the best workers you can find. Care about them all, but don't interfere with the chain of command. Don't dictate, but choose to agree and do so with consensus when it is at all possible. But, also remember you are the *cacica*, so you must take responsibility and wear your authority comfortably like an apron. The ceremonial dress is not for daily wear! That's why God inspired us to make aprons. Also, read everything out there until your eyes blur. And, when they do, as they will, then go for a long walk in the mountains—or, I guess, in your case, by the sea. And soak everything daily in prayer, like a gentle rain, giving life to your people through your love and respect, so the Great Cacique will lead you as you lead them. You *will* become the mother of the tribe. This is a good thing. It is only right. We love our mothers, when they love us. It is the natural way of the Creator."

"And my calling in Richfield?"

"It will all work together, if it is indeed from YaYa."

"I don't know how that could happen," objected Jo.

"Me either. But I didn't give you two callings and neither did the Tribe. God did that. So, God will sort it out."

"I hope you're right."

"I am the *cacica*. I have to be right! Or, at least, that's what I keep telling myself." And Mara laughed her beautiful, bubbling, rippling laugh.

Jo leaned over and kissed her on the cheek. "You are more a sister to me than I have—or deserve." And a tear began to form in Jo's eye and then it trickled down her cheek.

"If you need me, I will help you with that too," promised Mara. And they ceased talking and simply rocked slowly and watched the changing, constant sea.

28

STARLING FOUND DANIELA PULLED up into a fetal curl on a lounge chair under an umbrella on the outskirts of the pool area, crying. Star simply stood there for a long moment with her mouth open. She was accustomed to beauty having its privileges, which meant, of course, its arrogant sense of entitlement. But Daniela's was a case that completely baffled her: this yawning abyss within Daniela where an unduly expanded self-image should have been.

"Ah, honey," Star said in her most inviting coo, as she crouched down awkwardly next to the lounge chair, clumsily reaching to secure her hand.

But Daniela drew back. "No," she sobbed.

"What's the matter?" asked Star.

"You didn't support me! Nobody did!"

"What do you mean?" Star groped for some kind of meaning in all this emotion and then tried, "I've been calling you 'Daniela,' just like you asked me. . . ."

"That isn't it," sobbed Daniela. "What's the point of what you call me, if you don't take me seriously?" She began to heave great sobs and hid her face in her hands.

Star just stared at her in consternation. "Tell me about it, honey," she tried as softly as she could and then added, "I'm sorry—for whatever I did or didn't do." This one was going to be far more of a handful then she had imagined. Maybe she was not going to work out after all.

"Jo!" spit out Daniela. "I hate her!"

Starling waited. Here it comes, she thought.

"Everything I try to do, she puts it down!"

"That's too bad, honey," cooed Star, noncommittally. She had to be careful, she realized, because they still might need this Josefina's good graces, if Josefina really was ascending to the power her sister Ruby was indicating she would.

"And, you! You wouldn't support me!" cried Daniela.

"How did I not support you?" asked Star, straightening up. This crouching was starting to cramp her legs. "Let me get another chair and we'll talk this out." She went to a nearby table and dragged a straight back lounge chair over to Daniela's little makeshift lair, so she could lean over her in as solicitous a fashion as Star could muster. "Now," she said, "tell me all about it." She almost added "Tell Aunt Starling all about it," but refrained.

"You said Polarism was not a religion—that it was nothing. Nothing at all!" accused Daniela.

Wow, thought Star. She looked at Daniela like she was an even bigger idiot than she had supposed. She paused a moment, digesting this, and then prevaricated, thrashing around for an insight. "Ah, honey, ummmm, how to put this?" How indeed? "Well, see, this is a secret—that's it! You see a secret that is not for everybody."

Daniela looked at her through her tears. "What do you mean?"

"You remember about 'casting pearls before swine'?" asked Star, recalling something she had garnered from all her bored moments sitting in motel rooms, thumbing through countless Gideon-placed Bibles and shaking her head at all the altruism, waiting to see if some scam or other had taken or whether they had to grab their bags and run.

Daniela, still curled up, began to quiet down.

This was working. "You see," expanded Star, "what we have is only for a true believer. It's not just to be tossed before any scoffer who comes along."

"Like Jo?"

"Perhaps, like her" conceded Star, cautiously. "Only those truly in the know can fathom the full depths of Polarism."

"And Jo isn't in the know?" asked Daniela, sitting up.

"You know she isn't," agreed Star and then pulled Daniela in with: "Not like you are, uhhh, Daniela."

"I am in the know," agreed Daniela, sitting up and wiping her eyes. "I am a true believer."

"Yes," said Star, warming to her theme. "Many call, but few are chosen," she misquoted, unintentionally. But Daniela didn't seem to notice any more than Star did.

"I am one of the chosen," said Daniela.

"Yes," confirmed Star with import in her voice. "You are. The Pole has chosen you, Daniela. You are to be its spokesperson."

"I am," said Daniela. "And not Jo!"

Star nodded and added for good measure. "You, Daniela."

"I'm going to go and wash my face," said Daniela, with a new determination.

"Yes," urged Star. "We have a world to enlighten."

This time she let Daniela go by herself. This one was as hooked as she could be, Star reflected. She and Basil had dabbled in New Agey–type scams before, crystals and whatnot, but they had never encountered someone as monomanic, as far as embracing their rigmarole, as this one was. In a way, it was somewhat frightening. A scam is a scam, but creating a cult and turning people into fanatics is something else. There's an implied responsibility there, Star sensed, and it made her uncomfortable. Maybe this was not such a good idea. But she and Basil were into this all so deeply now with Balenzuela, and the promise of a big payoff finally was so appealing, that Star glimpsed no viable path on which to turn back that she would want to take.

Still, despite the heat of the day, Star shivered. Commitment always troubled her, as it was, but, again she thought, fooling with a false religion . . . What exactly was it that was giving her pause? Maybe it was that she had always tried to keep their scams controlled. Just in case they blew up, which they often did, she wanted to make sure they minimized the consequences if they got caught. She definitely did not want to accrue jail time, so her guideline had been: nobody getting hurt physically, just nicked monetarily. You do that subtly enough and, by the time they figured it out, you were long gone. And the damage wasn't so severe that anyone put that much energy into tracking you down. It was a living, if only barely some of the time—like these last few months. But starting a cult was a commitment that had greater dimensions than a mere salted mine, or bogus oil stocks, or even disappearing beachfront property. This bore thought, especially given Daniela's over-the-top reaction. With what exactly were they saddling themselves? Star frowned. And this is the unsettled state she was in when Basil and Ben arrived from the bar and right after them from another direction Ismael Balenzuela and—of all surprises—Daniela's sister Ruby right beside him.

"Yo, Ruby! You still here?" asked Ben.

"I am indeed," giggled Ruby.

Ben stopped and stared at her open-mouthed. She looked like Ruby, but there was some kind of change he didn't fathom about her. Ismael Balenzuela was also grinning at them all in a kind of supercilious way. Ben stared at them both and shook his head and then turned toward the business of the day. "How we doing?" he asked Daniela, as he noted her return.

Daniela's face was now washed and she had regained her composure. She seated herself in her lounge chair and even smiled at them all. "I'm doing better, Ben," she announced.

"Good. We'll leave it at that, then."

"Thank you," murmured Daniela.

"Don't mention it."

"How about I order some *piña col*—uhhh, I mean—what's that juice you all like?" Ismael Balenzuela began to offer and then broke off, looking embarrassed toward Daniela.

"*Chinola*," said Ruby and then added, "Passion fruit." And she giggled again.

Weird, thought Ben.

"Right!" said Ismael Balenzuela and added, "Thank you," and smiled at Ruby. "How about I order *chinola* juice all around."

"I'd actually like another beer," offered Basil, hopefully.

But Star glared at him and cautioned, "Passion fruit for everybody is just the ticket!" And she nodded theatrically at Daniela, who looked away.

"Oh, yeah," Basil corrected himself with consternation, mumbling, "it's too early in the day for alcohol. . . ."

Ben smirked at him, since they had just bellied up together at the bar.

But, when Daniela looked back at the group, she ignored everyone else and centered in on Ruby and Ismael Balenzuela with the intensity of a searchlight at a penitentiary. First, she stared intently at her sister Ruby, then over at Ismael Balenzuela, then back more closely at Ruby, and then again at Ismael, leaning slightly toward Ruby. An alarm went off inside her. She had seen that look before countless times throughout her life as boys and then men responded to her own breathtaking beauty. She herself had found Ismael attractive and she felt threatened, like she was confronting a prison break from the locked-down security of her own intentions. Ismael's obvious reaction to Ruby struck her as a clear rebuttal to what she took for granted was her own irresistible charm. Her first response toward Ruby was jealousy—not envy, her defenses told her, but jealousy. She felt slighted, robbed, in fact. She had had the prior claim on this dashing adventurer from ancient Spain.

She was confident that she had the power to take Balenzuela away from any other woman the moment she decided to do so. She had charm and allure and moves with every gorgeous part of her being that no man could resist. And to take him from her sister would be easy for her. It was something she had done countless times before to many competing women, simply because she could do it, and it was easy—just flashing her smile, striking a pose, glancing with eyes widening in unspoken supplication of the need for such a strong, capable man—moves that were simply part of a charade she had perfected, having become as natural to Daniela as breathing. And it would not be stealing at all, she assured herself. This was a case of her turf being invaded, because Daniela had met him first.

And then, as she regarded them both with a narrowing of her eyes and a tumult in her mind, determining which weapon to employ to put down this insurrection, a strange thing happened within Daniela. A change came over her she had never experienced before. Something deeper and more meaningful than taking away a man attracted to someone else took hold of her. She looked at Ruby and realized she loved her sister. She looked at Ismael and realized she did not love him, she merely liked him, found him fascinating, but not, ultimately, what she needed now. Now, she had found something much deeper, she told herself, than simply capturing one more man from a rival. She had a mission to polarize the world! She was becoming, in her own estimation, a deeper, better person now: an enlightened one. It was beautiful. It was fulfilling. It made her feel somehow complete. It was like signing off a prisoner to parole and letting this one go free. She relaxed and simply sat back in her lounge chair and watched them all benignly through her large, round sunglasses, content in her own "polarized" state.

Star, if she had been watching Daniela, instead of calculating the change in Balenzuela, their money ticket, as she and Basil persisted in thinking of him, would have given Daniela's condition another reading, a less charitable one, supplementing her earlier word with an adjective to read: *completely* hooked. But Star was no longer watching Daniela; she was intent on studying Balenzuela—and Ruby beside him.

"We have a campaign to plan," Ismael was announcing, oblivious to all this emotion erupting around him, for he was devoting his attention in the most tender manner toward Ruby, concentrating on her. "Will you join us?"

"I'll listen in," she said and added "sympathetically."

Star glared from one to the other. If it's not one thing, it's another! She fumed silently to herself. What kind of game is up here? I'll have to watch this closely.

"You know," continued Ismael, as a waiter delivered glasses and the great pitcher of orange-colored fruit juice he had provided, holding court now as his own captive audience gathered around him, sheltering themselves as best they could from the afternoon sun under two great umbrellas hovering over the two tables they had pushed together, "we need something special to really make our enterprise go. Something that will make people sit up and take notice. Something mystical. Something that will bring everyone in—including the locals."

"Like what? What do you mean?" asked Ben.

"Well," said Ismael, "just look at your own reaction, Benjamin. You yourself grew up half your life here—am I right?"

"Less than that," admitted Ben. "We came for visits every year, but mostly we lived in New Jersey—in Richfield."

"True, but even so, you aren't all that excited about the Magnetic Pole. And, if it's just commonplace to you, how is everybody else here going to regard it? Aren't they all going to continue to ignore it? I've been thinking about that a lot. And I've realized something. What we need is an extra perk."

"What's bigger than the Pole?" asked Basil, baffled.

"What you were mentioning before," said Ismael, speaking directly to Ben.

"What was that?"

"The relic."

"What relic?"

"The relic that everybody knows in legend, but nobody's ever seen."

"You're not talking about the Rosary, are you?"

"Exactly!"

"That's just a legend," said Daniela.

"No," said Ben. "I don't think so. I think it's real enough. And you're right—it's priceless."

Ruby looked at Ismael with concern. "If it does exist—and I've always personally thought it did—the Tribe must have it and it would be locked away somewhere. It would be next to impossible to get it. Artifacts are real important to them."

"But they must sell them from time to time."

"Coins," said Ben.

"Coins?"

"Yeah. Whenever the Tribe needs extra money they got kind of a 'bank,' so as to say, that nobody knows about."

"Do you know where that is?"

"Sure. In the water off Azua—it's in the Bay of Ocoa."

"In the bay?" asked Basil. "Whattaya mean?"

"There's all kinds of ships wrecked in the bay. So, whenever we need some extra cash, the Tribe sends one of our salvage boats out to a spot only the elders and the tribal treasurer know and the divers go diving. They bring up a bunch of rare coins and other treasure and they sell 'em on eBay."

"Doesn't the government want most of it for salvage?" asked Ismael.

"Nah!" Ben assured him. "Coins are everywhere here. The poor people even have 'em—Dutch florins, Spanish pieces of eight. Some of 'em go back to the time of Columbus and his maraud—I mean, his—uhhh—soldiers. Besides," Ben added, "the Tribe pays its taxes and we're on the edge of nowhere here. You think anybody cares what happens on this side of the island? Interest in developing the beaches is just recent. The Tribe has been doing this since like forever, and these kinds of relics are a good source of income for it."

"But the Rosary," Ruby reminded him, "the Rosary of Enrique is another matter altogether."

"Well, sure, that would have symbolic value," admitted Ben.

"Everything has its price," Ismael assured her.

"Maybe," said Ruby, hesitantly. "But this is from the greatest Chief himself."

"Even if they only let us display it," pursued Ismael, "Why, we could build a room for it and include other artifacts. It would be an attraction in itself."

"Like a history room," enthused Basil. "Kind of legitimize our whole affair."

"Hard to imagine," said Ruby.

"Yeah," agreed Ben. "The Tribe does have a treasure house somewhere—some kind of storage area all of us have heard about, but our parents never took us to it." Ben thought a moment. "I have a buddy who's been there, however, as a child."

"Really?" said Star and her eyes lit up with avarice. Even Basil put down his cup of juice and leaned forward. "Where is it?"

"He knows."

"Who's your friend?" asked Ismael.

"His name is Tomás," said Ben. "We were boys together."

"Always causing trouble," grunted Ruby.

"I'll say!" added Daniela, back in communication.

"Maybe we can buy it or rent this Rosary of Enrique," offered Balenzuela.

Or steal it, thought Star and Basil simultaneously, and, they both mused: Forget about displaying it—we could sell it on the black market ourselves. . . .

29

B Y MIDAFTERNOON, THE GUESTS had begun to gather and fill Las Olas with the camaraderie that had delighted Jo every time she experienced it as a child. The elders regarded each other as family, and it was more a meeting of the clan than simply a business meeting, though it was that as well.

Cacica Mara Luz Bayamancoel Collas, hereditary chief of the Yukayeke Collano Taino Tribe in the Central Mountains of Puerto Rico, had indeed been a blessing. And under her skillful guidance, and without Ruby's well-meant but underfoot officiousness, Ernesto and his young tribal friends had pulled the house together for the meeting in short order. Mara and Josefina herself had become the greeting committee as Doña Lucia supervised a company of chefs and waiters all drawn from their own southwestern district, while Don Ramón personally supervised the parking of vehicles, which was, in itself, no small task.

The countenance of every guest brightened the moment each passed in through the gate that was flung back in welcome by the distinguished Don Ramón himself. And this salute by leadership was heightened in pleasure by the gracious greetings of Mara and Jo as they stood on the porch, smiling each delegate through the great mahogany doors, after being kissed on the cheek by the women and saluted with a bow by the older men in the most courtly fashion. It always struck Jo how the centuries seemed to melt away when the chiefs arrived, as if traditional manners themselves had that power. Jo had a sentiment she was greeting the past, but she was also well aware that the meeting itself would be very much about the present and, particularly, about the future.

Mara had changed her sea-blue dress for a magnificent ceremonial dress, with sash and matching headband the color of the Tribal flag of the Collano Tainos. Big doings, indeed! thought Jo, recalling Mara's initial greeting to her. And she marveled as the *Cacica* of the Collanos greeted each guest with spot-on accuracy and unfailingly appropriate dignity that was far more than ceremonial. It was heartfelt: "Welcome, most distinguished *Cacique* of the *Yukayeke Inti Bajacu*: the Gathering of the Dawn in the Region of the Eastern Lands. You are most gratefully received." "Welcome, most distinguished *Cacique* of the *Cacicazgo Naca'n Guada Choreto Kiskeyanakán*: the Chiefdom of the Central Garden of Abundance of the Mother of Islands. You are most gratefully received." "Welcome, Most Honored Representative of the *Cacique* of *Yukayeke Oconuco Xaragua*: the Sub-Chief of the Families of the Mountain Farmland of the Jaragua Region, the Western Lands of the North. You are most gratefully received." This last was to a distinguished and commanding woman who threw her arms around Josefina in a great mother bear hug and murmured, "At last, *Nanixi!*" And then in Spanish, as she had always done since Josefina was a tiny child, she added the equivalent to this Taino word of endearment, "my love, my heart," "*mi Corazón*, your day has come!"

"Hi, Aunt Aña," came Jo's muffled voice, and then, as she managed to work her chin free of the voluminous clothing that enfolded her in her Aunt Anacaona's generous grasp, "I've been really wanting to see you."

"I'm so sorry, *Nanixi, mi Corazón*. I've been on the other side of the island—in Las Minas for Christian World Service, we've been monitoring a new Typhoid treatment to see if that will help the refugees. Most of our people are safe and the building projects have been going so well. But, as soon as they leave their little traditional homes behind, the new refugees flood into them and the water pollutes and the cycle begins again, "*Ayyy, ¡Dios mío!* My Lord knows I am existing on grace and good will alone!"

"Dear Aña," cried Mara, laughing, "you look as hearty as a twenty year old!—in fact, better than most!"

"Oh, I should add I am also sustaining on *platano maduro* too! Who could live without fried plantain?"

"And boiled plantain!" added Jo and then together with her Aunt, "and *tostones*, and *mangu*," and they both laughed, as this recitation had become nearly a proverb with her aunt since the earliest days Jo could remember.

"You're not afraid, *Nanixi, mi Corazón*?" asked her aunt, searching Jo's face.

"I am very much afraid, but not now as much since you and Mara are here with me."

"So it should be!" declared Mara.

"So it should be!" echoed her aunt.

Jo seemed to renew with life now that her aunt had arrived and she greeted the delegation from the *Cacicazgo Bohios Haity Sabana*, the Chiefdom of the Taino Homes of the Land of Mountains and Valleys, with deep gratitude that they had honored her possible ascendancy to *cacica* with their gracious presence.

Her new energy turned out to be delivered just in time, for, as the *cacique* from Haiti left her with a most cordial benediction, she looked up to see the austere face of Enrique Asenao, regarding her impassively, and beside him a short man about his age nodded to her without smiling.

"Welcome, Ricky, and Tomás, how good to see you!" Mara seized both their hands in hers and said, "*Natiao*, brothers, you grace us with your presence, *Taiguaitiao*, Good Friend," to each of them individually, and to Ricky specifically, "You are most welcome, *Nitayno*, sub-chief, and director of the voice of our nation," and to Tomás, "We are honored, *Manicato*," which Jo recognized immediately as a title of great honor: "valiant and bold warrior of good heart."

Both bowed to Mara and Ricky said, "You are too gracious, most distinguished *Cacica* of our brothers and sisters of the great Collano Taino Nation. We are in your debt for such courtesy."

It was traditional, of course, but Jo still found herself astonished that Ricky could respond with such cordiality. Mara had obviously won his respect. And though Jo's independent spirit railed against it, she realized that she actually wanted to win it too. That was a strange reaction of my heart, thought Jo, and then, it might bear thought for another, less busy day. She had not time to muse about it, for another delegation stood patiently waiting, as Ricky and Tomás filed with nearly military precision into Las Olas and Jo herself filed this encounter into her mental to-do compartment of grey cells.

And so the delegates came, sometimes in groups and sometimes one by one, some of them bearing messages of support and even suggestions from those who could not come for reasons of business or delays with visas or the sheer expense of travel. One group she had longed to see was the active Taino Tribe from Northern New Jersey, which held an annual *Areyto* celebration that she always attended. It would have been a well-met reminder of her other "home." She was also hoping to talk with the delegates from Florida and, perhaps, even be blessed with a visit from the distinguished Warocuya Felix of Oklahoma, who had served with the representatives of the entire Tribe when this chosen delegation representing many clans met with the United Nations and the Taino people were recognized once again as a sovereign nation in an historic meeting in the 1990s at the United Nations headquarters in New York City.

Inside the great reception hall, Ernesto and his team had set up *dujos*, the traditional cross between stools and U-shaped chairs with short legs that had been the distinguishing marks of tribal leaders since the dawn of

Taino time. Today, their use was more sporadic. Some employed them out of respect for their ancient sign of office.

The *cacique* of the central region of the Dominican Republic was by proclivity, personality, and practice a poet and was renowned for extending his art to his rule over a dual region which included not only the capital of the Dominican Republic itself, Santo Domingo, on the southern coast, but as well the lovely mountainous region of Jarabacoa in the central highlands. And his domain stretched up through the lowlands right to the northern coast and included such notable cities as Sosua, the cold-cut capital of the country, and even Puerto Plata, the traditional tourist mecca, famous for elegant beaches and fine cuisine. This *cacique's* demeanor was a work of art in itself: a pensive, well-respected scholar whose words were universally taken very seriously when he met with the country's president or the governmental ministers or the managers of finance and industry or the impresarios of the arts, but also he was well-known as a hiker of mountains who spun his oft-published verse from the misty heights of the great peaks of Constanza, not to mention his being held in well regard as a lover of sand and sea whose courtly air and casual grace charmed tourists who felt they had encountered Don Quixote himself, Dominican-style, whenever his presence graced the northern beaches—and ever, in each of these incarnations and in every one of these settings—he was at work on behalf of the Tribe. So, of course, he would be given the most traditional dujo, hoary with age and deeply scarred with memories.

One tribal chief from Cuba was so respectful of the great tradition of the *dujo* that she always insisted on bringing her own *dujo* as her carry-on, though it always had to be checked at the door of the airplane, because it was too big for the overhead compartment.

Of course, these days not every contemporary *cacique* preferred these traditional seats. The Chief of the Western Lands of the North was very old now and hardly traveled any longer, and most probably could not have gotten down into a *dujo* stool or safely back up at all without help. Jo's Aunt Aña, who was his named successor, was now running the region for him, since he was often infirm and frail on his best days and, though his mind was still clear, it would wander now and then. Aunt Aña, herself was by no means obese—she was sleek and strong—but she was a big, commanding woman of traditional build and preferred a large, comfortable rocking chair of *xiki*, very hard wood, so one was always set out for her.

The chief of the modern-day Taino district of the Dominican Republic, called the *Yukayeke Inti Bajacu*, the Gathering of the Dawn in the Region of the Eastern Lands, which was comprised of many prosperous families and towns and cities of the thriving eastern coastal region of the country, was a thoroughgoing businessman of great acumen and negotiating skill and had no patience for the *dujo*. What was he supposed to do, he wondered, spread his computer and all his printouts onto the floor? He often mused, when he looked around, that the "namesaked" chiefs who bore the ancestral names were less concerned about maintaining every tradition than the chiefs whose surnames were different and felt they had to explain continually their connection to an illustrious ancestor and squeeze themselves down onto these stools. He figured their legitimizing was owed to their skill in ruling, not simply to their ancestry.

What the neighboring chief in the central region beside his own did with style, for example, he himself, as the chief of the eastern lands, did with perspicacity, being accomplished, moneyed, definitive, generous, and shrewd. He invested tribal money wisely, funding numerous worthwhile projects, and these were routinely successful. A networker with nearly formidable personal skills, he was himself the owner of a popular chain of stores that ran not only throughout the island, but extended across to *Bimini*, that is, "Life of the Spring Waters" in the Taino tongue, or *Florída*, the land of flowers, as it is called in Spanish, or the US State of *Floor-duh*, which means nothing really in English, being a corrupted loan word. So much for an overdependence on tradition, he would scoff.

He was also a great supporter of Jo's Aunt Anacoana, whom he admired openly, and, since she was a widow and he a widower, tribal gossip wondered how they would ever get together, having their regions on the exact opposite sides of the country! But all such idle speculation always ended with the assurance: Miguel will work it out, and, if he doesn't, she will! They were both very practical. He, of course, always took a straight-back chair with a tray table routinely provided on which he could spread out those papers and always right next to an outlet. Business was business, and he was always prepared with charts and projections and plans to benefit every region, because "what helps one *cacigazgo*," he would regularly remind the gathering, "helps us all."

It is true that his ancestors had helped themselves, with the cooperation of what was left of their southern neighbors, to unite their chiefdom with their neighboring one to the south sometime after the invasion had taken place. The ancient tribal chiefdoms that Columbus stumbled onto when he and his marauders blundered upon the island were not precisely those that have come down to today's Tainos. The eastern coast, just as is true today, was a thriving *cacicazgo*, The Province of Higuey or *Caizcimu*, where the city of the latter name remains. It was ruled even then by a fine businesswoman, *Cacica* Higuanamá. And because she and the other noble women wore *caracuri*, nose rings often made of gold, and, because their peaceful chief wore her *guani'n*, her royal pendant, forged of gold, silver, and copper, the *conquistadores* assumed the area was a treasure trove of hidden gold. So, in their normal style of diplomatic relations, they hanged her and burned a teeming number of residents to death trying to extort the hiding place of the gold, never discovering that the residents had bargained for these pieces with others in the thriving trade industry within their own and across their sister islands. And, though the conquerors left the region in ruins, they could not destroy its one great legacy: its enduring penchant for business. The pieces were picked up by her successor Cayacoa.

When the survivors of what remained of this former capital of commerce eventually decided to fuse their region with the chiefdom to the north, they made a wise choice. That Province of Maguá—comprised of the eastern coast and its inland region—had also suffered through very hard times. Its Chief Guarionex was an artist, singer, dancer with strong personal skills and a big army. He fared well at first, teaching the invaders his *areytos*, his songs and dances. But the marauders mistook his cordial welcome for weakness and violated his wife, precipitating a war that their superior weaponry and ruthlessness won and, once he was chained, the gifted artist died. The loss of both these outstanding chiefs, Higuanamá and Guarionex, was devastating, so, in a way, their people's commiseration in time led to their union.

Once these two former *cacicazgos* united, they could choose their leadership from either or both regions, so they had a wide choice and over the centuries made many excellent decisions so, no matter how the country fared under a chance dictator or even another invasion, their careful, private rulers had been able to keep the Tribe stable and the families fed right to today.

The present chief of the combined *cacicazgo*, Miguel Luis Cayacoa, namesake of his illustrious ancestor, routinely joked that he thanked Providence that the family name that came to him was "Cayacoa," for, as he always explained, it was not only easy for him to write out, but, and he would chuckle, "imagine the phenomenal mess my business associates in North America and Europe would make in their emails if the name that I'd been saddled with was Cotubanama—not to mention Guacanagaric! Though," he would add, "it would not be a problem with my connections in Japan."

Privately, he reasoned that, if his region could unite two former chiefdoms (and if the traditional "breadbasket" of the island, the region next to him, could do the same—and more) why could he and the lovely and so capable Anacoana Behechio not somehow work out their own personal union along with their public rule of two separate chiefdoms, when she became *cacica* of the northern part of the Province of Xaragua, even if they were on separate sides of the nation (with that interloper between them!)—and if only she could find a way in her heart to return Miguel's ardent love for her. He had swung more complex business deals for his united region, he assured himself—why not this one?

Of course, he did have a rival—and a formidable one at that—whose ancestors had done just the same thing his had done. The "Central Garden of Abundance" next door had not been initially as big as it was now. Somewhere along the line, it had grown to its long, vertical length to become the showpiece that it is today, encompassing not only the nation's capital, and its largest and most imposing mountain, but also its oldest, most distinguished, and still quite moneyed beach resort on a coast, which he privately suspected, may have originally belonged to Chief Guarionex of his own northern coastal extension, the former Maguá Province. He was certain it had been gobbled up when someone wasn't watching! And the poet who presided over this expanded region today was quite the showman!

To be honest, he had to admit that the Province of Maguana had a lot going for it from the very beginning. It had always been the best agricultural land in the nation, well-watered inland soil, deep and rich, and, of course, as a result, the great cities from Santo Domingo up to Santiago and all those in between thrived in it. How could this region not have been a success? And its suave *Cacique* Juan Francisco de la Vega was, of course, Chief Miguel Luis Cayacoa's dear friend and all that. But "J. Francisco," as his neighboring *cacique* always signed his name, preferring his middle name to his first (as it sounded to him more traditional), was at the same time not reticent in manifesting quite clearly his own ardor for Aña and showering his attentions on her. He was, so as to say, the chocolates-and-flowers-and-original-verse type, who would take her dining and dancing and gazing at the distant starry lights on his yacht at Puerta Plata, while Miguel himself, he had to admit, was more the kind to introduce her as "the best real estate agent on the island" to newly arrived business reps who wanted the most upscale condominiums, or help her negotiate the best return on her property taxes, or engineer for her a great buy—wholesale!—on a wall-sized, state-of-the-art, flat screen TV—if she ever wanted one. If only the poet chief were not such a nice guy and his region were not smack in the middle between them both! And if only the mercantile chief of the East had inherited some of the artistic sensibility of Guarionex when the merger of his two uniting regions took place and not just the business sense of the Higueyan chiefs: Higuanamá and Cayacoa. Miguel sometimes sighed about his lack—but never when he was zestfully swinging a business deal!

Anyway, as both *Caciques* Miguel and Francisco did, every leader came to the chiefs' meeting with his or her own political and personal agendas, prepared in her or his own way, and each one of them was worthy of the great respect which had greeted them at Las Olas del Sol.

As Mara knew every title, Don Ramón and Doña Lucia knew every preference, and they had taught these to Ernesto, who followed them exactly. It was their own sign of respect to the annual gathering of the regional clan chiefs.

The tables laid out for their distinguished guests, for which Doña Lucia and her staff took personal responsibility, held a banquet worthy of being photographed for a gourmet magazine. They had created a cornucopia of traditional delicacies. If he had not been so hungry, the central region's *cacique* poet might have penned an ode to it—or an *areyto*. For, as Doña Lucia always encouraged her staff, if the chiefs' meeting did not go well, it was not going to be the fault of the provisions! And true to her pledge, the offerings were ample and succulent.

Hills of *cassava* bread bookended each table. Rows of *canaris*, vessels of water and juices both large and small, filled to nearly overflowing their own table with choices so numerous that no one suffered from thirst in the hot island climate. Between the liquid and the *yuca* bread rose what could only be called miniature mountains of piled plates of *guanajo*, roasted turkey, *ditas* and *jitacas*, traditional deep dishes and other receptacles of *hutia* and *qu'emi*, small and large rabbit in succulent sauces, *jaiba*, river crabs steamed to perfection, all manner of edible fish and even *cajaya*, slices from *tiburones*, that is, shark steaks for those who enjoyed them (and deep sea bass for those who did not), and, at the center of the meat table, a gift from the delegation of Ku-va, *yaguasa*, Cuban duck.

Mounds of white rice and beans, *criolla* style, savory with garlic, onion, coriander, parsley, green pepper, celery, vinegar, tomato paste, and brown sugar in equal proportions, sat beside chicken made with the same recipe, but with one key variation: fresh lemon as a nod to the central ingredient. And, beans, which the Dominicans call *habichuelas*, nestled down next to the rice in their own thick sauce, joining the other two of the three sisters of First Nation cuisine: baked *ñame*, yams and sweet potatoes, and maize in a sweet-smelling *axiaco*, a corn stew filled with vegetables, each of these dishes resplendently inviting as they waited for the chiefs beside *atole carraco*, red-toned corn stew, and with it yet another variation on the third "sister," *guanime*, fragrant corn bread. Next to all those vegetable-based dishes, *barbacoa*, Taino barbecue, redolent with tomatoes and peppers and heavy with spices, lured the forager and gatherer to move on. Piled next to these were baskets of bananas, and beside them heaping plates of freshly cut avocados, neither considered dessert, but part of the vegetable set.

The traditional place of honor, of course, was dedicated to vast plates of rich *platano maduro,* that banana-like staple, plantain, simmered in *canela en rama,* crushed cinnamon stalks in vegetable oil and brown cane sugar, and their leaves wrapped up in deep green *pasteles* of meat-filled, mashed, and baked *platano.* Numerous fruits: *yayama,* chunks of sweet pineapple, *guayaba,* large yellow and pink sliced-up guava, *guanime,* that tasty corn dessert, and yet one more mountain, this one of *tibiria,* watermelon, and even some *dulce de leche,* sweet rich milk bars with guava centers, promising to fill any remaining gaps before the final pile of *cassava* bread would leave the guests satiated and nourished with memories they could share with their families at home. Several of them even took pictures of the laden tables to email home to their families to show Papa or Mama was being well taken care of by the extended Tribe.

As they ate, they shared stories and family pictures and advised each other on issues arising in each particular *cacicazgo,* until the *alguacil,* the marshal, called them to order on behalf of the *Kiskeyan* Tribal Council. Each of the regions being equal in authority, the council was held this year in the Western Land in deference to several particular issues of pressing importance, not least of which was choosing a successor to the beloved *Cacique* Inti Saul (aka "Sol") Bohikio Archer, hereditary chief of the *Yukayeke Xaragua Ni Enrique Xiba Bahoruco,* that is, The Families, Settlements, Towns, Cities of the Jaragua Region of Enrique's Water, the Great Lake, and the Stone and Wood-Filled Mountains of the Bahoruco Range, or as the region was known, for short, in its more convenient form: The Western Lands of the South.

The Great Ceremonial Festival of the following evening, of course, was going to be far more elaborate, with dancing and music and storytelling and much more food and an afternoon traditional ball game and a night of great festivity, but, for the chiefs, this evening's meeting was all business, run by parliamentary procedure, with only a few variations, such as the passing of the conch shell to indicate who had the floor.

The *cacicazgo* of the Western Lands of the South was guided by a *Nitaíno,* a tribal council of elders comprised of seven members: an inner council of three and an outer council of four. The youngest member of the inner council was eighty-one years old. The inner council was chaired by another direct descendant of the great Chief Enrique and his wife, Mencia, and this elder herself was named not only for her great ancestor, Mencia, but also for the virgin Mary, the bee hummingbird, and the entire region, all of which turned out to be appropriate names for her, for Mencia María Guani Xaragua was a tiny woman, very devout, and very conscious of her connection with the Tribe and the land. She was deeply respected, and a mere wave of her hand brought silence. The natural chair, of course, would have been the *cacique*, but he had "passed on," so, in place of their leader, to whom they kept referring as "having his passing," she took command, aided by the other two council members. Despite her age of ninety, her voice was still strong and her mind clear and very integrated and insightful.

"All of you have been welcomed so graciously," she began, taking a moment to nod and smile at Don Ramón, Mara, and Josefina, who all smiled back with a certain amount of embarrassment to be so singled out. But the delegates all broke into applause, which made Jo's blush deeper and her eyes shine beautifully. "And," continued Doña Mencia, taking in the entire kitchen staff crowded in the doorway, young Ernesto and his seating team, and centering particularly on Doña Lucia, "we have been made comfortable and we have been fed with ambrosia and manna, as I imagine the tables of heaven will be laden for the Marriage Supper of the Lamb of God!" And then she grinned at the audience and added, "No doubt shortly I will know for certain." And at that the whole assemblage gasped and then broke into gales of laughter until the marshal reluctantly signaled for order.

Now that she had her audience's attention, the chairwoman immediately turned to the order of the day. "Thank you all for expressing your concerns, mailing or emailing your suggestions. All of what you shared is important, and we have tried to build each of your contributions somewhere into the agenda for today and tomorrow morning." She nodded at the other two elders who nodded back. "Some of your suggestions, of course, were late-breaking, so as to say," she explained diplomatically, and some of the elders looked down embarrassed, "and these are available in ecopy on your computer, though perhaps not in the printed version we are about to distribute. Our capable webmaster and director of the voice of our nation, *Nitayno* Enrique Asenao," she nodded and smiled at Ricky, "has ably updated the ecopy of today's meeting that you can access or see projected behind me. He has also duplicated agenda copies, as I noted already, which the young men who so graciously seated us all will now distribute to those who would like one," and she nodded at Ernesto, who was waiting with his crew, each with a fistful of printed documents.

I hope I am this composed, clear, and capable when I am sixty, not to mention ninety! thought Jo to herself, marveling at the efficiency of Doña Mencia.

Mara sensed the admiration in Jo's gaze and whispered, "She would have been *cacica* if it had not been for your uncle."

Jo looked at her startled. "I didn't know there had been a contest. . . ."

"There wasn't," Mara assured her. "Inti Archer was a superb choice and himself of hereditary succession from the great Enrique. The Tribe flourished under his leadership. He and Doña Mencia worked together seamlessly. There is not always competition for who is to be chief." And then Mara eyed Josefina, glanced over at Ricky, who was typing furiously on his computer, while an assistant filmed the meeting, and added, "But it happens."

Jo let that lie.

Doña Mencia was surveying the room from her chair in the front, alternately looking up at the marshal, who was carefully watching the progress of the distribution. Then he nodded for a signal from each of his assistants scattered throughout the room and, having received a nod from each, bowed his head to her.

She acknowledged that with a smile and a slight dip of her head and said into the microphone: "All right, you all have access to agendas. I'm going to run down some of the key issues. We will begin the official session with the blowing of the conch shell, as tradition demands, and our prayer for guidance to *Yocahú*, the One and Only Great God Who Is *Yúcahuguama Bague Maórocoti*, the Supreme Deity Who Grows the Yuca, Rules the Waters, and Is Without Ancestors" (and as she spoke, she translated these words into Spanish, French, and English, even though many delegates were wearing earphones, since the meeting was being simultaneously translated from the control room off the side of the kitchen, being fed by closed circuit television to those in that room).

This was all new to Jo, since she had never been allowed into this closed meeting, restricted, as it was, to *caciques*, representatives of *caciques*, and invited guests. She had also never been allowed into the control room, another strictly off-limits part of Las Olas. But, as a child, she had never minded, because her stepmother, Lea, when she was not required to travel with James and Sol on tribal business, had always planned an outing with the children and did the most creative things with them to their complete delight. Today, however, Jo was riveted by everything that was transpiring.

The first matter of business, Doña Mencia was announcing, had to do with the Jaragua-Bahoruca-Enriquillo Biosphere Reserve that embraced the complex network of ecosystems on the peninsula itself, the Great Lake Enriquillo, and the vast forest of the Sierra de Bahoruco. Particular concern, she noted, had been raised by development projections in the beach area of Bahia de las Aguilas, south of the city of Pedernales, in the southwestern corner of the peninsula, and just above the horn. She had asked the distinguished Elder Anacoana Behechio of the Western Lands of the North Xaragua *Cacicazgo*, who had achieved a rapport with the developers, if she would graciously prepare a report for this meeting and, she added, this distinguished representative has informed the chair that she is prepared to proceed. Jo's Aunt Aña nodded her assent from her rocking chair in the front row.

The next topic to be covered was the expansion of Lake Enriquillo, and Doña Mencia was delighted to report that in attendance as a guest was a noted professor from the department of ecological studies at the University of Santo Domingo, who had been studying the effects of the expansion and had graciously come to present his findings to them. The entire assemblage applauded.

At the final topic in this first omnibus entry, Ricky suddenly stopped typing, sat up in his chair to his full height, and raised his hand.

Doña Mencia paused and said, "The chair recognizes *Nitayno* Enrique Asenao."

"Thank you, Madam Chairwoman. I have invited a guest whom you all know, Tomás de Odnavo, who is in good standing with the Tribe, to share his firsthand knowledge with us of the depletion of our border forests by contraband runners."

"Thank you, that is duly noted and will be included in the Biosphere section."

"Thank you, Madam Chairwoman."

Doña Mencia continued, "We also have a report from an honored representative of the great *Cacicazgo Bohios Haity Sabana*, the Chiefdom of the Taino Homes of the Land of Mountains and Valleys, that oversees the interests of our tribal brothers and sisters across the great nation that we call Haiti today, from the borderlands of the northern coast to what some today call the traditional *Cacicazgo* of *Guacayarima* in the southwest. Under the auspices of the distinguished *Cacique* Louis Gama Manabauba Paix, we are privileged to have Professor Pierre Renault, a noted environmentalist at the University of Haiti in Port-au-Prince, enlighten us on his own findings on the effects of the plundering of wood, and it should explain much to us."

Doña Mencia continued to run down the agenda: a request from the International Caucus of Majority World Indigenous People Groups for solidarity in signing a declaration against industrial overfishing in the waters of Polynesia, another request for solidarity from the International Caucus to sign a "Statement on the Wellbeing of Indigenous Women and Children" to call for greater United Nations monitoring of the plight of women in countries torn by movements to institute a change of governing structure from the present legal constitution and its infrastructure to *shari'a* with its implications for gender-based violence. A further resolution from the same organization targeted honor-killing of women, and a fourth deplored the exposure of female babies in countries with legal limits set for population.

There was a universal nodding of heads indicating that those overtures would pass through swiftly.

Another more controversial conflicting set of resolutions were duly noted to be discussed, one calling for a resolution to present to the Dominican and the Haitian legislatures for consideration the changing of the name of the entire present island from *Hispaniola* to *Kiskeya*, while a competing resolution asked that the name be changed to *Haitey*, which the latter resolution pointed out was the actual primal name of the island—both separate overtures claiming they were putting forth for adoption the original name given by the original Taino inhabitants to the entire island. A similar request was made (but without conflict) to pass a resolution for Puerto Rico to be renamed *Borinken*, and a third to request that the United States' state of Florida be renamed *Bimini* were also put forth for consideration for a vote of support.

"That final one comes up every year," Mara whispered to Jo, "but hardly anyone except our chief poet, Don Juan Francisco de la Vega, ever votes for it. You can guess which delegations vote for the other two! But the coalition of all island chiefs has wisely ruled that the vote must be unanimous from all regions for a new name to be adopted. They don't want the Haitian delegation to be offended."

Jo nodded. All these overtures and all these concerns were a lot to take in. Was she going to become responsible for guiding her region of the Tribe through such a myriad of issues?

And then, after the duly noted reception of a report on the state of the rescinding of the Papal Bull Inter Caetera of 1493 and with it the rescission of the Royal Charter of the Church of England of 1496 in regard to the devastating effect on this island, suddenly Doña Mencia announced. "You will note that a cardinal issue for *Kiskeya* is the appointment of an acting *cacique* in light of the passing of our beloved Chief Inti Archer. The *Nitaíno*, the Council of Elders, including the three elders of the inner council whom you see before you and the four of the outer council who are all present today as well, Don Ramón Romero, Doña Lucia Romero y Consuela, Don Angel Moreno Cueva de Piedra, Enrique Asenao, who together comprise the seven members of the Greater Council, in consultation with the three other *caciques* of the *cacicazgos* of *Kiskeya*, have a majority and a minority report to deliver to you concerning the candidate recommended by our beloved passed *Cacique* Inti Saul Bohikio Archer."

30

Τhe report from the professor of the University of Santo Domingo on the expanding of Lake Enriquillo was very enlightening, and Tomás followed with an impassioned plea about the slash-and-burn nature of the carbon thieves and the devastation they were wreaking in the forests near the border. Jo determined she needed to research more deeply into the interlocking status of the vast components that made up this land the tribal leaders were threatening to have her steward. But now was definitely not the moment, since, at this very moment, she was herself the topic of discussion.

Doña Mencia began with a handsome tribute to Uncle Sol, followed by two more from the other two members of the council, and then the conch shell was blown again and a prayer was given in thanksgiving for *Cacique* Inti Archer by the *Behike*, traditionally the tribal medicine man and these days its chaplain (and still its designated healer through prayer and natural herbs).

Next came the majority report, and Doña Mencia presented it herself, excusing herself from the chair, which the elder Don Carlos Matos Morales to her right assumed. She began by saying, "It is no secret that, in his wisdom, guided daily by YaYa through the Great Spirit who is our exhorter and comforter, our *cacique* selected from among all of his family and all of us, whom he knew so well, his niece, Josefina Anacoana Archer, as his designated heir. All her life, he guided her into the wisdom of the Tribe, of the mountains, of the people. She responded to his deep spirituality and his love of people, becoming a caretaker herself, first as a community organizer and, second, an ordained minister. As his was, her vision is multicultural. She is Dominican born, of hereditary chieftains on both sides of her family: *Cacique* Enrique, whose direct descendant she is, as was her Uncle Inti, on her father's side, but also, she is a direct descendent of the great *Cacica* Anacoana on her mother's side. So, from both parents, she has inherited the blood of great tribal leaders. She is well educated, wise, universally respected, and, we believe, called by God for this task to our region. Appointed to it," she added, "from before the time YaYael laid the foundations of the world. Our choice has been confirmed by all three of the *caciques* on our island. I will now yield the floor to the minority report."

Jo waited breathlessly to hear herself critiqued. The report was delivered by Don Carlos, the elder to Doña Mencia's right, the one who had taken her place as chair. Jo wondered why she had expected the one to her left to be her opponent. She realized she had to be careful not to be carried away by all the symbolism that had been flowing around her since she had arrived in "Indian Country," as her brother Ben had jokingly called these western lands. "Symbols have a function to preserve tradition and are necessary to keep central tribal values consistent as the Tribe maps its pathway into the future," her Uncle Sol would lecture her. "But, Josefina," he would warn, "you must not let your perceptions of real life be funneled entirely through them. New challenges dictate new modes of actions—things we've never done—to preserve and forward those values in the changing contexts of culture." And he would wave his hands outward into the air, as if he were shooing these values like lovely green island parrots into the future. "Otherwise," he had joked more than once, "we'd still be communicating in the forest by imitating bird calls and not punching each other up on cell phones!" All this advice was still filed in her mind. Maybe it was time to let it all infuse all her thinking.

"Thank you, Madam Chairperson," said Elder Don Carlos, relinquishing the coordinating of the meeting back to Doña Mencia and rising himself to address the assemblage: "The minority report does not in any way impugn the heredity or the character of this most worthy candidate or in any way dismiss or deprecate her abilities." His voice was high and wavery and the control room cranked up the decibels to accommodate and amplify it. Immediately, a shrill screech shot through the sound system, and delegates winced and covered their ears. At once the control room shut the sound back down and there was a brief delay as the tech wing of the Tribe cautiously raised the sound until a balance was found. When the amplification was back in control, the eighty-seven-year-old elder, who had sat himself down in the interim to preserve his energy, rose again and continued: "We do not dispute the ability of the recommendation of the majority of our elders, but our reluctance to support this candidate is due to the fact that she has not grown up among us. She has been reared for most of her life in the United States. Our concern is that she cannot guide a people she merely visits briefly each year. She may be able to learn, but she has clearly been acculturated elsewhere. We felt that someone more cognizant than she is of our present situation is needed now, since our problems are timely and must be handled swiftly and with expertise. On behalf of the minority, I thank you." He sat down.

Suddenly, Tomás bellowed out, "That's right! We need a man for the job! A man who is aware of what's happening on the border. I say we elevate Sub-Chief Enrique Asenao! All of you know he is the logical choice to follow a strong man like Inti Archer!"

The group was stunned. Several hands shot up and Doña Mencia called for order and, noticing one of these hands was proffered by Angel Moreno Cueva de Piedra, she announced, "The chair recognizes the distinguished tribal elder and wise attorney, *Nitayno* Angel Cueva de Piedra."

"Thank you, Madame Chairperson. I have a point of order to raise. With all due respect, and great respect is sincerely felt, our distinguished guest has neither voice nor vote and may not address this assemblage, unless appointed to do so by the chairperson, as he did so ably in his previous report to us. If he wishes to make a counter-suggestion, he should be directed to apply to the spokesperson for the minority report."

"Thank you, Elder Cueva de Piedra," acknowledged Doña Mencia. She turned to Tomás, who sat up abashed, like he'd just been slapped, and she said in a diplomatic tone, respectful but firm, "The chair concurs with our wise elder's accolades of your great and most welcome contributions to the wellbeing of our people, but, it is my responsibility as chair to point out that the meeting of chiefs follows a strict parliamentary procedure. The sub-chief is correct. You may not address the gathering of chiefs, by ancient protocol, unless invited. In fact, I was remiss not to excuse you after your helpful presentation, but I will correct that now and excuse you with honor."

Tomás blushed completely. He stood up stiffly. Silently, he stalked out of the room. If the gathering had expected an apology, it was not forthcoming. Ricky's face was stone.

The chair recognized another hand: "*Cacique* Miguel Luis Cayacoa, Hereditary Chief of the *Yukayeke Inti Bajacu*: the Gathering of the Dawn in the Region of the Eastern Lands, you wish to speak?"

"Yes, thank you, Madam Chairwoman." The astute businessman rose up and let his friendly gaze sweep over the assembly, then he centered it on the three who sat before them all presiding over the meeting. "May we hear how many votes were in favor of the candidate and how many were opposed and then I would like to offer a recommendation, if this distinguished gathering would be so gracious to entertain it?" He paused, still standing in order to keep the floor.

The three tribal elders conferred among themselves, then beckoned the four outer council elders to join them. The rest of the gathering waited in a silence unusual, Jo thought, for any of the multitudinous meetings she had attended over the years. The gathering of *caciques* was very different from Richfield city meetings through which she had negotiated her requests while people shouted at each other when she was still "Spanish Community Organizer." And it was also very different from the desultory murmuring of pastors and church elders on various topics whenever there were pauses at presbytery, now that she was a minister of the gospel of Jesus Christ. The respect and the silence with which this meeting was conducted were unique in her experience. Even Mara was waiting in silence. Jo watched and waited.

Then the four elders of the outer council returned to their seats and Doña Mencia leaned forward and said, "The greater council is unanimous in raising no objections to having its vote shared with this assembly of leaders. The vote was five council members in favor, two opposed."

"Thank you, Madam Chairwoman," said the *cacique* of the Eastern Lands and then to the three presiding inner council members directly, with glances to include the other four elders of the outer council, "may I suggest that, given the fact that seventy percent of this *cacicazgo*'s leadership has supported the present candidate for chief, a trial period be initiated wherein the present candidate can attempt to accomplish certain key tasks chosen at the discretion of the entire greater council. A time limit shall be set with the goal of determining how efficiently and wisely this candidate performs these tasks so that both the eldership and the candidate herself can decide if the candidate is sufficiently equipped, sufficiently informed, and sufficiently successful in demonstrating she can handle ruling the region."

Doña Lucia's hand shot up, as *Cacique* Cayacoa sat down.

"Elder Romero?" asked Doña Mencia, adding, "You understand we cannot have discussion if a motion is not on the floor."

"Yes, Madam Chairperson. I am raising a point of order, suggesting that the distinguished Chief of the Eastern Lands allow his suggestion to be made into a motion so that I may second it."

Doña Mencia turned toward *Cacique* Cayacoa. "Is this your wish?"

"It is, Madam Chairwoman."

"Would you like to frame it in the form of a motion?"

"I would."

"Please do."

"I move that the candidate, Josefina Anacoana Archer, be invited to perform several important tasks appointed by the tribal council of the *Yukayeke Xaragua Ni Enrique Xiba Bahoruco*, The Families, Settlements, Towns, Cities of the Jaragua Region of Enrique's Water, the Great Lake, and the Stone and Wood-Filled Mountains of the Bahoruco Range, the region of The Western Lands of the South at the completion of which the council and the candidate by mutual agreement would determine if the candidate is to be elevated to the position of *cacica*. In the meantime, she should be appointed by the council to serve as acting *cacica*." He repeated the motion in French and English as well as initially delivering it in Spanish, despite the fact that the entire proceedings were being translated from the control room.

Jo noticed he was glancing down into a paper he had in his hand. Why, he must have prepared it quickly during the Tomás outburst—and in all three languages! And he had made his response look so natural. No wonder he and the Eastern Lands were flourishing. And she thought—I don't know if I could ever be this accomplished as a public orator. Then, she noticed, Aunt Aña was beaming at Miguel Luis Cayacoa from her rocking chair. Suddenly, it occurred to Jo, this support of herself was not just a matter of business—it was a matter of the heart as well. Smooth! Smooth! What a master negotiator he is! I really am being seated among the greats, she thought. Two campaigns, one official and one personal, in one adept presentation? Can I really rise up to this level of leadership? This is truly terrifying!

"Moved and seconded," Doña Mencia was saying. "Would the clerk of the meeting please read the motion one more time?"

He did.

"Is there any discussion?"

There was. Most of those who spoke did so in favor of Uncle Sol's right to choose and it being usually a matter of accepting that choice and only revisiting it if the candidate were unwilling to accept the responsibility of the position. But there was also a minority of responders who agreed with the two elders who had dissented. A *cacique* from Venezuela questioned whether a *reverenda* could really act definitively should the Tribe ever need to explore force in protecting itself or its lands—as theoretical as that may seem in as peaceful a province as the one in which they were enjoying such pleasant hospitality.

Doña Mencia pointed out that *Reverenda* Archer was not on trial, since the choice of candidate was solely that of the eldership of the *cacicazgo*, but the counsel of the guests was certainly avidly invited, so the candidate could be invited to answer, if she so wished to do so, but was not compelled to do so. She turned to Jo.

With heart pounding, Jo rose to her feet. She paused a moment to marshal her thoughts. "Distinguished *caciques* and elders of our people," she began. "I honor all of you and am grateful for the honor you are doing me. I have been trained in a great graduate school, one of the largest and most respected in the entire world, and I have wrestled with a number of issues, including this one. While the cure of souls is a task designed to bring peace, it depends on a theology of discipline. In the matter of nations, I deeply respect those who are pacifists, and, in matters of faith, I agree with their position. One cannot kill for Jesus. In matters of secular rule, however, in the traditional division between what in history was called 'the realm of the prince, versus the realm of the Pope,' just war theory has seemed to me to be the most viable approach. A chief must protect the people the chief has sworn to protect, the borders for which the chief is responsible, the interests of the Tribe of which that *cacica* is the chief custodian. While violence and conflict are to be avoided as much as possible, there are moments when careful, communal thought dictates that resistance must be instituted. Working closely with the Great Council and its advisors, I would not balk at armed action, if it were deemed necessary, and would participate in it myself."

A number of devout Roman Catholic elders shook their head yes in agreement.

Jo decided to add one more piece of personal information. "My father is well known as a leading pacifist, which is why I assume the question was asked. I honor his position. It flows from who he is and accounts for what he has been able to accomplish."

The delegation from New York, who had arrived just as the meeting began, all cheered and applauded and then lapsed swiftly into respectful silence.

Jo continued, "However, your passed leader, the distinguished Inti Bohikio Archer, my Uncle Sol—with my father's blessing—taught me how to use arms in our many excursions into the mountains. 'As all of us Archers,' he used to lecture me, 'your aim must be true.' It is." Jo sat down.

"Thank you," said Doña Mencia, and then to a delegate from Cuba. "You had a question—is this for the candidate as well?"

"It is, Madam Chair."

"You understand the freedom of the candidate to answer or not to do so at will, as already explained?"

"I do."

"Please, proceed."

"I understand that you have a ministry position in the United States. Will you leave that position to dedicate your full attention to the leadership demands of this region?"

Oh, oh, thought Jo. Why didn't they just ask me if I could do the job as well as a man, so I could preach equality of gifts at them? Something easy like that—something I am all prepared to answer. What am I going to say to this one? Jo rose again, even more reluctantly this time. She realized, it was difficult not to get swept up into the enthusiasm of her supporters. In fact, she was finding, it was irresistible. This was in truth the land of her birth. These were her people. Here was really where her heart was—now. But, she had a calling from God to her little church at Richfield. Oh, Lord, what was she going to answer?

Everyone was looking at her intently—especially those on the council—Doña Mencia and the other two presiding elders, Don Carlos Matos Morales and Don Martín Bautista Fernández Muñoz as well as Doña Lucia, Don Ramón, Angel Cueva de Piedra—and especially, with burning eyes, Ricky Asenao, the "man," as Tomás had declared, "for the job." Jo realized now was the moment to decide.

"I will not hide anything from anyone here. This has been a most difficult decision for me. Yes, the distinguished delegate is correct. My heart is torn. I do have a calling, but I am reminded," and this she said directly to Doña Lucia, "that I have a prior calling here. I have put my people in New Jersey into what I believe are trusted hands and I will give my heart, will, and strength completely to the tasks set before me until the council and my own heart, as guided by the Great Spirit of Y'aY'a, has given us an answer." She made certain to sound out the name of the Supreme God, the One Great Creator Spirit, not in its shortened form, but in all of its traditional Taino syllables. Then she made the plunge: "I vow I will discharge my duties as acting *cacica* with every aid to consult at my disposal and will do everything that is within my power to do to act upon these duties. This is my pledge to the council, the *cacicazgo,* and the greater Tribe itself." And then she added a flourish, unusual for her, but riding on the wings of the moment: "I am an Archer, and our aim is true!"

The lot was cast. And unusual, but not unprecedented for the gathering of chiefs, the entire assembly broke into a round of applause, led by the enthusiastic New York and New Jersey delegations, and all of them stood up—the least enthusiastic and the last to rise—but he did rise at last—being Ricky Asenao.

31

UNDER A DEEP GRAY cloud cover of swirls and waves that appeared for all purposes as secure as the sea below it, but in truth was as insubstantial as a dream, Josefina Anacoana Archer, about to become acting chief of the Western Lands of the South, stood vigil as she prayed to the Great God above all gods for guidance—and for confirmation for a decision she had already made publically—and far too hastily—and one that she had deeply begun to regret. As a result of her rash action at the meeting of chiefs, on this day would transpire a veritable sea-change for her life, or, more exactly in her reckoning, a seismic upheaval of her own personal continent. And— she told herself—it was entirely her fault.

Late yesterday afternoon, before she had even entered the chiefs' meeting, she had sternly warned herself not to be swept up into her supporters' enthusiasm. She had recognized clearly how irresistible the pressure felt upon her. She knew without a doubt she should wait until the very clear light of this morning to assess her commitments in order to discern carefully the path her calling by God would have her choose, and then she should proceed cautiously, weighing out the options being presented to her by calculating the positives and the negatives, consulting her advisors once more to be sure that she and not another candidate was truly the proper choice for each location for which she felt responsible, then soaking all of this decision-making in prayer, and, having asked for some time to decide, and having slept several nights on these choices, thereby letting her subconscious work them out, and, then, after waking for several mornings, consciously searching for the peace of Christ in her final decision, and, finally, having built into that cautious choice several careful bailout options, just in case the selection she made still proved, despite all this preparation, to be the wrong one, she should tentatively identify her option to the council. This was always the way she made an important decision: cerebrally and wisely. And, having developed and polished over years the practicing of all that wise procedure in every life-changing decision she had faced in her three decades of life, what had she done yesterday?

She had simply leaped up to her feet, leveled her guns of wit and dedication as response to the challenges being made to her leadership, and let her opponents have it, both barrels blazing. She had fired her reply across the room like a broadside from a pirate ship—something, she realized, more in character with that Ismael Balenzuela person with whom her sister Danny had become so entangled—rather than sounding the cautious set of protective (if barely adequate) salutes she should have issued from the fortress of her carefully constructed resolve. No, instead, she had declared in front of everybody she was not only taking the job, but pledging nothing less than dedicating everything in her power to make it work. Talk about making a public, decisive paradigm shift! What had she been thinking?

And now, finally, in the clear light of morning, here she was, skulking before God, begging the Almighty to make it all good and acceptable, because this very evening, in a great and elaborate ceremony, the Tribe, with the full weight of the authority of the council of elders, not to mention God's invoked blessing, would confer on her the title—and the full responsibility—of acting *cacica,* of the *Yukayeke,* "the great village," used in Dominican Taino parlance as a synecdoche, the "village" image to represent all the Taino families, settlements, towns, cities of the *Xaragua Ni Enrique Xiba Bahoruco,* the entire southwestern corner of the Dominican Republic, the Jaragua Chiefdom of "Enrique's Water," Lake Enriquillo, and the "Stone and Wood-Filled Mountains," meaning nothing less than the entire Sierra Bahoruco, the whole mountain range, not to mention the rest of the vast peninsula, which together comprise the Taino region of the Western Lands in the South.

And all of it was going to be up to her caretaking—she who had had her hands full with shepherding a little gathering of less than twenty immigrants, safely ensconced in the supportive network of a stable church back home in Richfield, New Jersey. And, she thought—as a climax to it all—she was about to lose her "home" in New Jersey entirely and rediscover another one—one in which she had not lived on a daily basis since she was a small child. It was a lot to pray about!

Four and a half hours later, Jo Archer, finally at peace with her God and, therefore, her decision, came into breakfast at Las Olas del Sol. She had been out on the promontory above the rocky beach since five a.m. and she was physically famished, but spiritually content.

Doña Lucia and Don Ramón had wisely left her alone, but they were praying themselves and watching. As she entered, just a glance at her face put them both at peace. "How about some *mangu*?" asked Doña Lucia.

"It sounds wonderful," smiled Jo and then hugged them both.

Wisely, they waited as she provisioned herself on the hearty breakfast of baked plantain and onions, pineapple juice, and one scrambled egg with a touch of ham and a tiny bit of cheese mixed in. And then, as she pushed herself away from the table and began to pick up her dishes to clean them, they could not restrain themselves any longer.

"What did you decide, *Querida*?" asked Don Ramón.

"What you hoped I would," said Jo.

"Thank God," said Doña Lucia.

The rest of the day was given over to preparation. The great festival in honor of the ascendancy of the new *cacica* was being held in a park the Tainos themselves had created, having apportioned off a great tract of the land that extended from their large Las Olas beachhouse holdings along the promontory above the shoreline toward Los Diamantes del Mar Hotel. The space between coastal Route 44 (the main road connecting the city of Barahona with the mainland towns to the north and the rest of the peninsula to the south) down to the shoreline of the Caribbean Sea was roughly a mile. So the park, extending from this road to the edge of the water, was large enough to accommodate hundreds of people. Though the Tribe had graciously left the park open for public use, since so much of the beachline was undeveloped, most of the year the great field stood empty and neglected, few visitors to this more remote area taking advantage of its spacious lawns.

Whenever a festival was in order, Don Ramón, as part of his work as custodian of the Las Olas property, rounded up a team of willing workers who were ever hanging around available in Barahona, and they cleaned and trimmed the park in preparation. Days before the chiefs' meeting, he had put them to work and, since the Thursday before the *caciques* and the other guests had even begun to arrive, the Tribe was in full force, setting up a bandstand and various stations for events and for food pavilions.

The festival was slated to begin at noon and to run all afternoon and on into the evening, so Jo had little time to consult anybody. Her main job was to get ready and coordinate with the elders her part of the ceremony.

The park was already in full bustle mode by ten thirty a.m. when she walked over from the equally bustling kitchen at Las Olas. What a transformation from the peaceful fields through which she had walked with her uncle! A huge grandstand was nearly completely erected in the far end of the great field near the promontory that overlooked the beach. Stations were provided for every conceivable traditional activity. An entire ball court was marked out in the center of the park with white chalked lines encasing the playing ground, a nod to current times, but also lined with carved stones brought in from the compound with great effort for the occasion, and portable bleachers flanking each side for the comfort of spectators. Several pickup games of soccer (or *fútbol*, as the children routinely called it in Spanish) were in progress before the official game of *batey* was initiated at two thirty p.m., after the siesta break for the babies and the *ancianos*, the honored elderly (and anyone else who was ready for a nap).

The children, of course, played with normal soccer balls. The adults, however, in integrated teams of men and women, played with a heavier ball made of several layers of rubber, though not as solid as the traditional balls of the past that were solid rubber, sometimes laced with cotton and with various fibers that could make encountering them a fatal experience. Though these days balls were lighter, players still wore protection on their limbs and what looked like abbreviated baseball catcher's padding over chest, stomach, and personal parts. These were cleverly customized to provide maximum movement, but it was still a rough game that called for being alert if one wanted to emerge without bruises or worse.

Storyteller stands, which used to delight Jo in her younger years, were also erected near the corners of the park, so the story weavers could spin their tales unimpeded.

Toward the grandstand, the dancing and singing area was roped off for now, but the ropes would be pulled back and the ground opened up to all after the great ceremony commenced.

As visitors entered, parking was available in the first quarter mile of the park, neatly organized by Ernesto and his team of young, future tribal leaders and, as visitors entered, the official greeters would welcome them in. To their right beckoned stands of *cocina criolla*, food of the country, succulent and redolent with enticing fragrances that lured all, and to the left glittered kiosks of homemade baskets, jewelry, simulated artifacts, handmade headdresses, and traditional garb spun, woven, and sewn in the traditional way. Each merchant gave a donation to the Tribe for the privilege to sell wares, and these donations helped set off the cost of the workers, the preparation, the cleanup, the trucks and crew for moving the equipment, and all the rest.

The big feature this year was to be a guest performance by the famous Native American, California-born and based, traditional yet immensely popular band and dancing troop, Sierra Tepee, whose global hit recording, "High Sierra Nocturne," had passed into the realm of legendary, universally loved songs, having been rerecorded by many performers around the world. Most of the older folks knew this music well, but there were always the young and the few uninformed visitors to be initiated to the power of the ever old/ever new classics of folk tradition: the music that speaks to many people.

Though the greeters had not yet taken their stations, Jo stopped first in the parking lot to chat with Ernesto and his eager team, then walked over to greet the hopeful merchants at the kiosks and stands, knowing many by name from past festivals. Then she strolled across the grounds, smiling a greeting at the workers as some installed the bleachers, others a tent toward the righthand corner of the dance area for an improvised nursing station, and still others setting a row of "job-side johnnies" to the right of the nursing station, edging the far border of the park. Appearing festive and being easy to spot, bright red trash barrels dotted each area in sets of three for recycling paper, food, and the rest of the refuse.

By noon, the parking lot was already filling up. The chiefs had left their vehicles at Las Olas, but it was obvious that by that evening a quarter mile square was not going to handle the traffic amassing, and Route 44 would be lined up and down with cars. In New Jersey, Jo mused to herself, the local residents might have rented out extra spaces in their driveways, but on this empty coast there were no neighbors—just Las Olas and Los Diamantes Hotel and the empty scrubland of the sand and stone of the promontory and the long stretch of beach below it. As it was, however, a local bus service had set up an excursion schedule for townsfolk and visitors at the Bravado Beach Hotel and for those of the other hotels and hostels who wanted to have an adventure and come home with something "native" on or under their arm to put on their walls or display on a table to show their friends and family what an exotic excursion this had been. So the bus service, along with every car that could be improvised into a "taxi" cruising the street for chance tourists, was more than ready for a lucrative afternoon.

At the zenith of the sun, a fully garbed greeter checked the sky and then signaled for the blowing of the conch shell. The first set of ropes was flung down and a sizable mob of "early birds" flew in, descending on the food stands like hungry pelicans, having been tortured for an hour by the wafting scents of the food pavilions. The craft merchants smiled and waited patiently, knowing they were next.

When it was safe from the prospect of being trampled, Jo went over and joined the greeters, helping welcome in a busload of camera- and guidebook-armed tourists, here on a mission trip, but taking Saturday off on recommendation of the church where they had been building an addition to expand a burgeoning Sunday School to see "a real native festival." Under their big sunhats and smears of sunblock, they were delighted to hear Jo greet them in perfect English. They all marveled at this stately young woman in her beautiful ceremonial dress, and one eager matron trilled, "Henry! Look at this!" And, fingering the sleeve of Jo's dress, she said to her,

"Oh, please, you must tell me where I can buy one exactly like this for my granddaughter."

Jo smiled warmly and said, "I'm afraid you can't buy one exactly like this one. This one is very old, but you can find beautiful ones in many colors with beads and everything right there," and she pointed to the dress kiosks section and waved at the knot of proprietors who all waved back.

"Thank you, dear. Let's go, Henry!"

"Wait a minute," said her husband, fumbling with his camera. "You want a picture?"

"Yes! Yes! Can we take a picture with you, Miss?"

"You may, indeed," smiled Jo and allowed herself to be hugged as the beaming matron, unknowingly, had her photograph taken with an authentic Taino princess, about to become a chief herself.

Greeting is an exhausting enterprise and one has to step lively to keep the scuff marks of clumsy customers off one's ceremonial slippers, so, after a bit, Jo left it up to the official greeters and headed off to the inner area. Before she became too involved in the proceedings, she wanted to enjoy herself and relive a little of her girlhood.

"Chief" Roberto Moreno Jabao, who was not really a chief, it being his stage name, was one of her favorite storytellers. Now in his late seventies, he was honored with being assigned the first storytellers' stand and his rendition of the traditional creation story was one of Jo's favorites. She went to him immediately and found him sitting on his own storyteller's stool, sizing up the crowd.

"Greetings, honored friend," she called out.

He looked around, smiled with delight when he saw who was addressing him, and rose up immediately, dipping his head in acknowledgement, "Welcome, our new *cacica*."

"Yes, acting *cacica*, but still the same little girl inside who so had her imagination stirred by the greatest of our storytellers—you who keep our traditions so wonderfully alive."

"I am ever grateful for your kind attention," he said, and the formalities now being over, he smiled and asked with genuine concern, "How are you, Josefina? I was so delighted to hear of your uncle's wise choice and of your gracious acceptance. The Tribe is deeply blessed today."

"I hope so," said Jo. "I am determined to do my best."

"I know you will. We all do."

"But it is very hard for me."

"It was hard for all the *caciques* since before the stories start. Shall I tell you one today of the Great Queen Anacoana, for whom you are named?"

"No, please," said Jo. "That one is so sad, betrayed as she was by the *conquistadores* and executed so cruelly at such a young age of twenty-nine—which just so happens to be my age today! Such a story would not portend well. And after all the kindness she had extended to them! No, today should be a day of gladness for me and for all of us. I was hoping you would tell the traditions of the creation—it is my favorite of the stories and you tell it so well."

"Ever sweet," said the elder, "and ever wise. That is you, Josefina." And then he added, "I have brought my own conch shell," and he picked it up and blew it shrilly, startling several visitors who were fumbling through the program they had been handed at the gate, gazing up toward the playing field, watching the children and wondering when the real *batey* was going to get underway. As they spun around, the storyteller, in his traditional garb, rose up on his stand and announced, "'The Creation,' as it has been handed down from legend keeper to legend keeper, since before recorded time began." And then, sizing them up correctly, and winking at Jo, he added, "The Shortened Version," and without missing a beat he began at once:

> Listen, all of you who would know the words of the wise of the doings of Y'aY'a and his son YaYael and of the Great Zemi, the Three Who Are One! When Y'aY'a decided to make the world, the king of the zemis—that is to say, "the heavenly spirits," begged for a place to muster his spiritual legions. Y'aY'a paused for one fleeting eternal moment and then, according to legend, taking up his most precious possession, the beautiful bowl that contained the bones of Y'aY'a's dead son, Y'aY'a flung it down between the stars and it smashed across the void becoming a land so beautiful the zemis gasped with awe. Today, we know the story more exactly. The Son of Y'aY'a, YaYael, who is eternal and very much alive, but still the most precious and beloved of his heavenly Parent, did indeed enter the void—but alive not dead—and forged this world through the power of the Greatest Zemi, the Eternal Spirit. It was later for this world that he had made he gave his life, then took it back up again, when he walked and lived and died and rose among the people he created But as the truth in the legend: ever Y'aY'a delighted in what was created.
>
> "This will be the Mother of All Lands," the Godhead ruled, "for you to inhabit, hold, and cherish. I will put creatures on it to nurture it and you may guide them, but you must not afflict them unduly."
>
> The king of the zemis acknowledged his Sovereign's will with humble thanksgiving, and he and his spirits took up

residence in every tree, stream, breeze, and sun shaft while YaY-ael fashioned the first man and woman. From their inception, these two lived among the spirits.

With practiced eye, the "chief" of the storytellers, watching his audience closely, could detect a fidgeting that meant that time was short, so he skipped over the elaborate middle and dipped in again at the end of the tale:

> But people were headstrong and greedy and became violent. When Y'aY'a threatened to flood the world to cleanse the bloodletting across the islands, the Greatest Zemi—the Uncreated Eternal Holy Spirit of Y'aY'a—guided a man and woman to board a giant coconut and bob safely in the Caribbean Sea until the world was purged. The zemis, once called emanations, but today we know as creations of Y'aY'a, protected humans in ways just like this, but some also sometimes disobeyed YaYa, their Creator, including the king of the zemis himself and plagued people in a most annoying manner. Therefore, whenever one feels the presence of a malicious zemi, one should always put a banana leaf over one's head so that it will lose you in the bushes—always making certain, of course, you have thanked the banana tree in advance, so as not to infuriate its spirit and have two angry zemis to contend with.

The visitors all laughed and waved, and one looked toward the bowl sitting suggestively before the storyteller, but they moved on, and Roberto Moreno Jabao shook his head and observed sadly to Jo, "It is the television set, more malicious than any bad zemi to a poor storyteller, for it steals the greatest treasure a storyteller possesses—the attention span of the hearers!"

Jo laughed and shook her own head and agreed, "So true. So true." Then she reached up as he bent down and hugged him warmly as she always did when she was a girl, and, after a few more pleasantries and warm thank-yous, she moved on (having surreptitiously slipped a two-hundred peso bill into his bowl, as he momentarily looked away).

Guessing by the sun's journey that it was now about one o'clock and high time to sample the traditional dishes before they were all gone, she turned back toward the food stalls, but as she began toward them, a voice called her name out in a ringing, unmistakable tone, and she stopped, astonished at what she saw.

Ruby came skipping up in company with the last person she expected to see.

Jo realized she was gawking open-mouthed and closed it, embarrassed. "Big day for you!" sang out her sister.

"Ruby and . . . uhhh . . . Señor Balenzuela. How good of you to come."

"Wouldn't miss it, Sis. Ismael wanted to come along, you know, to see us in our natural habitat. So, I had to bring him." Ruby actually giggled.

Jo gaped at her.

"How lovely you look in that dress," said Ismael Balenzuela, smiling warmly at Jo. And then he reached an arm around her sister Ruby and actually hugged her to his side. She smiled up at him, and Jo continued to gape, speechless.

"Besides," boasted Ruby, cuddling into his side, "soccer is my thing and I kill at *batey*. I thought Ismael would enjoy the game." And she beamed at him as she detached herself. He put down the gym bag he was carrying and grinned back at her.

Wonders never cease, thought Jo. "You do, indeed," she agreed, and then to Balenzuela, "Ruby is an accomplished athlete in many fields."

"I'm not surprised," said Ismael Balenzuela.

"Game's still on at two thirty, as usual?"

"Of course," said Jo.

"I'm going to catch up with the usual players and get in the game." And Ruby snatched up the gym bag herself, swung it over her shoulder, and touted both it and Ismael along.

"Watch out!" laughed Jo to Balenzuela.

"I'm going to get a ringside seat," he called back, trying to catch up with Ruby, who was all but sprinting toward the field.

It might amount to that, thought Jo, if it's anything like her usual playing. But the fact was that Ruby was on her best behavior. She found her friend Letty up in the back of a truck filled with equipment that was stationed by the field. Letty and two others were handing down protective gear for the players to Ricky, Rafael, and his cousin Pablo, and several other close mutual friends who were lining them on a bench by size as the pickup players sorted among them for the best fit. Ricky had his own equipment in a large gym bag, as did Letty and all those who were serious about the game. Letty, expecting her to come—and especially on such an auspicious day for her family—had packed along her spare set for Ruby, but Ruby had insisted on packing her own equipment as her carry-on luggage, and now she produced it from the gym bag. She and Letty were the same diminutive size, and both were solid muscle. It was one of the things that had bonded them together, though personality-wise Letty was her opposite: quiet and unobtrusive and as fleet as the *huron*, that small cougar-like hunting cat of the deep forests. Ruby was just as ferocious. They made a great team, and the organizers left them together, as they did every year. The field was regulation size, one hundred and sixty feet by one hundred and twenty-six, and guards were posted at twelve-foot intervals around the court in case the ball should fly out toward the spectators and do some serious damage.

The *batey* played today has discarded some of its traditional meaning, no longer serving as a reenactment of war, or for settling territorial disputes and thereby avoiding mass bloodshed. Neither has it retained the same religious significance as it did for the Aztecs, symbolizing the supposed voyage of the sun around the earth. In fact, the teams that formed on the day of Jo's ascension to acting chief were not even strictly regional, as this was a special day and not part of the island league's season. But, even during league competition between the *cacicazgos*, some of the players on the teams were friends of the Tribe and not even themselves Taino. Professional soccer players came regularly and marveled and begged to be allowed to play the swift *batey* to increase their speed and endurance, for it is a very arduous sport. But, though the game has lost some of its traditional meaning and mutated into what could be called an underground sport, known only to hyper-fans of *fútbol* in all its permutations, it still has a deep traditional significance for the Taino people, for it is wholly theirs.

Perhaps this heritage and the devotion to it explains in some part why Dominicans are so superb as well at *beisbol* throughout the island and also why they dominate the world of baseball in the United States as well. Though *batey* is more akin to soccer, the weight of the ball and its jarring impact removes all fear of being hit with a hardball, so Dominican players who have played *batey* are unafraid of being struck. The hardball of professional baseball, rocketing at ninety an hour miles, is still a mosquito to the thundering hornet of the *batey* ball. And no greater devotee of the risk, the pounding pace, and the thrill of a battle hard fought was the professional soccer coach, Ruby Archer. With an extra reason to shine today—and Letty also on her game—the twin *Guani* or "bee hummingbirds," as they were nicknamed, were everywhere. The team had placed these two small but fleet women as forwards, and the aggressive Ruby, with Letty at her side, was all over the field. If Ismael Balenzuela was serious about his infatuation with Ruby, this was the moment to take a lesson from her concentrated dedication—and her aggression. She was not a woman with whom to trifle.

Ricky was also playing on their side, and he played aggressively and very well himself. The other side was comprised of several members of the team from the central district. The Eastern Lands players had divided themselves between the two teams. Only two had come down from the north, where the ball game had fallen into shadow under the increasing incapacitation of their *cacique*, the aged and failing Pablo Manuel Moreno, and they joined in as best they could, but it was hard for them to keep up, not having a team on which to participate in the on-season leagues between *cacicazgos*.

On the siesta break from their meeting, which had been demanded unanimously by the chiefs so some could sleep and the rest could see the game, Jo's Aunt Aña, cheering from the bleachers, vowed to herself to make very sure that several age-divided teams got organized and going when she became *cacica* of the North Western Lands. It was one way to keep the youth identifying with the Tribe and not just with the Boston Red Sox and all the major league North American farm clubs spread around Santo Domingo and on up through San Pedro de Macoris—not to mention the lure of the Dragons of Chunichi of the Japanese league, which had a very strong presence and, of course, the stiff competition of the dream of most Dominican boys, which was to play on one of the superb local teams, the Licey Tigres, or their archrivals, the Leones, the *Gigantes*, or Giants, of the Cibao, and all the others.

But, as seriously as the Dominicans hallowed *beisbol*, so did the Taino warrior young favor *batey*—and it was one hard-fought battle waged that day in the new *cacica's* honor. Ruby came off the field, sweating and grinning. She had played one of the hardest—and least contentious—games of her entire career. Jo marveled at that from her cheering spot between Mara and Aunt Aña.

"What happened to Ruby?" asked Mara.

"I'm afraid to ask," laughed Jo.

"She seems so different," pursued Mara.

"Yes," was all Jo would say.

"And who is that man she keeps leading around?" asked Aunt Aña, undeterred by Jo's refusal to comment until she knew more herself.

"That," said Jo, "is someone we want you to meet."

"How so?"

"He is a developer who represents a firm in Spain. He wants to find resort land to develop here on the western coast. We have been veering him away from Las Olas del Sol."

"Las Olas!" exclaimed both women, simultaneously. And Aunt Aña added, "I should think so!"

"We all told him you were the one to meet."

"That's certainly true!" affirmed Anacoana Behechcio, smoothing her hair back—and Jo and Mara both laughed.

"Let's do it now," offered Jo.

"All right," said Aunt Aña. "Do you mind very much, Mara?"

"Not at all," said *Cacica* Mara. "This is an *Areyto* Festival. One can never be bored! But, just remember, we're supposed to be back at four thirty at the latest for the rest of the meeting, or Doña Mencia won't give us a break next year!"

"Check!" said Aunt Aña. "I'll just make it touching base with him and we'll set a follow-up."

"I'll go tell them you're on the way and smooth it over," said Mara, "but don't be long!"

"I have my orders, *Cacica*!" laughed Anacoana and saluted her friend.

Ruby spotted them coming as they worked their way down from the bleachers and immediately thought of the same idea. "Ismael!" she exclaimed, "here is the woman you want to meet: our aunt the real estate agent who knows every meter of beach around the entire island."

Ismael Balenzuela brightened up immediately. Jo brought the next *cacica* of the Western Lands of the North over to them and allowed Ruby to do the introductions. Then, as they began to talk, Jo faded away.

Her next destination was the grandstand to coordinate with the organizers how the evening's inauguration was going to go. But, as she walked away from the ball court, she passed the equipment truck and, as she stepped around it, she came face to face with Ricky Asenao. He looked none too pleased to see her.

"You played a wonderfully skillful game today, Ricky," said Jo graciously.

"Thank you," said Ricky curtly. And that line went dead. He simply stood there waiting and Jo, in the still air, could think of nothing else to say, but, "Excuse me," as she stepped around him and continued walking to the grandstand. Well, that was awful, she thought to herself.

The chiefs were back in session.

It was now about five o'clock p.m. and the whole area was mobbed. A group of drummers and dancers were entertaining the crowd, and Jo was relieved to see her brother Ben, not back in the casino, but here, sitting next to his friend Tomás, each of them pounding away on *tamboras*: wooden drums made from tree trunks and each one shaped into a long cylinder that narrowed at each end. They were beating the ends with sticks in an infectious traditional rhythm, while bare-chested muscular men in the traditional *nagua* loin cloth joined graceful women, dressed in ceremonial dresses with headbands and their long black hair in braids flowing down their backs, hunched forward in a circular dance that harkened back before recorded time.

"*Cacica* Josefina," called out a woman beside the stage and hurried over to Jo, signaling several others with her hand. "We must get you ready. It is already nearly five thirty and the dignitaries are beginning to arrive. Our special guest, the mayor of Villa Bahoruco, is already here, and we are expecting others any moment."

"The chiefs are not here yet, are they?" asked Jo, beginning to feel a twinge of nervousness.

"No, not yet, but Doña Mencia has promised to end the session by six o'clock and walk them right over. The food stands are closing by quarter of seven, and Ernesto, Doña Lucia's boy, is all set with his helpers to convert that area into special parking for the honored guests. If you will just come around with me to the preparation area behind the stage. . . ." She took Jo by the arm and guided her firmly—in Jo's feeling, like a steak on the hoof about to be poleaxed. Jo was right. The first thing they did was fuss with her hair, braiding it up, then touched up her lips with gloss, and they tried to touch up her face. Jo, who wore no makeup, argued for the minimum.

"But it will look so good in the firelight of the torches," argued her skin care consultants. They came to a hard if civilly fought compromise with a minimum and maximum each side could stand.

While this was going on, some of the women were moving equipment off the stage. "We're putting a *bohio* on the grandstand for the setting," the cosmetician explained as she worked on Jo's eyebrows.

"You're putting an entire house on the stage!" exclaimed Jo, adding "Ouch!"

"That hair was a little long," her torturer said by way of explanation, and then clarified. "And it's not a whole eighty-person *bohio*, just a little two-person one with an opening and a pointed roof, made to scale for the occasion. It's going to be very nice."

"What am I supposed to do—emerge from that?" asked Jo, beginning to flinch from the pinching and not at all showing the proper passive native Taino response her makeup crew was expecting.

"Oh, no, that's just for show. No, you are coming instate on a litter carried by ten warriors and heralded by flutes and maracas and the *guiro* to scratch out the rhythm of your ascendance and the drums to beat out the celebration of your arrival."

"Oh, good grief!" moaned Jo, always mortified to be the center of attention, having worked for years to push others forward instead, as all good ministers do.

But the head cosmetician frowned. "It is the way all the pictures show your great ancestor Queen Anacoana arriving instate."

"But it's such a fuss!" protested Jo, mortified at the prospect of being lifted up and paraded through a crowd of hundreds of people. Apparently, she had been hoping she could just amble onto the stage, receive her commission with a handshake like she was receiving a diploma, and then go heading off to work the very next day with a minimum of fanfare, if any.

"You'd better get used to the fuss," snapped a male voice. It was Ricky, still excused from the chiefs' meeting to oversee the arrangements for the evening. "You're *acting cacica* now." And he emphasized the word "acting."

"Aren't her eyes lovely?" asked the cosmetics expert working on Jo's face. Now Jo knew who she was—Ricky's second cousin. And she even remembered her name: Yuisa.

Ricky looked Jo over critically and grunted. "They are very lovely." Then he stalked off to search for the truck with the *bohio*, which he growled should have been here by now.

Jo didn't know if he sincerely meant the compliment or had simply responded appropriately because he could see how hard his cousin had worked on her to make her lovely. Jo just shook her head—or tried to without much success, because another woman was now maneuvering turtle shell earrings into her ears. "These earrings are the royal *tatagua*, your sign of office for now. If you succeed you will wear the *tao*, the chief's *guanin*. It is very beautiful."

"It is," Jo murmured. "I remember my uncle's pendant of office. I often used to play with it when I was little, but always so carefully because it was so special. Copper red and with gold filigree and in the center a crucifix like the kind on the great statue of Enrique Warocuya in Quito, Ecuador. It is very, very beautiful."

"I hope you win it, Josefina."

"Thank you, Yuisa. You are being very good to me and I know I am not being easy to work with."

"That's all right," Yuisa worked a ceremonial headband onto Jo's brow. "All this is very difficult for you. I can see that. But you are handling it like the great lady you are."

Jo almost burst into tears. All this faith everyone had in her! What she thought was: You don't know the half of it!

The finished Jo was resplendent in the eyes of all who had worked on her and they showed her off to everyone who came back behind the stage.

"*Nanixi, mi Corazón*, you're exquisite," exclaimed her aunt, who had just arrived with Mara and the leaders from Haiti, whom she liked immensely. "It's quarter of seven and the food stands are closing. They're converting the market area into parking—have you eaten anything?"

"No, and I'm starving."

"Oh, oh. I should have brought you something. I'm so sorry. Maybe I can get you something back at Las Olas."

"No, problem!" announced someone pushing through the crowd gathering around Jo, and in came Ruby in the lead, trailed by Ben and Ismael Balenzuela, all carrying large bags.

"We got you covered, Sis!" said Ben. And they began to shove the cosmetics to the side and bring out plastic containers of *cocina criolla*—the last at the stands—and invited everybody who was hungry to join in by courtesy of their distinguished visitor from Spain, Don Ismael Balenzuela.

Jo was aware of their mounting debt to this stranger and noticed, as young as he was, his generosity had earned him a title of honor and distinction. Ben was now proclaiming him "Don" Ismael Balenzuela.

"Thank you," said Jo, and acknowledged, "You are indeed very gracious and kind."

"It was my idea," crowed Ruby.

"And a good one too!" smiled Ismael Balenzuela and again hugged her.

Ruby beamed all over.

This time Ben just grinned.

The chiefs had eaten plentifully all day, so it was left to the cosmeticians to help the Archers and friends polish off their own ad hoc banquet.

By now the Bohio was up and the truck for the famous guest band had also arrived. The road crew was doing a sound test and Richard Little Bear, the legendary leader of the group, was brought over and introduced to Josefina.

"You are the youngest and most beautiful *cacica* I have ever met," he enthused and bowed before her, taking her hand.

Jo blushed a deeper tan and tried a little stylized half curtsy, which came off somewhat awkwardly, but her words were full of sincerity. "You do us such great honor, sir. We have grown up loving your music. You have spoken not only for your own Tribe but for ours as well, and you have given a voice to the voiceless all around the world with your wonderful, consciousness-raising songs. Thank you so much for coming."

"The honor is all mine. I knew your Uncle Sol well. He was very important in our lives. Back when we were still finding ourselves as a young singing group, I was introduced to him at an interclan gathering of First Nations People. We were just starting to change our image from the doo-wop group of children we were attempting to be back in the sixties to something more consciousness-raised ourselves. This was even before God graced us with 'High Sierra Nocturne,' the song that changed our lives. Your uncle took pity on us and invited us to come and sing at this very field. It was the first time any of us had traveled outside our own country, except, of course, to Mexico. Tony's mother was First Nations, but his father was Spanish, so Tony, our bass man, translated for us until your Uncle Sol arrived—he, of course, knew many languages. So we played for the first time in the islands right here—next to Las Olas—more than forty years ago. We listened to the *areyto* chants and jammed with the drummers and ate *cocina criolla*. . . ."

"Oh, you want some?" asked Ben with his mouth full of chicken.

Richard Little Bear shook his head. "We've been here since five o'clock. We hit the food stands pretty fast and pretty hard—I'm surprised there was anything left!"

Everyone laughed.

"Chief Richard." A beautiful young girl in a lovely red and gold costume, obviously one of the dancers who accompanied the group, stopped the conversation as much with her presence as her words. "I am so sorry, but they asked if you might come for the sound check."

"Thank you, Lolita." And then to the group, "My duty calls." And he bowed to all and left.

"Wow!" said Ben. "Richard Little Bear himself!" He spoke for them all.

Then Jo felt a hand on her shoulder and her aunt said, "It's time."

Jo stood up, reached over and gave Ruby a hug, took Ismael Balenzuela's hand and thanked him courteously, then hugged Yuisa and her team and stepped off, as she now thought of it, to destiny.

32

THE FRONT OF THE grandstand stage was cordoned off for about fifty feet. Marshals were walking down the perimeter, assuring the gathering crowd that there would be plenty of opportunity to see, that participants would be coming right in front of them, and to please keep their children outside the roped-off areas, because dancers and other marchers in the procession might not see them as darkness fell and they wanted to make certain that everyone was safe.

Jo walked beside her Aunt Aña in a gathering knot of chiefs and other dignitaries to the far opposite end of the field, directly across from the grandstand, above the nursing tent. Throngs of people were hurrying toward the stage, clutching their programs. Some would look over at the performers heading in the other direction, glance ahead of them and see no lights, and then hurry on toward the stage.

By the time Jo and her retinue arrived, she turned all about to see a burgeoning mob of garbed performers gathering from every direction.

The most disconcerting were several large men in parade dress uniforms marching directly toward her. Six of them, three in front, three in back, came within three feet of her and then stopped on command. The front three stepped to each side and carefully surveyed all participants arriving while the back three held their ground at attention. All were armed with side arms. Out from the center of the company of soldiers stepped a plump burly man in a uniform himself with gold braid on his shoulders. He strode up to Jo smiling and paused. One of his retinue announced to all and sundry, "*Alcalde* Nicolás de Odnavo," and then he added in English, obviously for Jo's benefit: "His Honor!"

"¡Bienvenida! Welcome," replied Jo in kind in Spanish and then English. "I am deeply honored by your presence."

"Do you know who I am?" the resplendent man asked, touching the brim of his dress hat as a salute to her.

"The Mayor of *Villa Riqueza* is always honored at our gatherings, being himself a member of our Tribe."

"You are well informed," he admitted. "Yes, I am a mixture of all the people I rule, Dominicans, Haitians, and," he paused and studied Jo's face intently, "Taino!"

Jo nodded, but said nothing.

"You are very young to be a *cacica*," he observed still studying her.

"I am being appointed acting *cacica*, not *cacica*."

"Yes, not *cacica* yet," he agreed and added, "and I am not yet elected to the tribal council. You may never be *cacica*, *Señorita*, and the closed company of those in power may never see fit to elect me elder. I hope you will take measures to rectify this very displeasing situation."

Jo paused and chose the noncommittal: "I'll look into it."

"Good," said the obviously ruffled mayor, "See that you do. It will benefit all. Just look at Villa Riqueza!"

"You have done very well," she tried to soothe him.

"You can't imagine how well!" he insisted. "No one has done with their territory what I have done with mine, and am I honored for it? No! To accomplish all one can and still be on the outside of the real decision-making body! It is foolish for them and totally not right for me. . . . And even my son, Tomás, is not treated with enough dignity. Here he is only playing the drum when he should be part of my honor guard—or at least yours!" He broke off as he saw the response of caution on her face. Then suddenly the grievance stepped aside to be replaced by charm. "But this is your day of celebration. Nothing must disturb the joy, dear Princess. We must have a chat someday soon. I will send an honor guard to escort you in style to my humble office where I will show you the appropriate amenities. And, as we get to know each other, there is so much more I can share with you that will benefit us both."

"Thank you," Jo nodded.

"Remember this," he replied, "I am always at home to the chiefs. For now, congratulations!" Then he paused for a last disconcerting observation. "You are very pretty," he mused, almost to himself. "People will follow you."

Jo was stung, but decided this was not the time to object to his comment's sexism and all that implied. She was certainly not about to be used, as she feared her sister Daniela was so obviously and willingly ready to be used by the people with whom she had fallen in. But Jo realized she was about the age of this mayor's son Tomás, and thus Nicolás de Odnavo was her senior in age, so the proper reply demanded respect. She chose simply, "Thank you, Mister Mayor, you honor me with your presence."

The *Alcalde* de Odnavo seemed pleased with that response.

"I salute you," he concluded. "And we are delighted to march in your procession," and he stepped back in among his retinue of bodyguards as the leader called to a knot of *alguacil*—the marshals who were attempting to bring order to the line of march according to a plan each of them was waving—demanding to know what was the place of honor that would be accorded to the mayor of the most illustrious town in the Republic.

Aunt Aña, who was watching all this, said simply to Jo once more: "It's time."

Reluctantly, Jo stepped onto the bamboo litter and sat down in the chief's chair that was fastened to it and waited.

By now, the great throng had converged. At the head marshal's signal, musicians in white embroidered ceremonial vests and long white waistcloths began to shake maracas, beat tamborines, the *mayohuaca'n*, the sacred ceremonial drum, and small *tamboras*, drums fastened to sashes slung over their shoulders to free their hands to beat the rhythms. Dried gourds, the *guajey* or *güiro* for scratching, added complexity to the rhythms, and ancient music sprung alive from the time of memory from the three-stringed *jab'bao*; the *caracol*, conch shell horns; *cascabeles*, bells; and *flautas*, flutes.

"*Ri' Guazabara!* Valiant warriors!" shouted a voice behind Jo that made her start and look up to see ten men in headbands surround her. Ricky Asenao directly behind her seized hold of the large central bamboo pole that supported the litter directly under her throne and shouted, "Easy now, men—up at the count of three. All together now as one, so we do not drop or injure our *cacica*." And to Josefina, he said, "Princess, you now begin your assent." Then to the men, counting off in cadence "one, two, three" in the Taino tongue: "*Heketi! Yamoca! Canocum!*" In perfect sync, the three at her head, the three behind her, and the two on either side lifted the litter up.

And at the rising of the new chief, the torches were lit, all the flag bearers of all five *cacigazgos* of the entire island unfurled their banners, as the flag bearers of all the guest Taino regions from each island and mainland represented surrounded them and raised their colorful yellow and green and blue and red flags, each featuring a traditional symbol in the center. Around them, all the dancers leaped, both men and women, beating and swirling and swaying to the rhythm of their feet, and to that rhythm, together as one, they all began to move forward, a great mass of celebrating flashes of color and music and rhythm and pageantry, crossing the half mile of the park with rhythm and chanting building as the crowd gasped to see this great company converging upon them, singing in one great syncopated, united voice.

Jo, high upon the litter, surrounded by swirling movement, as her warriors carried her steadily onward, felt a cataclysmic convergence in her own emotions of exuberance, fear, profound responsibility, as she felt herself swept into an inexorable current toward destiny that left her close to tears. Yet the smiles of the tribal council welcoming her as she hove into sight assured her of the friendly shore on which she was to land.

Up before the grandstand they came, as cameras flashed like fireworks and floodlights lit up the bells and the jewelry like thousands of fireflies escaping in flight.

Then the celebrants stopped and parted, and the Tribal council through the hand of Doña Mencia beckoned the first participant to mount the stage. The *alguacil*, the grand marshal, ascended first. He surveyed the gathering and then raised his hand. Suddenly, the drums stopped. The audience gasped. It was as if the earth had swallowed up all sound and movement. A single conch shell echoed out from a *nagua*-clad warrior, and in full regalia the *behike*, the religious leader of the Western Lands of the South, stepped out of the *bohio*, the little house on the stage.

"Thank you, *Yocahú*, for your blessings tonight," he shouted, raising his hands in supplication, "And may what we do on earth please you as in heaven!"

"*Amén*" shouted back all the celebrants in one great voice.

And then to the delight of all the onlooking guests, the grand marshal announced: "Please rise to honor a special guest, the Lieutenant Governor, the honorable Pedro Badilla, the administrative ruler of the entire region."

All who were not already standing came to their feet, ooing and aahing across the audience. Only Jo, by virtue of her precarious position aloft, kept her seat, as her ten warriors gently placed her bamboo litter on a base framework brought out from behind the stage by six more costumed youth, as, in symbolic support, her bearers remained around her.

The politician bounded up the stairs smiling and waving at everyone, working the crowd, so as to say, to thunderous applause. All the inner council who were already seated on the stage rose to greet him and Doña Mencia graciously offered him the empty seat next to theirs that had been set back on center stage. He took her hand courteously and then waved again at the crowd, which drew another round of applause, though less enthusiastic, and, gauging that, he sat down.

The next up was pageantry in motion. *Alcalde* Nicolás de Odnavo, who had hastily changed his military dress jacket and hat for a traditional vest and headband, mounted the stage accompanied by his six bodyguards and, after greeting the inner council, who nodded cordially at him, but did not stand, he proceeded to stage left where his honor guard fanned out behind him, standing at attention for the entire proceeding.

Then quietly came a single woman in a floral dress, unimpressive, perhaps, compared to her fellow mayor's entrance, but the *Alcaldesa* Flora Higuamota Guebera Hernandez, Mayor of Villa Barohuco, was renowned for her wisdom and universally respected. A descendant of Queen Anacoana, herself, and her husband, the great Chief Caonabo, Mayor Flora Hernandez was a distant cousin of Anacoana Behechio and therefore of Jo. And the elderly inner council all rose and embraced her warmly and seated her on their other side.

The mayor of Villa Riqueza, remaining seated on stage left, frowned at this display of affection, Jo noted, as she watched him carefully from her perch above the crowd, still making up her mind about him. Then he lapsed into a stoic silence free of all facial expression.

Mara and the other *caciques* and delegates from Puerto Rico were next, and then the chiefs from Cuba, Venezuela, New York, Florida, and on and on. Each was accorded full titles and enthusiastic response from the presiders, the performers, and the onlooking crowd.

This went on for quite a while until the climax: the presenting of the chiefs from the traditional Mother of All Islands, Kiskeya/Hatey/Hispaniola itself, where Taino legend claims life began. As each of the chiefs ascended, the grand marshal shouted out their full titles to the applause of the crowd.

These presentations began from the far east to the far west of the island. Each chief was dressed in the garb of office that each saw fit to adopt:

"*Cacique* Miguel Luis Cayacoa, Hereditary Chief of the *Yukayeke Inti Bajacu*: the Gathering of the Dawn in the Region of the Eastern Lands of the United Provinces of Higuey/Magua of Chiefs Higuanamá and Guarionex, and descendant of his illustrious Ancestor Chief Cayacoa" arose in a business suit that befitted his image as the progressive leader of the future of the Tribe's economy. But on his chest hung the *guani'n*, the great medal pendant of his office, its gold and silver and copper inset and interworked facets dazzling in the lights as he strode up to the stage to be applauded by all. He took his seat behind the council in the great place of honor of the five chiefs of the five regions that comprised the island.

When the great applauding of appreciation subsided, the grand marshal announced, "*Cacique* Juan Francisco de la Vega of the *Cacicazgo Naca'n Guada Choreto Kiskeyanakán*: the Chiefdom of the Central Garden of Abundance of the Mother of Islands of the Ancient Province of Maguana." To the delight of the crowd, the renowned poet chief rose to the stage resplendent in full traditional regalia. Crowning his brow was a large headdress of feathers: green plumes from wild parrots, white ones of cranes and herons, black ones and red ones in one united plumage, symbolizing the diverse *cacicazgo* guided by his rule. On his chest, his great *guani'n* was a *tao*, just as the great Enrique himself had worn, a traditional pendant with a cross in the center of it that, in Jo's eyes, rivaled even the beautiful *tao* of office of her Uncle Sol himself. The precious metals flashed in the torches, outlining with light the central cross, ancient and yellowed with great age. His robe was of the finest snow-white woven cotton, belted around with a leather thong skillfully embroidered with traditional designs. On his ankles, fastened on leather leggings, flashed a multitude of seashells sparkling white in the stage lights, and in his hand a great staff of office, its head a plumage of brown and black feathers. The applause was thunderous as he nodded with great dignity at the crowd. His reception took a while to subside, as cameras flashed and the *cacique* of the central region was mindful to pause graciously at several angles so the visitors could gather their photos to show their families at home what real authentic Taino dress and aplomb were all about.

"*Nitayna* Anacoana Deborah Behechio, Ancestral Descendent of the Great Queen Anacoana, Sub-Chief, Elder, Stated Successor, and Most Honored Representative of the *Cacique* Pablo Manuel Moreno of *Yukayeke Oconuco Xaragua*, The Villages of the Families of the Mountain Farmland from the Islands of Hinagua and Tortuga, off the Northern Coast, to the Ascobat, Hiatici, Cabay, down to the northernmost stretches of the Jaragua Region: the Western Lands of the North!" announced the grand marshal. And, befitting that long title and in answer to the performance of the splendid *cacique* who had just preceded her, Aunt Aña more than held her own. She wafted up onto the stage with great grace, despite her traditional build, with an elegance that made the women gasp. She was resplendent in a myriad of necklaces and armbands of gold and silver and seashells and so many semiprecious stones that they appeared to adorn every spare inch of her beautiful ceremonial dress. Her movement across the stage was as musical as wind chimes and her beautiful headdress rivaled J. Francisco de la Vega's for the splendor of its plumage.

The chief from Haiti, *Cacique* Louis Gama Magua Paix of "The *Cacicazgo Bohios Haity Sabana*, The Chiefdom of the Taino Homes of the Land of Mountains and Valleys of the Ancient Provinces of Marien/Bainoa and Guacayarima in the Southern Lands up through Maden and the Northern Coast in the nation called Haiti Today," had a formal title that had accrued so many facets over the years, as the region consolidated into one after the division of the Spanish and French into new nations and the final setting of the current border. Having arrived with an impressive retinue, filled with both young and old delegates who now grouped around him as he ascended, the chief mounted the stairs to great fanfare. Then his company returned to their places, hailing their chief and leading the applause with shouts and horns and rattles and drums.

At this point, at Ricky's signal, the ten warriors patiently standing beside Jo—still aloft on the framework—suddenly animated to life, seizing the litter poles and carefully shifting Jo's litter back into the air for the final moment. She felt suspended in time, poised like a hummingbird buoyed by the wind in penultimate stillness as the world shifted around her into place.

The grand marshal called for silence, paused a long moment, as many in the crowd of onlookers held their breath, wondering what was coming next. Then in a commanding voice he announced: "By the grace of *Yúca-huguama Bagua Maórocoti*"—which he graciously translated into Spanish for the guests and then in English for the gathered busload of short-term missionaries, snapping pictures and marveling at the pageantry—"the One Supreme Deity Who Provides Yuca for Us to Eat from the Earth, Rules the Oceans and the Seas, and Is Without Ancestors": *Y'aY'a, Padre Celestial,* God the Father, *YaYael, Yeshua Meshiha,, Jesucristo,* God's Only Son, Jesus Christ, and *Ti', Espíritu Santo,* The Holy Spirit, I present to all of you the new candidate to be inaugurated as Acting Hereditary Chief of the *Yukayeke Xaragua Ni Enrique Xiba Bahoruco,* that is, The Families, Settlements, Towns, Cities of the Jaragua Region of Enrique's Water, the Great Lake, and the Stone and Wood-Filled Mountains of the Bahoruco Range: The Region of the Western Lands of the South, Princess to Queen Josefina Anacoana Archer!"

A thunderous applause exploded. The guests joined in with the celebrants and the cheering went on and on as Jo blushed in a most humble fashion and, inside, was overcome with the most unquenchable longing to be simply walking again alone with her Uncle Sol on the cliffs above the Caribbean Sea with the only lights, those of the stars and of Las Olas, flickering in the distance.

Then the grand marshal waved his hand and suddenly all the celebrants fell silent. The visitors stopped a beat afterward. And in that split second of unexpected hush, a lone voice came arcing over the silence, "Why, Henry! The princess is that girl I had my picture taken with! Whoops!" And the matron clapped her hand over her mouth in chagrin while half the assembly glared at her and half broke up completely in laughter.

The ten warriors lowered the litter to the ground, and Ricky Asenao, the head of Josefina's new personal bodyguard, extended his hand to help her out. As she touched his hand a shock went through Jo. She glanced up at him and he blushed and looked away—but his hand remained steady. Then she paused, aware of her coming charge, turned toward the woman who had cried out from the crowd, and smiled gently at her and nodded, and all the woman's fellow short-term missionaries clapped and cheered for Josefina, joined once more by the whole assembly, as Jo stepped up onto the stage.

Doña Mencia and Doña Lucia of the Tribal council of the Western Lands of the South, and Jo's Aunt Aña, the heir to the chiefdom of the Western Lands of the North, all exchanged satisfied smiles as they rose and came forward to greet Josefina so the formal ceremony of inauguration could begin.

Then up onto the stage came the rest of the seven members of the *Nitaíno*, the tribal council of the region. They and the guest *caciques* and other dignitaries formed a huge half-circle around Josefina as the *behike*, formerly the medicine man but now the tribal chaplain, stepped forward to conduct a service of inauguration.

To each of the charges, Jo answered, *"Naboria daca!"* "I am a servant of God." All around her there was broad smiling from all three of the inner council members. Apparently her obvious popularity and her stately composure had won over the skeptical elders of the inner council, Don Carlos Matos Morales, and Don Martín Bautista Fernández Muñoz, for they both clapped with as enthusiastic an applause as the dignity of their advanced years and high positons allowed, and, of the outer council, all but one beamed encouraging smiles at her. She was not surprised to see the one face trying to be inscrutably passive ironically belonged to the director of communications, Ricky Asenao, unreadable and austere, though he had just been on the verge of cordial with her privately.

At the final question and Jo's positive answer a shout went up from the stage, immediately echoed by the audience, so loud that it would have awakened anybody who was still left asleep down the road in Barahona. And on that signal, the *areytos*—chanting and dancing—broke out in earnest, and the marshals dropped the restraining ropes and the crowd flooded into the center, mingling with the performers, everyone pressing toward the stage and Josefina, snapping pictures and shouting encouragement in four different languages—Taino, Haitian Creole, Spanish, and English.

Up onto the stage bounded Ruby, pressing through the throng to embrace her, announcing in a commanding voice, "She's my sister! Sister of the queen coming through! Make way for me! Jo, I'm so proud," she cried and dove onto Jo, hugging her tightly.

Jo looked around for the rest of her family. "Thank you, Ruby. You are so dear to me. You all are." Then she added, "Where's Ben?"

"I don't know," said Ruby, straining into the crowd. "It's easy to lose people in this mob. I saw him earlier with Tomás, but I haven't seen either of them for a while. Ismael left about six o'clock. He said he was sorry he had to leave, but he was really exhausted and, on top of that, he had something else he was involved in tonight." She trailed off. People were all pulling at Jo from one side to the other and shouting up to her from the ground to look this way and that, begging for Jo to pose for pictures with sundry family members, including children they were handing up to various chiefs on the stage who were graciously bending down and holding them up next to Jo. She felt like she was running for president of the country! A squalling, struggling baby was plopped into Jo's arms, so the last thing she heard her sister call out to her over the din of crying, as Ruby was swallowed up into the crowd, was: "I'm sorry, Jo, but I haven't seen Daniela at all—all day."

While all this confusion was going on, the road crew was deftly resetting the stage for an impending extravaganza to complete the night. Suddenly, they ignited huge additional floodlights which lit the stage and all around it like daylight. The grand marshal, who was poised and waiting, shouted, "Ladies and gentlemen! Now to bring our day of celebration to a fitting conclusion, we are proud to present the world-renowned voice of traditional First Nations music: Richard Little Bear's Sierra Tepee!"

Thunderous drum beats began pounding through the amplifiers, beautiful dancers resplendent in scarlet red and golden yellow swayed gracefully onto the stage, and, to the shock of visitors who did not know that Caribbean style is to play one's greatest hit first and then once again to end the program, the unmistakable strains of "High Sierra Nocturne" lilted out its message: "Two o'clock in the morning, I reined my pony in and the high sierra mountains were staring down. Made some coffee and I rolled my bedroll thin. And I laid myself on the cold sierra ground!" At the chorus, many began to sing along: "And the high, high, high sierra was calling down, talking to me in the night! It said, 'I nurture bears and bees and birds and, my friend, I nurture you. But, if you cut my forest—cut your life!'"

The audience was stunned, electrified, invigorated at the swirl of colors, the flood of music from the large industrial speakers, and the compelling ecological message of this legendary band.

Everyone, fixated on the performance, lunged toward the stage to be as close as possible to the epicenter of the action, so nobody noticed Jo slip down the side stairs and flee into the night in search of her missing family.

33

S UNDAY MORNING, JO AWOKE frustrated and exhausted. Her calls to Los Diamantes Hotel and even to the Bravado Beach Hotel had yielded her no news of either Ben or Daniela. She had not seen Ruby since the previous night, but at least Ruby had shared her moment with her. Frankly, she was worried—not, she assured herself, because they had slighted her honoring but because of what it might mean to their relationship: further estrangement from Daniela and who knows what reaction from Ben? But, as she thought it over, yes, she also had to be honest with herself, it did hurt her. Now that their parents were missing and their uncle was gone, all they really had was each other. Jo had always been the one to hold the children together. It would be such a pity if it were her ascension to acting chief that split them apart.

Mara was already up when Jo came downstairs. It was very early and Doña Lucia and Don Ramón and the rest of the *caciques*, obviously deciding to take to heart God's command to rest on the Sabbath, had not yet appeared. Even Ernesto was nowhere to be seen. The entire family had obviously spent all its energy to make everything work the previous night, and the festivities had gone on and on, long after Jo had slipped away.

"Good morning," called Mara, hearing someone arrive, as the chief from Puerto Rico rocked gently on the porch, soaking up the pleasant early morning air. When she turned and saw Jo, she added, "Well, Josefina, that certainly was some big doings last night. I'm surprised to see you."

"Yes," said Jo. "I'm shocked I'm up. I think I want to escape before anyone else comes down. I really feel the need for something simple and peaceful today. I don't think I could stand being the center of attention again. Are you heading over to see Pastor Remigio at that little church you like to attend when you come here?"

"The Pentecostal one? Absolutely. Are you up for that?"

"Yes, I am. I can be sure they'll focus on God and not on me—I need a break!"

Mara laughed. "First, we need some provisions."

"I am so with you," said Jo. "It's early enough, so let's make something that we can leave for the *ancianos,* our treasured old ones."

"We could do *mangu.*"

"We could indeed. There's plenty of plantain left over and a whole lot of stuff packed away in the refrigerator—even with all the tons of food they gave away after the chiefs meeting—as long as the call of the onions doesn't steal through the house, beckon everyone down, and give us away."

Mara, checking the first of the two large restaurant-sized refrigerators in the commodious kitchen of Las Olas, could see immediately they needed to change their plans. "I don't think we have to cook anything—there's enough here to feed the entire countryside! Let's forget making *mangu* and just forage."

They ate well, without making any observable dent in the leftovers, and then Mara insisted on taking her car, since she knew the way perfectly. The gate was not locked, since Don Ramón was not certain if any of their guests would be leaving early to return to their own homes and duties. So, together, the two women pushed open the iron gate and Mara drove down the gravel road. Turning toward the right, when they reached the highway, they headed to Barahona.

The little wooden church building stood on a crowded corner of the city. The curbs were high and the streets like culverts for the water runoff from the tropical rains that sometimes daily washed down through them to the sea. Little shops of all types crowded together. There was a park up the street, empty at this point, and they parked their car there next to a small statue dedicated to a benefactor and walked back smiling at the residents just beginning to awaken and several of them heading themselves to the church. The service, as Jo had hoped, was pleasant and restorative. The congregation clapped and sang enthusiastically through a number of *coritos,* gospel choruses that lent themselves to the tambourines the mothers of the church shook with such skill. Pastor Remigio was waiting at the door and he hugged Mara as she came in.

"So good to have you back, dear sister!"

"So good to be back, Pastor."

A woman handing out hymnals broke into a great smile and hurried over to her, crying, "Mara!"

"This is my friend, Josefina," said Mara to them both.

"I know you from past attendance," said Pastor Remigio. "Welcome once again to God's house." If he knew what she had become as of last evening, one look at the caution in her face warned him from making anything of it, so he simply shook her hand, without further comment and warmly ushered her into God's presence.

After two hours of singing, a sermon on the responsibility to serve God in whatever way God had called each attendee to do it, and an after-service meal of *pasteles,* meat-filled plantain pastries rolled into banana leaves; little sweet bananas called *gineos dulces*; and a treat of portions of *flan*, the traditional caramel dessert, all washed down with espresso-strength coffee from the nearby mountain that could jump-start a zombie, it was time to go—they had been nourished spiritually as well as physically.

As the pastor bid them farewell, he gave them a parting blessing: "May God bless each of you as you rule with wisdom, which comes when your will and God's will converge."

They thanked him and, as they walked away through the neighborhood now awake and beginning to bustle with people, Jo observed, "So he knows who we are."

Before crossing, Mara had to wait for a cart of avocados with a bicycle mechanism cleverly built into it to roll by, so she turned to Jo and said, "Of course, he was at the festival last night. I chatted with him. He was very excited that you were becoming chief. He knew your uncle well."

"And yet he didn't say anything when we arrived."

"No," agreed Mara sagely, "but you notice he was prepared with a sermon on leading with responsibility. He guessed correctly that I would come this morning. Besides," she walked a few feet and then stepped back out into the street again since a shop owner was washing down the sidewalk in front of his store with a bucket and a large mop, "all you needed was sunglasses and a scarf over your head to announce that you wanted to be left alone. He's very sensitive and wise."

They walked along the street for a bit as the washing water ran down the curbsides, but had to step back up on the sidewalk to avoid a large truck maneuvering around a tight corner, bumping up on the curb just ahead of them and then squeezing past a *publico*, a kind of public taxi, blowing its horn at them and anyone else that might be heading in the same direction as the other three passengers already crammed into the back.

The park was now filling up, and a knot of men were slamming dominos down on a card table with a determination strong enough to win a revolution.

"So, where to now?" asked Mara, as they crossed over to her car.

"It's probably a waste of time to check the Bravado to see if any of my family is there—mainly Ben at the casino. It's not open yet, this being Sunday. I saw Ruby last night, and I don't think Daniela wants me showing up at Los Diamantes. I think I'll need to wait for her. But there is a mission I want very much to do."

"What's that?" asked Mara, relaxing behind the steering wheel, waiting to see where Jo wanted her to go.

"Back to Las Olas to—well, I guess I'd say—confront Doña Lucia and Don Ramón."

"How do you mean?"

"Well, okay, so now that I am acting *cacica* and functionally in charge of the region, and I am in a waiting period until the chiefs decide what tasks they are going to assign me to prove whether I can do the job or not, I have my own agenda to do and, Mara, I mean to do it!"

"Which is?"

"I'm going to find my parents and—if I can—also find out what happened to Uncle Sol."

"Lots of luck with that," Mara muttered under her breath and said loudly, "Let's go try."

Las Olas del Sol was generally wide awake when they bumped up the gravel road. They both waved at the Venezuelan *cacique* as his van, driven by his son and heir, clattered past them on the way to the airport. The gate stood open and some of the young Haitians were out in the driveway kicking a soccer ball around with Ernesto. They stopped and greeted Jo and Mara cordially. Many of the parking spaces were already empty. The sandy ground cover was once again free of vehicles and not too flattened, or at least the strands of the vegetation were recovering, and Mara was able to find a paved place under the great lean-to that lined the wall to protect the cars from the elements and particularly the hot Caribbean sun, which could make a steering wheel feel as hot as a barbecue pit if there was no one nearby to rent a hapless driver a flattened-out cardboard to spread over the windshield.

Inside, the kitchen was bustling. Jo greeted the Cuban delegation on its way out and each traveler embraced her and wished her the best. Jo also received an enthusiastic blessing from the New Yorkers, who told her they were so sorry they could not hang out with her, but they really had to go— they all had a million things to do—and, besides, the gang from Florida looked like they were still sleeping in, so she'd have them for company. It was definitely an eat-and-run group of busy *caciques*. Jo pitched right in serving them in the great room and, by three o'clock, the bulk of the guests had turtled down and out—the elders from Florida being last, as it turned out. Jo was lugging a pile of dishes back to the dishwasher, as Doña Lucia, mopping her brow with a dishcloth, said, "Thank you, Josefina, we really needed the extra hand."

Mara was now upstairs packing, and Jo and Doña Lucia were finally alone. Don Ramón had been outside waving the last of the guests through and off, and Jo chose the moment that he stepped back into the house, came to the kitchen for coffee, and sunk into a chair, spreading his long thin legs out before him with a puff, to make her move.

"Ah, Lucia, my love," he sighed. "I think I may be getting too old for all this revelry. I think I'll need to sleep for a week or two to recover from all this festivity. I think it's easier to work than to celebrate!"

"I know what you mean!" said Doña Lucia, slumping into the chair next to him. "If it wasn't for dear Josefina here—and the wonderful Mara, who did what she could before she had to go and pack to make the ferry back—I think I would have had a heart attack and they would have had to fend for themselves!"

"Thank you, *Querida*," said Don Ramón, smiling wearily at Jo.

Jo sat down with them and smiled at them both. "You are my 'aunt' and 'uncle' and very dear to me. I am so honored and delighted to help you both."

They smiled back.

"But there is one thing I must do."

They waited quietly, watching her.

"I am now acting *cacica*. Am I right?"

"You are indeed," said Don Ramón.

"In a few days, if not sooner, the council will assign me tasks that will confirm or annul my appointment."

"Yes," agreed Doña Lucia.

"But, as I wait, I have before me my own tasks to which I am dedicated." This was the moment. "It is now time to find my parents." One thing at a time, she thought. Uncle Sol's fate would be next.

A look of such infinite sadness crossed the faces of both of these elderly gentle people so beloved by her that it almost broke her heart to see it. Almost.

Don Ramón sat up straight then leaned forward and took her hand. "You know that we love you, *Querida*."

"Yes, I know that. I have never doubted that." She left her hand in his and waited for what was to come.

Doña Lucia took her other hand. "As *cacica*—and you notice I do not say 'acting,' for I know that YaYa has selected you to rule. Well, as our chief, your mind will be the repository of many secrets. You will have a bodyguard, of course, but not all chiefs choose to employ them at all times, and you, Josefina, have always been the independent type. Am I wrong?"

"No, you are not wrong," admitted Josefina, leaving her hands in place.

"Well," said Doña Lucia, as earnestly as she had ever spoken to Jo before, and then in the Latin style pursing her lips and pointing them with a jerk of her head toward Don Ramón to include him into what she was about to say, she pleaded, "as two of the four elders of the outer council, we implore you to wait."

"This is not right!" objected Jo and, without thinking, pulled her hands away from them both and stood up.

"It *is* right, *Querida*," said Don Ramón, softly and with great tenderness.

"Please, Josefina, trust us," begged Doña Lucia. "Don't think just because you see no one when you go out, even with *Cacica* Mara at your side, that you are not being watched. You may lead evil men to where you do not want them to go. Please wait for the *Nitaíno*—the tribal council—to give you your tasks and then for you to perform them. When you do so, all will become clear."

"I don't think I can wait for that," objected Jo, stepping back a step and then forward again, unconsciously demonstrating she was ready for action.

"You must, dear. If you don't," cried Doña Lucia, "all might be lost!"

"What might be lost? What? I have no idea what all this secrecy is about! Name my enemy! I am not afraid!" She leaned on the table with both hands and said to them, "Believe me, I have the training and the willpower to muster whatever forces I need to have with me to deal with anything that has put the Tribe—or my parents—or this region in danger. And I will do what needs to be done."

"Yes, you will," said Don Ramón standing up slowly himself, using the same table for support.

He was followed by Doña Lucia, heaving herself up wearily from the chair. "We have no doubt about that. And that's why we have done everything in our power to help you become our leader. But, the wait is not long now, dear," Doña Lucia assured her. "Trust what we tell you, please."

As it turned out, trusting them did not take much effort. Two hours later, to the shock of all three residents of Las Olas, cars started to blow their horns outside the great gate and Don Ramón hurrying there was shocked to see the entire greater council of the entire country pour in.

"We must meet, and meet immediately," said *Cacique* Juan Francisco de la Vega as gravely serious as they had ever seen him. "The most terrible and shameful thing has happened and, though it may initially seem like nothing to you, it means treachery to the Tribe!"

34

A SOBER KNOT OF four of the five *caciques* of the island, Jo's Aunt Aña representing the fifth, along with the entire council of elders of the western south, gathered together facing Jo at the great conference table of Las Olas which had been pulled back into the middle of the great room after having doubled as a serving table for the conference of chiefs just the day before. No region was missing or not represented. The chiefs had also completely changed in demeanor from the previous night. Ricky's was not the only grim visage that confronted Jo.

Miguel Cayacoa of the eastern region was the first to speak, being all business, and, thereby, the ad hoc convener of the group by mutual consent. He did not waste time on amenities. "I was already half way back to La Romana when I received the call and had to turn around and come right back."

"I was already home when I had to get back into the car," complained Juan Francisco de la Vega, looking completely ruffled.

"Most of you don't know what happened yet, and," he looked pointedly at Jo, "I advise complete discretion as you choose with whom to share this."

"What happened?" asked Doña Lucia.

Miguel Cayacoa turned toward Doña Mencia: "Doña?"

The ninety-year-old spokesperson of the tribal council of the Western Lands of the South sighed. Her face was drawn, both from the exertions of last night and the sorrow she was about to share. "This morning, our *behike*, Don Bartolomé, went to the treasury to return some of the ceremonial items we used in your ceremony, Josefina. He saw immediately that someone had been in there before him. The Rosary—the Rosary of Enrique—was missing."

There was a gasp among the members of the outer council.

"You mean it's gone?" cried Ricky.

"Completely," said Miguel Cayacoa.

"We searched everywhere," said Doña Mencia, "before we troubled all of you. We hated to do that after so gracious a generosity of your time last night—and knowing how exhausted you all must be—but what could we do?"

"You did right, dear lady," said Juan Francisco de la Vega. "Its loss affects the whole council."

"You left early last night, Princess," said Ricky, narrowing his eyes at Josefina. "Would you like to tell us where you went and your subsequent movements—why you chose to leave your own celebration when one of the greatest First Nations bands was playing in your honor?"

Josefina was stunned. She stared back at him and said evenly, "I was worried about my family. I went to search for them."

"Don't be an idiot!" Sub-Chief Anacoana Behechio snapped at Ricky. "You think we would put her up for *cacica* if we thought she could be a party to something like this?"

The lawyer Angel Cueva de Piedra simply shook his head and regarded Ricky with what bordered on disgust, though he said nothing, which was his way. Instead, he said, "Although our friend and sub-chief Enrique Asenao has spoken out of the understandable pain that all of us are feeling, he does touch on something that may be relevant. Though," he added diplomatically, "not of course, Josefina, in any way implying your involvement in any of this."

"What is that, please?" asked Jo, deciding she had better take a strong hand in this and step up and assume her position as leader of the western south—even if it was only as "acting" leader.

Doña Mencia was the one to answer her: "We began some inquiries this morning when the theft was discovered. It came to light several hours ago that a proprietor of one of the curio shops in Barahona reported that that man whose company your sister Ruby has been keeping has been asking around about the Rosary of Enrique."

"Ismael Balenzuela?" exclaimed Jo.

"Is that his name?" asked Miguel Cayacoa.

"Yes."

"Who is he exactly?"

"He is a representative of a development corporation from Spain here to purchase and develop resort property."

"I am to meet with him tomorrow," said Aunt Aña.

"He's staying at the Bravado Beach Hotel in Barahona," said Jo immediately.

"All right," said Ricky, and flipped out his cell phone. "I have the Bravado on speed dial." And then at the quizzical looks, he explained, "They have function rooms I sometimes use for meetings." He put the phone to his head and turned slightly away, "Yes, good morning. May I have the room of a guest? Ismael, just a moment . . ." he looked at Jo.

"Balenzuela."

"Balenzuela. Ismael Balenzuela. He's staying there."

"What? Really? When was that? I see. Did he leave any forwarding address? No? Do you have any way to reach him? Yes, I'll wait." He drummed his fingers on the desk, his brow furrowed, and the phone clenched in his hand. "Just Cadiz in Spain. Hmmmm. Any name of his company? No? No way else you can help me reach him? No, of course, I understand. Once they're gone, they're gone. Did he pay by cash or by credit card? We can trace him that way. Yes, yes. I understand you can't divulge that. Thank you for what you could tell me." He punched off the phone and grunted what they had guessed already: "He's gone as of this morning. He checked out."

"Oh, good grief!" murmured Jo. A horror sprang up before her eyes that she did not want to look at closely. "Can you trust the police here?" she asked wisely, knowing that the positive answer was sometimes sporadic.

"I can in my region," boasted Francisco de la Vega.

"Most of the time in mine," muttered Miguel Cayacoa.

"We're not certain here," said Doña Mencia.

"The problem is that, even if this Balenzuela was guilty—and we don't know that," said Miguel Cayacoa, looking around the table—"there is no way he could have pulled this off by himself. He could not know where the compound is, could not know where in it the treasury is, and could not have gained access by himself."

"You mean . . . ?" began Don Ramón and then paused, frowning.

"Yes, someone in the Tribe would have had to have helped him."

"We have a traitor in our midst," said Aunt Aña.

"It looks as though we do," said Doña Mencia heavily.

"This is terrible," cried Doña Lucia, speaking for the first time.

"And I take it you have a guess?" asked Angel Cueva de Piedra, shrewdly.

"I'm afraid we do."

"Do you want to divulge it?" pursued Angel Cueva de Piedra.

"Not yet, not without more information," hesitated Doña Mencia.

"Then following your own lead in Saturday's meeting," spoke up Ricky in a tone unmistakably tinged with irony and directed at Miguel Cayacoa, "I suggest that we have our acting *cacica* look into it."

"It might be appropriate," murmured Doña Mencia.

Jo did not like the implication of that. It was much too closely pointing to what she herself had been thinking.

"While I have the floor," continued Ricky, "I would also like to suggest that we have our new *cacica* look into the charcoal thieving on the border and see if she can make any suggestions to stop the threat of defoliating our borders. That's relevant and necessary."

The chiefs and council paused and thought that over.

"This is really the chiefs' area to decide," warned Angel Cueva de Piedra. But this time his objection was not sustained.

"That has merit," observed Miguel Cayacoa, mainly to Anacoana Behechio, whom he seemed to be addressing directly. "These things are both timely and would prove her worth to guide the *cacicazgo* of these Western Lands of the South in a way that could be denied by no one." And he emphasized the last two words and stared back at Ricky Asenao.

Aunt Aña thought it over and slowly shook her head in agreement.

"Then it's settled?" hazarded Ricky, glancing from face to face.

No one disagreed.

"It would be very appropriate and—as you say—timely," said Doña Mencia, after receiving nods from her fellow inner council members and no objections from those of the outer council.

All of them turned now toward Jo.

"My tasks are to retrieve the Rosary of Enrique and bring the thieves to justice? Is that correct?" She looked around at the council and saw several shake their heads yes. Then she added, "And to research the stealing of wood from our borders by contraband runners and bring some kind of workable solution to address that. So," she summarized as much for herself as for them, "I am to deal with two forms of thieving. If I can accomplish these two tasks, you are saying my trial period is over and I am to be elevated to *cacica*?"

"This is correct," said Doña Mencia, the only one having the full authority to speak for the *Nitaíno* of the Western Lands of the South in selecting the rite of passage of their own chieftain, though, in fact, the recovery of the sacred artifact was truly the concern of the entire global larger Tribe.

"Then," said Jo, "I answer you with the same vow I made to serve last evening: *naboria daca*—I am a servant of God."

They all nodded. "Then, it's done," said Miguel Cayacoa. "But," he added, "since the Rosary is the inheritance of the entire Tribe, I suggest to the council we learn of her progress by report day by day and you, Josefina, do not hesitate to call on all our resources to help you recover it. If it leaves this country, we may never recover it and the loss would be immeasurable."

"Amen," said Doña Lucia, fervently.

"Yes, we should end in prayer—would all of you pray for me?" asked Jo, feeling the weight of two great burdens, the first of which may have already been a lost cause and the second a nearly insurmountable problem no one tribal or governmental had yet been able to accomplish.

As they rose and gathered around her, she thought: And after this, I must see how I will solve the problem of leadership in Richfield. It was then that she heard Ricky whisper beside her, "We will see just how far your resolve will go to serve the Tribe, Princess, when you delve into who's responsible for this outrage!"

35

J O WASTED NOT A second the moment the meeting was over. The *caciques* and the other elders had not even left Las Olas when she was back down from her room with a full knapsack and the car keys, and, without a word to anyone, she headed immediately out the door. She had almost reached her car when the *cacique* from Haiti, calling her name, caught up with her. "*Cacica* Josefina," he said, puffing up to her side, "I know this is very hard for you. Do not worry. Here is my card. Please call me. We must solve this robbing of trees for charcoal together. It is much more complex than I believe my fellow chiefs on your side of the border realize. It is not something solved in a day, for it involves the wellbeing of families who have nothing."

"Yes," said Jo, hurriedly. "I am thinking about this problem as a community organizer would. It seems very complex to me and it will involve research and field work."

"Yes, it will, and—please, remember, we will be watching over you as well."

"Thank you," said Jo, having no idea what he meant.

"Go with God." He had given her his benediction and he stepped back, his face full of concern for her.

Again, Jo thought, how can I measure up to the kind of people who rule this precious Tribe?

No sooner had she pulled out of the gate and started up the gravel road than she punched up her Aunt Aña's number.

Anacoana Behechio came on immediately. "Yes, Jo," she said.

"Are you near anybody?"

"No, they're all inside. I stepped out—my mind is all in turmoil."

"Yes," said Jo, "mine too. I don't like where this is leading."

"Neither do I."

"If you meet with Ismael tomorrow, will you call me and keep him there and wherever I am I will come over and we can grill him on this?" asked Jo.

"Absolutely. And you'll keep in touch?"

"Of course."

"And, *Nanixi, Mi Corazón,* Miguel wasn't kidding about the resources. Whatever you need, we can come up with."

"I'm going to need a wide range of contacts. Whatever else, I'll let you know as this develops."

"Good. Please do that."

"I love you!" and Jo hung up.

"I love you too," said her aunt, but Jo was already gone.

By now she was at the main road, but instead of turning south toward Barahona, she turned north toward Los Diamantes and, speeding up the road, pulled into the parking lot within a matter of minutes. She dashed out of the car and rounded to the back, bounding up onto the spacious back porch and into the open-air dining room which served as well for a reception area. No one was around, so she stuck her head into the kitchen, and called, "Anyone here?"

"Just a second," said a voice from the back. An efficient and lovely young woman in a long black apron came out and asked, "Can I help you?" She spoke in Spanish, but her accent was heavily influenced by French, or more accurately, Haitian Creole.

"Yes," said Jo, pursuing an idea that had suddenly come to her as the *caciques* and elders were entreating God for her. "May I speak with Ismael Balenzuela? I believe he is a new guest."

The young woman smiled and opened the big register book and perused the latest entry. "Yes, here he is. He checked in yesterday. At the top of the stairs. First room on your left, the big one."

"They're all big—and spacious," said Jo. "I've been here before."

The young woman smiled at her. "But I don't think he's here right now. He said something about going to Monte Cristi up on the northern coast for a meeting this afternoon. I think he went to Barahona to get some gasoline for the trip."

"Yes, it's about that meeting that I've come. He's going to be meeting with my aunt."

The young woman smiled at her puzzled.

"She's a real estate agent," added Jo.

"Oh."

"I actually have two sisters staying here too: Daniela and Ruby Archer?"

"Oh, yes. Daniela is very beautiful, is she not?"

"Yes, she is," agreed Jo.

"We were sorry to see her leave."

"She checked out?"

"Yes, she did."

"Do you have any idea where she went?"

"I believe she went over to the Bravado Beach Hotel down in Barahona. Do you know where that is?"

"Yes, I do. Can I ask you . . ." Jo hesitated, but then plunged ahead. "Did she go about the same time Ismael Balenzuela came to stay here?"

The young woman hesitated.

Jo said to her, "This is so much help. These are all my family and I want to make sure we keep track of each other. I know this is taking away time from your lunch preparation. Can I treat you to a soda or some sort of refreshment?" Reaching into her backpack for her wallet, she laid a 200 peso piece, the rough equivalent of a U.S. five dollar bill, on the counter.

The young woman beamed, thanked her and looked down into the book again. "Yes," she noted. "She checked out last night when he arrived."

"And one more," pursued Jo. "My brother, Ben Archer."

"Yes, he's still here. He's on the register, though I haven't seen him today."

"I see," said Jo, and then: "But I imagine my sister Ruby is still here?"

"Ruby, would that be Archer too?"

"It would," said Jo. "She's small and somewhat pushy. . . ."

"Oh, yes, she was here this morning. I think she went out running on the beach."

"Thank you," said Jo. "I so appreciate the help."

The young woman smiled again and closed the book, nodded to her, and went back to the kitchen. The 200 peso bill went with her.

Jo walked out onto the porch and punched up her aunt's number.

"Yes, Jo!" said her aunt's voice.

"Can you move your meeting from Monte Cristi to Los Diamantes Hotel and hold it today?"

"On Sunday? And at Los Diamantes? Why Los Diamantes? The property I wanted to show him first is up north in my region around the Bay of Icaquitos, between the beaches of El Morro and Monte Cristi."

"Plenty of time for that," said Jo. "I suddenly realized that he'd moved out of the Bravado to come over here to Los Diamantes to be near Ruby. I'm at Los Diamantes now. They think he's out getting gas."

"Great insight!" exclaimed Aunt Aña.

"I got it during the prayer," laughed Jo. "God's grace!"

"Let me call him," said Aunt Aña. "You got me just in time. I'm supposed to be in Monte Cristi getting ready for him tomorrow, but I've been sitting around chatting with Lucia and Ramón—two of my all-time favorite people." Her voice went a little distance from the phone and Jo could hear appreciative chuckling in the background. It didn't sound like anyone was unduly worried about Jo not finding and returning the Rosary.

Jo shook her head and sat down in one of the lounge chairs to wait.

The young woman appeared again. "Can I get you anything?"

"Why, yes, thank you," said Jo, knowing instinctively the right thing to do in this situation. "Do you have any *chinola* juice?"

Soon Jo was settled back luxuriously in an acacia wood rocking chair, sipping a long cool glass of passion fruit juice. And that is where her sister Ruby found her, when she came pounding up the incline from the beach, after her run by the sea.

"Hey, Chief!" puffed Ruby, coming to a halt and leaning over, both hands on her knees, gasping. "Twenty miles today! I was feeling good!"

"Sit here a second," offered Jo.

"Can't. Gotta take a shower before Ismael sees me."

"You look great," said Jo, "in that silver running suit you're like a photo out of *Fitness and Health* magazine."

Ruby hesitated, "But I'm all sweaty."

"Or *American Runner*. You know, sweaty is sexy. It makes the nylon cling to you like another skin, and you have a great body—all sleek curves and muscle."

"I do, don't I?" said Ruby, sitting down. "It's my best feature."

"You've got a lot of great features," Jo assured her. "You're smart and beautiful and a real sparkplug."

"Thank you, Jo."

"And yesterday you were magnificent in the game!"

"Was I?"

"You know you were—and you didn't fight with anybody!"

"Yeah, I was real good, wasn't I? Everybody said how happy I looked. I didn't want to fight with anybody. Jo, you're so sweet, I'd give you a hug—but I'm so sweaty. I better go take a shower."

At that moment, Aunt Aña pulled in, and, slamming her car door, was soon striding around the back. Spotting the proprietor, who was an old friend, she detoured and went over to greet him by the pool.

"Wait!" said Ruby. "Isn't that Aunt Aña?"

"Yes, it is," said Jo.

"What is she here about—Danny? Danny's not here anymore. She moved out."

"We know."

"And for that matter, what are you doing here, Jo? Haven't you got some kind of tasks you're supposed to be doing?"

"I'm doing one of them right now."

"Wow!" laughed Ruby. "I hope I get to be chief someday so I can sit around on Los Diamantes porch and drink *chinola* juice."

"I wish it were just that. I have to tell you something that may be troublesome," warned Jo.

"Uh, oh," said Ruby.

By this time, Aunt Aña and her friend, Los Diamantes's director, were mounting the steps of the porch.

"Josefina!" he exclaimed. "When did you come? Welcome! We've just this month come across a new cave in the countryside, in the mountains behind Baul and Carrizal, that I know the Tribe is going to be excited about. I was just telling Anacoana."

Jo smiled. He always insisted on calling her aunt by her formal name, a courtesy from his background in Spain.

He looked them over and, with the sixth sense that the best hoteliers can muster, he perceived immediately that something private was troubling them. He bowed cordially and said, "Let me bring a pitcher of *chinola* juice to refresh you all. Things go better with passion fruit." In a moment he was back, serving them himself, as his assistants went on with their preparation.

"Thank you, dear friend," said Aunt Aña. "In just a few moments we'll be begging to sample some of your delicious fish dinners, just as soon as we complete our business."

"I am at your orders," he said graciously and then added, "Oh, and Josefina, my most sincere congratulations on your inauguration as chief. The Tribe is always wise in its choices. I applaud the council and you."

"Thank you," said Jo humbly.

"Okay," said Ruby. "I'm staying. What's it all about?"

There was no beating around the bush with Ruby, thought Jo, you just have to run your stick right in and poke the *hurón*. "The Rosary of Enrique was stolen last night!"

"Oh, no!" cried Ruby. "That's awful. Who would do such a thing?"

Neither woman said anything.

"Uh, oh!" cried Ruby again. "You think Ismael had something to do with this?"

"Do you?" asked Aunt Aña.

Ruby paused. "Honestly, I don't know. I love him, Jo," she confessed. "But I don't really know him that well. I'm being honest now. I would hope not, but what can I say?"

"You're not defending him to the hilt?" observed Aunt Aña.

"No, how can I? He's very interested in the Rosary. Ben was shooting his mouth off about it, and Ismael asked Ben all kinds of detailed questions. But he never talked about stealing it. Only buying it or renting it."

"What on earth for?" asked both women simultaneously.

"Oh, for that crazy magnetic pole thing Danny's in such an uproar about."

"What's that?" asked Aunt Aña.

"Danny fell in with some pretty shaky looking opportunists who have some health and wealth thing going on with the magnetic pole," explained Ruby. "They sound like they stepped out of some other era, and they certainly don't appear to be above some skulduggery like this." She hadn't touched her passion fruit drink, though she must have been nearly overwhelmed with thirst.

"What pole?" asked Anacoana Behechio. "You don't mean the one over near Lake Rincon?"

"The very same one," said Jo.

"That's absurd," said her aunt.

"Don't we know it!" exclaimed Ruby.

"Nobody's going to get rich from a load of iron in the ground, or whatever it is that pulls the cars up the hill."

"Well, they think they will," said Ruby, and began to cough. She finally took a long pull from her juice glass and wiped her lips with her sleeve. "The way they're going about it, they're probably the only ones who will get rich."

"I'll bet," said Aunt Aña. "So, what's your Ismael's connection with all this?"

"They've talked him into footing the bill."

"They're very smooth," explained Jo.

"His company went for this?" asked Anacoana, astonished.

"It's his own money," said Ruby. "And Danny and Ben are a part of this too."

"Oh, the poor lamb," moaned Aunt Aña, rolling her eyes. "And where does the Rosary fit in?"

"Ismael thinks if the Tribe could lend it to them, it would be an extra added attraction." Then Ruby paused, "And I think he's a superstitious kind of guy. I notice he has an amulet on his bureau that is supposed to bring good luck in his business."

"You've been in his room?" asked Jo.

"Naw," said Ruby, "just noticed it when I was waiting for him in the hall and he left the door open. Don't worry, Sis. I'm not stupid."

"I'm sorry," said Jo, "that was out of line. I'm just worried about the Rosary and you and Ben and Danny. I don't want to see any of you get hurt. And I'm worried about Ismael too. I appreciate the fact that you like him, Ruby, and so I don't want anything to happen to him either."

"What could happen to me?" asked Ismael, himself, who was standing down at the bottom of the stairs, looking much the same in a half opened white shirt and dark slacks as he did the first time they had met him at Las Olas in what had been only a matter of a few days previously, but felt to them all like a lifetime before. "This looks like a meeting. Am I intruding?" he asked, hesitating to draw nearer.

"No, not at all," said Jo. "Please join us."

"Thank you," he sat down. "And please accept my warmest congratulations for your inauguration as acting chief."

"Thank you," said Jo. "You are always so gracious and generous and cordial."

"Ismael, dear, we've got a problem," said Ruby.

"How can I help," he replied immediately.

"You can tell us where the Rosary is," said Ruby.

"What? What are you talking about?"

"The Rosary of Enrique—we know you have been making inquiries about it!" said Anacoana Behechio, becoming chief all over on him.

Ismael Balenzuela looked astonished. "I have no idea," he claimed.

"You better have an idea," snapped Sub-Chief Anacoana Behechio, "or you'll bring the whole Taino tribe here down on you and you'll be out of this country quicker than you got here."

"Easy does it, Aunt Aña," said Ruby. "Ismael has been nothing but kind to all of us."

"What? Is it missing?" he asked Jo directly.

"It is missing."

"Oh, no, they didn't!"

"Who didn't?"

"I mean, yes, I was asking around, but I would never hire anybody to steal it. I don't work that way. I wanted to make an offer for it, sure. I'm not hiding that fact."

Both women's mouths dropped open.

"You wanted to buy it?" exclaimed Aunt Aña.

"No, no, I wanted to rent it. Ruby already told me that buying it would be out of the question, if it even existed."

"Rent it? What on earth for?" demanded Aunt Aña. She was a great fan of imported cop shows on cable and decided she would be the bad cop to Jo's good cop even before Ruby had arrived. "What could that possibly do for you? It's not a talisman."

Ismael Balenzuela left that last statement alone. He wasn't sure about that.

"You met Bo and Peep at the Bravado," he replied directly to Jo. "You heard about their spa. You even offered to do what you felt you could to help us."

"It didn't include the Rosary," said Jo firmly.

"If you know who might have it, please tell us," Ruby pleaded, an action very un-Ruby-like.

He vacillated.

They waited.

Then he said, with great hesitation, "If I do, you might hate me, because it would involve someone that you love."

"Ben," said Ruby.

"Well, yes, Benjamin. I had been asking him about it, and he came later and said he had a friend who could get it for me. I thought it meant 'could make arrangements.'" He turned to Ruby. "And that's the honest truth."

"I believe you," said Ruby.

Neither Josefina nor Anacoana looked like they did.

Ismael saw everything he had been working for and what he had come to value most slipping away. He looked at Ruby for a long moment with tenderness laced with fear, and then he made a fateful decision. "All right," he said, "I'm going to tell you the full truth. And this is honest to the bottom of my heart. You know my last name? Balenzuela? I changed it. It is Valenzuela. I am a direct descendant of that villain who plagued the great Enrique's life and raped his wife and oppressed him severely. I've known about the Tainos for all my life and what was inflicted on your people. So I changed my name before I came here because I thought it might make business negotiations difficult. That was the only reason. But I never took to heart the implications of what happened so many years ago. I never really thought about them. These were just words on a page. And then I met all of you, and I saw it all through your eyes. Now I feel entirely different. I realize these were real horrors done to real people like you who I've come to regard highly. Now I am ashamed of my name and I hate my ancestor. I didn't want you to know who I was because I didn't want you to hate me. But I was sent here to do a job. Now I want to try to do it within my small and limited power in a way that atones. I know I can't change history. No one can do that. But, in a small way, I feel like I am a second chance for my family, like the great-grandchildren of a Nazi commander who can do something to save the Jews of a new time. It will never atone for what the ancestor did. But it will change the course of life now for new people living in a new era. And that change of course will make everyone's life now and the future of all people better. And that's all any of us can do. In my small way, I hope to work here to benefit the people."

Balenzuela paused and looked earnestly at the women weighing his words as he shared them, and then he gambled everything for the pearl of greatest price that he realized was their regard. He made a confession. "Now, I will tell you something else. I am *not* free of my ancestor's genes. I can relate to the Heitzes—Starling and Basil—because inside I realize I am much like them. I can wheel and deal and it comes easy to me. I know their quasi-religion is a scam for them, but I can see it is not a scam for your sister. I plan to make money out of it, of course, but I am convinced the people who come will be made happy by the hope it gives, and I was not lying when I said I was hoping to create many jobs for the people of the area. It will never atone for what my ancestor did to yours—I've said that!—and you may still hate me for it, but, know this: I would never steal your relic or your property of Las Olas del Sol from you, or anything else that is yours. And, believe me, I have been tempted to do just that. I don't deny it."

And then he turned to Ruby. "But, you've stolen something from me. I never figured on meeting you, Ruby. You've stolen my heart. I hope you will let me keep yours in its place."

The moment was electrified, as if all the static electricity of the island was suddenly focused on Los Diamantes del Mar.

All three women were silent for a long moment. Ismael held his breath. Whatever was going to happen now, he felt he had glimpsed the man he really wanted to be.

"I love you the more for it!" said Ruby through clenched teeth.

He reached over to hug her, but she drew back and warned, "But, I'm all sweaty!"

"I don't care," said Ismael and crushed her to him.

"Let's go get Ben," said Jo.

"All right," said Anacoana, "but first, I want to eat. I missed breakfast, and we always know where to find Ben! He can't find a pawn shop or antique store open on Sunday in Barahona if that's his game, and the owners would call the Tribe the second they saw what he was handing them. They well know what would happen to their businesses if the Tribe boycotted them."

"Ben couldn't have done this by himself," pointed out Jo.

"No," Ruby agreed, "and we can guess who was in on it with him."

"Yes, we can," said Jo.

"About those fish dinners!" Aunt Aña shouted back toward the kitchen.

"I'll pay for it all," Ismael Balenzuela offered happily.

"Not this time," ruled Jo. "You're practically part of the family now. So we'll start history over again. Once more, we want you to be our guest."

36

Starling and Basil Heitz were having a very bad day. First, Ismael Balenzuela had suddenly moved out of the Bravado Beach Hotel without a word of explanation. They had no idea where he'd gone. Second, Daniela had moved in and was expecting them to do all their mumbo jumbo on the beach every night! And, third, to top it all, their meager money was completely running out. The best scam they had ever had was being sucked down into the quicksand of penury and, so as not to jeopardize it, they couldn't even fleece somebody of a credit card or some extra cash to keep it afloat. What a perfectly miserable day they were having! When Ben stopped by their room, they thought the day was now complete. The first time he rapped, they thought it was the manager having finally discovered they were not Arthur and Bee Beaumont (that hapless couple whose extra credit card had disappeared at the main desk of a hotel in La Romana—a fact that at some point soon these elderly tourists must discover) and they both froze. Then Ben rapped again with a brief tattoo and they recognized it was him. Basil muttered, "It's the wastrel, probably trying to dun us for money."

"Well, we don't have any," yawned Star, stretching her arms out and twisting her tense shoulders and back muscles in relief, "so we have nothing to lose. Might as well open it up and we can commiserate together."

Basil got up off the bed, slowly ambled over, and swung back the door to reveal two people—Ben and another young man.

"This is Tomás, a good friend of mine. He has something to show you," announced Ben, stepping inside. Tomás could sense an immediate hostility, so he hesitated.

Star was glowering at him. She couldn't imagine this miserable Indian had anything that was going to brighten her life. As usual, she was wrong when it counted.

"Come on in," said Ben, motioning to him. "They're not as out of it as they're looking right now." He grinned at Basil, who was scratching his belly through the large T-shirt that barely concealed it. He hadn't shaved yet today.

"We're broke," said Star, for an opener.

"That's okay," replied Ben. "It's your friend we want."

"Ismael? He's . . ." began Basil, but Star cut him off.

"Why do you want to see him?" Star asked, suddenly interested. She looked Ben over and recognized an excitement more than his normal enthusiasm.

"Well, last night my sister Jo was made the chief of our region."

"We missed it," grunted Basil.

"I figured as much," acknowledged Ben. "But while everybody was busy hooping and hollering, we went over to the Tribal center—it's like hidden away, but Tomás here knows where it is—he's like really into the Tribe and all."

Tomás winced. He didn't want to share too much with these people. They were exactly the kind of Anglos he despised.

"Anyway, he knows where the secret treasury is and he got in and," Ben ended with a flourish, "he's got the Rosary of Enrique!"

"It's real?" exclaimed Basil.

"It's very real and it's very here! Tomás?"

But before he could answer, Basil asked, "What else did you get? What all have they got there? What else can you take?"

Tomás was stunned. "Only the Rosary!" he exclaimed. He was deeply affronted. "Benjamin," he said, "we're wasting our time here."

"Wait," said Star, her eyes rounding as her brain raced. She slid off the bed and opened the little room refrigerator in one deft continuous movement. "Please, gentlemen, sit down. Bo, pull out a chair from the desk for our guests!"

"Uhh, sure!"

"Dear Ben and honored guest, I'm so sorry that you caught us at a bad moment. We were a little stressed this morning. Working on our great plan has been so exhausting and I think the pressure has been catching up with us. Ben, you could use a beer, couldn't you?"

"You bet!"

"And, Tomás, would you like one too?"

Basil winced. There were only two put in the refrigerator by room service each day. He was going to have to do without all day, since there was no longer any spare change to go to the bar.

"No thank you," said Tomás.

Basil breathed a sigh of relief.

"The only reason I consented to take the Rosary for this man is because we are in a crisis situation. Our forest is being invaded by contraband runners. They are burning our trees. I have seen it myself. They already killed someone, but the rangers are unable to find them and stop them. The Tribe needs to act and some of us are ready to hunt them down, but we need weapons and equipment superior to theirs. They have a militia from somewhere that is guarding them. It's full of seasoned mercenaries. No one seems to care enough. We mean to stop it. That is the only reason I consented to do this!"

"And," Ben chimed in, "I want to get my part of our inheritance one way or another. Why should my sister get it all? If I didn't get in on the beach house, at least I can get a part of this!" He looked at Tomás and added, "At least a small cut like we agreed! I did, after all stand guard."

Everyone looked back at Tomás. He leveled his eyes at them and shot out, "I want a million U.S. dollars for this priceless and rare relic."

"Yes, this unique charm of great power!" added Ben in his coaxing, salesman's voice.

"Nobody's got that kind of money," scoffed Basil.

"Fifty thousand tops," agreed Star.

"We know how this black market thing works," Basil assured them, realizing this was not the moment to be coy. "You get one-fifth the value if you're lucky for normal items. A stolen relic would go for about five percent of the true value. They're very hard to unload."

Tomás raised his eyebrows and stared at Ben.

"We got a buyer," Ben assured them.

"Ismael?" guessed Star.

"Who else but?"

And then, as if it were scripted for the stage, a rapping came at the door.

Both Basil and Star froze: their constant reaction these days.

"It's Ismael," said a muffled voice.

"Look at that!" said Ben and then to Tomás, "I told you this was the right place to come."

"Open the door! Quickly!" ordered Star.

Ben pulled it open and Ismael Balenzuela came in and smiled at everyone cordially. "Ben, how are you?"

"Good," said Ben.

"Bo, Peep," he chose their working names in view of the stranger in their midst. "And you, sir? Whom do I have the pleasure of meeting?"

"Tomás, a friend of Ben's." They shook hands.

"We got something for you!" said Ben. "Something you want very much."

"Please sit down," offered Star.

Ismael looked around. There was no place to sit. "I'll stand," he said. "What have you got for me?"

"I want a million U.S. dollars for it," growled Tomás, obstinately.

"A million dollars? For what?" laughed Ismael.

"It's the Rosary!" exclaimed Ben. "The Rosary of Enrique. You wanted it. We have it for you!"

"The Rosary of Enrique!" marveled Ismael. "I thought it didn't exist."

"I told you it did," Ben assured him.

"I want a million dollars for it!" insisted Tomás.

"Well, I'm sure you do, but you're not selling it to a museum now. This, I presume, is stolen property. It's almost impossible to find a buyer for it. May I see it please?"

Tomás hesitated.

"Show it to him," said Ben. "He's on the up and up. We're working together."

Tomás paused for a long look at Ben and then slowly produced it from his pocket. It was wrapped in a great white cloth and was very simple and of great age.

Both Basil and Star craned over to see it. It looked very, very old to Star and probably pretty fragile and dusty from what she could tell. Who would want this decrepit piece of junk? she wondered. But that was the way with these collectors. It also didn't look like much to Basil: just an old set of beads and a crucifix. The difference was he inadvertently blurted out his disappointment. "Looks like a piece of junk," he snarled.

Ben and Tomás were stung by this dismissal. "No! No!" Ben protested. "You're missing the point. This is five hundred years old!"

"Yeah," conceded Basil, underwhelmed. "So what is it made of?" he demanded. "Just wood? It just looks like wood. I thought it was going to be valuable—like gold or something. Who would want all wood?"

Tomás, deeply insulted, scoffed in disgust, "For your information, they offered gold. The great chief's people did, from the hands of their finest craftsmen. They wanted to make it for him as a thank-you for saving their lives. But he refused!"

"What?" Basil was shocked.

Tomás sneered at his avarice, and from the lofty height of his own convictions he lectured, "The tradition tells that the great *cacique* agreed that gold was beautiful and celebrated the glory of God, but it had become such a source of pain and suffering from these Spaniards' greed that he could never use it without his prayers being drowned out by the cries of the people they slaughtered for it!"

"That's right," broke in Ben, unable to restrain himself. "Then they offered him black coral, a tribute from the African slaves he had rescued and welcomed into his band. These also wanted to carve him something to show their own beauty reflected in the blackness of the coral, revealing the God who made them as beautiful and precious as they are. And again Enrique thanked them and said, 'Please make it for the church we will build when we are finally free. It will celebrate all people who come to join us from the hand of our Creator God.'"

"Did they ever make the church?" blurted out Basil, wondering if he could locate it and loot it one night.

"Yeah," said Ben. "But, after he died, his wife built it. It's in ruins now, nothing there but fallen stones."

Basil was disappointed again.

"So what did he settle for?" broke in Ismael Balenzuela, wanting to get this all back on track. "What is it?"

"Acacia wood."

Everyone stared at it. No one looked impressed, so Tomás explained, "Again, the great chief agreed such a rich gift would honor him, but like Ben said, he redirected it to honor God. Instead, he kept this," and he held the old rosary up for closer inspection. "He told them, 'This simple rosary was given to me by my teacher, the priest who rescued me and gave me a home and taught me the wisdom of God. It is not just any wood. This is acacia wood!'"

"What's so special about that?" demanded Basil

"Didn't you ever go to Sunday School?" asked Ben. "It's the wood they used in the Ark of the Covenant in the Tabernacle."

Basil stared back blankly.

"Oh, for crying out loud!" snapped Star finally having enough of Basil's ignorance for one morning. "It's the tent the Israelites used to carry around for the box with the Ten Commandments in it!" Again, the Gideon Bibles were paying off.

"Yeah," said Ben, "Enrique explained it would last forever, just like the faith itself. As the tent moved with the people, so does the faith go wherever we go." And then Ben broke off self-consciously and looked down, feeling suddenly an inexplicable tinge of shame.

There was an awkward silence.

Then, Ismael Balenzuela spoke up in a cautious tone "How do I know it's authentic?"

"You can trust us," said Ben. "Tomás has been my friend all my life. He's grown up with the Tribe. His father is a very important man. We went together to the compound last night, while the celebration over at Las Olas's field was going on. The whole place was practically empty. He slipped in easily. Nobody guessed we were even there. Tomás knew exactly where it was. He took it from the tribal treasury itself. It's the real thing."

"Okay, it is what I want for a number of reasons, but, fellows, I couldn't raise a quarter of that sum if you put a—uhhh—bow and arrow to my head. Nobody in the world would give you that. I don't think the Tribe would ransom it back for that."

"We can't ransom it!" said Tomás firmly.

"It's a thought," said Ben. "That kind of thing's been done . . ."

"Absolutely not!" cried Tomás, and once again explained his motivation for the theft—this time to Ismael Balenzuela.

Ismael saw his moment to make his move and win over the seller. "Ben," he warned, shifting his attention dramatically so Tomás could see, "what are you thinking? Your friend is a man of honor. He has put himself at great risk to take this and his honor is at stake. He can't hold up his Tribe. That would be shameful."

Tomás nodded.

So, Ismael handed his attention back to him. "I understand the sacrifice you're making to win all. It is a great gamble." Ismael was all concern, displayed in his tone, in his facial expression, in his posture, and in the great sigh he gave as he shook his head in ostensible admiration.

"A great sacrifice," echoed Star with equally great commiseration.

"It's killing me," said Tomás sadly. "I've never done anything that bordered on the dishonorable before."

"It's for a great cause." Ismael shook his head up and down in affirmation. "I understand."

"Thank you."

"I wish I had the courage to do the same."

"Me too," said Basil, catching up with the wagon train.

"The problem is," said Ismael, "this is my own personal money I'm investing. I can't use company funds for such an enterprise. It would surely be discovered and we would all be in jeopardy. I have to work with what I myself hold." He eyed Tomás. Sizing him up, he hazarded: "How about twenty-five thousand?"

"I could sell it on eBay for more than that!" objected Tomás.

"Try it!" sneered Ben, the consummate wheeler-dealer. "See how fast you end up in jail!"

"What do you really want?" asked Ismael in a kind voice.

"One hundred thousand U.S.—not a penny less!"

"Ooof!" Ismael sounded like he'd been hit in the solar plexus. "I honestly haven't that much to my name. And that's the truth. I only live in an apartment at home. The euro is weaker now than the dollar. I could do maybe thirty thousand. . . ."

Tomás looked him over. He appeared so sincere. "Black market guns are expensive," he said, "and so is ammunition. Seventy-five thousand."

"I could do thirty-five if I scraped it together from all my accounts." Ismael frowned, the picture of a man straining to reach a great height.

"Fifty thousand, and I'm really serious—I won't go lower."

"Listen, I understand. And, because it is a worthwhile cause, I will give you every euro I have to my name. I plan to stay here and, after you succeed in saving the forests, and the word gets out what you've done, and the whole Tribe celebrates you as the savior of the forests, I'm banking on this helping me with my building projects. If I close every account I have, I could squeeze it up to forty thousand. It's all the money I have in the world. And that's the truth." He pulled out his check book. "I can call and consolidate all the accounts into one omnibus check today. Give me one night for the transfer to take place and you can cash it at the Iberian International Bank where I have my account tomorrow."

"How do I know your check is good?"

"It's been good so far every time," said Ben, rallying behind the lead horse.

Tomás faltered. "Are you sure you can't make it forty five?" he pleaded.

"If I did, the check would bounce. This is everything I own in the world," said Ismael, reeling him in.

"Do it!" urged Ben. "We can't keep waiting. We've got to hit the tree thieves now and quickly."

Ismael closed the deal: "I'm staying over at Los Diamantes Hotel with Ben here. I'm not going anywhere. If you want, I'll go to the bank with you tomorrow and verify my signature and approval." He asked Star for a pen and motioned for Ben to get up out of the desk chair, whereupon he sat down himself, opened his checkbook, and paused, the pen poised above the paper. "To whom do I make this out?" he asked.

"Tomás de Odnavo," said Tomás. And he added, with a challenging look toward them all, "By the time anybody figures out what I did, we will have hit hard and saved the forest!"

Ismael stood up and handed him the check. "If I don't honor the deals I make, I can't stay in business. This check is good."

Tomás took it and stuffed it in the pocket of his jeans.

"Wait!" said Basil suddenly. "Star, let's get out of here right now, before he hands over the relic. We're in enough potential trouble and I don't want us to be part of this too. I'm sure nothing will happen, but this way we won't have to testify!" He caught Star's eye.

"Right," said Star jumping up. "Don't change hands yet. The less who see this the better. We didn't see anything. We know nothing!" She and Basil converged on the door at the same time. In his haste to leave, Basil lumbered into Tomás, hitting him hard.

"Hey, watch it!" shouted Tomás, banging back into the door.

"I'm sorry! I'm so sorry!" apologized Basil, and literally ran down the hall, Star in close pursuit.

"Geez!" Tomás was disgusted. "What cowards!" He handed Ismael Balenzuela the relic.

"I'll leave first," Ismael cautioned him, taking the Rosary in his hands, opening the cloth quickly and rewrapping it carefully. He slipped it into a vinyl shopping bag he had brought along with him. "Wait six minutes exactly and then come down and leave normally like nothing has happened. I'll head back to the hotel. You can tell Ben what you want to do about tomorrow."

"You'll be there?" queried Tomás, giving him the eye.

Ben laughed. "He's been hitting on my sister Ruby. In fact, I think he's head over heels for her." He grinned at Ismael.

Ismael hung his head as he went out the door. "There's a time for every man!" was the last thing he said, and he heard Ben laughing as he walked rapidly down the hall.

Basil and Star, dead ahead, nearly jumping up and down with impatience, focused on desperately punching the elevator button. It was sooooo sloooowww! Ismael ducked into an alcove and paused to watch their reflection in the window of a snack machine cater-cornered across from him until he glimpsed them enter into a full elevator. Immediately, he dashed into the stairwell, leaping down the two flights, two and three stairs at a time, swinging around the railings.

As soon as Ismael hit the lobby door, he paused and peered cautiously out toward the elevator. Sure enough, the dial was stopped at the second floor, emptying and adding people before it began creeping again down to the first. He swung open the stairway door and dashed across the lobby, glancing over at the dial above the elevator constantly, gauging the rate of its descent between the second and first floors, as it crept downward.

Ismael raced up to the three women, sitting sentinel on a sofa in the lobby, themselves watching the stairs and the elevator, and motioned to them, lifting his hands like he was reading a newspaper. Then, pointing to himself and the stairwell door, he raced back to it. Jo understood immediately and snatched up some magazines and a tabloid newspaper from the center coffee table next to them, switching her seat to put her back to the elevator. Aunt Anacoana looked at Jo for orders. "They may not know me," she muttered.

"If Ben is part of it, he will. You're hard to hide. You switch here!" Jo patted her hand on the seat next to her.

"I'll take the paper," said Ruby. She opened it up and disappeared behind it, just as the elevator opened, spewing Star and Basil out. In their haste they hurried right by the three women as Star ran and Basil lumbered directly toward the parking lot. The second they were outside, Ismael flung open the stairway door and called, "Come on! Let's go after them!"

The rental truck was parked as close to the front of the hotel as they could get it, the third vehicle over, and they jumped in and started it. "Go! Go! Go!" ordered Star.

But at that moment a minivan pulled out of the space on the other side, came right across the driveway, smack up behind them, and touched their bumper with its large, almost cowcatcher sized front-work.

Both Star and Basil turned around to pull out and stared into the grim faces of two uniformed men.

"Pull forward!" screamed Star.

"I can't!" yelled Basil. "There's a divider there!"

They flung open the doors just as two burly police officers strode up on either side of the truck.

"You are the Taylors?" one of them said in accented but fluent English. "You rented this truck months ago and never returned it?"

"No! No!" cried Star. "That's not us. They're in the hotel. We're just borrowing the truck."

The second officer took a photograph from his pocket and waved it in front of them.

"It looks like you," said the first officer, narrowing his eyes at them and blocking their exit completely.

"That's them, officer," said a well-dressed man in perfect Castilian Spanish in company with three distinguished-looking women who came up and surrounded the truck. "Gentlemen, these are the people I called you about. They stole this truck and they just stole something from me. I am Ismael Balenzuela of E-corp, the property development company. These women with me are the leaders of the historic Taino nation for this region."

The two policemen took off their hats and nodded at the women.

"Give me my check," demanded Ismael severely through the half open door to Basil, still sitting in the idling truck.

"I don't know what you're talking about," blustered Basil.

Star began to cry in loud, dramatic wails.

"Don't be a fool," warned Balenzuela. "It's incriminating evidence. Don't you realize it will pile another set of charges on every crime you've already done here—grand larceny of the truck, the stolen credit cards, the swindles . . ."

"Wait a minute, *Señor!*" said the first officer, now in Spanish. "If it's evidence, we need to impound it."

"It is only personal evidence, valuable to me—it's merely a piece of paper, Sir," replied Ismael Balenzuela smoothly, and then, indicating the truck, he observed, "They are sitting in the great piece of evidence. Please, let me pay any expenses that may accrue for returning my property. I am so grateful to both of you gentlemen for apprehending these miscreants so effectively and efficiently," and, as he spoke, he pulled out his wallet and opened it to reveal a wad of bills. But, first, he produced his card and gave it to them with a flourish. "This verifies my name and connection with a respected development company. I am in conversation not only with these astute leaders of the Taino nation, but with many local distinguished leaders—like the Mayor of Villa Riqueza." At that name the eyes of both officers opened widely and they nodded at Ismael with great respect.

Basil began to shout something, but the second officer leaned into the truck and gave him a hard buffet on the shoulder. "Shut up, you!" He commanded.

Basil began to whimper, as Star was now yelling, "Ismael! Ismael!"

Both policemen slammed the truck doors.

"Gentlemen," continued Ismael, still holding his wallet open and displaying his cash, "you understand that we need at all costs to avoid any scandal that might jeopardize the progress of the development projects here. I cannot be involved in any court case—even as a victim! If the projects become embroiled in any bad press at all, that might mean the loss of jobs and much needed income for the people of this area. It might be disastrous."

The policemen were half listening to his words and half concentrating on watching the fistful of one-thousand peso notes Ismael was now pulling out of his wallet.

"Please," he begged, "as a favor to me, please pay any court costs for me," and he began laying thousand peso notes into each officer's hand. One, two—he watched their faces. Then another. He paused. They were still waiting. Then he laid a fourth peso note in each hand and they both nodded and smiled. It was the equivalent of two hundred U.S. dollars: one hundred each.

The first officer swung the truck door open. "Give him his property back, ¡Puerco!" "Pig!" he snarled at Basil, still cramped miserably in the driver's seat. Basil just sat trembling, so the burly officer grabbed him and yanked him out of the truck, dragging him forward, spinning him around, and then, slamming the door closed, he splayed Basil up against it, kicking his legs apart and deftly spreading him across the top.

Basil fumbled out of his pocket the check he had light-fingered from Tomás as he bumped him hard on the way out of the hotel room and proffered it backhanded to the officer, who grabbed it from him and, without looking at it, handed it to Ismael. "Is this it, sir?"

Ismael glanced at the crumbled paper. "It is. Thank you, gentlemen. And, when the time comes for us to testify, we will note to the court the superb job both of you did in apprehending these dangerous criminals."

The first officer nodded and then yelled to Star, "Out of the car, you!" The second officer roughly motioned to Star and she squeezed out trembling.

"You want to pay your fine, too?" the first officer demanded.

"We have nothing," she cried, and then, "Please!" she implored Balenzuela.

He stared back at her stoically.

The officers nodded at Ismael and the three Taino descendants and then he and his partner began dragging the Heitzes toward their patrol car. "Let's go, you!" the first officer commanded. "There's a reward out for the return of this truck from the rental company and we mean to have it!"

"Please, Ismael!" was the last plea Star screamed as the second officer roughly pushed her head down and shoved her into the back of the van.

"He stole a relic! A relic! Arrest him!" the last words Basil began to shout, but they were cut off as he was stuffed into the police van. He was still shouting incomprehensibly in English as the vehicle wheeled off.

Immediately, Ismael looked at his watch and ordered the women, "Run back inside! We have a half minute left to clean up the rest of this!"

At once, Ruby wheeled and sprinted across the short space to the hotel entrance. Ismael caught up with her and they banged through the door.

"You face the elevator," he yelled to Jo and Aunt Aña, motioning them to stop there. "Ruby, come with me!" He slammed through the stairway door and held it open. "Dear Ruby, please crawl beneath the stairway and retrieve a green vinyl bag. It's to the left in the corner!"

Ruby slipped underneath, stooping.

"Oh, and be careful with it—it's very fragile."

She crawled back out, cradling it as if it were a baby.

"Come on!" he urged her, and they both exited the stairwell just as the elevator door slid back. Out stepped her brother Ben and his friend Tomás to confront Jo and Aunt Aña, who was standing with her arms akimbo, like a truant officer invading an arcade during school hours.

The two young men stopped stock still and stiffened in the elevator entrance, their eyes widening. "Wow! You're all here?" exclaimed Ben.

"Come out right now!" demanded Sub-Chief Anacoana Behechio, Ben's aunt. "We have some words to share with you both."

"I'm in a hurry! Let me by!" snarled Tomás. "I have important things to do!"

"Not any more, you don't!" snapped Ruby, joining the other two women. She held up the green vinyl bag and waved it at them.

"Busted!" exclaimed Ben.

Right behind her was Ismael Balenzuela. He held up the check and displayed the front of it to Tomás. "You have to be more careful with your property. You wouldn't have gotten very far without this. . . ."

Ben stepped forward, Tomás in tow, and pointed at Ismael! "He did it!" he yelled. "He's got it! I had nothing to do with it!"

Tomás stepped back away from Ben and stared at him with chagrin. "What?" he demanded. "What are you saying?"

"I think I actually have it now," said Ruby, ignoring Ben and Tomás's outbursts, and fishing in the bag.

"Let's all sit down and talk this over like family," said Jo. "We've caused enough of a scene here for one day." And she nodded toward the hotel staff, all gathered behind the reception desk, watching this melodrama unfold.

"We are so busted!" muttered Ben as the two empty-handed men followed docilely enough and Jo led them outside to a far table with five chairs around it.

Ismael, dragging a sixth chair over to them, signaled to a waiter and confided, "We will let you know when we want you to come over. We will be conferring first and then I will signal you," and he gave him a two-hundred peso tip to stay away.

Ben and Tomás slumped down in two chairs and the women surrounded them. The next *cacica* of the Western North, Anacoana in her most imperious fashion, planted herself right next to Tomás, and Ruby took up her post smack up against Ben's side, glaring at her brother. Jo sat down directly across from them both, and Ismael Balenzuela, dragging up his chair, sidled himself over next to Jo.

Ben looked up at Ismael, and Ismael said to them both, "It was a sting. Neither of you is very smart." Tomás hung his head.

Jo gazed at them both stoically for a long time. No one spoke until the two would-be saviors of the forest began to fidget like schoolboys. Then Jo spoke. "What were you both thinking? That none of us care about our homeland? Did you think the land means nothing to us? Did you think as *cacica* I would do nothing? Was that it?"

"While you two were drumming," broke in Ruby, "and you—Ben— were squandering your life away at some crooked casino, Jo here was saving the whole Spanish half of Richfield as its community organizer. Why do you think we made her chief? It was because she's a woman who gets things done!"

"Listen," said Jo, directly to Tomás, "what you did was wrong and it was foolish, but," and she paused so long he had to look up at her and stop staring down at the table so she could capture his eyes with hers, "your motivation was just. Therefore, we are prepared to make an arrangement with you."

"What arrangement?" he faltered.

"I am going to address this issue of the stealing of trees for charcoal directly and start our Tribe's coordinated involvement in some kind of solution that will work. This issue is not as simple as recovering the stolen Rosary from you two *boys*." Both Ben and Tomás winced at the mild but well deserved insult, as Jo continued: "There's a lot of parts to this. It's complex. I listened carefully to your presentation at the chiefs' meeting on what you saw in the forest, and I also listened carefully and took notes on the report the professor made, and I am going to be working closely with our Haitian brothers and sisters with the full support and cooperation of their *cacique*, so we will address this from both sides of the border. I will also contact the rangers and the army and whomever else I need to mobilize. I will get to the bottom of this. I will discover who is behind the militia and what will begin making a lasting solution to the problem."

She paused at the open-mouthed stare of Tomás as she outlined a campaign plan so far above anything he had envisioned when he had set his sights simply on engaging the unknown militia in battle. "To get to the heart of it," Jo assured Tomás, "I agree with you that I need to see all this myself, so, as recompense for your foolish actions, which I consider partially ameliorated by your good intentions, I want you to take me to the places in the forest that you went and show me in person what you saw."

"It's dangerous, *Señorita*!" he protested. "The forest is deep and these people are murderers."

"We will not go alone," Jo assured him. "We will bring a handpicked expeditionary force and we will reconnoiter the area carefully. And," she added, "you don't have to worry about me. I am versed in woodcraft by my uncle. I will bring a weapon, just in case, though I will avoid using it at all costs except failure, and," she ended, narrowing her eyes at his before sitting back and letting his go, "I am an Archer and our aim is true!"

Ismael felt like applauding, but noting the impassive stares of the women, he copied theirs.

"Now," said Jo, looking toward the two women, addressing Aunt Aña primarily, but generously including Ruby in her consulting team, "What shall we do with these two misguided lambs?"

"What do you recommend?" asked Anacoana Behechio wisely, thereby affirming Jo's authority in this matter in her region.

"If you agree with me that they appear truly repentant, we could allow them to return the relic to the tribal treasury and alert the leaders of the compound that two thieves have been captured, and here is the recovered stolen item. If you gentlemen put it that way, you need not lie."

Tomás began to wipe rough tears from his eyes. Though he tried to constrain it, his voice broke as he spoke. "So much mercy," he said. "I have misjudged you completely. I am truly sorry, Josefina."

"Then, that's done," said *Nitayna* Anacoana Behechio. And she said to Ben directly. "This is a great trust. Do not betray it."

"I won't Aunt Aña," he said. "I'm sorry too, Jo. For everything."

"Ruby?" said Jo.

Ruby handed the bag to Tomás. "I don't have to tell you to guard this with your life. Your honor is completely at stake in this."

"Yes," said Tomás. And standing up he said directly to Josefina, "Thank you, *Cacica*."

37

A s soon as Tomás and Ben left, Jo rose at once to her feet and said to her aunt, to Ruby, and to Ismael Balenzuela, "Please don't look for me for the next several days. I will need you, and I will call on each of you as the need arises. I plan to do some extensive traveling here on the island and some continuous research on the net, and seek the advice of the available experts until I get a line on this."

"Should I go with you?" asked Ruby, leaping up herself.

Jo smiled. "You are such a gem. And so well named! No, precious sister, I don't know where I need to go and with whom I need to talk just yet, but I will keep you apprised of it and you can all share what I learn with each other. For now," and she nodded, smiling at Ismael, "you should give our new brother some well-deserved attention—both of you have earned a vacation. And, Aunt Aña . . ."

"Yes, *Nanixi, Mi Corazón?*"

"As a favor to me, please show our brother Ismael the best of your properties and help him bargain for the very best prices."

"My thought exactly."

"Thank you, Chief Josefina," said Ismael. "I am very grateful. This is a gracious act that neither I nor my ancestors ever deserved."

"It is the Taino way," said Jo simply.

Aunt Aña smiled at Ismael Balenzuela, as she said to him, "Let me speak to you now not as a sub-chief, the *Nitayna* Anacoana Behechio, ancestral descendant of the great Queen Anacoana, herself, et cetera, et cetera, and all the rest of the history that goes into my title, but as a potential aunt."

Ruby blushed and giggled, and Jo smiled as she began to move away.

"Please, *Nanixi, Mi Corazón,*" Aunt Aña stopped her. "Would you stay just a little longer, because I have something to say I wish all to hear."

Jo paused, frowning, but she loved her aunt and she sat down.

Immediately, Ismael Balenzuela signaled over toward the waiter, hovering on the edge of the pool area, waiting for guests to order drinks but watching this generous gathering which promised to order big and tip big. At once he scurried over. Ismael turned back to Aunt Aña and said, "Please, I don't want to miss a word of what you have to tell me, but," he turned toward Jo, "a chief cannot fight a war if she has no provisions. Please, eat and then run."

"It's wise advice," consented Aunt Aña, "and you are always wise, Jo."

Jo thought about it. "Only if we pay this time."

"I am on an expense account from the *cacicazgo,* so I'll pay," ruled Aunt Aña.

"Thank you!" said Ismael.

"I'm starved," piped up Ruby. "All this intrigue and apprehending of criminals and now plotting to save the world has given me quite an appetite!"

Everyone laughed except Jo, who merely smiled. The weight of that world was a burden she had never felt so heavily as at this moment.

Ismael Balenzuela turned back to Aunt Aña as soon as the orders were in and leaned toward her so his body language could highlight his words: "Please continue," he begged her.

Aunt Aña smiled broadly and did indeed continue: "What I'm trying to tell you is something that will help you keep from repeating any part of the mistakes of the past. What you should understand is that I think we Tainos use all that history that goes into our names and our positions to locate ourselves within a family—a great family that reaches down the millennia since our ancestors arrived in these islands some fifteen hundred years or so ago—the exact time no one knows for sure. You see, because, instead of conquering the people who were already here—the Ostionoides, and any of those that remained of the people before them, the Saladoides, the Arcaicos, and all the rest—we simply absorbed them, or, to put it more accurately, welcomed them into our family. There were no wars, except with the Caribes, who did not wish to assimilate. But, this is the Taino way. It is what our people wanted to do when Columbus and his marauders arrived. Our people were generous and forgiving and we wished to make an alliance. We have never changed that wish. We live at peace with everyone when we can. We are not a people who want to fight and conquer and rule. We are a people who want to coexist and help our neighbors so everyone can thrive and prosper. If you are sincere, this is what we want for you. I don't know your heart, Ismael, or yours," she turned to Ruby. "This may be an infatuation and nothing develops from it. Or it may be authentic and the love of a lifetime. But, either way, the family embraces those of good heart. Do you have a good heart, Ismael?"

He paused, chagrined at the question. "I . . . I don't know. Honestly, probably not. But," he added hastily. "I sincerely want one." He looked around at the three women, one by one and asked them, "What can I do to be free of the worst parts of my heritage and start again?"

"¿*Reverenda*?" asked Aunt Aña, nodding at Jo.

Suddenly, Jo was no longer in a hurry. She prayed a moment silently as she looked deeply into Ismael's eyes and then she said, ""You must embrace the Source of forgiveness."

"What is that?" asked Ismael.

"The One who has forgiven us everything—including those of your ancestry who come in true sorrow."

"You're talking about—what do you call him?—YaYael?"

"Yes," said Jo, "*Jesucristo*."

Ismael looked around the gathering once again. "This is very hard for me. My family, as you know, was Catholic, down through the ages. But, I'll be honest with you still, it did not seem to help my ancestor Andrés de Valenzuela. He was a scurrilous villain from all accounts. Everything I have learned about him brings me shame—what I learned in school, what I learned at home. I have always thought that his faith was a sham." Ismael saw the smile was gone from Ruby's eyes. "I know I put myself in great jeopardy with this admission. Ruby, I love you. But, you will know sooner or later that in college I was attracted to socialism. I know! I know!" he waved down the response he knew was coming, because it always came from his own mother. "There are many socialists who are also Christians. Why here in the Dominican Republic itself you have a Christian Socialist party!"

Aunt Aña laughed. Here in such a serious discussion that might directly impact the future of young love, which was always a favorite with Anacoana Behechio, she still laughed. "Here in the Dominican Republic, the Communist party puts a large Christmas tree in front of their headquarters in the capital and strings the whole property with festive colored lights!" she chuckled, shaking her head at the wonder of it.

"But, my family only goes to church on family saints' days and on holidays, and I don't even accompany them then. There is no place for a god in my life," Ismael confessed. He spoke only to Ruby now. "This will be a problem, beloved?"

She nodded. Ruby, to the shock of all, was actually tearing up. Not sobbing, but her eyes were damp. "Don't make me choose," she pleaded.

Ismael Balenzuela sat back in his chair, his face troubled. He sighed, but he could think of nothing to say, except, "If I make you choose, I will be the loser?"

Jo stepped in very gently. "Friend Ismael, you are not an atheist, are you? Aren't you an agnostic? I mean, you don't really know, do you?"

"That's true," he said. "I don't really know. But you don't either, do you? I mean how can anyone be sure?"

Aunt Aña spoke up: "Answers come only with experience. As you live and age, you feel an emptiness—a question continually nagging at your mind—what's it all for?"

"I've asked that all my life."

"I understand," said Jo. "You see, before the marauders came, our people already knew YaYa. They saw the Great Spirit at work everywhere. They tried to reach out in foolish ways through *cohiba*—that only made them vulnerable to enemies, both spiritual and physical. Why would they have needed an hallucinatory anesthetic, when the actual awakening Spirit of God was ever poised to grant authentic visions of truth in response to prayer? Why settle for a substitute? It was disastrously foolish. And this self-anesthetizing of much of their leadership helped lose them their homelands. But at the same time, they also knew that YaYa had a son who died, YaYael, and that the dead divine son of God was involved in creation. The Caribes were working their way northward from island to island and our Tribe across the entire Caribbean was praying for a deliverer. When Columbus arrived, our people welcomed him with open arms as YaYa's answer to their prayers. Columbus, as a supposed man of faith, should have been that answer. Had he simply told them that the death of God's Son was God's act for their deliverance, defended them against the Caribe invaders, and lived among them as brothers in Christ, there would have been nothing our people would not have done for them out of gratitude."

"Instead," mourned Ismael Balenzuela, "they pillaged and burned and enslaved and killed."

"They made sport of the faith," cried Aunt Aña. "They bet each other they could make our ancestors worship a stick and set up crosses that they forced them to bow down to, as if the wooden cross itself was a talisman. It was a great disgrace—a blasphemy—an abomination. Why our northern continent celebrates the day of this villain in their country and why they named it after a *bobo*—that nincompoop Amerigo Vespucci—has always been a mystery to me. Such a great nation, such a great people, calling itself by the name of a fool."

"Ismael," said Jo, "our direct ancestor, the Great Warrior Enrique, saw through the deceit and recognized the affinity of our knowledge with that of the priests, and he discerned the missing piece that made our faith complete. He was the greatest warrior chief in our history. And that is because he relied fully on God, praying his rosary—the very rosary that you rescued for us—as he walked the perimeter of his troops at night. And in his actions he showed the wisdom and then the mercy of God as he led his pursuers up into the mountains until their horses failed and they laid down their arms in exhaustion, and then he forgave them. This is something. Do you understand? It is something wonderful that we treasure. It is the lodestar of most of our lives. If you are indeed a man who admits he does not know, then you are choosing between something and nothing. As a businessman, you know already that having something is far better than ending with nothing."

Balenzuela thought that over. "You have a point there. It is foolish to end up with nothing. Still, I have to know that something is real. It is not just like bogus stock." He looked directly at Ruby and pleaded, "I really *don't* know. I won't lie to you. Lying comes too easily for me. It is how I got the rosary back. I can play a part so easily. But not with you, Ruby."

Ruby wiped her eyes and reached over and took his hand tenderly in hers. "We'll work on this together," she said.

This, thought Jo, is definitely a new and improved Ruby. Ismael had understood a profound truth about her sister. She had to admit that to herself. Ruby was not Daniela. She did not put personalities on and take them off like costume changes from her wardrobe. This gentleness was a new addition to Ruby's character. Her love for Ismael had given it birth. It was a wonder to see.

"Thank you, Ruby," said Ismael, taking encouragement from her touch. "I want to please you, but it has to be real for me."

"All right then," said Aunt Aña, beaming on them both. "We've got ourselves a deal!"

Ruby laughed and wiped her eyes once more with her napkin.

"Just practicing up the making of deals for the whirlwind of business we're going to start together tomorrow," Aunt Aña confided to Ismael, to his delight.

The food arrived—no sandwiches for this active crew—and they fell to it like the warriors their actions were simulating, nourishing themselves on a full expanse of Dominican delicacies. *Paella* this time—a full, gigantic plate of shrimp and rice that served them all. An array of juices for the women and a better wine than house wine for Ismael at Aunt Aña's insistence ("The Tribe can cover this, as it stands to benefit from your development projects"). Of course, Aunt Aña insisted on a large plate of *platano maduro*, which she informed all of them once again was her staple food in life. All the rest was accouterments, according to her—even the main dish!

"I'll have to work this all off with a couple of extra miles tomorrow," Ruby promised herself through a mouthful of succulent plantain.

"Yes, the calorie clock is ticking like a fat bomb," laughed Aunt Aña, heaping paella on her plate. "But we're all running around ragged anyway, so we'll burn it off easy. You girls," she observed, "are always so slim and trim. Obviously, you didn't get your figures from my side of the family!"

"But, you're not fat," protested Ismael. "You are very attractive, *Nitayna*."

"Why thank you, Ismael. You can call me Aunt Aña—at least for now!"

"That's right," urged Ruby, "put on the pressure! He's a big boy, he can take it!"

Not exactly how they taught us to share the faith back in Boston, mused Jo to herself. No subtlety here. These laypeople were cash on the barrelhead!

"You know," mused Aunt Aña. "If I were only twenty years younger, you might have a real run for your money, Ruby!"

Everyone howled with laughter. Even Jo.

I love this family, thought Ismael. I would so much love to be a part of it. But, he cautioned himself, what they believe really has to be real for me. I don't want to live any more lies, if I can help it. I'm facing up to my family debt to these wonderful people, but I need to base everything now on truth, as much as I can, or I'm just replacing the lies of my ancestry—that they really did something worthwhile when they decimated this island—with a gentler lie, but a lie just the same.

They ate happily and they ate well. Long gone were the days of ascetic starving and then purging and then drugging to reach God and understand life. This mistake in the Taino's own heritage had departed when a full understanding of YaYa entered. So, at last, well nourished and very satisfied, they were ready for the business at hand.

"Where will you go, Jo?" asked Ruby, the first to express the concern they all felt.

"Don't worry," Jo assured them all, "not into the forest yet. I think I need to pray by myself for guidance and then my plan at this point is to start with the supposed head of my 'bodyguard,' the very difficult Ricky, and then I'm going to seek some legal advice. After that I hope to interview the professor who spoke at the chiefs' meeting, get myself well informed in the offices and labs at the university, talk to the anthropologists, the chemists, everyone who can give me helpful information. I want to examine the satellite pictures and the studies done on the defoliation and the reasons for it and then get an intellectual take on the nature and extent of the problem and the reasons this stealing continues to happen. When I feel I have a basic understanding of what we're confronting here, then I'll come back. I'll meet with the *cacique* from Haiti and his experts and see for myself the effects and the benefits of this thievery to the other side of our presently divided island. All that I will do before I organize my patrol to go into the woods and survey the devastation myself. Then, when all this is done, I will formulate a strategy, contact the rangers, the border guards of the army, and whomever else I need to consult, and put together a game plan that I will then bring to the chiefs."

"This will take months—a year—five years!" exclaimed Chief Anacoana Behechio, shaking her head.

"I will do this in one, not more than two weeks," said Jo, firmly. "That is why, now, I must leave you all."

As she walked away, after receiving their expressions of solicitation, promises of prayer, pledges of support, she texted Mercedes Del Rio, her good friend and fellow minister back in Richfield, to get one more piece of vital information: how her church planting was faring there.

38

WHEN JO LEFT HER family, her first stop was one she did not mention to them, because it was private to her: She needed a vigil, even if abbreviated. She drove to Las Olas del Sol, left her car on the road and did not enter the grounds, but circled around its walls and sequestered herself on the cliffs overlooking the Caribbean Sea. And then the substance of her hours of prayer was this simple plea: "Lord God, I am so small and insignificant. How can I guide a people so great? Everything Ricky said was true: I come from the outside. I know nothing. But, Dear God, these are your people and you are our Great Parent and you know all. You are the God of Wisdom and the prayer for wisdom is one you always answer. Please, Lord, give me ears to hear and eyes to see what is the true nature of this problem, and guide me to its solution."

It was late afternoon when Jo rose from the rocks and went down to her car. She paused at a bodega for a simple set of whole wheat multigrain (called *integral*) bread and meat and cheese and several bottles of water and a banana, which is always a trustworthy fruit for a supper on the road, and then she drove off on her quest.

Jo's announcement that she was planning on meeting first with "the very difficult Ricky" Asenao contained no misnomer. Again, she pounded on his door. Again, he was back at home—and, again, he was none too pleased to see her. At least this time he asked her in. "I'm very busy," he said in English.

"I've been very busy, too," she replied in kind.

"I can imagine."

"Good, because I need some help."

"That I can imagine too!" He grunted this at her from what sounded like a lofty perch high atop a mountain of information that was probably going to be revealed as inaccessible.

"I want you to take me to the Sierra del Bahoruco, where the trees are being stolen. May I sit down?" asked Jo, eyeing the rocking chair.

"What?" Ricky looked like he needed to sit down.

"I'm asking if I may sit down."

"Yes, of course, you may sit down. Be my guest! But, as for your other request, well, we don't always get what we want now do we, Princess?"

"And why is that?"

"Because you're asking me if I'll take you into the heart of a battle and the answer is no, I won't!"

"And why is that?"

"Because it's no place for you. I don't want the responsibility of reporting to the Tribe why I lost its acting *cacica* in the forest when you fell behind, or why you got yourself captured by the enemy as you lumbered about making a racket, or whatever inept thing you do in the woods."

"You really think low of me, don't you?"

"Not at all. I think in your place you are probably very competent."

"And what place would that be?"

"Back in the States where you belong—leading your church. You don't belong here—you belong there. You don't even know where the thieving is taking place. It's not only in Bahoruco that they're striking now—it's elsewhere as well. See? You know nothing—nothing at all!"

Jo paused and regarded him for a long moment as he glared at her, standing over her like an executioner's assistant—all threatening and frothing, but powerless to do the deed—and then she said in Spanish, "You are right about one thing—and I have never denied it. I do not know enough about what is happening in these borderlands, but just as I learned my work when I was doing community organization in a land that was not my motherland, so will I learn what is happening here—in the land of my birth. And I will do it with or without your help."

"Well, if I have a choice, I won't lead you into danger."

"What do you mean, if you have a choice?" demanded Jo.

"Well, you are the acting *cacica*. You could order me to do it," admitted Ricky with obvious reluctance.

"Why would I do that? You think I need to compel one man to help when I can find willing supporters to take me there and show me what I need to know?"

"What makes you think anyone would do that—take you there? Why don't you realize that everyone would think just the same way that I do?"

"You really think no one will help me?" demanded Jo, astonished.

Ricky stared at her in his own amazement and retorted, "Well, of course! This is a job for a man. Tomás made that so clear at the chiefs' meeting. Look at a man like our *Cacique* Inti Archer. What woman could handle what he did?"

"For that matter, what other man could do what he did?" shot back Jo, all but getting up and pointing at Ricky himself. She was sitting forward in her chair, her eyes blazing. "But Anacoana did it—and she did it so well she became a legend for it! She was queen and tribal mother and ruled as the *cacica* when her men were murdered, with dozens of sub-chiefs loyal to her. Uncle Sol always held her up to me as a model."

"And you think you are another Anacoana? Is that it?" sneered Ricky.

"No, I don't. Though my Uncle Sol seemed to think so," replied Jo steadily. "Anacoana was gifted in ways that I am not. She had personal skills so great and wisdom so profound that everyone took heed of her and everyone loved her."

"Well, there is so much more involved today in being chief than you probably imagine," Ricky lectured her in the most pedantic manner. "It is vastly complex. And at this moment there is real danger. This is what I am trying to explain to you—if you would only listen! You are named for Queen Anacoana, but are you aware that she was executed?"

"Of course!" cried Jo. "How could I not know? I am her namesake! She was hanged at the age of twenty-nine—the age, I might add, that I am now! The marauders feared her power and they tricked her and murdered her. I have grown up all my life knowing her sad story. But here's something you need to understand, and so does everyone else in this Tribe!" And Jo narrowed her eyes and they bore into his face like lasers. "I am another kind of person, and we live in another age. The Tribe is established. It needs a different type of leader. Uncle Sol felt that my aptitude for organization is what it needed. And I am now convinced he was right. I will not be swayed from my duty and my pledge."

"Humph!" grunted Ricky, and then he added the oddest thing: "Your eyes are lovely. They flash when you're angry. But," he examined her face carefully, still standing over her as she sat forward in the chair, "your face is too long."

Jo's mouth dropped open. What was this all about? "I can't help the shape of my head!" she replied, once more astonished.

"Of course, you can't," he agreed. "Yours is the traditional Taino face. It is your ancestry."

"And your face would be more pleasing," Jo shot back, "without its perpetual scowl!"

Ricky laughed and then took a chair and sat down. He was so irritating! thought Jo.

"I'll tell you what, Josefina." His tone was suddenly reasonable. "I can see you are determined to stay, no matter what I say. I am just in your way. How about I step down from sub-chief and director of communications and make way for someone else who can support you in a way that I cannot?"

Jo stared at him, trying to see if this was more ridicule, or if we was actually sincere. But his face remained serious and the sneer was gone from it.

"No, thank you," she said, quietly now. "I would not want to accept this responsibility without you."

"Even if I don't take you to the forest."

"You are the head of my bodyguard, but, yes, even if you won't take me there. I consider you very competent in what you do and a benefit to the Tribe."

"I'm relieved to hear you've given this foolish idea up, because I really don't want to put you in danger or watch someone else do that."

Jo stared at him. She had not said she was not going herself. This man jumped swiftly to a lot of conclusions. She began to think of him as electricity. He could light up a room with his capabilities, or burn it down when he short-circuited, which appeared to her to be rather often. Maybe *he* would actually be a liability in the forest. She never knew what he was going to do. But now he was on a new topic.

"This is a hard place to fix," he was counseling her. "You may not find your skills as up to the problems here as you imagine they would be."

"I have no illusions about my capabilities, even in my ministry in the States. There are many things I can't fix that are wrong: We need cleaner air in Pasadena. Better law enforcement against human trafficking in Portland. Serious tax reform throughout Massachusetts—where is all that money going? Fewer executions in Texas. Better safeguards for retirees in Florida. A more effective seawall projection off of Galveston and New Orleans. Better controls of offshore oil retrieval in the Gulf of Mexico and in Alaska. Protection against international overfishing and red tides off Gloucester and the rescuing of Plum Island before it disappears completely into the sea. Not to mention the victimizing of the poor by gentrification in all our major cities. And the list goes on and on. You want somebody to concentrate on? You can concentrate on ridding the world of terrorists! I'm just one little voice, working among good people who know they are not perfect, but they're doing their best with what they have to work with. They are well-meaning and that's what I am expecting to find here, because that's the way I think of Dominicans and Haitians in general and my Taino family in particular: good, well-meaning citizens who each want their families not just to survive, but to flourish, and sometimes that causes conflict."

"It's a pretty speech," grunted Ricky—and the sneer was back. "But what we need is force to stop what's happening to our trees."

"Shoot 'em up, eh? Go in there with both guns blazing?"

"Well, something like that."

"Then, you're right. We probably wouldn't get along in the woods." Jo stood up. "I have another visit to make tonight, before it gets too late. Thank you for your time."

Jo had turned formal and Ricky answered in kind, "At your service."

Jo thought ruefully as she returned to her car that the last thing he was was "at her service."

Angel Moreno Cueva de Piedra's office was just across town, and she arrived there within ten minutes. He was surprised to see her, but ushered her in graciously. "Is there something wrong?" he asked, concerned.

"No—other than the fact that everything is wrong—at least according to Sub-Chief Asenao."

"Ah," said the little lawyer wisely. "You are just coming from an interview with him?"

"If you can call it that," said Jo. "More like a battle."

The lawyer smiled, but said nothing.

"I am so sorry to invade your home at this hour."

"It is also my office," he said charitably.

"Yes, and that's why I am here—as the acting *cacica*."

"Of course, you are a woman of action."

"Thank you," said Jo.

"Please sit down."

Jo did.

"Would you like something to drink?"

"No, thank you. I know it's the polite thing to do, but time is a commodity I must spend in short measure."

"I understand thoroughly," said *Licenciado* Cueva de Piedra, and he seated himself behind his desk and looked toward her expectantly.

"I have a theory, and I would be so grateful if you could gather some data for me, so I can test it. Of course," she added, "I would make sure the Tribe reimbursed you for your efforts."

"I am on retainer," he smiled at her. "You needn't worry about that."

"The rich farmland in and around Villa Riqueza. Who owns that?"

He stared at her in surprise. "Why I imagine the people do. The citizens of the town."

"Yes, so would I. But, I would be grateful if you could run down the names of the owners on the deeds of the properties. Is that much work?"

"It can be done," he observed, looking puzzled. "And you need this why, if I may ask?"

"It's just a theory I want to test. I don't want to say anything more until we can look at the data."

"All right, I'll make a note of it." He wrote the note to himself on a pad on his desk. "Do you want original owners? Do you want to trace the property back to land grants? Or do you want present owners mainly?"

"Just the final piece," mused Jo. "I think I only need to know in whose names particularly the prosperous farms are listed. That's all—in and around Villa Riqueza."

"All right, I'll get it for you. Please give me a few days to do this."

"Of course," said Jo, "and I thank you."

"Is there anything else?"

"Well, not that you can do. I asked Ricky if he would take me to see where the deforestation is taking place, but he refused."

"He was probably worried about your safety."

"That's what he said."

"But you doubt it?" asked the lawyer.

"Well, not entirely, but, yes, in part."

The lawyer thought: You know he wants your job. But he said nothing. Looking at Jo, he could see he did not need to say anything.

"It is his responsibility to show you what you want to see. He is the coordinator of your personal guard," he informed her.

"Yes, I know that."

"You could order him to do that," the lawyer explained. "You have the power as acting *cacica*."

"Yes, I know that too."

"But you don't want to do that?"

"You're right. I don't."

"You know," said the lawyer, "your Uncle Saul would not have hesitated to order him to do whatever he wanted him to do."

"Yes, I have no doubt that is exactly what Uncle Sol would have done. But I am a different kind of leader, though I honored my uncle and admired him and deeply appreciated his style and what he could accomplish with it. It was expedient and effective. But it is not mine."

"Well, you are your own person," affirmed the lawyer, "and you will get on well, I have no doubt. You have done so already."

"Thank you for your support."

"That, you will always have."

"I could not accept this responsibility without the support that you, my Aunt Aña, Doña Lucia, Don Ramón, Doña Mencia, the *caciques*, and so many others have given me."

"Yes, you are well liked and well trusted. The great majority of us are convinced that you are the person for the job. And—don't overlook one fact. For all his bluster and what must look to you like overbearing entitlement and his sometimes ill-advised and exploded self-reliance, Enrique Asenao is no fool. He is very smart, if a bit precipitous. And, a little-known fact is that his mentor is our own mayor of Villa Bahoruco. She took him in when his parents died and reared him from his middle years to maturity. He is devoted to her, and despite his *macho* inclinations, he is totally supportive of her leadership as mayor. There is much more to our Ricky than even he realizes."

"I'll keep that in mind," reflected Jo, standing up. "For now, I have a journey ahead, so I must leave you."

"Not a long trip at night, I hope," he asked, concerned.

"I'm afraid so. I want to arrive in the capital before it gets late. I have some early appointments tomorrow at the university."

"It is not good to drive so far alone. Would you like me to accompany you?"

"How gracious you are," said Jo. "And I am tempted to say yes, because I would really benefit from your wisdom as I try to piece together what is happening in the forests and why it is happening. But, to be honest, I very much want the data that I requested from you as soon as you can dig it out. I think it may prove to be very helpful."

"I will ferret it out starting tomorrow morning," he promised.

"Thank you," said Jo. "I completely rely upon you and your wise discretion."

The small lawyer bowed his head and smiled a very pleased smile.

"Besides," Jo assured him, "I won't be alone. I can pray undisturbed and be in the Lord's company, and I am also ready to spend some time on *Into the Nite with Laura Lamar* as soon as I've traveled far enough for her signal to come in on my dial. I am more than ready to relax with some much needed bachata and merengue! I find them so therapeutic!"

39

THE ROAD OUT OF Villa Bahoruco to the capital is just over a hundred and twenty miles, winding around the southeastern edge of Lake Enriquillo. Before turning northward and starting its serious cross-country trek, it needs to throw its lot in with some friends to become a main caravan thoroughfare. Beginning as Route 46, a country road, as it turns toward the north, skirting Lake Rincon, it joins up with 533, a tough mountain highway cutting down from the western ranges, and then spices itself up with 44, the scenic beach route lounging up from the south. Altogether, the united road is now ready to handle the traffic. Had all those numbers converged as well, the result might have been the combined Route 623, a name impossible to remember, so it wisely strips down for its journey to just what it needs to be: an easily identifiable major passage traversing the kilometers as simply Route 2. As such, it meanders along through a plethora of major cities and little towns, each one attempting to slow down or divert its travelers in order for each to hawk its distinctive wares, before the road pumps back up a few numbers to widen out and flex some extra lanes as Route 6, the main thoroughfare entering Santo Domingo.

Had Jo taken on that challenge by day, she would have had to contend with the biggest obstacles to any traveler: speed bumps ostensibly protecting the entrance of every town from high-roller speeding, particularly by powerful, cross-country commercial trucks attempting to cut delivery time by zipping through straightaways and careening into road detours through congested business districts. Slowing down both day and night was a given, but for Jo, travel by day posed a greater difficulty in the reality that Ismael Balenzuela had also come to realize: that every "sleeping policeman" breeds "a family," and her generous nature made her particularly vulnerable. Her progress could always be charted from beggar to beggar, so early evening was her only real choice if she wanted speed. Still, the price one paid for careless dark driving was risking ripping out the bottom works of one's car.

So the night's task was, therefore, slow and steady driving and peering carefully ahead with the brights on as much as possible.

This night, however, was helpful, clear of clouds with a moon full and bright, and Jo invested her rapid rates between towns and her crawls through them in a languid and refreshing time of prayer of thanksgiving for the swift return of Enrique's Rosary and a detailed set of petitions for wisdom in unpacking the enigma of the persistent stealing of trees from her region's borderlands.

When her prayer was complete and she reckoned the evening was late enough, the hills far enough behind her, the competition of local stations largely stilled, and the strong signal from the capital powerful enough, she switched on the radio and found "your fellow traveler of the airwaves: 'Into the Nite with Laura Lamar.'" The mellifluous voice of "the traveler's best friend," "the 'other girl' on the night shift," "the late-hour waitress serving up sound," and all the rest of Laura's slogans brought memories rushing back. Many were the vacation evenings a sleepless Jo had listened to Laura as she spun out her meringue, and these days her bachata, and her simple, wholesome, encouraging advice helping many a young girl grow into a woman who felt good about herself and her world, because that was what Laura Lamar projected. Tonight, Jo was in for a very pleasant surprise. As she caught the signal, the warm voice came on announcing, "And here she is, dear, dear friends, the surprise guest I've been promising you. It's my own sweet girl, my daughter Lana Lamar—her second year in college and ready to help Mama for a few hours each week. Say hello to the travelers, *dulcita*."

"Hello, everybody," said a pleasant young voice.

Wow! thought Jo. The dynasty continues! And, suddenly, Jo felt very old. How long have I been listening to Laura Lamar? she wondered. I guess I was, maybe, twelve when I first started? Why, that was seventeen years ago! And now that little baby that used to sleep in the studio and even cry from time to time is—what?—a sophomore in university? Eighteen maybe? Nineteen? And she's on the air with mom?

And, then, Jo thought: I wonder if I'll ever have a daughter? I wonder if I'll ever have any children? Will anyone ever want to marry me? Am I going to be wed to this calling? Is a *cacica*—especially a female one—ever able to find a relationship and invest the time needed in one to make a marriage successful, nourishing both husband and wife? Will it make me neglect my husband and my children, as I'm running all around solving the problems of my people? Actually, can anybody—male or female—be a chief and maintain a family? After all, Mara's not married. Neither is Aunt Aña. Of course, she's a widow. Actually, Jo realized, and almost stopped the car in the dead center of the road as the thought struck her, even my namesake Queen Anacoana only became *cacica* when her husband and her brother were murdered and she was now alone. A big truck bearing down on her from behind honked a warning and Jo floored the pedal, jumping her car forward while still mulling this over in her mind as a recent bachata melody began to play: Miguel, the chief over in the east, used to be married, but he's also a widower now. And Don Juan Francisco of the central region never married to my knowledge. I think only the Haitian chief is married. It certainly bears thought. So, that's now something else to pray about.

And so, between petitions to the Great Spirit and the playlist of Laura and Lana, the road emptied her at last into Santo Domingo, her gas low and her spirits lower. Laura Lamar's joy was Jo's wake-up call. She had to think this chief thing over carefully, once she solved the second challenge.

These thoughts were uppermost in her mind as she sped down the boulevard named Twenty-Seventh of February, turned on the road named for Maximo Gomez, cut across a corner, and then down Maximo Cabral to her present destination. The guard, sitting out in the bright warm moonlight, was expecting her, and, as soon as she pulled up, he opened the electronic iron gate. He greeted her pleasantly, gave her a key, and, making a concession by taking the elevator and not the stairs up to the sixth floor, she soon entered the empty condominium of former New Jersey friends of the family now living and teaching in Massachusetts. These had become her teachers at the Center for Urban Ministerial Education in Boston, after urging her to come and study with them, and their relationship had deepened, tied together by a common love of the Dominican Republic. Their condominium was available now to the Tribe whenever its delegates on tribal business needed a reasonable place to stay in the capital. From the sixth floor balcony, one could catch the pleasant breezes of the trade winds, glimpse the ocean between the buildings, watch the moon rise and race across the city, and all this above the range of the mosquitos that rarely ventured that high because of the twilight's hunting birds sweeping the city sky.

For Jo this evening, the balcony was only a quick stop for a few breaths of the air off the ocean to quiet her soul, and sleep in the guest room came immediately. The next morning, she awakened early enough, refreshed and determined, up at the "alarm clocks" of the truck horns on nearby Avenida Bolivar.

Professor Raymondo Ortiz was waiting for her in his office in a laboratory when she arrived at the University of Santo Domingo, and he had a similar set of graphs, charts, and satellite photographs to those Jo had downloaded from the internet. But he also had a wealth of helpful insights and, after they reviewed the data sheets, he shared some of these. His knowledge was extensive and detailed.

"This is not an easy issue to address, Chief Archer," he said, spreading out anthropological analyses, environmental reports, books and papers and agricultural studies, soil analyses, sociological studies, and on and on until his desk was a disheveled mountain of data. And then he swept his hand toward a large bookcase and observed, pointedly, "A good portion of all that material deals with the highly complex and very difficult relationship between those who are now French Creole–speaking nationals and those who are Spanish-speaking nationals, divided by linguistic and cultural borders far stronger than today's tenuous frontier demarcations drawn by politics and history."

Jo nodded and waited.

"I have a class at four p.m., since most of the schedule I teach these days consists of late afternoon and evening classes, but I am prepared for today's class in anticipation of your visit, so you have me for the rest of the day, if you need me for all that time." He smiled.

For reply, Jo lifted a basket she had filled at the *supermercado* on Maximo Gomez, brimming with fruit and those whole-grain rolls called *integral*, cheeses, bottles of fresh fruit juice, sliced turkey, both plantain and *yuca* chips, and several more delicacies, including some *dulce de leche,* the sweet milk bar with its center filled, in this instance, with thick guava jelly, and she said, "We won't go hungry."

"And," Professor Ortiz laughed, "we won't waste any time, either, pausing to go out for lunch, I see!"

"My thought exactly," said Jo.

"Well, let's unpack this all then," he said, and started right in: "First of all, you must realize that the act of cutting down trees and forming them into an oven and reducing them to charcoal and proceeding to sell that charcoal is not illegal in itself. People do it openly all over both nations all the time. If you have a tract of land you want cleared and you hire workers to clear it—especially if you hire Haitians—slash and burn is the preferred way to clean fields. Charcoal production is the natural follow-through. But what is illegal is doing it on public lands, yet even that is only sporadically enforced. You're in the Barahona area—right? I heard the other day of a Haitian caught with a kiln in the woods just off the beach! The police arrested him, but then one officer said, 'He's so dirty from the work, he'll mess up the squad car.' 'And,' said his partner, 'if we send him to jail, we'll have to feed him!' So, they told him to get out of there and never do it again. As soon as he left, they took the charcoal themselves and sold it. Do you think that kind of law enforcement is going to deter anyone?"

Jo stared at him, amazed. And then he proceeded to take Jo on a very detailed historical tour of the conflicts at the border, the impoverishment of the Haitian side, the centrality of charcoal in the lives of the Haitian people, the alternatives being proposed with a careful analysis of the benefits and problems of vast implementation associated with each possible solution, the specific cultural attitudes of the Haitians toward the Dominicans, particularly, and the Dominican side, in general, and its bounty of woodlands, and much more.

Since she had received this assignment, Jo had been reading assiduously on the net, and this diligence helped her to keep up and keep pace, or at least stumble along gingerly, as Raymondo Ortiz raced through the studies and analyses and graphs and speculations from inside the country on both sides of the border, from the United States, from abroad, and even from multinational businesses and international banks offering their solutions. When three thirty p.m. arrived, Jo, lugging an armload of photocopies and notes so plentiful on her computer that she joked it made it five pounds heavier, walked him to his class amid expressions of profound thanks.

"I have always admired the Taino people," he confessed to her. "They arrived amicably, stewarded the land, and never lost their gracious generosity right up until today. It is an honor for me to advise you on their behalf, and I am available, just as my colleague was from the University of Port-au-Prince, to advise you in any way I can to help us all work on a solution. If we all find one together, it will help the people of both sides, if it is done correctly."

"Thank you," said Jo, setting down her burdens and taking his hand. "May God bless you for your own gracious generosity of time and expertise. I am seeing my way much clearer. And now, if you will be so kind as to point me to several other offices and laboratories I hope to visit, I have a five p.m., a seven p.m., and an eight p.m. to touch base with several other professors in other departments, but you were my main informant here. Oh," she added, "I think I neglected to mention that your book, which you so graciously made available to all online, contained a brilliant analysis of the situation, which is why I came to see you and why I am so grateful for the time you invested."

He bowed his head to her and smiled a somewhat self-conscious acknowledgement.

She nodded back and smiled her farewell, gathering up her data and lugging it to her next appointment.

By ten p.m., she was back in the condominium and, after heaping all she had gathered onto a large mahogany desk that practically filled the little office there, she spread all her findings out, organized them by category, then put large decorative sea shells from its little office bookcase on each pile to keep this precious gift of knowledge from blowing together from the breezes of the open window, and was asleep by eleven thirty.

The next day, she visited several other universities.

When the data began to duplicate, she made one more visit. But this one was to a different kind of information center: a large military surplus store in the midst of the *Conde*, the walking mall in the center of downtown Santo Domingo.

"You are the *cacica* who called?" asked an armed guard outside the door as soon as Jo asked for the name of the contact with whom she had made an appointment.

"I am," said Jo.

"Please come this way." He opened the door for her, nodded to his fellow guard, who picked his rifle up from the sidewalk, where he had carelessly placed it, barrel down, to assume a more professional stance, and the first guard led her into a warehouse-vast store, unusual for the little shops that typified the *Conde*, both in size and in the fact that all the walls behind the counters were filled with guns.

A fit woman somewhere in the midst of life came out to greet her, signaling to a man about the same age, as she ushered Jo into an office and closed the door. "Welcome, Chief," she said. "We are honored to have your trade."

"Thank you," said Jo. "I appreciated your helpfulness on the phone. I did not want to communicate by email."

"Understood," smiled the woman. "You've looked at what we have to offer on our website?"

"Yes, I have." Jo produced from her briefcase a number of downloaded printouts of various weapons and passed them around to the two employees.

"These are nonlethal," observed the woman, studying them and passing them on to the man.

"Let me see what we have in stock," replied the man, swiveling the computer on the desk toward himself and beginning to punch up some numbers. From their style, and their accents, and, particularly, their penchant for switching back and forth between Spanish and English, peppering their speech with neologisms, blending both languages together, Jo guessed they were "*NewYoricans*," Puerto Ricans reared in New York, extending their business to *La Republica Dominicana*, bringing the "Big Apple" to the "Land of the Mango."

"Just a second, please," said Jo. "I've read about these options and I have some questions to check."

"We need to know your targets," said the woman, leaning forward. "You realize, of course," she added, "that, though you don't need a permit for these here in the Dominican and we try to maintain strict confidence for our patrons, this is not a confessional, and, if a customer is investigated, we have to hand over our records to the police or the courts."

"I'm intending to work with the authorities," said Jo, calmly.

"That's all we need to know," agreed the woman. "What do you want to look at?"

"Well, I'm interested in tranquilizer rifles and stun guns, mainly."

"Tasers too?"

"Maybe. . . ."

"Here's what you need!" offered the man, swinging the computer around on its swivel toward Jo.

"What's that?" she asked, peering at a rainbow of snug little items that looked like toy guns next to others that appeared to be keychains or flashlights or purse-sized digital recorders.

The man pointed to one of the little toy guns in pastel green and explained, "It's the Donner Pepperpot—in designer colors."

"What does that do?"

"It shoots a pepper spray that nails an assailant up close."

"I was thinking about a little less painful," confessed Jo.

He pushed the up key. "Well, how about the Donner Spouse Gun?"

"The what?"

"It's the Donner D-42. They make a line of stun guns specifically for women. We all call this baby the 'spouse gun'!"

"The spouse gun?" asked Jo.

"Sure, it's the friend of the abused wife—a particularly effective tool. Say you're trapped, hidin' in the bathroom. See, you keep this little baby hidden in the medicine cabinet. Here comes hubby with a snoot-full of booze. Bang! Bang! on the door. You just slide it open, touch him with it, and then stroll out of there, stepping over the flopping body. Or, if you want to put him out for a while, you could use a blow gun."

"A blow gun?"

"Sure—stand it up in the back behind the toilet. Put this to your lips, puff up your cheeks, slide the door open, pfft! Put it back in the medicine cabinet."

"Doesn't a tranquilizer take a while to take effect?" Jo protested, glad she had done her homework. And then, slipping into English, she observed, "I was thinking more of the stun guns like the 'spouse gun,' but these look awfully small and inexpensive. Two hundred and forty pesos? That's only about six bucks. Do they really work well enough?" And then, before they could answer, she quickly added, fearing all the prices would skyrocket, "It's true, I don't have a lot of money to work with, but I don't want something that's not reliable."

"Don't want him laughing at you and chasing you out of the house and up the street after you zap him, huh? Well, don't worry. If you switch to the spouse gun, he'll be floppin' on the floor. These are minis and plenty powerful. New technology. It's almost like a Taser, but remember, you have to touch him. It's for up-close and personal. The Taser, of course, shoots out prongs—so you've got more range. But, it's still whamo!" he smiled too easily for Jo's sense of precision.

"And don't worry about the money. We've learned nobody has any here," added the woman.

But Jo was momentarily distracted, thinking about her reflections during the Laura—and now, as well—the Lana Lamar show. "Hopefully, I won't need that," she concluded.

"No wife thinks she needs it . . ." he began.

Jo broke him off, "I'm not married, and I'm picky, but, just for comparison, what's the range of the Taser?"

"About fifteen feet. Both prongs have to hit, but the effect is instantaneous. It's good night, papa!" the salesman promised her. "Still, the spouse gun is plenty—it's a matter of degree."

Jo fought down the urge to buy one just to use it on Ricky. Tempting as it was. . . . She did order a dozen of the little stun guns of various shapes and sizes as side arms, but promised herself: The second this is over, I'm getting rid of mine! "What else do you have?" she asked.

"Rifles are available," the woman assured her, "but before we look at those and seal the order, I want Raul here to show you the 'Doomsday' Crossbow."

Jo looked horrified.

"It's just a name," the saleswoman explained quickly. "It shoots a .50 caliber dart, that's 12.95 millimeter, depending on which way you calculate. It's like a flying syringe, which is what any tranquilizer weapon is."

"Yes, right—not arrows—darts, of course. May I see one of those?"

"Raul, would you please check the warehouse and see if we have one in stock?" ordered the saleswoman, and then, without missing a beat, turned to Jo, "Two point four pounds is all it is."

"I may have a candidate to use that," murmured Jo, taking this all in.

"Eighty pound pull," the saleswoman assured her. "All you've got to do is hit one leg and they'll be too busy flailing around to shoot back."

"I thought it didn't knock them out immediately," questioned Jo.

"Right! You need a Taser for that. But a dart—especially in the butt—will keep them occupied!"

"Well, what's the difference between a tranquilizer gun and a Taser?" asked Jo, trying to find her bearings in this sea of data.

"Good question! It's time and effect. Let me lay it out for you." The woman leaned forward and smiled warmly at her—sort of girlfriend to girlfriend, sounding like she was sharing a recipe or a better hair-color product. "See, with a Taser you're the queen for fifteen feet. You can nail anything or anyone and, unless they've got a suit of armor, your probe can zip right through a couple inches of protective clothing. They're going down! It's instantaneous. Of course, you've got to get both prongs you're firing into them, like Raul said, but at such close proximity that's a pretty sure thing. We're talking about fifty thousand volts here, so they're not thinking about anything else for a full half minute, that's for sure! That's fifty thousand volts! And our stun guns start at one hundred thousand volts. We peak out at five hundred thousand volts. When you're getting in the higher echelons, you're talking about a police weapon. We don't want any lawsuits. Anyway, fifty thousand is more than enough. They're completely down and out for thirty seconds! You've got plenty of time to head for the hills, but you don't have to break your leg doing it, 'cause they're not feeling too chipper after they come to, either. See, it's strictly a shoot-and-run deal for you, 'cause no assailant is up for the chase after being Tased. No, they're down on their knees wondering what hit 'em. Some of them couldn't get up if you paid 'em! They're all confused and nothing's working right—they look like a box full of newborn kittens. See, it messes up the brain and everything gets disoriented. Oh," she added, picking up one of Jo's downloads and holding it up before her, "and this one's got a built-in laser. Puts out a red dot you just train on 'em and shoot, so you can nail 'em at night—really put out their lights, so as to say! Or make 'em see a new set of stars!" The woman laughed.

But Jo shuddered. "This all sounds very painful!"

"Well, it's not fun," agreed the woman, "but what they had in mind was no fun for you either!"

"Can I do them any real damage?"

The woman paused. "Well," she said, "normally, no, not at all. But I won't lie to you—there's always a risk. These kind of weapons, as harmless as they look and as nonlethal as the companies tell you they are, well, they're still extremely potent and not for practical jokes. These are strictly defensive weapons to save your life and your safety from rape and battering and any deadly assault. You use them only when you're in peril—to save your own life. You also don't want to hit anybody in the liver with a tranquilizer dart, if you want them around afterwards. You don't have time to ask them if they have an allergy to whatever drug you're got in the dart you're using, and you've probably seen already that the literature is full of warnings about 'excited delirium,' which can be a fatal reaction in drug addicts, especially ones on uppers like cocaine. It can also happen to the mentally ill. It's not common, but it can make them stop breathing or have their heart stop. So, this is very serious—strictly a 'you or them.' You don't want to risk getting a manslaughter rap and going up yourself for using a tranquilizer rifle or a Taser or a stun gun that's shot in the wrong place or too powerful a voltage just because you wanted to make completely sure you could walk away! So, that's why they call it a 'stun gun.' You just wanna stun 'em—put them out of commission, not out of their misery." This time she smiled, but did not laugh.

"I think I'm finally getting the difference," pursued Jo, deadly serious about the whole thing.

"Okay, here it is," said the woman, spelling it out like a third-grade teacher, "the Taser or stun gun delivers an electric shock at close range— touch him with the stunner, or shoot him with the electrode barbs. That takes away the control of those muscles an assailant wanted to use on you. The Taser's is a fifteen-foot range because both metal probes have to hit them, and the cost of it is pricey too. These on the screen start around three hundred bucks. But, they're awfully comforting at close range. The stun gun is also electric and really short range, but way cheaper. It sends out an electric shock, and, remember, you have to touch them with it. With the Taser, if they fall on you while you're zapping them, you're gonna get it too!"

Jo looked at her baffled, so the woman explained, "You see, they've become an instant conductor of the electricity you're shooting into them. While it's going in—it will nail anyone touching them."

Jo nodded her head, so the woman proceeded. "If you're doing hand-to-hand combat, then you want the stun gun—the Taser's for short-range distance. Up close, then you would need, instead, an electric night stick you can wham 'em with—we carry those as well."

Jo looked confused, so the woman spelled it out again. "Look, it's simple. The stun gun is bam! He's got a hold of you—you wiggle your hand out of the stranglehold and touch him with the stun gun—it's bam—he's down and you're out—out of there! The Taser is a thirty-second full body treatment. A deluxe charge! It keeps on giving. He's still touching you and you're gonna get it too. It's not so sweet dreams for both of you! You wanted range? The Taser is done with range!"

Jo nodded.

The woman raised her eyebrows and patted Jo on the hand. "See, you just zap and run—with range or without! Oh, and the Taser has a built-in stun gun feature—just in case you miss. You get your money's worth!"

Jo's own head felt like it was being stunned with data. She was processing as fast as she could.

The woman smiled and raced on, "See what I mean? Anyway, the tranquilizer is a whole other affair. It shoots a dart at a greater range. This also knocks them out, but it takes a while—like five minutes. That's okay if you're a game warden and hunting down caribou to band or something. You'll have plenty of time to stick a band on their ear while they're out 'nighty night.' But, you don't want to shoot 'em and immediately head right out of the bush to see how it's taking effect. They're gonna be flailin' around—and some of these tuskers weigh tons—so give 'em some space. All of these I'm showing you are CO_2 driven and considered very humane." She paused and looked Jo over. "They are for the careful. You're not even noticed by the target, if you don't screw up the shot. Nobody will know where it came from if you don't telegraph it, because these are practically silent. They're lightweight, too, so they're versatile. And they are extremely accurate—if you can shoot. That depends on you."

"I can shoot," confirmed Jo.

Just then, the salesman Raul returned with an armful of items and more carried by two assistants. "Just put them down. Thanks," he said. And the assistants left. Neither of them looked at Jo. She could see discreetness was the rule here.

The salesman opened a large box and brought out the crossbow. It looked to Jo like a bow on a modified open gun frame—something like a miniature skeet pull you could do by hand.

"It's light," pointed out Raul, handing it to Jo. "Right, Abby?"

"Right!" agreed the woman. "Like I said, two point four pounds, eighty-pound pull. And a crossbow is even self-cocking."

"How much are we talking here?" asked Jo.

"About thirty dollars U.S."

"That's in my price range." Jo hefted it. "This may work for one of my people," she murmured.

Raul and Abby exchanged glances.

"You planning to start a war, *Señorita*?" Raul asked.

"I want to protect my family," said Jo, quietly.

"Uh huh," grunted the man, noncommittally.

"How much were you planning to spend?" Abby ventured.

"I have a ceiling of a thousand dollars to work with," said Jo, firmly, looking at them both. "I need tranquilizer rifles and my budget is a thousand. I can't go over that."

"The rifles are expensive," said the woman. "What we've been showing you is low budget. Don't forget, we've got cheap blow guns for twenty bucks and less. Did we say they're modeled on the kind they use in the Amazon? They're very effective. And the darts they shoot—you can't swallow them. They're very well made. Even the cheaper ones."

"And the rifles?" asked Jo.

"That's another world. You want one with a scope, we're talking half your budget or more."

"You've got used items as well," Jo reminded her.

"Well, yes, we do and those are all guaranteed. What do we have, Raul?"

He was back on the computer and punching away. "Wait!" he said, "Here's a honey. This is a $600 gem, scope and all. Great shape. We can give it to you for half price." He ran through the stock offerings. "I have a $200—shows a bit of wear, but the mechanism is all replaced. How many do you need?"

"I'd like to buy two, if I can, plus one Taser and some of your other items."

"I don't know," hesitated Abby. "This may run you a bit over a thousand. . . ."

Jo paused and shuffled her papers together. "I've been looking at a similar store in Santiago. In fact, I'm going near there on my way back. I was thinking of stopping and seeing what they have to offer. Doing a little comparison shopping. There's also the net. I notice if I sign up for a gift card program, I can drop some of these prices drastically." She paused to let that sink in and then added, "Oh, did I mention I am prepared to pay today in cash when the price is right?"

"I think we can make the thousand dollars work," the woman assured her.

"Good," said Jo.

All four of them helped her carry her purchases out to her rental car, filling the trunk and the back seat. A seriously shaken Jo drove away with Abby's last warning echoing in her head: "Remember this, ma'am. These things can kill if you hit the wrong spot. Hit them in the butt to be safest with the tranquilizers and then run, because a lot can happen in a five minute lag time. If you can't get away and they catch up with you, then use the stunners. That will do it! The Taser is your close-range guarantee. Good luck!"

Whew!, thought Jo. I'll need more than luck to pull off a nonlethal encounter that is actually going to work, if it comes to that, Jo told herself. This is all crazy and may not be the right way to go. I may have just wasted a thousand dollars. But I can't come back here tomorrow. I'm going to need a lot of wisdom to think this through and a lot of grace to pull it off. And not having the time or the company to treat herself to an elaborate restaurant, she worked her way from the Conde over to the Hermanos cafeteria on Independencia, stood in the food line, bought two meat *pasteles* wrapped up in plantain leaves, side orders of rice and beans and some *platano maduro*, all washed down with pineapple juice, and, so fortified, headed out of the capital and back home to Barahona, her car a moveable arsenal of nonlethal equalizers and her computer, briefcase, and head also loaded with data.

40

WHATEVER RICKY EXPECTED WHEN he opened his door to admit his friend, it certainly wasn't "Hey! I'm going to take the new *cacica* to see the problems beyond Las Lajas and I want you to come along with us." Ricky stood, stilled, in an instant disorientation so complete he vaguely wondered for one wild moment if this is what it felt like to be "tazed." Tomás handed him back his gun, wrapped in burlap.

"What?" Ricky stared at him dumbfounded, simply holding on to the gun.

"You heard me," said Tomás.

"Are you crazy?"

"Are we going to stand in the doorway or are you letting me in?"

"I'm thinking about it," grumbled Ricky, stepping only grudgingly away enough for Tomás to squeeze in. "What's all this change of heart about?"

Tomás turned one of the straight-back chairs at the table around and nodded toward the rocking chair. Ricky sat down in it and leaned back. If there was anything in body language, he was saying volumes, drawing as far away from Tomás as possible. The wall was next, and then he would be outside the window.

"I'm just seeing things clearer," said Tomás.

"Well," said Ricky, "she's got to prove herself by herself. I'm not getting involved."

"Who ever proved themselves by themselves?" scoffed Tomás.

"Well, why should I help her?"

"Maybe because all you and I have been to her so far is a pain in the butt. I spoke up against her at the chiefs' meeting."

"So?'

"So, now I'm thinking they were right to kick me out. I wasn't thinking through anything. I was just parroting back my prejudice."

"Somebody tell you to say that to me—like her?" demanded Ricky, leaning forward now in the chair, getting more aggressive.

"Naw! I just thought about it. Even the great Enrique surrounded himself with an army. She's doing the same thing. She's got everybody working for her."

"Ahhhh!" exclaimed Ricky, exasperated. "I can't believe I'm hearing this from you."

"Well, believe it," said Tomás, firmly. "She's been gracious to me, and I'm going to be the same with her."

Ricky completely ignored what he said and hit on one of his main concerns. "So, are you going to stand around and watch her turn the Tribe into a church?"

Tomás paused and thought that over for a minute. Then he replied, "I never considered this, but just look at our ceremonies—like the one we had when she was inducted—all those prayers and invocations to Yocahu. Sounds like we got one foot in already. And, again, look at Enrique."

"Well, I'm not putting the other foot in!"

"Suit yourself," said Tomás, standing up.

"I can't believe you're saying this," protested Ricky, getting up himself and now all but blocking the door. "What has she got? Some kind of magic incantation that's got you mesmerized? Is that it? Maybe she's a shaman after all." If it had not been his own floor, he might have spit out his disgust.

"You know," said Tomás, leveling his eyes at him, "I think you've misjudged her completely. I think you could use a bit of the attitude she's got. She doesn't think she knows everything. . . ."

"Well, that's for sure," snapped Ricky.

"She's thoughtful and kind and firm at the same time. I think the chiefs were right in testing her out for *cacica*."

Ricky's eyes widened. "What? Did you fall in love with her?"

Tomás thought that over. "I guess I could, but, no, I just think that she's going about things carefully but progressively. I like the old ways, but she's not changing them. No, she's preserving them." He was thinking about the Rosary, but, if Josefina wasn't going to reveal what he had done, why should he?

Ricky was speechless. His mouth dropped open. He simply stared at Tomás, trying to gauge the depth of this damage. Neither spoke, but just stared at each other. Finally, Ricky broke the silence. "Whatever happened to 'We need a man for this job'?" he sneered. And then, less aggressively and more toward cajoling, "What about how her own uncle, Inti Archer, accomplished so much with his over-the-top, seize-the-reins, get-it-done-now personality?"

Tomás paused and then said, "Another person for another age. He did what he did in his time because he was the best person for it—gifted by YaYa to lead."

"I can't believe I'm hearing this in religious terms. What's happening to you, my friend?"

"I think I'm growing up. You could certainly use a bit of what she has to offer. I certainly need it. The religion is part of our heritage. The thoughtfulness before she plunges in is part of our age. Anyway," he started heading for the door, "I think she should see the devastation. Maybe even watch the *contrabandistas* as they strip our forest and make it like the ruin they leave behind in Haiti. I think she should see the army they've got there protecting them."

"What can she do?" scoffed Ricky.

"She's trained as a community organizer," Tomás reminded him. "Don't sell that short. I think with her training she can do a lot more than I can do. And," he put his hand on the latch, "I think she's better equipped for a job like this than you are—Mister Communications Expert."

"Well, that was a nasty cut!" protested Ricky, affronted.

"No," said Tomás, as he headed out the door, "that was a wake-up call."

He left Ricky standing in the doorway, affronted but pensive.

41

A s soon as Jo had driven into range, she punched up her aunt on her cell phone.

"Nanixi, Mi Corazón, what do you need?"

"Aunt Aña, can you get me an anesthesiologist and a ranger we can trust?"

"Hmmmm, let me think a second." There was a pause, then Anacaoana's voice was back on but broken up as Jo rounded a hill.

"Just a second, I'm losing you," Jo shouted into the phone. "I've got to find a place to stop. I'll call you back."

"No," crackled Aunt Aña, "I'll hang on, if I can." But the phone went dead.

What seemed to Jo an interminable set of minutes turtled by until she saw a break in the hills ahead. On a rise, she squeezed her car over to the side and tried again. She hit redial and then, "Are you still there?" she shouted into the phone.

"I'm here—and not deaf yet!"

"What did you say when I lost you?" asked Jo, and then she added, "I never want to lose you, too."

Aunt Aña chuckled. "You won't. We have a man from the Tribe who's an anesthesiologist just over at the hospital in Jimani—right in your own jurisdiction—but why on earth would you want to talk to someone like that?"

"I'll tell you later," Jo parried. "And the ranger?"

"Yes, I know someone who is connected up with Cesfront—*El Cuerpo Especializado de Seguridad Fronteriza,*" then she switched to English, "You know, the agency that specializes in border security? I guess it's something like your Homeland Security in the States, but this one focuses on the border with Haiti."

"I got it," said Jo.

"Anyway," continued her aunt. "This is a good woman from the Tribe. You'll know her when you see her. The man is less active, but also faithful to the Tribe. He's a good man. They're both very loyal to us—each in their own way."

"You're a lifesaver!" said Jo.

The next call was to Haiti. Jo had put on speed dial each of the cell phone numbers of her ruling counterparts across the island, but it still took her a number of kilometers' travel to connect with *Cacique* Louis Gama Manabauba Paix. "¡*Bendiciones*! Blessings, *Cacique*," Jo greeted him in Spanish and then English and then, switching to French, she identified herself, "*C'est Josefina Archer.*"

Immediately, he switched to English. "Good day, *Cacica*," he greeted her in his low, guttural voice. "How can I be of service to my new colleague?"

"May I come and visit you? I have some questions as I follow up the tasks I have been given."

"Absolutely not!" he replied immediately. "I will come to you. The border roads are not safe now for a woman traveling alone. I assume you are driving by yourself? Is that correct?"

"I am. But, I could switch to a bus."

"A bus would be better, but, as a matter of fact, we are driving too. I am in the van with Professor Renault—you remember him from the meeting of *caciques*?"

Jo gasped. "I do indeed! Meeting with him is one of the chief reasons I am coming to see you! Where are you now?"

"We're coming up from Port-au-Prince on our Route 102. We're heading to Santo Domingo to meet with a professor there. . . ."

"It wouldn't be Raymondo Ortiz, would it?" Jo gasped again.

"It is," said *Cacique* Paix. "How did you guess?"

"I was just in to see him yesterday. Would you please hold the line for a second—please!"

"Of course," he replied cordially.

Jo checked her rearview, signaled for a good quarter of a mile to let everyone know her intentions, and then squeezed over to the side of the road and stopped again. The horns still blared in warning as they shot by, but Jo ignored them. "Let me check the map," she said, fumbling it out of the glove compartment and spreading it out over the steering wheel. "Let's see, where are you crossing the border?"

"At Mal Paso. Then we're going through Jimani, where the roads divide."

"I'm not far," said Jo. "Do you know the hospital there?"

"Everyone knows the hospital!" exclaimed the chief. "We had many of our countrymen treated there during the great earthquake. We owe those generous people a great debt."

"I am already outside Barahona, I can be there in about an hour."

"We need to go through the border guard and the traffic is congested, so it will take us about the same time. Where would you like to meet us?"

"How about in the visitors lounge at the entrance?" suggested Jo. "Or, better yet, at the new cafeteria—I will treat everyone to a meal."

"You don't have to do that, Josefina," protested the chief.

"I want to do it," she said. "All of this is a great boon to me. I have spoken in depth to Professor Ortiz and I heard the excellent presentation of Professor Renault, but now I need to be schooled from your perspective and learn of the human side of this thorny problem of the contraband charcoal trade. It seems to me it is as much or more about culture and survival as it is about business."

"That is correct," said Louis Paix. "Many Dominicans don't really understand that dimension, even in our own Tribe, divided as it is itself by this border. But, without an understanding, we can solve nothing."

"Then we're set," said Jo. "And I thank you from the bottom of my heart." Then revving up her motor, she insinuated herself into the traffic by flooring the pedal and, after a heartstopping entry, flew down the winding road with everyone else, pausing only to bump over the speed bumps in each town and hand oranges out through the driver's window like she was running for the mayor of each *pueblo* as she moved inexorably on. She had distributed a bag of fruit to all who asked before she cruised into Jimani and found a place to park at the famous hospital there. She raced in and checked the cafeteria, but the Haitian travelers had not yet arrived. Port-au-Prince is just on the other side of the border, and she had covered twice that distance in the time that had elapsed since her cell phone call, but that was the way of the official border crossings: crowded and often complex. Immediately, on seeing she had some waiting space, she dialed her Aunt again.

"*Nanixi, Mi Corazón*, what do you need now?"

"I'm sorry to bother you again, Aunt Aña."

"Never a bother. What can I do for you?"

"I am at the hospital at Jimani. I am waiting for *Cacique* Louis Paix, Professor Renault, and their party. I am wondering if I can touch base with the anesthesiologist. Can you give me his name?"

"Wilson Perez, but I can do better than that. I will call him and ask him to stop by and see you—where are you now?"

"In the new cafeteria."

"You mean where they put in that little food court?"

"Yes, that's what I mean."

"Wait there by the chicken kiosk—I call it the chicken shack, but what's its name? —Ummm, oh, ah! —the Pollo Más Supremo booth—and I'll have him stop by, It's right by the door."

Jo waited ten minutes when a man hurried in, looking all around. He had on a light green coverall and a large plastic head cover. He had a face mask pulled down and plastic gloves in his hand. Jo rose up immediately and hurried over. "Are you the new *cacica*?" he asked immediately.

"Yes, Doctor Perez! Thank you so much for taking this time to meet me."

"I have only seven minutes," he said.

"Here is my cell phone number," said Jo proffering a small slip of paper at him. "I am based at Las Olas outside Barahona," she said.

"I know Las Olas and, of course, your uncle Inti Archer—a great man."

"Yes," said Jo. "May I bring a small group to meet with you at your convenience tomorrow or the next day? Could you find a way to fit us in? We need advice on the use of tranquilizer darts and stun guns."

"You're hunting big game?" He looked at her quizzically.

"You might say that," hesitated Jo.

"You're using them on people," he answered sagely.

"We're going into the forest to check out the contraband runners, and we need some protection. I am opposed to lethal weapons."

He nodded. "Stay away from opiods like M99—one drop can kill a human! They didn't sell you that, did they?"

"No, they didn't. "

"What are you using—air propulsion? CO_2? What kind of weapons?"

"We have two tranquilizer rifles, about a dozen little stun guns, a Taser, and some pepper spray, but that's only if we're desperate. In fact, it's all only if we're desperate."

"What's the drug they sold you?"

"It's a barbiturate. They said it was like a form of valium strong enough to put anyone to sleep, but there's a lag time, so we have the stun guns too."

"And you're planning to use these on workers cutting down trees?"

"No, not at all," explained Jo quickly. "There's a small army guarding them. This is the group against whom we are protecting ourselves. But, if all goes well, we should remain undetected. We are, after all, Tainos. I'm bringing the best of our Tribe schooled in woodcraft."

The anesthesiologist nodded his head. "Shoot them in the backside," he said, "and then get away. They will be preoccupied, because the dart hurts and they will thrash around, but, if they're soldiers, and they catch on, they can shoot at you, even if wildly, or they can give chase, at least for a minute or two. If they get near enough, you'll have to stun them, but remember that all this affecting their nervous system can be dangerous to them. Just do one thing: Tranquilize them, or taze them, or stun them, but don't do them all, unless they're ready to kill you. You don't want to murder somebody if you can help it. What I'm trying to say is don't overdo it. Act defensively, not offensively."

Then he added, "I have to go now, but here, copy down my number as I give it to you." Jo punched it into her cell phone. "Call me and bring over your delegation and I can tell you what else I know about this. I don't know a lot about the weapons themselves, but I do know about Azaperone and Combelen and Etorphine—which you never use on people—and Immobilon and Sodium Thiopental and all the rest. I know the drugs. Did you go to the shop on the *Conde* in the capital or the Santiago one to get them?"

"Yes, in the capital."

"Good. They're both fine and they won't sell you darts with a lethal dosage. So, you're probably okay. But, again, be prepared, and don't take any of this lightly. Different people react differently to different drugs. You gave yourselves a good choice, but do everything with great care. Lives are in your hands—your friends' and your enemies.'"

"Yes, thank you," said Jo. "Thank you, so much."

The man nodded and hurried away.

A pensive Josefina sat down and waited for the Haitians to come, mulling all of this over in her mind.

When the Haitians finally arrived forty minutes later, Jo was completely prepared. She had satellite maps spread out on the table and was listing the coordinates of her target area pinpointed as best she could from the report to her by Tomás. She had put together a two-page summary highlighting each major point from her conversations at the University of Santo Domingo and a one-page summary of Professor Renault's diagnosis of the ecological dimensions of the situation. The Haitian experts were suitably impressed, but Jo swept it all aside and said, "What a trial you must have endured at the border check."

"Yes, from both sides!" groaned *Cacique* Paix. "Why they imagine we would be smuggling fresh eggs in or out of the country is anybody's guess!"

"At least they didn't check our trunk for bags of charcoal," smiled Professor Renault. "We were going the wrong way!"

"Maybe, they'll do it on the way back," said a young man, smiling at her—probably a driver, thought Jo.

"We have two vehicles. Border guards are always interested in the second vehicle. They take forever checking it—hoping for bribes."

Everyone nodded.

"But, now," said Jo, "let us ease the strain of that ordeal and have some refreshment. I'm having a full meal here at the Pollo Más Supremo—chicken, rice and beans, salad, maybe even ripe plantains, if they have them. I would like to order full meals for all four of you."

"You don't need to feed us," said one of the young drivers, humbly.

"Yes, I do," said Jo, "and I want you to eat well or my feelings will be hurt. The capital is a long drive and the roads demand a full stomach and a watchful eye."

"Thank you, *Cacica*," they said, nearly in unison. And the second added, "I see they have tacos. We never get tacos."

"Yes, they're the rage in Santo Domingo right now, and they're springing up all over. It's the Mexican invasion. By all means, order what you want, but, please eat enough for the journey." Jo looked to the chief and the professor.

"*Cocina criolla* is fine for me," said the chief. "I like the different style from the way we do it at home. It may all be rice and beans, but it's a world of difference."

"I'll join you too, and thank you, *Cacica*," said Pierre Renault.

Jo rose and said to the eager staff of the new Pollo Más Supremo kiosk, "Please put these gentlemen's orders on the same bill, and I'll be back in a moment to add mine and pay it all. Please come," she said to the two young drivers, "and we'll see what the Dominican version of Mexico has to offer."

The last thing the chiefs heard as Jo guided the two young drivers across the cafeteria to the taco stand was the voice of the second driver announcing, "I don't know what an *enchilada* is, but I've heard of them and I'd love to try some."

The meal together went well, and so did the briefing. Pierre Renault was impressed at how much Jo understood, and all of them added vastly to her knowledge of the social dimension of the problem. "It's about people and history as much as it is about business—but at base level it's all about survival needs." This was the message each shared over and over again and in many different ways. And Jo listened and wrote notes and felt the voice of an entire people speak to her through these colleagues, united with her by the common First Nations bond, but, yet, so different, so very different in perspective and culture and historical understanding. To say a new world was opening to her in this study would minimize the way she felt. She had grown up a good portion of her life here in the Dominican Republic and took the Haitian connection for granted, but she felt now that she had understood next to nothing of the burdens on these people who shared the western tip of this same island, roughly a third of it.

Jo remained for the rest of the day in Jimani and took a room at a small hotel near the central park, where she mapped out her plans for the next two days and began making cell phone call after cell phone call, leaving her room only to buy phone cards, replenish herself with meals, and walk through the park and the streets of Jimani for exercise before returning to plan her reconnoitering campaign as carefully as she could so as little as possible would go wrong. Much, she realized, for her and for her people on both sides of the border was at risk, and she felt so thoroughly inadequate to handle it—so she soaked each step in fervent prayer.

42

Two mornings later, the meeting took place very early, and long before Wilson Perez had to report for his seven a.m. shift or the hospital
opened for visitors. Jo had used the intervening day to rest, and she had
spent much of it sleeping. Now she was fresh and ready to go.

The ranger was already there and waiting for them when she pulled
in at five thirty a.m., the same time she was gratified to see that Tomás and
those he had gathered arrived. The moment Jo stepped out of the car, she
recognized the ranger as Eridania Rosario, an active tribal representative
in her own district and a fast friend of her Uncle Sol. About ten years older
than Jo, so in her late 30s, the ranger was about five feet, eight inches in
height, well muscled and sleek as a wood nymph, dressed in forest green
and thick army-style boots. She had a side arm holstered at her waist and no
doubt more artillery in the jeep. Her partner remained behind, sitting in the
vehicle, out of earshot, obviously on her request. After Eridania gave a brief
greeting to each one she knew in the gathering assembly, she left nothing
vague. "I can't officially approve of what you do, or sanction this invasion of
the woodlands. But I can't stop you, because they are public lands."

"People live in them," growled a familiar voice. Jo looked away from
the ranger and to her astonishment discovered Ricky standing on the edge
of the gathering. She had assumed he would not come. But here he was. . . .

"That's right, *Nitayno*." The ranger replied matter-of-factly, as much to
Jo and the rest of her company as to the acerbic Ricky. Obviously, she knew
him well and was unperturbed by him. "But they do so at their own risk,"
she added. And then she said to them all, "At the same time, the agency
understands the Tribe's attitude toward the forest and its prior claim on the
mountains and the undeniable history of deliverance that took place there
in the ancient days, and all of this counts for much. If you will keep me
posted, I will look the other way."

"We will let you know each step of the way—where we are, what we discover, if anything, though it is doubtful we will discover anyone, since hit-and-run seems to be the way they avoid detection."

"It has been their style," agreed the ranger. "But," she warned them, "there has been a disturbing change being reported to us—in rumors mainly—and it has caused a lot of concern in many places. I tell you this, because I have to warn you that the Dominican army is also involved now and you cannot make a deal with the general the way you can with me."

"Understood," said Jo and looked around at her group for confirmation. All of them nodded, even Ricky, she noted. As she looked at each, she thanked God for these Tomás had gathered. In addition to himself and the recalcitrant Ricky were all four of the original party Tomás had brought into the woods with him when they had discovered the *contrabandistas* at work: Letty, Sergio, Rafael, and his cousin Pablo. All of them were children of the forest. They were joined by four more. Ariadne, a much larger woman than Letty, who had herself been a former ranger, decorated for her bravery and now retired, and her daughter Adelina, an athlete who had participated in the *batey* game at Jo's inauguration and had played a hard and fast game for the winners, creating space for Ruby and Letty to score. New to Jo were two young men who were identical twins and went by the nicknames *Uno y Dos,* "One" and "Two," tagged on them early by their playmates. Both of them were reared in the forest and knew woodcraft from birth, as, essentially, did all of her team. Watching the begrudging Ricky, Jo decided he had come along not so much to help her, but to keep tabs on the proceedings and, hopefully, watch Jo fail. And, when Jo overheard his not-so-disguised side snarl to Tomás, "We're Christa and her twelve disciples!" she felt her impression was confirmed. Jo ignored him, but as she turned away, she caught a glimpse of Tomás glaring at him. Perhaps she had made one convert to her leadership. The rest of the group remained impassive, as if the remark had not been made.

"Thank you both for coming out at this early hour," said Jo, indicating it was time to begin. And Wilson Perez immediately began in detail to describe to the gathering the effects of the barbiturate, which he had now read on the label of the dart packets. He warned them all of the probable impact on their targets and the dangers of overdosing and lag time to take effect. There were no questions.

Then Eridania Rosario gave everyone severe warnings about the dangers of missing their targets and what would happen to them when an enemy discovered them and how contraband runners had even killed a ranger. So, her advice was to stay away from any militia whether in force or even individually: "These are drawn from soldiers of fortune and they are ruthless, if the rumor is true and there truly is some kind of militant involvement!"

She cautioned the gathering that the only sensible recourse was to approximate a count of the soldiers and workers, steal away from the scene as quickly as possible, and text message her immediately the strength of the *contrabandistas* and their coordinates and she would alert Cesfront who would alert the military. This was the only wise route to follow. She added that they should not be surprised to find that the contraband runners were gone already, since this had been the greatest frustration with tracking them. Unpredictability had been the poachers' greatest weapon to avoid detection. So, for the Tainos to avoid confrontation, they should proceed carefully and, if the woods were indeed empty, do a reconnaissance of the extent of the damage and report that back to her. Then she turned to Jo and asked, "And you've made me a map of where you are going, its coordinates, your timetable, and how many of you there will be?" Jo handed it over to her without a word. "Good," said the ranger. Then she turned to the group once more. "Understand," she cautioned them one final time, "These weapons you are bringing are strictly defensive. Only a fool or an untrained and unthinking civilian would face an armed guard with them." She frowned at them all severely.

Ricky, in turn, glared openly at Jo. His disdain was nearly palpable.

Jo continued to ignore it, used to him and everyone else throughout her whole life who had dismissed her either as an "Indian" or a "broad" or both. She was a First Nations' Woman, heir to a legend, and nothing was going to deter her from her duty. She warmly shook the hand of Wilson Perez and, on an impulse, gave a brief sisterly hug to Eridania Rosario, and then turned to the gathering. All eyes were on her as she simply ordered, "Let's move out!"

43

Two four-wheel-drive transports commandeered from the Tribe carried the team up into the mountainous region north of Jimani. They climbed up Route 48 well enough, but, when they turned into the little town of Boca Cachon and began in earnest to ascend the gravel road into the mountainous interior, the occupants could hear the strain of the shifting. This was high dry forest country. The little villages of Tierra Nueva and Las Lajas seemed like lonely sentries forgotten at the top, and beyond these were mainly birds and locusts until the frontier cut the mountain across the north, while far off over the hills, providing a nearly mirror image, the little outposts of Camillon and La Toison stood sentinel like counterpoints on a corresponding mountain gravel road in Haiti. To the east, more empty highlands awaited the fate of the far western hills, while to the southwest the mountain sloped down into the waters of Lake Saumatre, shared as it is between Haiti and the Dominican Republic.

In the vans, the group was a silent one, as befitted those reared in the woods, and so the ride was a quiet one. Jo herself had no desire to talk. She felt uneasy, yet the chance to think was not helping her either. One of the worst parts of this whole period, she realized, had been her utter sense of being alone—with or without others around. Without constant prayer, she realized, she would have been lost, for she felt the utter lack of human community. Certainly, she had her aunt, but Anacoana was not here. The *nitayna* had her own tasks to do and responsibilities pressing her in the northern region—as did Mara back in the mountains of Puerto Rico. Jo's own family was completely missing. Ruby she could not invite, for, small as she was, Ruby would have tramped through the forest like a raging heifer, ready to give those "contrabanders" a piece of her mind! Besides, she was wrapped up now in her budding love affair with the half-reformed Ismael Balenzuela—of all people! Ben was simply out for himself and currently untrustworthy and in disgrace for the Rosary escapade. Jo had no idea where

Daniela was, where her parents were, or even where Tomás, though present in the transport, was locating in his thinking.

Jo was a community organizer and the last thing she was working with here was a community. Nobody in either van had come along on her account. They were there for the forest only and would be here with or without Jo—and Jo was not certain whether, in their hearts, each of them considered her to be in the way. Ricky had come along clearly on account of her, but not at all to support her, but instead to watch her fail, she assured herself. She couldn't trust him to do anything to help. As far as the action/reflection model was concerned, Jo knew she herself was always strong on reflection and careful on action, so, for her to be successful, she had always relied upon a team to prod her forward. She needed that. Even the recovery of the Rosary of Enrique had been driven by Ismael's admittedly devious, unscrupulous cunning. His had been a morally equivocal strategy to adopt at best. Now, here she was again, in a moral dilemma, with no one here on her "team," with the possible exception of Tomás, with whom she felt comfortable enough to talk this issue out. And she was not sure if his support had only been momentary—a warmly grateful response ignited by her kindness that had flamed and now cooled. So, there was no one, really, to depend on and talk things out before acting, which was always what she did with past teams before finally acting. The simple fact was that she had had no time yet to build a real team with which to work.

As a result, all the immediate actors in this drama were basically unknown to her, and the few she did know—Ricky, for example—were not the best choice for the position they were holding. Case in point: Ricky was her director of communication, the one to report her activities to the world at large! That was so ironic, she thought. The one who communicates least with me and is rarely civil is my conduit to send my information to the world at large! But, right now, he was her only choice. She was stuck with him. She was stuck with all of these present participants, and how they would respond to her leadership under fire she had no idea. She hoped she would not have to find out.

Most people carry an ache around in themselves. Josefina Archer was no exception. Others won't necessarily see it, but it's there just the same. It may not be always in one's consciousness, but it's constantly present like the dull aching of a tooth or a softly pounding cramp in the side or a throbbing muscle pull—it's there to tell us something's wrong, and it shoulders its way into our consciousness when we pause and reflect. Something's always wrong, it asserts in an endless monotony. And, in Jo's particular case, it continued to lecture, whenever she had a free moment to reflect, it will stay wrong with you until the ones you love are fixed.

For Jo, sitting there morosely, everything seemed to be wrong with her family, and worry about them was the default position to which she continually regressed whenever the opportunity was thrust upon her. I can't do an operation on myself, she complained to herself. And even God won't do it. Mine is a long-distance pain that needs a remedy in someone else—several someone elses—and these I have not been able to fix. If I can't keep my family house in order, how can I expect to rule a Tribe? She put her face in her hands, as the van bumped along. Any onlooker would have assumed she was getting carsick. In reality, she was heartsick.

The rocky path beyond Las Lajas toward the edge of the border is pitted with holes and rugged with loose gravel, and the transports bounced and slid along until Tomás broke the human silence announcing in a voice grim and taut, "This is where we stopped before." The area was desolate and had not a sign of human life for miles: nothing but the ceaseless whirring of insects.

They pulled into a copse of twisting guacan trees that sufficiently hid the small troop carriers from anyone not close up in the sky or land, and they all piled out. In addition to the five and six passengers in each large vehicle were the boxes that Jo had purchased, and all her fellow travelers looked on with interest as the thousand dollars of surplus weaponry was unloaded.

"All of this may be unfamiliar to you, so please be careful with it. This is why we have such an early start" Jo explained. And, building on that morning's presentation by Ranger Eridania Rosario, she invested the next hour in taking them carefully through the paces of how each weapon worked, preparing to have everyone practice with dummy darts in trees right at the road's edge so as not to put any of their fellows in danger. "All of this is hasty. None of us is familiar with this equipment sufficiently to handle it in combat," she warned them all continually, "so this is just a precautionary measure." Several of them, however, appeared unconvinced.

"A gun is a gun," snorted Ricky. "How complex can these tranquilizers be? You load them. You shoot them. I have grown up with guns all my life."

"So have I," retorted Jo. "But I've never used one on anyone, have you?"

"Well, no," he admitted.

"I'm sure it's a whole different world—plus, don't forget—these people we are seeking are killers. They're armed with real guns and they've murdered a ranger already. They may not hesitate to kill any one of us, or all of us together. So, remember, we are not here to engage them. Not at all. The point of having Eridania Rosario involved is so that she can have highly skilled and armed rangers and army troops on call if we encounter anyone.

We simply text in our coordinates to her and she alerts them. We never even have to be seen or detected in any way."

Jo gazed around into totally impassive faces, registering neither assent nor dissent, so she plowed on. "Therefore, we need to exercise the greatest caution and simply view the scene from a distance, take as many pictures as we can, and then fade back here. Only in the direst unexpected conditions, if we stumble on any activity and if we absolutely have to, let's take the advice we heard this morning to heart: Shoot for the butt and then get out of there, because it will take five minutes to take a large soldier down, and any of them might start shooting wildly and actually hit one of us. Caution is better than calamity, so let's not court any emergencies." She looked around to still no response and figured, well, that's that.

All this time, Tomás had been eyeing the crossbows, and, as soon as he sensed it was time to divide up the weapons, he called out, "I'll take one of these. It's more traditional and so more fitting." Sergio immediately commandeered the second bow.

"I'll take that three hundred dollar tranquilizer rifle," grunted Ricky, the sub-chief, snatching it up. "I want the best I can get if I need to put someone down fast."

"I'll take a stun gun," said Letty. "I want a small and potent one. They aren't going to see me at all, but, if anyone does, that's all they'll see before the big flash. Wait! Let me have a couple of the hundred thousand volt ones!"

"Two-gun Letty," laughed Tomás.

"Who can tell these are guns?" countered Letty. "This one looks like a flashlight and this one's the size of a cigarette box."

"You don't even smoke," scoffed Ricky.

"I won't be the one smokin'!" grinned Letty.

Jo shook her head. She wanted this to be taken more seriously. "Someone's got to stay with the vans," she broke in. "Two drivers." She looked around.

"We'll do it," said Ariadne, "Adelina and myself."

"Ahhh, Ma!" protested her daughter. "I want to be in the action!"

"You're seventeen and you can drive like the wind. Everything in this venture is 'in the action.' The whole thing is dangerous from start to finish. I was a *guarda bosque* myself. I know exactly the kind of risks we're running. We will need cool heads here at home base to barrel these transports out and off the mountain the instant they all come tearing back." And Ariadne pointed her lips at the arming-to-the-teeth patrol. "You and I will be on guard the entire time, not playing dominos, or sleeping, or strolling around looking at the wildlife. For one thing," she explained to her daughter, "the closer they get to the devastation, the less they're going to find for shelter. There won't be much of anything. This is no stroll in the garden. These *contrabandistas* rip the trees out by the roots and any iguanas and other wildlife they find they capture and sell across the border where they eat anything that moves. It's going to look more like a desert than what we're seeing on this dirt road. The trees will be gone! So, be careful," she ordered everyone. "Don't plan on having too much to hide behind. This land is already very dry, and cutting swaths in the foliage destroys everything and turns it all to wasteland."

She paused: "Do you have your cell phone, Adelina?" she fired as a sudden request at her daughter.

"Well, yes, Momma."

"*Cacica*, give her your number and text us the second you are on the run out. We'll start the two transports and have them revved up and ready to fly as soon as you all appear."

"That's what we'll do," Jo ordered. "First of all, everybody put your phone on pulse. All we have to have is somebody calling in to alert our quarry someone's lurking about. Lizards don't have cell phones! And we've also got to stick together for safety. We should go out in two sets," Jo reasoned. "The first five to leave the forest must go at once, Ariadne. Get them out of here. Don't wait for the others. Tomás, you know the place we are seeking already. Can we divide up your former group and put each of us newcomers partnered up with one of your veterans?"

"A good plan, *Cacica*!" He looked around at his former companions.

"I'll go with Chief Jo," said Letty.

"So will I," volunteered Ricky to Jo's surprise. He saw her quizzical expression and growled, "Someone's got to take care of you!"

It figures, thought Jo, but what she said was, "Thank you."

Rafael, who was armed with their only Taser, stayed with Tomás, as did Sergio, and they added both twins, who always worked together. This gave them a team of five. With Jo were now Letty, Ricky, and Pablo, Rafael's quiet cousin, who carried the second rifle, which made four of them. With Ariadne and her daughter back at the jeeps, this made eleven of them in all—ten plus Jo—so Jo suddenly wondered about the point of Ricky's snide remark at the briefing section outside the hospital earlier that morning about "Christa and her twelve disciples." What was that all about? And then she realized he was including Wilson Perez and Eridania Rosario in her following. That was Ricky! Always choosing up sides! He was impossible to win over, and she found herself loathing the fact that he'd opted to come along. Well, there was nothing for it now but get it over with, and she looked down into the box. All the weapons were gone but a flashlight stun gun and the blow guns. Apparently, nobody wanted them. She looked around at the group, all familiarizing themselves with their weapons and those with tranquilizers already testing the empty practice darts she'd bought against the trees. "What about these extra blow guns?" she asked.

No one said anything, so it was left up to Ricky to growl, "Do we look like *jibaros* to you? This isn't the Amazon!"

Jo nodded and reached in and took one herself. They were sleek, and the woman at the store had convinced her they were easy to use and the dart was in no danger of being swallowed. "Feed it in and blow it out—it's designed to work and it works well!" she had been assured. The flashlight stunner would be helpful if night came, as unlikely as that seemed now so early in the day, but one never knew. Besides, she had no choice. That's what was left.

Jo had packed a knapsack for herself and she zipped the flashlight stun gun into it and fastened the blowgun to the side, and then she shouldered it.

"You planning to camp out?" challenged Ricky.

She considered ignoring him, but opted for the soft answer to turn away wrath. "I like to come prepared, and I don't want to lose anything I might need in the forest."

He nodded grudgingly. He eyed her water bottle and grunted, "You're certainly prepared. I'll give you that."

She nodded and called out to the others, "I packed in a case of water. Everyone should take one." They all did, and Ricky didn't question that. "Tomás," she called out again.

"*Cacica?*"

"Let's get a game plan!" and she brought a briefcase out from under the back seat of the transport she'd ridden in and produced a dozen aerial maps of the immediate wooded area surrounding them. They all crowded around and took one and she put hers up against a back window and said, "We're here, right?"

Tomás studied it. "Yes, we are."

"And, please show everybody, we're going—where?"

He stepped forward and in a moment pointed to another spot to the upper right of the map. "Here. You see the barren land over the border and this space here down the western slope? It's the devastation."

"Why don't we come in from two sides?" offered Ricky.

Jo nodded. "A good plan. I was thinking that myself."

"Are we ready to go," asked the eager Tomás.

"No," said Jo. "Now we need to be sure that everyone has everyone else's cell phone number in case we get separated."

Young Sergio groaned. "Everyone's?" he whined.

"Everyone's!" ruled Jo.

"I did the same with my party," Tomás confirmed her order. "It's foolish not to do so." He glared at Sergio, who went quiet.

"And," said Jo, "everyone especially needs to give their number to Adelina, so no one is lost." She looked into Sergio's silent, exasperated face and explained like a parent to a child, "A few moments of proper preparation now might save us hours of anxiety later." Young Sergio did all but hop around in anxiety, but he and all of them did as she directed and, finally, Jo judged they were ready to leave.

"Do we have to do bathroom stops now?" Sergio complained, glancing at Tomás out of his peripheral vision, but Tomás simply stood impassive, waiting.

Jo smiled and said, "You can do that in the forest, if there are still enough shrubs left." A burst of laughter eased everyone's tension.

And then Tomás said, "You should pray for us *Reverenda*. For safety for us all and for the wisdom of your God."

She stared at him, astonished, and then she understood. He had done it to support her. It was out of continued gratitude for the mercy she had extended him. She nodded and said, "Let's pray." And she did—for all of them.

And then, the strategy set, the two teams blended into the woods, each pursuing a different path, as quiet as lizards slithering over the moss.

Tomás's team was the first to enter. He grouped them behind himself and, having distributed machetes he had brought along in the transport van, he began to cut a swath through the bush for his team to follow him in.

"Did you remember to bring one?" challenged Ricky.

"No, I didn't," Jo confessed, "Tomás reminded me."

"Humph!"

"Did you?"

He showed her the machete in his hand.

"Thank you," she said.

And then, mollified, he admitted, "Tomás reminded me too. I didn't think of it on my own."

So, thought Jo, he can be fair! "Would you lead us in, please?" she asked.

"With pleasure. Let's go!" Ricky ordered their little team of four and, glancing at the map, he led them about twenty yards to the left to a fairly clear spot and then started slashing their way into the woods, following a series of herders' paths to minimize how much they had to cut.

Underfoot, the ground was basically stones and dirt. Several feet in, the dry vegetation closed around them. It was thick and tangled, all interwoven thorns and vines and dried branches. Cactus spiked up in clumps, and they worked their way around large rocks half obscured in the tangle of growth as the interior became small hills and hollows.

What they did not know is that a jeep with a single occupant had followed them undetected and was now secreted two hundred yards back up the road. Its lone occupant had crept through the woods and had lain in the brush off the road within earshot of all they had said. And now he shadowed these team members to the left, Jo's team, as they worked their way carefully through the high dry forest, he as stealthy and unexpected as they were.

44

BY A HALF HOUR into their trek, Jo was already slashed up from the thorns and the myriad of limbs. Her backpack kept getting caught, and she had to take it off in spots and cradle it in her arms to get around some of the boulders, thickly inlaid with brush. She had had the presence of mind to pack work gloves with her. Ricky was a surprisingly attentive leader, and he made sure all four of them were together in a tight band and no one was straggling. To Jo, skilled by her uncle in woodcraft, the other three still appeared to be moving much more effortlessly cutting through the tangle. Letty was nearby flitting like a small bird from limb to limb. Pablo was also small and agile, slithering like a lizard over the rocks, while Jo, as adept as she was, felt herself gangly and awkward and only muddling along. At least she was glad Ricky was not noticing what she considered her haphazard progress as he deftly slashed his path, and only what was needed to let himself squeeze through, as his muscles undulated with the rhythm. Step by step, he paused and listened.

Tomás and his group were now completely out of sight.

Jo and her team were working their way through a very thick hollow and could see nothing more than a few feet ahead when suddenly Ricky paused and stiffened. He cocked his head to the side, his right ear up. Jo and the others paused too and waited. "I think I hear something," he said in a hushed voice. "Letty?"

She slipped up beside him, "I've been hearing it for a while," she confirmed.

"I think we're going to see more than simply remains," he cautioned. "Let's proceed carefully."

"I'll take the rear," whispered Jo. "Letty, Pablo, you both should take the lead with Ricky, since you've been here before and will recognize the terrain as we approach it." They both stepped forward and, as Jo turned, her eye caught a glimpse of what looked like movement about thirty yards behind her. "Wait!" She paused and strained into the distance, but nothing else was forthcoming.

"Let's move on," said Ricky.

"Yes," said Jo, but she kept glancing behind herself.

Another half hour of careful progress and the sounds of work became unmistakable. They heard what sounded like chanting. Jo realized it was a work song, but she could not yet make out the words. Then Ricky stiffened again and this time he wrinkled his nose and pantomimed sniffing. Jo took a conscious breath and caught the acrid scent of burning.

"It's wood," whispered Ricky. "Our wood."

"Maybe I should go a few steps ahead," offered Letty.

Ricky thought that over and looked at Jo.

Jo nodded. "All right, but not too far."

"Right! Not too far!" echoed Ricky.

Letty smiled. "Who's worrying now?" she mocked him gently, and then crept forward. The other three stopped and waited. Pausing, Jo became aware of her immediate surroundings. Even seeing only a few feet ahead, she could identify roble and cambron and *caoba* (mahogany) trees, while all around her fluttered *mariposas*, small yellow butterflies. The sound of rustling was incessant, both from the endless whirring of locusts and honeybees and the strong day wind from the south rattling the mountain foliage. One thing she took note of: No one should ever starve here, for everywhere were saona and pocolobe cactus with their edible fruit, but, at the same time, water was scarce. She also wished she had made *viha*—that reddened natural insecticide the Tainos had adapted from carbon—because what she had put on earlier had been sweated away. At least she had had the presence of mind to cover up completely in camouflage and wear thick boots—even though everything was now soaked through with sweat and her cap nearly floated on her damp head.

She glanced forward and saw Letty lying prone now on a small rise ahead and then creep back down and signal to them with hand outstretched and flattened. Jo read: proceed slowly and with great caution.

Trees—thorns—cactus—hill—hollow rock—trees—thorns—cactus—hill—hollow rock—had all seemed to be rotating in nearly monotonous, endless repetition when, suddenly, Jo realized, they had arrived. Now she was glad her Uncle Sol had made sure that she would be perfectly fluent in "forest." Avoiding an ant colony, she inched her way over the stones, minimizing the crackling of fallen leaves, until she hunched over and crept up the rise as silently as did the others. She peered over.

There in what should have been a natural hollow a great ugly gap was torn out among the trees. Huge rounded piles of dirt over barely visible circles of logs had been constructed. Every foot around each pile's perimeter a stick poked out and holes had been made that puffed up smoke—the scent they had caught.

It looked to Jo like the fire mounds of hell.

About thirty Haitian men and some women with axes and hand saws and even twenty-inch-blade, gas-operated power saws were making a devastating gash in the trees that continued the forest across the clearing. A great, dark dirt path disappeared to the right toward the border. Jo, surveying the devastation and the workers who were attacking tree after tree, caught a movement in her peripheral vision and saw Tomás and his team on the far side of the same rise. Their view of the clearing was not impeded by the vast circles of smoldering wood, as was Jo's, and Tomás waved cautiously, out of sight of those in the newly hewn-out valley and then raised his clenched fist and put up his fingers one by one until all five were extended. Then he pointed back at the marauding.

Ricky shook his head no, vigorously, but far too close to resort to the bird calls each Taino used for self-identification or to signal retreat or attack, Tomás gave a pause signal with his hand and then fished something out of his pocket. In a moment, Ricky felt a pulsing at his side and pulled out his cell phone. The text message read: "Only 5 guards. 10 of us. We're going in."

"Ahhhhh," groaned Ricky and swished his hand back and forth in a hasty negative gesture. "He says there are only five guards. He's going to do something!" he warned Jo.

"No!" gasped Jo, and snapped her phone off the side of her backpack, starting to type a text message, but, before she could do so, Tomás had carefully leaned the crossbow down in a clear space on the top of the rim, steadied it and sited for a moment, and then he pulled the trigger. The bow was virtually silent. Jo and Ricky heard nothing from the shot.

But a second later a voice bellowed out, "OW! OW! I'VE BEEN STUNG! SOMETHING STUNG ME!" And there was a great commotion and a flailing about as a man in a uniform spiraled along the ground up and down, reaching behind himself, as four others came running. No sooner did they arrive when two more shots now from two crossbows hit the first two—one in the thigh and the other glancing off a kneecap. Both of these went down.

"They're darts!" screamed one in Spanish and ripped the dart out of his leg. "There! On the hill!" The fourth and fifth men swung their automatic weapons up and began to pour fire into the hillside. Tomás's team slid down the hill wildly and stumbled toward brush cover as the soldiers charged.

"Pablo!" hissed Ricky and both men stood up, took aim with the remaining two tranquilizer rifles and fired at the charging men. Even up close the firing was simply a muted rush of air. The two syringe darts caught the soldiers near the top of the rise. Ricky's hit his target in the top of the arm near the right shoulder. Pablo's entered his man in the side of the thigh. The one hit in the leg stumbled against the other and they both toppled down the rise back to the bottom. But just as they were falling, the fifth soldier, whose knee had only been grazed by the fleeing Sergio, limped to the top of the hill and paused as the five Tainos of Tomás's patrol were still scattering for the woods. But before he could raise and level his gun, Letty, leaping from cover, raced down the rise and across the space as fleetly as on the batey field. By the time her movement caught the soldier's eye, he turned to find her dashing upon him. He tried to swing his gun around just as she jumped upon him and triggered an electric arc into him—dead center. He went down like he was poleaxed, and then she waved her stun gun at the two soldiers writhing on the ground and, pointing at their rifles, said in heavily accented, but fully legible English: "Don't even be thinking upon it!"

Instantly seeing this insignificantly small native woman with no uniform or rifle attacking her militia guard, the huge woman overseer Tomás had seen before was suddenly galvanized into life. "Hiyahh, *Tu!*" she shouted and bounded forward, reaching out huge hands to clamp on Letty to shake the life out of her. In one sinuous movement, Letty swiveled down out of her reach, snapped up her second hand, and let go another arching blast that caught the woman full in the chest. Letty dove to the right and rolled out of the way as her huge opponent sprawled down where she had been.

The workers, all leaping forward, following their leader, instantly skidded to a halt, dumbstruck at the collapse of everyone protecting them, not knowing what to do, what to think.

Jo snapped, "Show of force!" and rose up in full view of all, waving her backpack back and forth like a flag. Ricky reared up next to her, following her lead, holding his long gun up in full sight, and Pablo leaped up, waving his next to them.

"On the ground—all of you, now!" bellowed Jo, in a tone as low as she could go. Letty, snapping up from the ground with a kip, shot off a warning arc that crackled in the air, and all the workers went down prone in full force all across the clearing.

The entire attack had hardly taken more than a minute.

Tomás and his team, clamoring back up the rise, skidded down into the arena, Tomás distributing something from a knapsack he carried as he ran forward. Jo could see what looked like ropes as he and his team began moving from fallen soldier to fallen soldier, expertly binding up each guard as they writhed more and more slowly on the ground, the tranquilizer darts beginning to take effect. Both stunned targets of Letty's were still unconscious.

The makeshift kilns, quietly smoldering all about their nearly thirty-foot-oblong expanses, were sending up grey plumes of smoke. Some of the workers on the ground were shouting, some crying. But over top of their din, Jo detected another sound.

"Quick!" she screamed. "Let all the workers go!"

"What?" several of her company shouted back.

"Send them up the road! I hear something coming!"

Jo ran to the edge of the mass of workers spread-eagled on the ground and shouted in French to go—now—up the road they had cleared toward the border, and never return. No one moved. She nudged a small man closest to her with her foot and said in a kind but commanding voice— "Go! I am setting you free, but you must run up the road to be safe." He got warily to his feet, flinching and staring at her from half downcast eyes. She nodded at the road and he began a loping run toward it. Several others came up to their knees and then Letty let off another crackling electric arc and Jo screamed, "*¡Vayan y nunca regresen!*" No one needed a translation for this command to "Get out and never return!" and they all scattered up the road.

The huge woman overseer began to stir and Letty shouted at her, "Come on you! or I'll stun you again!" But nothing worked on the leader and she lay on the ground bewildered. Jo was filled with great pity and remorse and she shouted at Tomás, "Did you bring handcuffs?"

"Yes, two pair!"

"Put one on the soldier you choose and one on the leader here and take them with you—now! Rafael, you go with them, and you too, Pedro. With the twins you can put one on either side and walk your prisoners into the woods as fast as you can. Listen to the shouting on that new road. I think reinforcements are arriving. Leave either captive behind if you have to—but go! Get out now! And get through with one of them!"

"Check!" yelled Tomás. "Come on!" Three Tainos surrounded each prisoner. The twins and Pablo helped the large woman up and half helped, half dragged her to the top of the rise and started down. Tomás and Sergio quickly lifted the smallest militia man, got him to his feet, and started off with him on a stumbling run. But as Rafael, who had been trussing the farthest soldier, ran across the clearing to catch up with them, a platoon of men filling two heavy dump trucks burst into the shouting, scattering mob of workers. A driver slammed on the brakes, dove out of the cab, and ran forward at enormous speed and collared Rafael, grabbing him in a headlock and began pulling him down. Rafael, half on the ground, jammed his arm between them and shot off his Taser.

"No!" screamed Jo, but too late, as the shock hit the soldier, instantly rebounding through him into Rafael himself, for he had not let go of him. They were still connected. Both went down unconscious.

"Help me here!" shouted Jo to Ricky and Letty. "Help me drag Rafael over the rise!" All three of them pulled him through the billows of smoke as the truck began to empty. Jo ordered, "Give me the rifle and I'll cover you! Get him out of here—take him back the way we came!"

"But," Ricky began to protest.

"Now," yelled Jo, snatching the rifle from his hand and sliding over the rise to double back. She fired an arc into the air from her stun gun in her other hand, screaming at the soldiers.

"Over there!" yelled a militia man and opened fire. Jo dove off the ridge and slid down its side as a burst of automatic fire slammed into the trees ahead of her.

The first militia man scurried to the top of the hill and Jo turned and fired a dart point-blank into his leg. He shrieked and toppled back down the hill. Then she threw away the large awkward rifle as she ran into the thick entangling woods.

Seeing their comrade fall backwards, wounded, the group of militia men paused at the bottom of the rise, not knowing how many were lying in wait on the other side. But one huge soldier of fortune leaped up the hill in full pursuit and tore into the woods after Jo, firing a burst that smashed a tree right by Jo's head. He was only a few yards behind her, thundering up fast, and Jo, as she ran, was punching up Eridania's number on speed dial and screaming into the phone, "We're under attack!" She gave the coordinates, hastily. Then she raced on, still clutching her cell phone.

She could hear the huge man crashing through the bush behind her. Fleet and adept, Jo ran, working her way back toward the forest entrance, keeping larger trees between them to foul his shots. And then, as she slid around a great boulder festooned with bushes and undergrowth, a fallen branch caught her foot and she went down hard on the stony ground. Before she could scramble up, he was above her, the tranquilizer rifle she had cast away in his one hand and his own gun in the other. Jo crawled backwards away from him as far as she could go until she hit a tree. He strode forward, standing high over her, and said in heavily Nordic-accented English. "So, it is a wood nymph with a blow gun!" Jo glanced down at her pack, now twisted around beside her. She had forgotten she had the blow gun. "Raise it to your lips and it will be the last thing you do," he snarled. Then, without stooping, he carefully laid his own weapon on the ground and, taking the tranquilizer rifle in both hands, he grunted, "First, I will quiet you down—and then we'll have some fun with that body of yours, wood nymph."

"You wouldn't shoot a lone woman, would you?" pleaded Jo, stalling for time.

"Sure, I would," laughed the mercenary, raising the tranquilizer rifle to his shoulder and taking aim through the sites. "Right between the eyes," he murmured. Then—suddenly—he flung the gun up into the air with a shriek and crumbled to the ground. Behind him was a slim, young, very dark man with a Taser in his hand.

Jo stared at him. Her mouth dropped open.

"¡Corre!" he yelled at her, and then in heavily French Creole-accented English, "Ron!"

Jo scrambled to her feet and without a word dashed into the forest.

45

A BATTERED AND BLOODIED Jo, reeking of carbon smoke and sweat, burst from the woods well over an hour later. Thorns and twigs had slashed her face and tangled in her hair, for her hat had fallen off when she'd sprawled out by the boulder before her inexplicable deliverance. She was streaked with dirt and soot and totally winded. She stumbled out from between the trees, put her hands on her knees, coughing in the dryness and trying to catch her breath. Nothing was in sight. She glanced at the early afternoon sun judging which way to go and then started up the dirt road, trying her best to keep behind trees to avoid being spotted by any pursuers.

"Here!" called a voice softly.

Jo paused, and the former ranger Ariadne appeared from behind a copse of small bush guacon trees. "I sent the others ahead with my daughter. Come!" And she started toward a new spot where she had moved the second transport vehicle.

"That was right," gasped Jo, trying to keep pace, though everything hurt from the scrapes and slashes and insect bites of the forest. "Thank you so much for following what I asked! Did they bring any prisoners with them?"

"Yes, they did. Here we are." Ariadne cleared huge fronds of cuchero palkera palms away from the vehicle.

"All of them fit in the other van?" asked Jo, helping as she could. Her right knee on which she had fallen ached, as she stretched to pull off the leaf cover.

"Yes, the 'guests' were tucked into the back space behind the last seat, out of sight."

"Wisely done."

"When we get on the stone road, we can get you some water. I saved a bottle for you,"

"You're a lifesaver," croaked Jo.

"I've done these kinds of wood excursions before when I was a ranger. One can get as dry as the land itself!"

Suddenly, both women stopped cleaning off the transport and scurried into the woods as they heard a roar building overhead. Moments later a half dozen helicopters raced across the sky and over the mountains toward the way Jo had come.

"Let's get out of here! Looks like the next fight is about to start," shouted Ariadne in the receding din. Both women dashed to the van, pushed the rest of the palms off, scrambled inside, and Ariadne fired it up, crunching it over the rest of the palm cover, sliding and popping out gravel as she maneuvered the little troop carrier out of the woods and up the road. Bouncing about, Jo rolled up her trouser leg and washed the cuts and bruises on her knee with some of the water from the bottle.

"First aid kit's under your seat," recommended Ariadne.

Painfully, she slid it out and doused stinging alcohol on this and all the cuts she could reach. Now she hurt everywhere, but only for a moment, and then she finally slumped down in her seat and began to relax.

As they bumped through the little villages and eventually onto the main road, Jo could feel herself beginning to doze, dropping down into an exhausted somnambulant calm.

"It was bad?" asked Ariadne from what seemed to Jo like far away.

"Yes," murmured Jo from even farther away. And then she drifted off.

The scraping of the gate at Las Olas awakened her. She was stiff and sore and eased herself out of the van. Ariadne reached out to hug her good-bye, but Jo warned her, "I'm filthy."

"I don't care!" said the older woman. "I'm just so glad you're safe."

Ernesto, who was taking a turn at the gate, gasped when he saw her. "Do you need help, *Cacica*?" he asked uncertainly.

"No, but thank you," Jo assured him. "I can limp quite well back to the rocking chairs, drink in some of the trade winds' relief, and then navigate my way to a solid clean-up."

"As you wish, *Cacica*."

"But, thank you, Ernesto, and thank you, dear sister Ariadne."

"I am at your service."

"And I at yours."

"Oh, and *Cacica*, you have visitors," Ernesto called after her.

Visitors? Jo just shook her head. Fully bedraggled, dirt streaked in sweat, her hair still tangled in some briars she had not clawed out, Jo trudged around the corner and slowly up the porch stairs and then she stopped. Staring back at her, open-mouthed, was a shocked Lawrence Fennelman of Richfield, New Jersey, neatly outfitted in safari jacket, white pants, white shirt, and white ashen face, gaping at Jo, speechless. Beside him in resplendent beauty sat her sister Daniela, as equally shocked, but not speechless. Confronting Jo, who stood wearily on the top step, holding on to the railing, Daniela railed at her in a loud voice, "What did you do to my friends?"

"What?" faltered Jo.

"What did you do to Bo and Peep? How could you?" demanded Daniela.

Lord give me strength, moaned Jo in her mind. "Do you mind if I sit down? I've had a trying day. . . ." Jo sunk into a rocking chair.

Both her visitors continued to stare at her—taking all this devastation of the usually natty Jo in to process. And then Lawrence Fennelman gave voice to his uppermost thoughts: "You're dirty and unkempt!" he exclaimed.

"Yes," admitted Jo, sinking even deeper into her chair. "I've been out saving the rainforest." She stretched her legs out. The khaki camouflage could not hide the caked dirt smudges on everything she wore. "Actually, it was a dry forest. . . ." she corrected herself.

"Is that what you intend to do and the way you're going to look all our married life?" he demanded.

"Our what?"

"Our married life!"

"I wasn't aware we were going to get married," retorted Jo, glad she had had the opportunity to rest in the van, not knowing another ordeal awaited her!

"Why, I've come to propose! You must have figured that out!"

"No, not really. I'm shocked to see you. But, welcome to the Dominican Republic," and she almost added *el pais del sabor*, "the land of flavor," but guessed correctly this was not the moment for levity. Post-exhaustion hysteria was her surmise for her odd frame of mind.

"Well, I *have* come to propose," and he showed her a diamond ring that he dug out of his top pocket. "But now," he warned her, "I'm thinking it over. Are you going to look like this often?" And, hesitatingly, he got awkwardly down on one tentative knee.

Jo sighed and leaned farther back in her chair away from him. What a day! "Well," she said, "I guess I'll have to look like this whenever the forest needs saving."

"And how frequent will that be?"

"Hard to tell."

Daniela was watching all this and wondering if Jo might want to say yes, but was just embarrassed about her appearance, because appearances, after all, were extremely important. This would be a great way to get back at Jo, it suddenly occurred to her. "Larry," she said.

He looked around, frowning. No man wants to be interrupted in such a key moment of his life. "Yes?" he snapped, peevishly.

"I'd like to get to know you better."

Lawrence Fennelman's mouth dropped open once again, and he struggled off his knee and stalled there for an astonished moment. Crouching tentatively, he turned himself toward the radiant Daniela and faltered, "You . . . you would?" His amazement was almost palpable—something that, if it could be distilled and bottled, could be used in the movies. So, frankly, was Jo equally, completely astonished.

"Yes, I would. But you have to support me in what I think is important," said Daniela, leaning forward and displaying, whether consciously or not, a glimpse of much of what she had to offer in her low-cut, designer blouse.

Lawrence stood up immediately. His heart was pounding in his chest like a Santeria drum. His brain was punching and pulsing within him like the Black Orchid boxing champ herself was in there jabbing. "Anything— I would do anything for you!" He drank in the full splendor of what was Daniela—this breathtaking goddess of a woman.

"Anything?" she checked him out, coolly, sitting back and leveling a calculating gaze at him.

"Absolutely anything!"

"Would you support my great mission?"

Jo groaned.

"With everything I have," he promised solemnly, and reached for her hand.

Daniela let him take it. In fact, she gave it to him and took his in her other hand. "You must support me in everything I want to do," she repeated.

"Everything!" he agreed. "Will *you* marry me?"

"I will, but you have to understand, my mission is costly."

"Daniela, I have been a bachelor for forty-two years. In those years I have worked steadily in finance and amassed a sizable fortune. I will lay all of it at your feet."

Daniela smiled at Jo, the kind of smile she used to bestow on her girlfriends as she walked off with their beaus. All that was left to say was, "Done!" This deal was sealed. And all Daniela needed to say was "Come!" to lead him away from Jo.

Jo sat forward. Now she was the open-mouthed one. She had begged God to let her see her little sister again, the little lost girl, the one she used to comfort so many years ago. As Daniela began to descend the first step to depart, Jo reached out her hand to her as she had done so many times over the years, the way she had done it long ago, when Daniela would run into her arms, crying. Jo leaned forward, reaching out, and touched her arm, "Danny," she murmured softly.

Daniela jumped back like she'd been stung and slapped Jo's hand away.

"Don't touch me! I hate you!"

Jo was cut to the core.

"All you've ever done is destroy everything of value to me! You even put my friends in jail just to keep them away from me. I will never forgive you for that! I hate you so much!"

Even Lawrence glared at Jo.

Tears began to well up in Jo's eyes. She said nothing for fear her voice would crack. Only two doleful tears slowly worked their meandering way down her cheeks to betray her feelings. Otherwise, she sat impassively, but Daniela saw the tears.

"Good," she gloated and then, with a haughty toss of her head, she stalked down the porch stairs, Lawrence Fennelman, the financial key to her dreams, in tow.

Jo wiped the tears away, but she could not stop them and she sat long afterwards, slowly letting them fall, hardly moving, saying nothing, even when Doña Lucia came out and stood by her for a time and then softly walked away.

46

THE NEXT MORNING, CLEANED up and nourished up and shored up in spirit as best as she could manage, Jo set out for Villa Bahoruco and the office of Angel Moreno Cueva de Piedra. This being daytime, his office assistant, Octavia Belgrada, ushered Jo in, and the lawyer rose up in his inner office and greeted her, closing the inner office door behind her.

"*Cacica*," he confided immediately, all amenities set aside this time. There was a suppressed excitement in his usual deferential tone. "You have come upon something that is important. You have perceived something that none of us thought to ask."

Jo waited, still standing. But he did not ask her to sit down. Instead, he leaned very close and whispered up to her ear, "I have checked out the ownership of the farms in Villa Riqueza. Nearly everything is in the name of a corporation called 'VillaRica Land Holdings.'"

Jo nodded her head slowly.

"You knew?" he hazarded, watching her closely.

"I guessed," she said.

"This is very bad," he said. "Those people who live there are no more than—well, tenant farmers. Share croppers, if you will!" He shook his head. His eyes were very sad. "It is the most prosperous of all of our towns. But, who gets the money?"

"Who indeed?" questioned Jo.

"It would be important to find out," he said, "but I think it might be very dangerous to know." And then, noticing Jo lean a tentative hand down on his desk, he exclaimed suddenly, "Please sit down—where are my manners?" She sank gratefully into his client chair, but rather than seating himself behind his desk in his office chair, he dragged it around to the front and sat himself across from her, but so closely that their knees were nearly touching. "I won't lie to you, *Cacica*," he whispered, leaning even more closely, "but there have been very strange things happening in the area."

"Would they involve the presence of a militia?" she whispered back.

"They would indeed."

"Do they have anything to do with my parents' disappearance?" Jo leveled her gaze at him with sudden, almost muted ferocity that began to equal Daniela's open hostility toward her.

The lawyer could see she was exhausted and exasperated and he bowed his head humbly. "Yes," he said simply. "But, please, understand this. Your parents are safe. Completely."

"So everyone tells me. And I don't know where they are being kept away from me or why this is happening in order to keep me safe—is that it?"

"Yes," he assured her. "That is it exactly."

"Well," she informed him. "I have seen the militia. In fact, I am hesitant to report this news, but I will. I went in the trouble area with a team. We attacked the militia and took two prisoners with us when we left."

The lawyer's mouth dropped open and his eyes widened. "You did what?" he exclaimed.

"Just what I said! It was not what I had planned, but you of the inner council asked me to check out the deforestation of our lands and that's what I did."

"But," he protested, "we never meant for you to go there personally and put yourself in danger!"

"I am a research scholar and a community organizer," she stated frankly. "What I do is field research."

"The Lord preserve you!" he murmured fervently.

"That's what I'm banking on!" she assured him. "Now give a breakdown, please, on all you discovered about VillaRica Land Holdings."

After an hour, her briefcase filled now with even more photocopies and notes, she took her leave.

Shortly after Jo drove away, Octavia Belgrada slipped from the outer office and went outside to make a call on her cell phone.

As Jo started down the road, she was mulling over in her mind a number of possibilities, but moving toward one inevitable conclusion. Nearly ten miles up the road her thinking and her progress halted. Out of seemingly nowhere, three military troop carriers, a tow truck, and a limousine suddenly roared off the largely empty perpendicular highway that intersects the main road, leading to the towns toward the north. One of the carriers skidded across both lanes, blocking all oncoming traffic. A man in a uniform leaped out and started directing traffic as other uniformed men leaped out of the backs of the troop carriers and began checking all the stopped cars in the left lane. When they got to Jo's car, they wrenched open the door and dragged her out. The uniformed man waved the trucks and cars behind her to back up and make room for the tow truck. Jo was thrust into the back of the black limousine and her car was hooked up to the tow truck. "Move on!" ordered the uniformed man. The three troop carriers dispersed themselves to positions before and after the tow truck and the limousine. The man waved the traffic on, and the troop carriers and their prisoner took off up the perpendicular road.

Jo was terrified, but she had no doubt where they were heading. When they arrived at Villa Riqueza, the limousine rolled to the back of the government building, and she was pulled out and taken through a basement door to a cellblock and thrust into one of the cells. There was no one else in the area. All of it was new, immaculately clean, in fact, sterile looking. No one was in either adjoining cell or across the way. Jo was completely alone. A small camera was trained down on her. She decided this was not the moment to use the open toilet in the corner. In fact, it was not the moment to do anything but sit on the small bed attached to the wall and pray, and so this is what she did.

About an hour and a half later, she heard noises and the metallic clanging of keys in locks. The outer door opened and then two large female guards came in and unlocked her cell. One of them patted her down, frisking her for weapons, but Jo had brought none, not even a pocket stun gun, intending only to visit the lawyer. "Come with us," ordered the one who had not checked her.

Jo remained silent. What was there to say to that?

She accompanied them out the prison door to an elevator and they went up to the third level, the second floor above the street level, Jo guessed.

She was ushered into an opulently appointed office to confront the frowning face of Nicolás de Odnavo, the mayor of Villa Riqueza. He glared at a very wan Josefina Archer, noted the bruises with a critical scowl, let a few moments of silence elapse, and then observed, 'You don't look as buoyant as you did the night of your inauguration.'

"A lot has happened since then."

"I can believe it!" he exclaimed. He stared at her for several more empty moments, hoping no doubt to let the tension mount. And he liked less and less what he saw in her impassiveness. If he had expected her to plead with him, he was changing his mind on that option. Finally, he broke the silence. "Well," he snapped at her, "you've been busy, haven't you?"

Jo said nothing.

"What do you think you're doing?" he demanded. "You've been causing all kinds of trouble!"

Jo decided to answer. "I haven't been the one causing the trouble," she corrected him.

He ignored that. "I told you you needed to work *with* me. Why do you not pay attention? What do you know about anything?"

"I know that I am the *cacica* of hundreds of Taino warriors! That there were many people on the road who saw me abducted and can identify my abductors. I am already in too prominent a position simply to disappear."

The mayor scoffed at her. "Do you think they will say anything? Do you think anyone will? What do you have to bargain with? I could make you 'disappear,' as you say, permanently and no one would know anything and—believe it! —no one would *say* anything! No one at all!"

"I think not," said Jo carefully.

"And why is that?" he sneered. "This room is soundproof. Do you see the thickness of those windows?" he jerked his thumb toward the street side. "Well, the walls are equally insulated. Anything can happen in here and no one would know! Why do you imagine you would be safe if you defied me?"

"Because I know the answer to the right question to ask," Jo shot back.

"And what is that?" he demanded.

"Are you VillaRica Land Holdings?"

He paused and his eyes narrowed.

"I also know the answer to another question," and, on a gamble, Jo turned toward a slightly opened door to the left and said, "and I know who is backing you up. All of this," she added, "is documented and in several hands. If I disappear, that documentation will immediately be given person-ally to the governor. Assure yourself on that count."

Nicolás de Odnavo paused. She could see a reflection in his eyes of rapid calculation and then he said more gently, "Just a second. We're get-ting ahead of ourselves." And, before her eyes, his whole demeanor changed. "You're the one who said 'disappear,' not me. You're reading this all wrong. I was just making a point. I have no intention of hurting you. I already offered to have us work together. That is all I have in mind."

"Work on what together?" asked Jo.

"Let me show you something—something exciting. This is something that will enrich your Tribe and turn the whole western section of our island into a paradise like you see here in Villa Riqueza. Wouldn't you want that for your people?"

"Of course I would. Who wouldn't? But what's the cost?"

"Nothing to you. Nothing at all! Let me explain something to you you may not have fully understood. It is a fact of history no one denies and it puts things in a different perspective for me."

He was pouring all his charm out now and came around and sat in a chair next to Jo. "Equal to equal," he was communicating.

"You know our history, of course," he cajoled her. "Originally, the French and Spaniards divided our island up between themselves. The border was just beyond Azua and the Haitians occupied all these lands of the west. In 1844, the Spanish on this side declared themselves an independent country and took over all the area from Azua on to the present border—a bleak year for Haitians and the reason today they believe they are entitled to all the woods of the Sierra de Bohoruco! Dominicans have been lax over the years. In 1861, we asked Spain to come back and take over! Between 1916 and 1924, we let the North Americans take over the whole country until the great leader Rafael Trujillo bought it back for us. Did you know there are countries today who want us to relax our borders or start a third country between us? Well, like the Generalissimo, I am a visionary, and I mean to take the lead in the future of this land!" And he leaped up, strode behind his desk, snatched a cylinder from his bookcase, and spread a map out on the desk, beckoning her to step around and see it. It was a map of the entire island, but, instead of the usual borders, there was a new division encompassing the eastern lands of Haiti and the western lands of the Dominican Republic, cordoned off from the two formerly adjoining countries.

"What is this?" demanded Jo.

"It is The Republic of Riqueza. A new country—a country designed to be prosperous and a model not only to the other two nations, but to the entire world! What we have done here in Villa Riqueza we can do to the entire region. Haiti was once the most prosperous side of the island. Mismanagement ruined it, but we mean to change all that. We want to help it regain its former glory in the new nation we are creating. And the Dominican Republic can benefit too. These are forgotten lands—all the real action and concern of the government is in the east now. Watch and see! No one will miss the western lands. Together, we can make this happen. You and the Tribe could be key to its success, for you have a prior claim on the island and you are connected across it by blood in ways that no one else is. You can help us immensely. And you personally and the Tribe generally will be richly rewarded. You have everything to gain and nothing to lose."

"With you in charge?" asked Jo.

"Well, yes, in a way," he admitted.

"Let me guess the way," said Jo, throwing all she had figured out on the table. "Lieutenant Governor Pedro Badilla is the first president or at least the titular head. You are the secretary of state and the real brains behind the operation. He is simply your frontman. Your militia becomes the trainers for a people's uprising—either peacefully by a call for a plebiscite vote or by an actual takeover and secession, if you thought you could pull that off, but I'm guessing you want to work things around to the first. How am I doing?"

The mayor's mouth dropped open. "Who told you all this? Who's the traitor in my midst?"

"No one," Jo assured him. "I'm a community organizer. That's the way I'd do it, if I were creating a country."

"I've picked the right person to partner with!" exclaimed the mayor, practically fawning on her. "You see the vision! You deserve to be chief! This is wonderful. You are so much smarter than I imagined, even smarter than your uncle, who wouldn't listen to reason. So," he beamed on her, "are you in with us?"

There was a slight muffled sound like something heavy falling outside and the mayor shouted, "Keep it down out there!" Then there was silence. "Well?" demanded the mayor.

"No," said Jo.

"No!" he scowled. And then in a more conciliatory tone: "Don't you want to think about it?"

"No, there's nothing to think about. The history you recount means little to me. I am Taino—as are you—but *my* loyalty precedes the invasion and division. The Tribe has decided to honor these divisions God has allowed and so I am loyal to my birth country and the Haitian chief of our Tribe is loyal to his. We would no more countenance an uprising or manipulating a plebiscite than we would condone the contraband trade that you're furthering to create unrest so you can capitalize on it." Jo glared at him.

"And, about the history you've just offered, let me mention, by the way, the earlier Treaty of Ryswick in 1697 basically divided the island as it is now, by its natural boundaries, its rivers and lakes. And, when Duarte and his commanders led the revolt against Haiti in 1844, all the eastern towns decided to align with them, not Haiti. The North American military did take over the D.R. in 1916, as you noted, but, remember, much earlier Buenaventura Báez and the legislature in 1869 asked to be annexed to the U.S.! And, Trujillo didn't even come into power until 1930! How could he have bought the country from the U.S. when he was preceded by Horacio Vásquez six years previously in 1924! Besides, Trujillo was no friend of Haiti's. He ordered his troops to kill Haitians on sight. They slaughtered at least 20,000 innocent Haitians in the Dominican Republic and had to pay recompense for that later. This monster was no hero for you to follow! You have no argument here!"

The mayor glared back at her and then spoke very slowly, spelling out the consequences of this position. "So, you know your history! Well, understand this! I am not threatening you. I am promising you what will happen to you if you persist in this position. I put up with your uncle's refusal because he was old and about to be gone. But, you're young and too smart and you've guessed far too much. Believe me! You will have a car accident. And it will be very convincing. You will be dead. Is that what you want?"

"That plan didn't work for that monster Trujillo, when he had the 'butterflies' bludgeoned in the cane field, put the sisters' bodies in their car, and pushed them off a cliff. Even then any forensic doctor could see the difference between wounds inflicted by accident and those by assault—and the tribal council will get the best doctors, spurred on by the iron-willed Anacoana Behechio—my aunt."

Muffled sounds of commotion outside barely resonated off the sound-proof windows, but the mayor shook his head in exasperation and cried to the walls, "I'm trying to negotiate here—will we have no peace at all! This is a day of great frustration for me!" he snarled directly at Jo. "And I deal swiftly and terminally with those who frustrate me!" Then he scoffed, "Yes, you're well connected, all right, but we'll brave that out. We'll have plenty of police reports to corroborate our story and we'll show great sadness at your demise. I can be very convincing. We have too much at stake and you now know far too much to let you remain a living adversary. You must choose and you must choose now!"

Jo was quaking inside—as terrified as she had ever been. The momentum had stopped. Now was the moment of decision. But what could she choose? "I don't want to die," she said.

He grinned malevolently and shook his head yes.

"But I will not join this treason."

He exhaled a great sigh of air, shook his head theatrically, and said, "Then you give us no choice. You are obstinate and altogether disagreeable. Well, we have people who can fix that. They are experts in changing a contrary mind. I will return you to your cell where more persuasive methods will be used on you. You will soon be crying out to join me. Let's hope it's not too late. For, if I give the order, you will die, little acting *cacica*." He left that hanging in the air, paused one more moment, eyeing her closely, then his eyes snapped down to slits. "Guards!" he shouted toward the door.

The door opened, but instead of the two female guards, a young Haitian man came in. "Excuse me, your honor," he said humbly. And then he trained a Taser right at the mayor's chest.

"What is this!" shouted the mayor deeply affronted.

Jo stared at the young man in consternation and then she recognized him. "You're the man from the forest!" she gasped.

"Just a moment, please, *Cacica*. Your honor, this is a Taser."

"I know what it is!" snapped the mayor, imperiously. "What I want to know is what it is doing pointing at me!"

The young man held his gun steadily and said humbly, "We've come for our *cacica*." He was joined by Eridania Rosario and several others, slipping through the door and surrounding him.

At that, the mayor of the dominant town of the region, propped on the pinnacle of its wealth and power, pulled himself up to his own full height, peered down imperiously at the young man, and demanded, "What makes you think any of you will ever leave here alive?"

"I am prepared to electrocute you temporarily to secure your complete cooperation," said the young man carefully in studied Spanish. "To avoid that measure, if you would be so kind as to glance out your front window." He motioned with the gun.

The mayor decided it would be prudent to comply.

Jo heard the slamming of internal doors over to the left behind the cracked open door and decided the eavesdropper had made an exit.

The mayor stalked to the window and glanced out. The street was filled with hundreds of Taino warriors from everywhere close enough to come. On the ground of the street lay several dozen militia men, their hands behind their heads. The mayor stared, his eyes fully rounded, his jaw went slack.

"Who are you?" asked Jo of the young man, as many others now poured into the room.

"I want to see my son!" shouted the mayor, turning back into the room. "I want to see Tomás!"

"He's down in the street, roping the hands of your army," said Eridania Rosario, as she stepped around the desk and cuffed the mayor. "Do you really want this patriot to see you—the traitor?"

"I demand to see my lawyer!" screamed the mayor.

"You'll be seeing him, all right," snapped a uniformed man with army braid resplendent on his shoulders. "You are wanted for questioning in the death of Emilio Rosario and his wife, Sophia, who were pulled from their home two weeks ago and shot to death."

"I had nothing to do with that!"

"You had everything to do with it!" Eridania Rosario clamped a hand on his shoulder and walked him away from the window.

"You can't prove I did!"

"Sure, we can and we will! They were executed by your militia men!"

"That was Pedro Badilla's army!" he cried, his voice beginning to crack.

"Is that right?" snapped Eridania sarcastically. "Well, Mister Mayor, we've heard an interesting confession from a militia man captured in a recent skirmish between your private army and a Taino land protective unit. He claims your orders are responsible for the murder of the Rosarios because

Emilio was your political rival for mayor and in great favor with the people. And we also have two eyewitnesses who saw the act take place and were pursued by this man and others of your army before they eluded them!"

"I know nothing about that!"

"What you need to know is that Emilio and Sophia Rosario were my uncle and aunt. I am Eridania Rosario, a ranger of Cesfront, and I took the confessions from both the captured soldier of fortune and the overseer of the charcoal thieves they protected. We have sent copies of them to the Minister of the Interior, who also wants to know about the legality of your deed arrangements for the lands around Villa Riqueza—how they were obtained, why a militia was involved, whether strong-armed tactics were used. Oh, and the army's border patrol also wants to have a few words with you about the disturbances on the border. Your lawyer's going to be very busy." And she nodded toward the army officer beside her.

"I have nothing to say," growled the mayor, but his confidence was shattering. It was echoed in the cracking pieces of his voice.

"Well, that's predictable. Perhaps you'd like a place where you can gather your thoughts?" offered Eridania Rosario, nodding again to the army officer, and each of them took an arm of the mayor and began to walk him out. "I understand," she continued, "you have a temporary holding bin in your basement. How about we try your own cellblock out for size—shall we? Cesfront and the army interrogators are on their way." The last thing they heard her say as she and several other camouflaged rangers, Dominican soldiers, and officers of the national police led him away was: "A lot of interesting charges here, your honor. Yours will be quite a celebrated case. . . ."

Jo turned to the young man. "How can I ever thank you?" she asked with wonder.

"I'm hurt that you don't recognize me," said the young man. And he was clearly hurt.

"Why, you're one of the drivers of the Haitian delegation. I recognize you now," Jo assured him.

"I'm Jean-Jacques!" he exclaimed. "Don't you remember when our chief said we would be looking out for you? I volunteered to be the one. It was my right!"

"Your right?" Jo was baffled.

"Yes, of course. I'm Jean-Jacques!"

"Jean-Jacques," repeated Jo, groping for the meaning.

"Don't you remember? You supported me when we were both little, right until I turned eighteen! I'm your former foster child from Christian World Service!"

"You're Jean-Jacques!" cried Jo and threw her arms around him. "And you saved my life!"

"Of course! And you mine! Now you know me!" And he hugged her back.

47

A MISERABLE STAR AND Basil Heitz had been separated ever since their arrest, and now they were sharing a rare moment together, sitting in a little room of the police headquarters in Barahona, waiting for an attaché from the U.S. embassy to come. How many warrants were outstanding in the U.S. they could not guess. But here in the D.R. they had been piling up misdemeanors and felonies over $250 U.S. like ripe mangoes in season—in their case, a truckload, so as to say, and certainly enough here in the island in petty thefts and credit card fraud to put them away. The question for both of them was how many could be traced to them. The most obvious was the truck, and that was the topic of discussion once they had done the obligatory contest of comparing whose miseries of incarceration had been greater.

"We could plead that we thought we had unlimited miles . . ." offered Basil with what still sounded like hope.

But Star was crying. "We'd have to grease some palms for that, and we have nothing left—nothing!"

"Well," snorted Basil. "If we did have anything, they would have taken it away from us as soon as they busted us." That was certainly what he himself would have done had he been the police, he reasoned.

"Everybody's turned against us," whimpered Star, "even that Ismael Balenzuela. I thought we could trust him."

"You can't trust anybody," snarled Basil. "The only possibility is that Danny. And—let's face it! —there are a couple of hoofers missing in that chorus line! Look at how zonko she's gone on the scam. Hard to believe anybody's that dumb."

"That's the way with some lookers." Star rubbed away her tears with her hand. "They get so much handed to them that there's no reason to use the upstairs for anything but storing old prom tickets, and dead corsages, and love letters from cruelly jilted admirers!" And Star started crying again, blubbering, "We can forget about any help from there! That one's got the attention span of a canary! She's probably forgotten us already." And she continued to sob out her remorse, taking a kind of comfort in what a pathetic picture she was portraying.

"Yeah," mumbled Basil to his no longer attentive audience, "she's probably just laying around on some lounge chair working on her tan and . . ." Suddenly he broke off and became as alert as he was capable. Star sat up too. They both heard voices outside the door to their containment room and they both turned automatically to watch the entrance. Neither felt particularly terrified; it was more the feeling of uneasiness one experiences when one is waiting in an inner examination and procedure room and hears the muffled fumbling of a doctor extracting a chart from the plastic container on the outside door and perusing it in consultation with a nurse before entering. As far as avoiding more unpleasantness, well, that option was all over. Star and Basil kept telling each other they had been caught with the goods—literally *in* the goods—and more people would yell at them, and then they'd go to trial and, after that, prison. It was inevitable, thought Star, overwhelmed with indignation and self-pity for the unfairness of it all. Such a waste and such a shame it had to happen on the eve of the greatest con game of their entire career—and, the rub was, this one was at least half, if not three-quarters, legitimate!

The door opened and an officer in an open-collared white shirt came in and regarded them with an appraising eye.

"You are the Heitzes? Yes?"

"Yes," said Star. She could think of no reason to deny it now.

"Is the U.S. embassy official here to see us?" asked Basil, ready for the worst.

"No. You will come with me now to an official visiting room. Your visit will be monitored by a guard."

"Fine," said Star, getting up. At this point, they had to be careful what they chose to hide. Denying who they were was a waste of time. It was going to come out anyway. But, at least, she reasoned, we didn't kill anybody. They can't execute us.

They stepped into another small room—all they had in this building appeared to be small rooms—and they were seated at the wall side of a large table. Across from them was a mirror, no doubt two-way, Basil concluded. They waited.

In stepped a man they had never seen before. He had on a sports shirt that showed a stomach beginning to round and an expensive grey pair of dress slacks showing a waistline beginning to widen the hips. His sandy-colored hair was beginning to thin. He looked like an accountant who had spent his life at his computer and it was beginning to show.

"Are you the ambassador?" asked Star.

"What?" The man looked confused, "I'm Lawrence Fennelman. Wait a second, she's just talking to the officer outside the door."

"Who?"

"Daniela, of course." And, as if on cue, in stepped Daniela Archer followed by her brother Ben.

Star gasped and Basil gaped. If they felt any remorse for their cutting remarks and dismissal of Daniela as a player in this drama, they showed no indication.

"Oh, Daniela, we were hoping so much that you would come quickly! We knew you wouldn't let us down!" lied Star. "It's all just a big mistake! You must know that! We would never intentionally do anything to hurt anyone!"

Basil swiveled his gaping head toward her.

"Of course not," said Daniela. "I know you have good hearts. You are very spiritual people and care nothing for the material."

Ben smirked, but said nothing.

Star summoned up a few designer tears to confirm that diagnosis, while Basil simply sat open-mouthed and continued to gape at Daniela. He couldn't believe she was dumb enough to come to their rescue. A robot designed for dishwashing would have been smarter, he was concluding.

"We're trying to see what we can do for you—oh, this is Larry, he's my friend."

"I'm her fiancé!" announced the man with aplomb. Looking at her "all gooey-eyed" is how Star summed up what she was observing to herself. She did a quick calculation. No doubt about it: She could play him as well as the twit. He was already a sucker for Daniela. That was clear enough, so that made him just one step away from being Star's patsy too. It was like standing dominoes: Knock down one and it knocks down another. Even Basil was already calculating how to exploit this obvious lack of judgment on Daniela, Ben, and their friend's part. Both Star and Basil had forgotten what mercy looks like. They had convinced themselves it was a sucker's game for so long that gratitude had dropped entirely out of their mental vocabulary.

"The officer was telling me there's no way you can avoid jail time," said Daniela sadly.

Both Starling and Basil groaned—and this display of emotion was real.

"I can't understand how you ended up with someone else's credit card!" Daniela looked at them, baffled. "Maybe it got switched by mistake at the car rental company? But why would you sign someone else's name?"

Star and Basil simply stared at her open-mouthed. "Because we had nowhere to stay so we had to do that until we could get our own card back and settle the difference of the accounts?" tried Star, wondering what this market would hold.

"Two somebody else's cards," corrected the man with her, eyeing them both suspiciously. That hung for a moment in the air.

"Anyway," continued Daniela, "they're going to let us bring some meals in for you both for a price, and maybe we can get a good lawyer to help shorten the time."

Now you're talking, kiddo! thought Star. What she said was, "Oh, you are so kind to us and so wise to think of such a thing. We, Bo and myself, have been so distraught over these misunderstandings that we have been unable to think."

The man calling himself Lawrence looked carefully at Star and said, "The police say you also boosted a truck!"

Hmmm, he wasn't that dumb, thought Star. She'd better be careful.

Basil protested. "Not at all! That's a lie!"

"We misunderstood the contract," explained Star, picking it up from Basil, but her voice was shaky. "We thought we had unlimited miles." She knew that was a hard sell.

"They said you had it over six months."

"We were going to pay it all at the end."

"What do you do?" Basil suddenly asked the man, trying to veer the conversation away from their crimes.

"I'm an accountant with a firm in Westfield, in New Jersey. I specialize in investigating fraud cases for Ledger, Taylor, Bond, and Campbell, a firm that services Wall Street."

"Oh," said Basil. He decided this was a good moment to clam up.

"Can you get us out on bail?" asked Star, hopefully.

"I'm afraid not," said Lawrence. "You haven't been arraigned yet. They're still adding up the charges, the credit cards, the truck, seeing if there's anything more, but, mainly," he added, eyeing them some more, "they think you are both at risk to bolt."

Basil's instant protest died on his lips. This guy might look portly and somewhat socially challenged, but, when it came to business, it was obvious he was sword-sharp.

"It's time," said a heavily accented voice outside the door, following a sharp rapping. The monitor stood and motioned them out with a pursing of the lips and a nod toward the door.

"I'll pray for you," said Daniela. Her worried look told Star volumes. She would obviously have hugged them both if the guard had allowed it.

"Wait here!" ordered the guard and escorted their visitors out.

"Like we can go anywhere!" grumbled Star.

"Well, it ain't the Ritz," cajoled Basil, "but we got some kind of room service! We're almost back!" and he flashed a lopsided grin at his sweet patootie.

"Shut up!" snapped Star, disgusted. "We got less than five minutes. We got to get a single story and a game plan now that we got a couple of marks on the outside." She was obviously not depending on Ben. There was a commotion outside the door, and Star's face flashed a warning. "Better yet, just shut up and I'll think it through. Just go with whatever I say whenever we can get together again."

"Gotcha!" said Basil.

"In the meantime, just take one thing to heart."

"Anything," promised Basil, "what is it?"

"Don't shoot off your fat mouth to anyone—ever!—or we'll never get out of this hole."

48

As Jo awakened, a gentle rain began to descend upon Las Olas with the reluctance of mourners: first one hesitant drop, then a second came calling, then a barrage of weeping visitors.

After a fitful night full of strange dreams and a foreboding sense of loss, an even more wan and exhausted Jo sat the next morning with the *Nitaíno* as the steady pelting rain delivered its condolences at the great windowed doors of Las Olas del Sol. She hardly felt up to standing and welcoming Eridania Rosario and Tomás de Odnavo, the guests she had invited to address the local tribal council to help her explain what was happening.

"You look so tired, my dear," said Doña Mencia, filled with concern. "Are you certain you are up to this?"

"Doña, if the eighty- and ninety-year-old elders can meet this morning, so can a twenty-nine-year-old employee."

"But I'm not sure we've been having the same adventures that you've been having, or so I've been told," replied Doña Mencia.

Jo smiled, "It's true; I can't remember a week when I've been shot at by militia men, chased through the forest, abducted, arrested, and imprisoned by a government official—it certainly makes all the past stories I've saved up to tell pale in comparison."

Nobody laughed, but Jo still smiled as reassuringly as she could at them.

"We haven't lost you, have we?" asked Don Ramón, searching her face. It was the first time he had had a chance to speak with her since she had returned to Las Olas.

"No, you haven't."

"This job isn't too much for you?" asked Ricky, but with no sneer this time. Jo glanced at him. It sounded to her like genuine concern, but she was, after all, tired and not at her perceptive best.

"Frankly," she confessed, "if I had to do this by myself, yes, this would be far too much for me. But I had a long talk with *Cacica* Mara Collas and she advised me to select the most capable people in the Tribe to help me guide it. It is sound advice and I will take it to heart. It is what I've always wanted: to be able to work in an intentional community. This is what I had been seeking in social work. I also sought it in the church. And, yes, I found it there. But not to the degree I found it here with the Tribe, because this is my actual family—and it follows YaYael. But now I have to be honest with all of you. Coming home has shown me something about myself. Since you gave me the tasks, I realize I have been tempted to do them all by myself, for myself, to prove to myself and others I could do them, that I could fulfill my Uncle Sol's belief in me and honor the memory of my famous ancestors, Great Chief Enrique and Queen Anacoana. But, over and over again, people have had to come forward to help me—my Aunt Aña, Doña Lucia, Don Ramón, Tomás and his warriors, even Brother Ricky here, Señor Cueva de Piedra, this council itself, our tribal family in Haiti, a fleet of advisors, and on and on, everyone solicitous for me, everyone caring for me, coming alongside me, guarding me, rescuing me, and even Jean-Jacques saving my life. Sister Eridania here was poised with a strike force combination of rangers and border guards of the army to intercede if we called—and the helicopters were already overhead before we'd left the forest!

"Why, even the information I am about to share with you is the result of research done at great length by others that I had the privilege to glean. In fact, the little new church development I pastor back in Richfield in New Jersey I have had to put in the capable hands of friends. And all of the time I have been depending on God's Spirit. So, I have done nothing completely by myself. I realize that I have always worked with a team, always wanted a team, even wished for my brother and sisters to form a team with me—and this is a great part of the sense of sorrow I bear today, for I have come to realize I have nearly completely failed at that. Only Ruby has stuck by me. How can I hope to guide the Tribe or a fledgling church if I cannot keep my own family together in the absence of our parents? To put it simply, yes, this has been a learning experience for me—that's for certain!"

The council listened carefully, some nodding.

"This, I know, has been a very personal and human way to give a report to the leadership, and, perhaps, because of it, you will change your mind and decide I am not really capable to be the *cacica*. If that is your decision, I applaud it. I wholeheartedly agree. But, for myself, I have been given the task in good faith and I labor beneath a burden of trust down through the generations and I cannot slip it off as if it were a mere knapsack—it is precious to me, like the weight of a child one carries. My uncle Sol honored this burden all his life and he transferred it carefully to me, and I will shoulder it in honor of him, if for no other reason."

Jo paused and looked around into sympathetic faces, so she continued. "I give you my honest personal feelings, because what I have to share with you is also very human. You asked me to look into the destruction of our trees, the motivation for it, the ways to address it. Well, the answer is that this, too, is a very human issue. Some things I've learned you already know. Professor Renault did an excellent job at the *caciques* meeting sharing the extent of the ecological impact of the damage. I do not need to repeat it. I had the privilege to talk with him further and I also gathered data from my visits to the University of Santo Domingo and from other stops at universities and institutions in the capital. And I have downloaded studies from international environmental and economic organizations on the internet. And I will make these available, but what I think I need to explain to you today is the human face of this problem, for understanding that is what is going to help us address this defoliation most effectively. And this human face *Cacique* Paix revealed to me. It evokes mourning at the end of a great tragic catastrophe. And this is why I begged this expert, Ranger Eridania Rosario, to attend this meeting as a resource to help us understand the complex interworking of need that itself is being victimized by greed to produce the persistent problems we are all enduring today on each side of the border."

Eridania Rosario nodded, but said nothing. Jo nodded back and continued.

"So, now let me take you into a different kind of forest—one overgrown with the complexities of culture. Do you see this familiar photograph?" Jo distributed an aerial view of the border, showing a dramatic contrast of lushly wooded mountains to the right and practically barren hills to the left. Eridania, Ricky, and Tomás simply passed it on, but some of the others studied it carefully. "This is our border," explained Jo. "Our neighbors have less than two percent of their forests left. But, I want you to see this not simply as a contrast in the land, but as a contrast of peoples. We Dominicans may not consider our own as a prosperous country, but our neighbors and brothers and sisters of Haiti have inherited little at all from their ancestors. There are only two small wild mammals left alive in most of their country, the *hutia*, something like a small mole, and *nez lounge*, a rodent, and these too are nearly extinct. Everything else has been eaten by desperate people. All the birds that are left are mainly in parks and nature reserves, but these are being poached daily and eaten or sold to tourists—as are all the snakes and bats and parrots and flamingos, which are also dwindling away. The problem appears insurmountable. Even domestic animals like goats and horses and donkeys and cows, key resources to an agricultural community, are starving as the people starve. Charcoal is a costly way to cook a family's normal meager daily meal of rice and beans and at least three quarters of the population cook on charcoal or wood.

"This forest I am telling you about is nearly impenetrable, because it is a forest of ancient cultural habits that are not easily broken. They distinguish our Haitian brothers and sisters from us Dominicans, and so such practices as burning wood and agricultural refuse for charcoal are deeply ingrained in the understanding of what it means to our neighbors to be distinctly Haitian. These have become an intrinsic part of their sense of identity. Chief Paix explained it to me when we met at the food court at the hospital at Jimani. He was so insightful; I wrote what he said down, word for word."

Jo selected another page from her notes and read: "The poor have no electricity! They have no gas! They have no stove! How can they cook their food, except with wood and carbon? In addition, they have their tradition. It's almost impossible to change the customs of a *campesino*! I lament for my people. They are living for today, but they are killing tomorrow."

Jo looked around earnestly at the gathering. "You have to understand, a family would have to spend up to a quarter of all it earns on cleaner-burning charcoal or it must continue to risk inflicting lung infections on its children and even premature deaths from the carbon monoxide from wood burning inside the home. But few can spare anything for cleaner fuel, even if given a stove free, and, rather than let their children starve, they will burn what they can afford. Traditionally, wood is preferred. It's what they were taught to burn for fuel down through the generations, but, whatever they can get that will burn, they *will* burn for cooking. Our forests are an available commodity for them and borders mean nothing to people who are starving."

Jo looked over at Eridania Rosario, who said, "This is the conclusion we have reached as well. We cannot let our forests be destroyed, but every one of us is filled with compassion for the plight that motivates the workers to cross the border and steal what they can. It is a business for them, certainly, but their consumers must buy—or die. It is as simple as that!"

"Yes," agreed Jo, and everyone could see the sadness in her eyes. "It can't go on like this. Our neighbors will lie dying next to us at the foot of the unbuilt wall which is the border and behind which we pursue our busy and relatively prosperous lives. I won't say we have been oblivious to this, because we haven't. Our nation rallied around wonderfully during the earthquake and daily we let countless day laborers come across to work all through our region. But the problems of poverty mount and, if these are not addressed effectively, the border will not hold the desperate back. Eridania?"

"That is the truth," the ranger assured them, "and the reason I came today to add my voice of support. We cannot protect our own resources against undernourished families. Either we share them or we will lose them. Undernourishment will end in widespread starvation and the emaciation of a population. That will end in war—whether guerilla or formal war, but war nevertheless. How can it not? This is what we must address, for we can protect ourselves just so much. Then we must all reach out and survive together, if any of us are going to survive at all," and she turned back and nodded to Jo.

"Yes, thank you," said Jo. "So, clean energy cooking is paramount because it accounts for a full seventy-five percent of all energy used on that other side of our island. Have we wondered why this problem is so widespread? Why we can't keep it from spilling over our borders? We think we should have wondered why so many of our neighbors are restraining themselves from pouring over in masses!" Jo looked around for emphasis, and then she added, "But there's hope."

Eridania nodded, "Yes, she's found some hope for us," indicating Jo. And the tribal council turned to Jo with interest and even a suppressed glint of eagerness.

"The Germans," said Jo, "have been developing a briquette made of sun-dried coconut husks. A family can live on the coconuts and cook over the burning husks, or buy the briquettes and help us save our forests and help them redevelop theirs. Researchers from a North American school, the Massachusetts Institute of Technology, have also been working on the development of briquettes not made from charcoal. Even the United Nations has been supporting the development of clean stove cooking too. What I am saying is that we are not alone in our concerns. There are many who are concerned with the plight of pollution, and one thing I have learned from community organizing is that there is no reason to try to invent our own wheel when someone else is already working on a bus that will carry the people we want to help to a better destination.

"And, there's so much more! Did you know that makeshift shacks that are open to the elements can be replaced by used shipping containers for homes, sunk cheaply in concrete to make them secure? That will ensure the minimization of homelessness should another earthquake strike. Think of that! Also, did all of you know that a number of nongovernmental organizations composed of both Haitians and Dominicans are studying the problems of devising non-fossil-fuel energy for irrigation, improved strategies for more effective nurturing, more responsible harvesting for offshore fishing, building family outhouses set up to produce compost out of waste—this and other ways to drop the cost and ensure a more productive yield for organic gardening for every family? It is amazing!

And these innovative ideas—late as they may appear to be—are all focused on addressing the root problems and, as a byproduct, together they will eliminate the need for robbing our forests. We can become an aware and contributing part of the solution. Our Tribe can support these efforts. We can save the forests and the lives of our neighbors!" Jo sat back. It was obvious to all that even her enthusiasm was draining her energy. Doña Lucia felt the urge to leap up and brew Jo some creole tea, but she didn't want to miss a single word, so she sat still, as Jo went on.

"Look," said Jo, "Let's be honest about this. If we were to stride over the border and start to implement such things we would be considered imperialistic by our neighbors and be suspected, shunned, and our money would be wasted. That's the human side, and it's built on conflict and distrust on both sides that originated long before any of us were born!" Everyone nodded in agreement. The cultural clashes were redolent with misunderstanding. "But," continued Jo, "at the same time, we are in a unique position. We have a firm bond already with our fellow tribal members across the border. They are studying the problem themselves with Professor Renault and others—in fact, the chief and a delegation were on the way to several universities in Santo Domingo to compare notes with their experts when they graciously paused to meet me at the hospital at Jimani, at my request, to increase my understanding of the situation.

"So, what I am saying is that what we did in interrupting one case of tree thieving and the subsequent invasion of Villa Riqueza that was orchestrated by Ranger Rosario here and a delegate of the Haitian *cacicazgo* secretly assigned to follow me and protect me—for which I am personally deeply grateful!—well, this taking out of one greedy entrepreneur and his small militia even though its goals were large—fomenting unrest to make way for a political takeover—well, that was, at best, only a temporary step." Jo looked over toward Tomás, who was sitting with his head down, his eyes downcast.

"But, it raises an ethical issue for us: If starving people will do what they can do to feed their families, is it actually moral to stop them? I am not certain it is moral if we offer no other solution. But, at the same time, we must look to the wellbeing of our own families. If we let them destroy our trees, we will all end up in the same condition. Then no one can help anyone.

"There is only one solution: a sophisticated networking of resources with every organization that is addressing this problem, working closely with the forest rangers and the border guard for the temporary containment of it and with our Haitian Taino counterparts and all the organizations, domestic and international, that are developing ways to address it for a permanent resolution. We can choose the levels to which we can contribute, guide our youth to study in these areas and become the leaders of the future, and invest what we can afford—without impoverishing ourselves, of course! What I mean is: we can help a specific area right directly over our border to discover another way to thrive, besides robbing us. We can help introduce fuels and cooking techniques, improved gardening and health and educational practices, and so on, but we cannot change the traditional mind of the people. Professor Renault made it very clear to me that right now we could fill a truck full of clean-burning stoves or even pour our resources into improving the development of a highly efficient solar-powered stove and cart those over the border and give them away tomorrow morning free of charge, and tomorrow night the poor recipients would lug them back over the border and sell them to Dominicans. We could plant coconut palms and they might cut them down and burn them to cook supper. All they are doing is what they have always done, and what they can point out is every day that's being done on our side of the border as well. To clear land by cutting down trees and building dirt kilns to make charcoal is normal border life, and many of them believe the border should still be down at Azua and that we are 'disobedient brothers' who have stolen the land from them, so why should they listen to thieves who call them thieves? They resent us as interlopers and would rather starve than be handed what they consider to be insulting charity when they think we should simply vacate the land or act like guests toward them and not proprietors.

"Therefore," and Jo paused and searched the face of each member of the council individually before she continued, "it is absolutely imperative if we want to help bring about a peaceful resolution that is effective to benefit all involved that we do all we do in partnership and under the guidance and leadership of the *cacique* and the *Nitaíno* of the *Cacicazgos Bohios Haity Sabana*, our family in Haiti! This is what I recommend."

Jo paused to look around again. The tribal council stared back, and then one of the two inner circle leaders who had opposed her began to clap. That was joined heartily by all the others, even Ricky and Tomás de Odnavo. Doña Lucia beamed on Jo, and the lawyer Angel Cueva de Piedra and Don Ramón exchanged broad smiles.

When the clapping had subsided, Doña Mencia called for order and then asked for what Jo had been dreading was coming: a report on the other theft.

"And the second matter of business?" Doña Mencia said firmly. "The return of the Rosary of Enrique?"

"It is returned to its place," said Jo simply and paused.

"Yes, we are grateful for that, but now we would like to know what happened exactly," Doña Mencia pursued her.

Jo was uncertain how to proceed. Isn't it enough it is back? She was about to say, when Tomás lifted his head and interjected. "I am afraid I am responsible for that."

"For what?"

"For the return of the relic!" offered Jo swiftly.

Doña Mencia simply gazed at her, suspiciously. Jo subsided.

"Suppose you tell us about that," Doña Mencia ordered Tomás, as if she were his own grandmother, demanding to know what happened to the tin of *dulce de leche* she had left on the kitchen table.

"Thank you, *Cacica*, for standing up for me," Tomás said, and this time it was his turn to smile wanly at Jo, "but I came today to make a clean confession. I think I should leave the Tribe." The *Nitaíno* became very quiet; even Ricky stopped and held his breath.

"I have been thinking over my actions. They were very foolish. What *Cacica* Josefina said earlier of herself I now believe is true of myself as well. I think I always suspected my father was involved in the robbing of the trees. Even as a child, I could never face him. Now I am thinking that all of my concern and fervor for the forest was out of my concern for him, for stopping him before he went too far. This roundabout way to address the issues of people we love is a foolish waste of time. I'm afraid even now to think what he might have done, what he might be facing. I am glad for the first time in my life that my mother died and did not have to live to see this. She died in childbirth—my birth," he looked around at eyes where only pity shone. "I took the Rosary of Enrique to sell to arm ourselves to go in and fight my father's troops and stop him and save our forest. I am glad I did not succeed. Our new *cacica* had a better way. Under her guidance, we did not hurt anyone. We took two prisoners who confessed and we verified the truth. It broke my heart, but it had to be done."

Jo nodded.

"Was anyone else involved in the theft of the Rosary?" asked Don Ramón with great concern.

"I entered the tribal treasury myself, took the Rosary from its place, hid it and carried it out, and offered it to a buyer. I am entirely to blame by myself."

"And why was it not sold?" asked Doña Mencia.

"Queen Josefina devised a strategy that let it fall into the hands of a better friend of the Tribe than I have been." Tomás could not help but lower his eyes again before all those of the leaders. His shame was nearly palpable.

"How is it the artifact is back in its place?" asked Doña Lucia.

"Tomás saw the error of his ways and voluntarily returned it," spoke up Jo. "He also bravely secured the two prisoners he mentioned that helped bring his father to justice and he helped lead the charge into Villa Riqueza that captured the militia unawares and rescued me from possible torture and death. All of this he did since that one previous foolish decision."

"I can verify that, your honors," spoke up Eridania Rosario. "One of the reasons I came today was to attest to his courageous dedication to the wellbeing of the Tribe. He helped lead the surprise and bloodless invasion of Villa Riqueza. It was planned and done so adroitly that no one was hurt. They were all taken completely unawares!" Eridania paused and indicated Ricky. "*Nitayno* Asenao was part of the planning and execution as well and of course *Nitayno* James Archer." Ricky looked down embarrassed before Jo's surprised gaze.

"I didn't make it upstairs to rescue you, *Cacica*," Ricky mumbled, "though it was my duty as head of your bodyguard. We were still doing the rounding up. We took their armory first. They were all playing cards in their long house. The next thing they were looking at our tranquilizer guns!"

Jo's mouth dropped open.

"Oh, yes," Ricky assured her. "We had plenty of darts left over and we recharged the stun guns. We decided to use them again."

"Right!" spoke up Tomás. "They took one look at the equipment and decided they didn't want any part of that again!" He and Ricky and Eridania all chuckled. They restrained themselves from giving each other high fives in deference to the presence of the elders. Jo knew it was time to make her move.

"As your acting *cacica*," she said, "I would plead with the council that these acts atone for what is now past." Jo stopped and projected pleading into her gaze at each member of the tribal council.

Don Ramón smiled but said nothing.

Doña Mencia looked around at the other six members of the council and asked, "Are you satisfied with this decision?"

Several nodded. Ricky spoke up quickly, "I think it is very just—gracious."

"Does anyone object?" Doña Mencia continued after a pause. No one indicated that he or she did. "Then this matter is done."

Tomás looked up. "I can stay in the Tribe?"

"Yes, but in the future, please consult the tribal treasurer if you are planning to remove any of our artifacts. According to the bylaws of the Tribe, you need a majority vote of the eldership to do so!" lectured grandmotherly Doña Mencia, as the other elders nodded their assent at the young miscreant.

"I will never touch another one again!" Tomás vowed.

"See that you don't!" ordered Doña Lucia.

"I believe that concludes our business of the day?" asked Doña Mencia, glancing around at contented elders.

"Does that mean that the report is accepted?" asked Doña Lucia.

"It does indeed," said the chairwoman.

"In that case, having brought her assigned tasks to successful completion, does that mean that Josefina is now our regular *cacica* and not the acting one anymore?" she demanded.

"I myself don't know what that 'acting *cacica*' business was in the first place," confessed Doña Mencia, her face splitting into her usual wry smile. "Privately, to my knowledge, we don't have any such ceremony. We did it for your sake, Josefina, to give you a little space to adjust to your new calling. You were always the chief of the Tribe since the moment you were inaugurated, as far as the majority of the council was concerned. You just had to feel confident in your ability. In other words, to feel the confidence all the rest of us already had in you. And, of course, the minority of elders who were not sure had also to be convinced. We always prefer to build consensus."

"You mean I've been chief all along?"

"That is correct."

Jo couldn't help but look over at Ricky, who simply shrugged his shoulders and then—to her wonder—smiled at her.

There was a pause as Jo searched his face. All the elders could see it, so no one spoke.

Finally, Ricky admitted, "You opened my eyes in the forest, *Cacica*. Tomás here had been telling me I was wrong about you. And then I saw you risk your life so that we could rescue Rafael, drawing all the fire toward yourself so we could—and did—escape. How many others would do that? Only the true leader risks her life for her people. You have the gifts of your forebearers—you are wise as King Enrique and courageous as Queen Anacoana. I am proud to serve beside you now."

Jo felt herself near tears.

"Shall we end with prayer for our *cacica*?" asked Doña Mencia, diplomatically.

Suddenly, Jo felt seized by desperation. "Wait! Please! Just a moment," she blurted out. Then she leaned forward, taking the attention of the entire *Nitaíno* captive to what she had to say. "I have done the tasks and secured your approval. I am now the *cacica*. I have done my part of the bargain. Please, may I see my parents now?" She sat back in the chair. The exhaustion mingled with hope was evident to all.

"Yes, you can. We will take you personally to the compound," said Doña Mencia, and the rest nodded and bowed to pray.

49

NO SOONER DID THE car bearing Jo to see her parents, driven by the gentle lawyer Angel Moreno Cueva de Piedra, edge out of Las Olas del Sol and begin to hum down the highway than Jo felt a great drowsiness seize her and, fight against it as she did, she fell sound asleep before they had covered half the distance. She was asleep when they arrived at the little stands run by the elderly selling produce along the road—stands that doubled as outposts to alert the compound if any unwanted visitors tried slipping through the paths in the brush. She was asleep as a bit of the brush was moved aside and a small obscured access road was exposed, into which the lawyer's car disappeared to be swallowed up by the dried bushes that were then moved back into place. She was asleep when they passed the plantain orchard on the right and the sugarcane field by a stream on the left and on the right a clearing with little *bohios*, country houses, with grazing cattle that made the entire area appear as a simple farming community. She did not awaken until the car gently stopped at the main administration-reception building, a replica of the thatched roof/branch-constructed longhouses of Taino history that regularly housed eighty residents, but now contained several modern bedrooms, two bathrooms, a kitchen, dining room, living room, and an office on its left side. The thatch and branches were a decorative overlay on a solid frame, so as to appear merely quaint from the sky, much like a large stable.

Despite the gentleness of the stop, Jo jerked awake, momentarily confused. "Are we here? Where?" she gasped, befogged.

Don Ramón and Doña Lucia, who had been sitting quietly in the back, stepped out and Don Ramón, in his most traditionally courteous manner, extended his hand in courtly fashion and helped Jo out of the car.

"Where are we going?" she asked.

"We want you to rest up just a little, before we go on."

Jo began to protest, but Doña Lucia was persistent and persuasive. "You look exhausted. You can't see your parents this way. They will be terrified for your health. You don't want that—do you? A little *siesta* would be just what you need to look fresh for them." All the while, she was ushering Jo up the stairs to a bedroom appointed for her. Don Ramón and Angel Cueva de Piedra stayed downstairs and knocked on the door of the office to visit the administrator, an old friend of Don Ramón, one with whom he used to cause plenty of trouble a half a century ago when they were boys.

Upstairs, Doña Lucia was saying, "Let's just step out of that dress and slip into this nightgown. Even for a little twenty-minute power nap, it will help you relax." She pulled down the shades and coaxed Jo into bed and then tiptoed out.

Fourteen hours later, Jo opened her eyes to a new sensation. Gone was the cataclysm of sound that was ever the tone poem of Las Olas, the susurration of ebb within the booming of flow, awakening one to a drumming of waves on rocks, and, beyond that shoreline, the brushed-cymbal reverberation of the ocean, undulating below the morning batterie of sky with modal clouds, resonant in the white foam of the surf. Instead, a gentle stirring of breeze wafted in through the open windows the scent of flowers, heralded by those encased in her bedroom's own window box, splashes of cherry pink, light orange yellow, and blueberry blue, set off by coconut white petals of a climbing vine, gripping the side of the window and overhanging the top, representative of all the beauty of the land that now lay around her.

As she climbed out of bed, she tried to shake the sleep from her head, wondering if it were early evening, but suspecting her twenty minute power-nap had turned into an all-night slumber marathon. She stepped to the window for verification and gazed beyond the flowers to the unmistakable signs of dawn. Early morning hawks reconnoitered the mountaintops, searching for breakfast prey, soaring above clouds like great furry hunting cats creeping down the mountain toward her. Far below, deep green palms, some stately with fronds fanning out, rustled beside extensive orchards of gigantic mango and avocado trees, behind which nestled small cashew and banana plants, some in season, some not, and some, like the acacia trees that dotted the wide expanse, always available for aesthetic beauty and practical function, and all of this gilded in increasingly dazzling sunlight.

Jo discarded the nightgown and soaked herself in the shower, washing off all but the memories of the past week, hoping the trauma would wash away too. This is the subtropics, she told herself. Clothing that fit her perfectly hung from a hook on the door. Jo smiled at Lucia's consummate gift of organization and dressed, letting her long hair hang damp so it could sun dry and, perhaps, lighten a shade. Now her interest was completely captured by the perfume of browning toast, punctuated by the deep rich scent of mountain coffee. Invigorated by the peace, Jo nearly skipped down the stairs to the kitchen and found Doña Lucia and three helpers serving up a mini-banquet.

"Good morning, *Cacica*!" called the first of the chefs to see her enter. All four looked up, themselves beaming with the glory of the outside sun. "We are so honored with your presence this morning."

Jo felt like she was walking in every forgotten, undervalued, and marginalized woman's dream. Maybe she could get used to this life!

"Good morning!" smiled Jo. "Is some of this bounty for me?"

"You know it is!" laughed Doña Lucia. "Come and eat and we'll go and see Don Diego and Doña Lea."

Jo smiled even more broadly. Her "Aunt" Lucia always insisted on calling Jo's father by his Spanish name, not James, as Jo knew him, or "Baiguanex," as was his Taino name.

"It is only because my whole body has refused to accept the marching orders of my brain until it is provisioned," grinned Jo, sweeping her hand down the long length of herself. "I am having my own comestible revolution this morning, or to put it succinctly: I'm famished!"

"Then we'll set it up in the dining room," said Lucia. "Please call Ramón and Brother Angel for breakfast. They're already up. They both got pulled into a project last night at the office and we better get them before they get too involved in it today or we'll lose their company on our trek to see your parents. The office is the last room down at the end of that hallway," and she pointed with her lips.

"At your orders," nodded Jo, and added, "thank you all so much."

Everyone smiled happily and redoubled their efforts to complete the meal.

As Jo walked down the hallway, she wondered why her Uncle Sol had never brought her here to the headquarters of the Tribe. At the same time, Jo experienced a strange sensation of calmness now that she was finally here. Somehow, all the haste and anxiety had fallen away from her. She had imagined she would hit the sanctuary running, dashing into her parents' arms, but now that she was here, she felt no need to rush. She would eat a leisurely meal, stroll across these living, productive grounds, and there would be her parents, alive, well, and joyful to see her. Why not enjoy each moment of their reunion? What's happening to me? she wondered.

Jo knocked softly at the office door. There was a stirring inside and—of all people—Ricky opened it up. "Good morning, *Cacica*! Did you sleep well?" he asked in a manner that was undeniably cordial. Now she knew she must be dreaming.

Don Ramón and Angel Cueva de Piedra, both hunched over computers inside, rose at once in her presence. "Good morning, *Querida*," smiled her "uncle." "*Cacica!*" bowed the little lawyer.

"I've come to invite all of you, I guess, to breakfast."

"We're certainly ready!" Ricky spoke for all.

"It's still early," the lawyer reminded him, a hint of disapproval in his voice. One did not complain, correct, or adjure the chief lightly, he seemed to be intimating.

Ricky just laughed and patted him on the shoulder. "Let's go soldier it down," he chuckled affectionately.

The little lawyer shook his head. The young—what can one ever do with them?

Jo was placed at the head of the table and the breakfast was indeed a banquet. Doña Lucia's hand was evident everywhere in the opulence and the succulence.

"I'm going to grow very fat and lazy if this keeps up," Jo warned her and ladled in another mouthful of *mangu*.

"Not the way we're going to run you ragged," laughed Doña Lucia.

I have no doubt of that! Jo assured herself.

When everyone was satiated— and after making up for missing a meal the previous evening so that now Jo could hardly move—Don Ramón announced, "It's time, *Querida*. Your parents should be up already."

"I thought my folks might come to breakfast," Jo confessed.

"No, no," Doña Lucia patted her hand and kissed her on the forehead. "They were up hours ago. And they have a lot to do. And some of that we have not even been told! So we are curious to see them too."

"Would you like me to help with the dishes?" Jo offered, remembering her manners.

The three workers shot glances at one another and all smiled, while Doña Lucia exclaimed, "Of course not! If you can't be pampered in your own headquarters, where will it happen? No, you go with Ramón. Your parents are waiting and very anxious to see you."

"Well then, let's go!" said Jo.

"This way, ¡*Querida!*" Don Ramón opened the door for her with traditional gallantry.

"I'll come with you," said Ricky and together they strolled across the grounds toward the fruit trees Jo had seen from her window. Butterflies from the mountains flitted everywhere, some with small bright orange wings, some black and medium-sized with yellow stripes, yet, even in the daytime, the ever-present hunting mosquito lurked in ambush in every patch of shade.

Behind the orchards, they passed several buildings, and Jo looked her question at her "uncle." Before he could answer, Ricky did: "These are the homes for the single women—the center of greatest interest for all the single young men who live on the exact opposite side of the encampment, near the mines."

"We have mines?" asked Jo. This was a dimension she could not recall her Uncle Sol mentioning.

"We do indeed," said Don Ramón. "This is where we get our steady wealth. Oh, and that reminds me!" He stopped suddenly and Ricky nearly walked into him. Don Ramón pointed at the great rise that rose up to the right, but whose expanse banked most of the rear vision of the compound. "Do you see that mountain?" He indicated it with an outstretched arm. It was the same mountain she had seen out her window earlier this same morning.

"Yes?" said Jo, wondering why on earth they were pausing to peruse it when they were just about to see her parents—finally!

"That is your inheritance!"

"That hill? I mean, that mountain?" Jo corrected herself. To her, it was a hill like any other hill in the whole elevated vicinity of the Sierra de Bahoruco, the great mountain range of the western peninsula.

"This is where we get our wealth, Princess!" said Ricky, with just a hint of the old Ricky lurking beneath.

"Tell me about it," ordered Josefina, suddenly interested.

"This is where we mine for gold!"

"Gold? We have a gold mine? Nobody ever told me that! Not even Uncle Sol!"

"Yes, it's our best-kept secret," Ricky assured her. "No one really knows but the elders and the workers—and, of course, the chief. So now you know, *Cacica*!"

"Yes, and, of course, we have the offshore 'bank,'" added Don Ramón.

"Oh, right!" said Ricky,

"I actually know about that," said Jo.

"I think everybody does," Don Ramón assured her.

"Even the tax collectors," Ricky agreed. "One third of what our divers bring up off Azua goes to local government, one third goes to some charitable outreach—a sizable amount of that in my estimation—to your Aunt Aña and all her ministries, *¡Reverenda!*" he punctuated the last word, so that Jo glanced sharply over at him for his sudden switch of titles for her, but he was smiling. The playful Ricky. That was better than the alternative: the snarling one! "And one third goes to the Tribe," he concluded.

"Yes, and we always hand in all our debts scrupulously and swiftly to the government so that they never have to come and collect—everyone is satisfied." Don Ramón almost sounded like he was lecturing these young neophyte leaders.

"He means they never have to come and snoop around," Ricky confided.

"Yes, exactly that," agreed Don Ramón.

By now they had passed the women's quarters and they could glimpse ahead, behind more vegetation, a large building canopied over by trees that let in only leaf-kissed sunlight looming up before them.

"What is this?" asked Jo.

"We call this the *Naca'n*—the center. It houses some of our key offices. This is where your parents are staying. It is our sanctuary for fugitives. And it houses our infirmary, for those sick and injured we do not want to trust to the hospital—even to that excellent facility in Jimani. It has state-of-the-art health care. All the equipment is new and the best we can buy, and our staff is highly educated and thoroughly trained. Much of our budget is invested here."

"New worlds are opening to me every moment today," reflected Jo.

This building was guarded, but the armed guards stepped deferentially aside as they saw Sub-Chief Don Ramón and Sub-Chief Enrique Asenao accompany in the new chief. Everyone knew who Jo was because everyone who could do so had attended her inauguration. She was their new celebrity. Only Jo, as she now fully realized, had thought her own status was temporary.

But her guides paused before the entrance and did not take her inside the building. "Before we go in on our tour, let's go to the opposite side of the compound to the cave where your father is."

"My father's in a cave!" exclaimed Jo in consternation.

"Of course," said Ricky. "That's where my actual work center is!"

Out of a cave, thought Jo. This man's a troglodyte—no wonder his manners are like someone "drug up in a cave!"

"Don't get the wrong impression!" Ricky warned her. "Suspend opinion for several hundred yards." They crossed over a huge living area filled with little traditional family homes, built like *bohios*. All of them had large antennas and small satellite dishes stuck up through the designer thatch roofs. Children were running everywhere.

Then Jo and her guides passed through a grazing area of cattle and well-trained guard dogs, who quieted down as soon as they caught scent of their guests. A row of windmills, rearing into the sky, stood waving everywhere, some sentinel high, set upon the top of the mountain.

"These account for a good deal of our energy in the compound," explained Don Ramón. "Ahead is the mine, and this cave is Ricky's center." He indicated a series of large cave openings. "In this one is our treasure, our present, our future." People were everywhere—like worker ants going in and out of the apertures.

"I want to see it all—in detail," Jo pleaded with them, "but now, please! I want to see my dad first!"

"Of course, you do!" sympathized Don Ramón, and nodded: "Ricky?"

"Come this way, Princess—or, more exactly, I should call you Queen Josefina, because this is the heart of your domain." And he stepped aside and ushered her in.

Jo stepped through great mahogany doors, opening up to a vast operations room, flooded with light. A huge set of screens and consoles lined all four walls, allowing only space for the colossal doors. The room was filled with people working on keyboards, while a series of large liquid crystal screens flashed a myriad of images.

"What do you do here?" asked Jo in wonder.

"Everything," said Ricky. "Look over here. This station has been working with marine biologists in Puerto Rico. We are helping track propeller-driven boats that have been colliding with manatees. There are only several hundred of them left. We are serving as a communications center that helps store information in our great data center, and we relay messages from ships to the Center for Endangered Marine Animals at Ponce. Not everything we do is focused on our own nation. But a lot of it has to do with the wider interests of our Tribe. We are conservation-driven," said Ricky, proudly.

"Of course we are," agreed Jo.

"And we monitor potential dengue fever epidemics, and we check seismic readings with the Tectonic Center for the Caribbean in San Juan in case another earthquake disaster threatens Haiti, and at this console we check out the latest deforestation satellite photographs and data, and this is where our brother Tomás got his information on where to strike, and. . . ." Ricky trailed off, because Jo had been searching through the horde of people and finally discovered a familiar figure far on the other side of the room. Jo immediately left them and "Excuse me! Excuse me! Sorry!" she "*Con Permiso*-ed" her way across the room until she was within earshot and could call out, "Dad! Dad!"

It took a minute for James Archer to hear his daughter because he was wearing headphones, but, when he recognized her voice, he glanced immediately around, saw Jo, flung his headphones down, leaped up from the keyboard, and ran, like the father in Jesus's parable, to embrace his daughter.

"Oh, Dad! I'm so glad to see you!" cried Jo. And, as her father took her in his arms, Jo couldn't help it. She began to cry.

"It's okay, JoJo. We're all safe. And what a splendid job you've done!"

After a time, Jo finally let go, and her father wiped her tears away and hugged her again and kissed her on the cheek and said, "I've been very proud of what you've been doing."

"Do you know about it?" asked Jo, puzzled. "I thought you were in seclusion."

"This is seclusion!" he assured her. "Who's going to find me here? Actually, I've had my hands full coordinating that invasion of Villa Riqueza."

"You were involved in that? How?"

"I was on top of all that from here. This is Ricky's communication center. He supervises the whole thing. He was very concerned about you and co-opted every workstation he could to facilitate it. I coordinated it all, since I've had a long relationship with Foresta and the agency's concerns. Yes, we were in touch with Cesfront, the army, the national police—we even had a direct line with Governor Franco Barrio's office. The governor's a good man and has always maintained the best relations with the Tribe. That's why he's been in office for twenty years! All of us vote him back in again and again. He's coordinated the pursuit for Pedro Badilla. He began to suspect him of being involved with a conspiracy and alerted us to watch out for him. We monitored Badilla's visits to Villa Riqueza and had our own team shadowing him constantly."

"Hah!" said Jo, her eyes widening. "And where is he now? Do you know?"

"We do indeed. We were following him when he fled from Villa Riqueza to see if he would lead us to others. But he went over the border where our jurisdiction stops, so we let our Haitian brothers pick up his trail. The lieutenant governor's going to have a tough time of it there. He'll have to tap one of his banks for money, and we are not above hacking into his accounts."

Jo raised her eyebrows. This was her strait-laced Dad?

James Archer recognized the surprise in her face and squeezed her hand, "JoJo, dear, I'm a diplomat—I do whatever it takes to keep the peace— the true peace. And Ricky here is a master at hacking!" He smiled at him, and Ricky, who had caught up with them and was standing deferentially aside, trying to look like he was not listening in, had the grace to blush under his already deep olive tone and look away.

"Sweetie, I was involved in every step of your adventure, even though the Tribe and the national police insisted I stay out of sight. Your mother and I saw something we shouldn't have seen and we had to flee for our lives. You almost lost us there, but we know this compound well and all its secret entrances. We utilized one that terrible night and fled to its safety. We lost our pursuers because we knew where we were going. And it was raining too—and that helped. God's grace!" He shook his head and paused. Jo could see the pain of loss in his eyes and felt it in her own spirit. He noticed her reaction, but, not certain what it meant, he explained," I was afraid, if they discovered we were in contact with you, they would use you to find us—we were the only eyewitnesses I know of to a great crime, besides those who perpetrated it."

"The murder of mayoral candidate Emilio Rosario and his wife Sophia?"

"Exactly."

"Wait!" cried Jo, putting it all together. "Did you tell Aunt Aña to recommend their niece Eridania the ranger to me?"

"Yes, of course! I've known that family for years. They're very dedicated to the Tribe. I just asked Aña not to tell you about the connection. It was not only dangerous, but it would have cramped your style. And let me tell you," he returned enthusiastically to his original theme, "you did splendidly. And I'm not the only one who thinks so. We all do! Your Aunt Aña told me to tell you she's so proud you turned such a dangerous situation into a positive one and got everybody out safe—and with prisoners intact! And she's glad Wilson was helpful. And that Ismael and Ruby are loving the properties she's showing them. Between us," confided her father, "I think Ruby's sort of taken over and is driving poor Aña ragged, and Ismael's head is spinning with all he's seeing.

"And, something else," he thought a moment. "Oh, yes, great work on getting the Rosary back! She told me all about it. But right now Aña's afraid Ruby's going to make her show Ismael the whole coast all around the entire island!" Jo laughed. "Anyway," concluded her father, "we all want to tell you what a great job you did coordinating the sting and the return. It was a masterpiece stroke for a *cacica* and her community—so swift, so effective, and so adroit at utilizing all the human resources on hand!"

Jo felt warm all over, blushing and taking this all in. Then she said, to take the attention off herself, "Anybody else you orchestrated into all this, dad?"

"Well," he paused a moment. "I didn't know about the nonlethal weapons deal, if that's what you mean. That was your innovation. Your aunt knew the anestheologist, Wilson Perez, because he's in her district. The excursion into the forest was your idea, but I talked to every member of Tomás's original team and asked retired ranger Ariadne—who had had twenty years on the force—to go along so that there would be some mature thinking involved in it. As it was, it turned out pretty wild, I understand, from Eridania's report to me—much more precipitous than I would have liked."

"Yes," said Jo, "that was Tomás, I'm afraid. But it yielded us our own eyewitnesses and helped us clinch the truth! So I'm not pointing any fingers there. Sometimes one has to act swiftly!" and then she stopped. She was sounding to herself like his attorney for the defense. She noted Ricky was grinning at her, so she changed her style from public defender back to *cacica.* "Well," she mused, "I guess I can still take some credit for contacting Cesfront, even if it turns out to have been a follow-up! They in turn recruited the border guards." She looked to her father for confirmation and he nodded, so she went on, "But I guess I owe you for the first contact with the army and the national police and the governor and I don't know who all—the Haitians too?"

"No, that was Jean-Jacques LaCaye, himself. As soon as he learned you were going to be elevated to chief, he dedicated himself to serve you, but out of sight. You know who he is?"

"I do now. I'm sorry I didn't recognize him myself."

"Children grow," her father acknowledged gently in a consoling voice that allowed for small omissions as a regular part of life. "You, for example, have turned into a stellar leader. And I am so proud of you!" And he hugged her again. Jo basked in his continued praise. "And now," he said, "let's go see your mother."

"Where is she?" Jo asked, "I have been wondering."

"She has a very important job to do here—and has quite a big surprise for you, Jo, and for you all. Ramón?"

"Yes, sir?"

"Is Lucia here?"

"She's where she always likes to be—in the kitchen supervising some banquet or another. It relaxes her."

"Would you please ask her to come over to the infirmary? This surprise is for her too."

The walk to the faraway center of secrets from the reception building was about the same distance as it was from the caves and the mine, and near the end they mirrored each other, walking across the fields through the trees, coming up nearly together. Lucia, arriving moments earlier, smiled as they joined her.

"Come upstairs with me, please, all of you," invited James. "Lea is working there."

They all followed without question. Jo had the feeling that all of them would have followed the beloved James into the center of a battle as vast as Armageddon, had he asked them to do so.

At the top floor of the hospital was another set of guards and a sealed-off unit. James Archer paused before gaining admission. "You must all contain yourselves for what you are about to see. Please make no sudden noises or movements, do everything as peacefully as you can." Everyone gazed at him in astonishment, but nodded yes. "All right, let's go in quietly." And the guards gently swung back the hospital doors.

Inside were two more guards, then a totally white expanse and a set of sunlit rooms behind a nurses' station. Equipment was everywhere. James Archer led them down the hallway to a room that encompassed the entire back of the wing. He knocked gently at the door. It opened slightly then swung open gently. Jo's stepmother stood there in the uniform she used in her work as a coronary care nurse, complete with face mask, and she stepped outside and greeted them all, but guided them back to a scrub room and said, "You must all scrub up your hands and face and put on these gowns and head coverings and face masks." Her tone had no hesitation at all in it. Jo had visited her at the hospital many times over the years and always marveled at the different side of her stepmother that emerged there—definitive in every matter.

A scrubbed, gowned, face-masked, quiet set of puzzled visitors followed her docilely back to the end door where she paused and ordered, "No sudden movements or sounds. Come in peacefully, stay no longer than ten minutes, leave at my signal." Jo felt like a salute was in order, but simply nodded her complete acquiescence like the rest. "All right, prepare yourself for a shock now," and she gently swung back the door.

A figure was in a large white hospital bed, hooked up to monitors. Jo and the others came diffidently forward, hesitant to take each step. And then Jo stopped and gasped. Before her was her Uncle Sol, aged, drawn, and so much smaller than she remembered him, but with the back of the bed raised, he was regarding them and smiling at them. "You're alive!" she gasped.

"Is that you, Jo? Everybody looks the same to me in those get-ups. Let me see, who else do we have?" His voice was very weak, nearly gasps. But he was alive. And he was clearly himself.

"It's Lucia and Ramón," said James, his brother, softly. "And Ricky's back again and this is indeed Josefina."

"You've done so well, Jo," gasped her uncle. "I'm so proud of you."

Jo marshaled all of the strength of will that she had not to throw herself on the bed, pounce on her uncle, and squeeze him with all her strength. Instead, she gasped, "Uncle Sol, how is it you are alive?"

"God's grace! That's all," he murmured.

"What happened to you?" asked Lucia, unable to restrain herself any longer. "We all thought you were dead! We were all grieving!"

He spoke softly and it took several moments for him to get it all out: "I *was* dead—for several minutes. I had a massive heart attack. They tell me it was too much tobacco over the years—that's the problem being Taino: We had to smoke in every ceremony and, of course, we discovered tobacco." He swiveled his head slightly toward Jo, "Take it out of the ceremonies, *Cacica*, like we did *cohiba*—that was our downfall with the Caribs and Columbus's marauders—we were all drugged into passivity and they all walked in and took away our lives!"

It was the old Uncle Sol—that was for sure!—thought Jo. He was lecturing already.

Lea patted her invalid on the arm and he subsided immediately. "Whoops! The boss says to put that on the shelf," he murmured. "Anyway," he smiled, a soft, sweet smile, "I'm not chief anymore—you are now Jo. That was the best choice I ever made, no offense, Ricky, for you are indispensable in your current position, keeping us in communication with the world."

"None taken, *Cacique* . . . uh . . . *ex-Cacique*?" Ricky fumbled.

"Just call me retired *Cacique* or maybe *Cacique-emeritus*? Anyway, it's Jo's problem now. The doctors tell me, I'm done."

"Inti, you never told us," said Don Ramón. "We thought you were dead. We were grieving for you. . . ." The hurt stood out in his voice.

"That was such a hard decision. I wanted to take you all into my confidence as I have always done, but they wouldn't let me."

"Blame me," said James. "I made that decision as any diplomat would have." He took Ramón and Lucia by their gloved hands and said with a voice filled with love, "Our dearest brother and sister, you are both so honest I was compelled to insist we do this, because it was imperative to make certain Jo felt she was on her own in this decision to become our chief."

Then he turned to Josefina herself. "My precious daughter, you were so wrapped up in your work in Richfield, you were only looking at what the Tribe had to offer you so you could use it to shore up your ministry there. You were so utilitarian about it all—hyperfocused as you always are—it's your nature. So, I thought you needed to have the space to decide." Then he turned back to Lucia and Ramón. "Dear friends, how could I saddle you with the burden of prevarication? It is not in your natures to deceive. Relief would be everywhere in your demeanor, in your speech, in the way you handled each new issue—Jo is far too smart to be fooled for long." All he could see were their eyes. But, as they glanced at one another, James could tell they were mollified.

At this point, Lea stepped forward and said with that soft command that registered nurses possess that brooks no opposition, "It's time."

"Thank you, Lord, he's alive!" breathed Jo in ardent prayer and that captured everyone's feelings—even the doubting Ricky's.

As they exited, Jo seized hold of her stepmother and squeezed her as tightly as she had wanted to squeeze her uncle. Her father joined in the family hug, as the rest of their small party stepped thoughtfully out of the unit and waited for them behind the doors. "I want so much to tell you about what's happening to Danny," started in Jo. "I'm so worried about her."

"Tonight," said her stepmother. "I'll be off at nine o'clock, when Uncle goes to sleep. We have a wonderful nurse spelling me for all night. We'll talk then." Jo felt an enormous sense of relief.

Outside the unit, their gowns and headdresses and masks neatly folded on a chair, the three other visitors were putting together the pieces of what they had just witnessed.

"Well," Lucia was saying, "the language everybody was using was always so strange. I noticed that! No one ever said clearly that he was dead— they only kept saying he had 'passed.' It was strange."

"And there was never any viewing or any funeral or any body. That was unusual—I thought so all along," said Ramón.

"Me too," said Jo, joining in. "I kept asking about it!"

James smiled and said, "Let's go see some other wonders, shall we?" And he led them out.

50

W ITH AN ENORMOUS SENSE of relief, Jo walked with restored agility in her step. Already this morning, she had felt invigorated. Now she was feeling like a younger woman in her twenties again, if only barely hanging on to her twenties, and not a tribal elder in her nineties, full of the weight of responsibility for absolutely everything. What was making the difference? Nothing had changed in all the trauma she had endured. She had still been through life-threatening ordeals—in the forest, in Villa Riqueza. But, what she realized now was, beyond all that personal stress, what was obviously continually the overriding issue for her was the fate of those she loved. Her parents and her Uncle Sol were safe. Her brother and sisters were now back in her parents' hands. These were the cardinal concerns that affected her most. She saw herself more clearly than she had ever done before. What happened to those she loved was what was central to her wellbeing—hers was a personality in relationship. The realization had never been more clearly presented to her.

As she walked, a wide vista of thought opened to her, commensurate with the growing fields through which she now strolled. This was also the center of her faith: not the "smells and bells" as some called the trappings of worship, but the point of it all, the relationship with a caring God who was already in an eternal triune relationship of love and was graciously extending that love to earth to include humans through the generous, sacrificial act of one eternal personality of the Godhead, choosing to become human as *YaYael*, *Yeshua* the Messiah, *Jesucristo*, Jesus Christ, the anointed *Salvador*, rescuing humankind from the consequences of its own failings. This was the Great Community Organizer reconciling the world to Godself.

Deeply invested in that relationship, Jo had pursued her training in reconciliation, and now, as she completed her first decade of service to humanity, she could see that everything she did was constantly engaged in networking everyone she could into that beautiful divine love.

I think in concentric circles, she realized. The center of my being has become my relationship to God. Then the wider circle is my family. And then the circles extend out, like the stone of my spirit was dropped by the Great Spirit into the pool of humanity. How then could I not hurt deeply when those closest to my own center simply ignore or neglect divine love? I see why I feel such mourning, when the vast concern of the celestial Parent is taken for granted just as the sacrificial caretaking of loving earthly parents is taken for granted by foolish children too busy, too self-centered, too overinvolved in the bustle of life to reach out and take these hands of love.

Jo's pace slackened and she nearly stopped walking as her disparate vision focused on the screen of her mind. So this is why I have been so deeply troubled in my core and why I feel such great relief. I can give my sister and my brother back to my parents and, through them, to God. The rest of it—the people I love in New Jersey, my people here in my Tribe, our extended family in Haiti and across the Caribbean—these responsibilities I can embrace more confidently now. And, as for the rest, like the threats to my safety? Important, of course. I'm not an ascetic at heart. I don't welcome pain as if it were somehow purgative and life-giving. I'm all about seeking that which is life-enhancing for the people I serve. I love this earth and all in it! I thank the Great Creator for it! This is the First Nations way and what my ancestors strove to teach all of those who came to them. And it is my way. This is primal truth. It's just that I have made more gains with strangers than I have with those closest to me. This has been my greatest burden all along. I see that now. . . .

"What would you like to see first, *Cacica*?" The voice startled her. Jo had fallen into such deep reverie she had continued walking slowly on when everyone else had paused a dozen feet behind. Jo stopped and glanced back, deeply embarrassed. But at least they weren't regarding her as one would a zombie who had just stumbled into their village after twenty years' absence. Don Ramón and Doña Lucia were waiting patiently without any other visible expression. Ricky was looking bemused. Her father was smiling, as he observed, "A lot on your mind, Josefina." It was not a question.

"I am so sorry," she apologized, abashed.

"Don't be. Sol was often that way. He was thinking all the time. You are very much like him."

"Thank you, but I hope I am like you as well."

"Of course," laughed her father with delight. "And all the best traits!"

He paused.

Jo noticed they had stopped about a hundred feet from the entrances to the caves in the mountain. People were constantly moving in and out, so this would be the last time for any personal discussion before they inserted themselves into the crowds. Jo did notice that most people were moving out of the two most prominent of the caves and smaller figures were grouped around the entrance to the third. "What is that other cave besides Ricky's?" she asked to show she was interested in what was obviously important to them.

"The supply depot," said Ricky. "It's deep and it's got everything we need in the way of equipment and—well—pretty much everything we would need to store in a large warehouse. Do you see that fourth entrance? The one set much farther away from the others? Way beyond? Yes? That is the entrance to the gold mine. We cordon it off and enter it when we need it. The nearest entrance is, of course, as we mentioned, the one to our treasury."

"That's where we're heading next," James Archer assured him. "The new *cacica* will want to see that."

"And, Jo," continued Ricky, "I hope you won't be offended, but I probably should check in with the Communications Center. Let me go while all of you see the wonders. Everything appears to be under control there, of course, but I like to see for myself what's happening. I've found it's always wise to be checking in constantly—which is why I live in the town and not the compound, or I'd never get any rest! Anyway, I'll be back before you leave."

"Of course," said Jo's father, and Ricky hurried over to join the crowds pouring in and out of the two farther entrances to the mountain, which was Jo's mountain now.

He called me "Jo," thought Jo. He hardly ever does that—it's always "Princess" or "*Cacica*" or whatever. She was about to muse on that, when "Humph!" the lawyer Angel Moreno Cueva de Piedras snorted sharply. He was right at her elbow now, and Jo jumped. What's happening to me? she asked herself. This is no time for more introspection. I've got to get hold of myself. Even more deeply embarrassed, she realized the Tribe's central lawyer had been so deferentially hanging back, so silent this entire time, and she so wrapped up in the shock of the discoveries and her precipitated self-absorbing reflections she had quite forgotten he was even along.

But now she began to concentrate on him and, as she did, the thought came to her: How curious a reaction he'd voiced. . . . And, immediately, in one of those unusual, preternatural moments of inspired insight, Jo realized with absolute certainty that Ricky was escaping because he did not want the topic of the Rosary, which was without a doubt back within the treasury, to raise a discussion and force him to implicate his friend Tomás further when Jo had so effectively rescued him. As Ricky apparently had, Jo too realized that this quiet little lawyer hardly ever missed anything. And he was probably always in waiting for the appropriate moment to reintroduce whatever it was that troubled him until he was satisfied. Maybe he was a bit obsessive-compulsive—but what a boon for the Tribe. Still, she thought, what a wise move on Ricky's part to make a tactical retreat. It was, she reckoned, the measure of this man, as well. There was subtlety here, even if he tried hard to disguise it. . . .

"Before we enter," her father called a halt, "you should realize, Josefina, that what you will be viewing we consider the center of our Tribe—its heart of heritage and the material center of its wealth. It is what we treasure most in earthly items, subject of course to our overriding loyalty to YaYa. And, JoJo, I've been thinking about your whole dilemma, really your crisis of identity over your calling to minister by Yocahu, the God of the Trinity, who rules all and sustains all. You are a minister ordained to preach the gospel of Jesus Christ, YaYael. Clearly, we of all people, the descendants of Enrique, would never seek to annul that calling. We are simply envisioning that God is presently redefining the description of *cacica*—"chief"—back to being the spiritual as well as organizational leader, which was the model that the great Enrique forged for our people. In a sense, you are *cacica* and *behika*—though you should still maintain a *behiko*, as Enrique did his for ceremonies as a kind of assistant minister. Our present one is a devoutly faithful follower of YaYael who has completed the promise of the ancient shaman with God's deeper knowledge."

"Of course," agreed Jo. "I would never have dreamed of replacing him. He is a fine man of faith."

"Good," said her father. "I have no doubt that you will discharge your duties adroitly and loyally. You will be chief for your calling—a material and a spiritual undertaking. And, Jo, about your other heart's concern, well, we can work with you on what is best for your new church planting in New Jersey. That is not unimportant to us, for what is important to you is important to us," and he looked around at the other sub-chiefs who all nodded, so he continued. "What would you say to picking the best associate minister you can find as your delegate and the Tribe donating the salary as part of our mission? You can still check back regularly whenever you need to do so. It is only a plane ride away, if it comes to that. At the very least, your money worries are over. As *cacica*, you have great power in determining where tribal money is invested. And this looks to us like a good, solid investment." Her father looked at her expectantly.

Jo caught her breath. No one knows you like your parents, she thought. Ample funding at her fingertips! "That sounds workable to me!" she said, visions of all the things she wanted to do for her people back in Richfield parading through her head.

"Then we have an accord!" her father said. And, each *nitayno* and the *nitayna* of the *Nitaíno*, the sub-chiefs of the tribal council, would have cheered and patted them both on the back except for the restraints of their dignity. As it was, Jo received a warm handshake from the lawyer, a bow from her "Uncle" Don Ramón, a kiss from Doña Lucia, and a hearty embrace from her dad. "And, now," he said, with an uncharacteristically dramatic flair, "The Cave of Little Faces, the center of our Tribe." And, Jo thought, the goal to which I have been drawing since I arrived here, and indeed the one I've been moving toward my whole life!

They crossed the space and Jo was surprised to see children playing around the entrance.

"Watch your head," warned her father, and Jo had to dip it to enter in. She looked down at the children, scurrying in and out around her feet, and she wondered why the Tribe had never chosen to heighten the entrance so adults could pass through as easily. And then, as she lowered her head even further, Jesus's words flooded her mind, "*ean mē straphēte kai genēsthe ōs ta paidia, ou mē eiselēte eis tēn basilian tōn ouranon*": "Unless all of you change inwardly and become as little children, you will not enter into the reign of heaven." The treasure is obviously not in the money, if they give children access to it, she told herself; it must be elsewhere.

She thought, as she continued to bow through the entrance, how many of us down the ages have realized the intention here? Did even the small Tomás have to bend his head when he entered to steal the Rosary of Enrique? Did her brother Ben stoop in or wait outside? Did it make any impact on either—this enforced humbling—as it's making on me?

As she finished her crouched shuffling in and raised her downcast eyes, she did indeed confront an amphitheater of wonders. The cave was large and well lit by hooded lights that glinted on carvings everywhere. Predominant among them were childlike stick figures with snowmen's round eyes depicted like nuggets of coal and mouths often frowning but interspersed with some that were grinning. Standing out was what was called the "swaddled baby motif," a curious drawing where a little head and body were emerging out of the top of the head of a larger body encased in what appeared to be tight wrappings, the spirit emerging in death to return to the Great Creator. Other figures festooned the walls as well and some nearly leaped off of them in their vividness. A square-headed, slit-eyed *zemi* ferociously frowned, a demon here to cause trouble for humanity, but it had been surrounded by simple crosses, imprisoning it to ward it off, and it appeared furious at being so impeded. Another head with the unmistakable tracing of a rough armored helmet and lines beneath the circle of chin, depicting a beard, told of the *conquistadores*, armed and insulated against the gentle culture they had invaded. But most of the faces were plain little circles with round black eyes and lines for mouths, nestled beside each other, the simple work of ancestors to record that, "Yes, we were here before you in these sacred places."

One entire wall had a high shelf on which sat the *iconos tricusipidos, trigonolitos*, those three-sided stone icons, symbols of the sacred to these ancestors. At the apex of most of these was simply smooth uncarved stone, not representing any figure. On one side of the triangular shape were swirls to show the movement of the Spirit, and on the final side a face, often in agony, "Three points in one stone," her Uncle Sol had lectured her, "Father, Son, and Holy Spirit represented in our sacred age-old icons, but so much more as well. The entire history of our migration is often told in these *zemis*. So read them carefully."

On the other walls sat so many other treasures of pottery, crafting, *dujos* of famous ancestral chiefs still preserved, whole displays of ancient coins under plexiglass, ornate swords and muskets captured from the invaders and now on display beside bows and arrows and stone axes and hatchets and, in one corner and on the floor to be easily accessible, an entire *bohio* in and out of which the children ran, and, all over, the floor was filled with toys. None of the children could touch the actual treasures set high above them, but the toys, often representing them, were everywhere. All of the children were playing games with teenage attendants whose work it was to entertain them between lessons and explain everything that surrounded them.

In the center of all this activity, on display on the central wall one faced upon entering, were beautiful crosses and religious items, and off to the side a very simple rosary sat apart, darkened with age, its wooden beads cracked, inexpensive even for its day, but precious beyond comparison, the only clear possession that had come down from the great liberator, Enrique, besides his bones that lay abandoned in the ruins of the church at Azua.

"Look," said her father, and pointed at a crude representation of the evening sky, adorning the top of the control wall. "I've often thought, when I was a child, that my brother Inti, your Uncle Sol, was very much like the sun in my life, all boisterous and fun-loving, and giving of himself to exhaustion, a natural ruler, gifted down through the ages by rulers. Your regal, natural mother was like my moon, a ruler herself, but in a style far more gentle and thoughtful but thoroughly as effective. Had she lived, she would have become a *cacica* in *Borinken*, or as some say *Borikua*, Puerto Rico today, but the Great Spirit took her from us. Though Saul never married and Raquel left us as all of us must do one day, still they were my two centers of light. And Raquel and now your wonderful stepmother Lea, regal herself in her own delightful and capable way, gave us you children as our stars—and now, Jo, you are the one star that shines forth as the new center of light. All of us bow to you, our new *cacica*."

Jo looked at her father, astonished, as he broke off speaking and tears began to trickle down his face. "I had no idea this meant so much to you," she gasped, and she took him in her arms and held him.

Finally, he wiped his eyes and faltered his apology, "I don't know what came over me."

"It doesn't matter," said Jo. "You are a great man and I have always admired you and relied upon you. I still intend to do so."

He nodded, and his heart was so full he could not answer.

Jo looked away to give him a moment to recover. She watched the little Dominican-Taino children playing with antique toys and balls and little traditional Taino games and figures she had played with herself, but not here. And then she stopped and gasped again—it was a day for revelations!

She turned to her father, still standing at her side and asked, "Why did I never play in this cave?"

"We did not understand it fully when you were born. This cave had become sealed off in those days from all but the few. In the last decade or so, your Uncle Sol became much more introspective than he had ever been. He'd been all action as a young chief and built up our store of treasure—it's down that corridor, you can see it when you want to, vaults of gold coins and bullion and precious jewels from shipwrecks and all the traditional kinds of treasures you have ever imagined. He had long talks with Doña Mencia, whom he had personally elevated to head of the Tribal Council when her aged predecessor died. By that time, no one questioned his judgment on nearly any point, as I know they will come to trust yours, Jo. Your Uncle Sol had these display shelves built and the sacred *zemis* and Enrique's Rosary and all the treasures you see set out on high where they were out of the reach of young ones who could swallow them or be cut on them or hurt themselves in some way, and he had the Tribe open up the anteroom of this cave again with all its wondrous carvings that tell the entire history of our Tribe and display in synecdoche its treasures. He wanted the children to grow up with them as very familiar poignant illustrations of their identity and their heritage. And he wanted them to become so familiar they would be commonplace and no one would lust after them."

"To make Enrique's treasurehouse a place where children can be safe and loved, a haven he created to go down through the generations. I think I understand it," said Jo as she gazed around at everything and everyone, the children initially ignoring her and her father as just two more grownups in their little world of today, with no expectations but to continue to be loved and cared for. Then Jo sat down on the floor next to a group of children copying the little faces on the wall and coloring these in and adding their own designs. "These are so good," enthused Jo.

"I like pink faces," said one little girl, shaking back her long dark hair.

"I like green ones," said another and lifted up her drawing so Jo could see it.

Jo looked up at her father, smiling broadly. "I think I will come here often," she told herself as much as she did her father. "This 'cave of little faces' is truly a holy place. It is full of treasure. I will check with Uncle Sol and Doña Mencia, but I'm sure that I am right. The real treasure is the happy little faces of these children as they learn to live together in harmony in our great family. I am so blessed to be a part of such a holy body of Christ."

"I'm so glad you think so, Jo," said her father, as they emerged from the cave of the tribal treasury, amidst one bevy of children crowding out and another one dashing in. "I've come to my own thought about children, though it took me all these years to do so and, of course, the lesson of having four of my own, which, believe me, was very, very humbling."

He and Jo laughed together, she a bit self-deprecatingly. "I realize something about our sense of identity," and he paused and looked deeply into Jo's eyes. "I've been waiting for the opportunity to share it with you, because I think you may find it helpful. You see, when we are infants, our identity is wrapped up completely in ourselves. We can't go and get anything for ourselves or even explain what we need or want to have, so, in our frustration, we call out our cries and survive. Our world is our breastfeeding mothers and ourselves. That's the limit of it. Dad comes in early on, too, if he is nurturing, as I've always tried to be, and soon a child's identity is nuclear and so is its whole world—though I doubt if Ben, even as a little boy, ever claimed that his Dad could lick any father in the world!" Both of them laughed uproariously this time. It was good to laugh with her father.

"All right," said James Archer, "the next phase: As I grew, my identity was defined by myself and my brother and soon our friends joined us, so our parents couldn't object successfully to even the worst of them! I went through my saving-the-world stage too, but that was only presaging adulthood, for, when I met your mother, that and everything else fell immediately down—not to second place—but thirteenth, fourteenth, and what have you—all the top twelve spots in my attention were commandeered by my love for young and lovely Raquel. All those words of Genesis 2:24 hit me like a *batey* ball—I was bowled over—and I discovered that 'one flesh' with one's spouse meant I had a new expanded identity. She and I were now one flesh—a new creature in God's sight!"

They had emerged completely from the cave by now and were standing outside it so James Archer could use his hands in fine Dominican and New Jersey style to express his points. So he repeated, "We were now one new identity in God's sight! One flesh!" And he clapped his hands together to illustrate that solid bonding. It was a booming clap and several frightened children dashed back into the cave. "And then, when you children were born, my personal identity expanded from two to be defined by three, four, five, and then six, and your little lives were my life, just as Sol and I had been part of the identity of our own dear parents. Today, my living wife, Lea, and you, my children, are my identity—who I am. But, lately—and this is why I'm telling you all this, what I want you to know—is that, as I live on, I realize that all the children in the Dominican Republic and all the children of our neighbor, Haiti, and indeed, all the children in the entire world are really my children too. I see now increasingly that we are—all of us—intrinsically tied together in macrocosm in God's creation, just as we are tied together inseparably in microcosm in our own Tribe. It is who I am becoming now: not just a diplomat, but a father to the world."

"And you are a wonderful leader and a great model for any of us young men!" said an all-too-familiar voice, and Jo looked around to see Ricky, back from checking out his center, regarding them both. "Thank you for the lesson." And then he asked cautiously, peering around himself, "Where are Don Ramón, Doña Lucia, and Don Angel?"

"I don't know," said Jo, glancing about in surprise. Just she and her father stood together amidst the playing children and their tutors.

"Well," he grinned, "then I am able to tell you now, plainly, Queen Josefina the First, without fear of correction," and he looked to James Archer, who merely bowed and swept his hand in a "go to it" gesture. "Well, I want to say that I will never believe in Columbus and his good intentions, that's for sure. But, let me state this even more surely, my *Cacica*. I now believe in you."

Glossary of Taino Terms

alguacil: the marshal(s) who brings order

areyto(s)/areito(s): traditional songs and dances

azua: "A—zu—a," the chant that could synchronize rowers

batey: a ball game, traditionally serving as a reenactment of war or for settling territorial disputes; also name for ceremonial ball court

behike/-a/bohiti: traditionally the religious leader, tribal medicine man, and healer through prayer and natural herbs

Bimini: "Life of the Spring Waters," Florida

Bohio: a traditional round house

Borinken/Boriquen/Borikua: "Great Land of the Valiant and Noble Lord," Puerto Rico

cacique/cacica/cacike: hereditary or selected regional chief

cacicazgo: the territory over which a chief ruled

Cacicazgo Bohios Haity Sabana: the Chiefdom of the Taíno Homes of the Land of Mountains and Valleys

Cacicazgo Naca'n Guada Choreto Kiskeyanakán: the Chiefdom of the Central Garden of Abundance of the Mother of Islands

canaries: vessels of water

caracol: conch, spiraled sea shell

caracuri: nose rings often made of gold

cassava/casaba: bread made from yuca

cemi(s)/zemi(s): three-sided stone icons, symbols of the sacred to the Taíno ancestors: at the apex of most of these was simply smooth uncarved stone, on one side of the triangle shape were swirls, and on the final side a face, often in agony—three points in one stone

cohiba/cohoba: an hallucinatory anesthetic snuff made from the Cojobana tree that gave visions to *behikes* and *Nitaínos*

Diosa: of God

ditas and *jitacas:* traditional deep food dishes

dujo/duho: the traditional ceremonial stool or U-shaped chair with short legs that had been the distinguishing mark of tribal leaders

Guakia Baba: Our Father

Guami-ke-ni: the Lord of Land and Water

guanajo: turkey

guani: bee hummingbird

guani'n: the traditional royal medal pendant of chief's office, forged of gold, silver, and copper, a shiny metal, symbol of authority; see also *tao*

guajey/guiro: small dried gourds, which are scratched to add complexity to the musical rhythms

jab'bao/ja'bao: the three-stringed musical gourd instrument

jan-jan catu: "so be it," *amen*

Jukiyu-jan: good spirit—yes

Juracan-ua: bad spirit—no

Kiskeya, Quisqueya: "The Mother of All Islands," Dominican Republic, Hispaniola, Hatey, Bohio

Maboya/Mabuya-ua: ghost/spirit—no

Manicato: "valiant and bold warrior of good heart"

mayohuaca'n: the sacred ceremonial drum

nabori daca Diosa: "I am a servant of God"

naca'n—the center

nagua: traditional loin cloth made of white cotton

Nanixi/Nanichi: "my heart, my love"

Natiao: brother(s)

Nitaíno/Ni-taino: a tribal council of elders of the region

Nitayno/-a: sub-chief of the tribal council

tai: good

Taiguaitiao: Good friend; *guatiao* is "friend"

Taino/Taíno: the aboriginal inhabitants of Cuba, Hispaniola, Puerto Rico, Jamaica, and other Caribbean islands, "good people"

tambura/tambora: long wooden drum made from hollowed tree trunk, shaped into a long cylinder that narrowed at each end, fastened to sashes slung over shoulders to free hands to beat the rhythms with sticks

tao: synonym for *guani'n,* a metal plate made of gold and copper in the form of a cross for a chief

tatagua: earring, made of gold or sea shells

Ti': the good great Spirit, "height, highness"

Xamayca: "the Land of Wood and Water," Jamaica

YaYa/Yaya: the Great Spirit, the Creator; *Y'aY'a/Y'ay'a*, the name of the Supreme God, not in its shortened form, but with all of its traditional Taíno syllables

YaYael/Yayael: son of *YaYa, YaYa*'s son who died, according to Taino tradition

Yocahú: the Supreme Deity, Creator who is *Yúcahuguama Bague Maórocoti,* the One Who Provides the Yuca, Rules the Sea, and Is Without Ancestors, *Y'aY'a*

yuca: tropical root crop, like potato

yukayeke/yukaieke/yucayeke: "the great village," the gathering, the "village" represents all the Taíno families, settlements, towns, and cities

Yukayeke Inti Bajacu: the Gathering of the Dawn

Yukayeke Oconuco Xaragua: the Villages of the Families of the Mountain Farmland

Yukayeke Xaragua Ni Enrique Xiba Bahoruco: the Families, Settlements, Towns, Cities of the Jaragua Region of Enrique's Water, the Great Lake, and the Stone and Wood-Filled Mountains of the Bahoruco Range

zemis: "the heavenly spirits," traditionally called emanations, creations of *Y'aY'a*, which protected humans; see also *cemi(s)*

Acknowledgements

Thank you for reading our novel, a labor of love on which we've worked for more than a decade. If this were a movie instead of a book, we might call this addendum: "The Making of *Cave of Little Faces*." The majority of it we researched and wrote in the Dominican Republic, which is where Aída was born. It started as a conflation of two ideas we had. Some twenty years or so ago, Aída envisioned writing a contemporary tale about a woman who retreats to a cave periodically to sort out issues in her family life. Bill, reared by his father in New Jersey with a raised consciousness about his Native American background (Leni Lenape), was contemplating writing an historical novel about the great liberator Enrique, the Taino chieftain whose devout Christian faith, astonishing courage, and phenomenal skills as a military strategist rescued his people from extinction by the marauding *conquistadores* and who holds a great share of the credit for the existence of the enclaves of the Taino nation that exist today. When Aída was inspired to unite these two ideas in one story featuring descendants of Enrique today, loosely structured on the Joseph story in the Bible (Genesis 29–50), our projects came together. Both Enrique and Joseph were minority believers in antagonistic majority cultures. Despite a vast separation of time and culture, each struggled with the same question many of us face today: How do we negotiate a personal, national, and spiritual minority identity in an often hostile majority world?

Pursuing this idea, we spent several years creating biographies for our characters and structuring our story. Aída focused the trajectory on Jo's search for identity and the parallel recovery of a symbolic religious artifact. She also designed the major locations: the beach house, the compound, and the two opposing imaginary towns of Villa Barohuco and Villa Riqueza. The rest of the setting, including the magnetic pole, the two lakes, and all the other towns and cities, are all authentic sites. Armed with this roadmap, each morning Bill would write a chapter, fleshing out the narrative. He added the contraband deforesting/adventure theme, the Polarians, the meals and ceremonies and meditations and conflicts between the siblings, and added in various supporting characters and incidences including the batey game; Jo's tribal meetings, coronation, and tests; Ruby's romance; etc., to become a story. Then each day, Bill and Aída went over that morning's chapter carefully together, Aída critiquing everything and making many suggestions for improvement, which we'd toss back and forth until we were both satisfied. Our goal was to create a world within a world into which readers could enter and inhabit. Sadly, while statistics suggest that many Dominicans retain fifteen percent Taino DNA heritage, there are no organizations of those who identify themselves as Taino of which we are aware here in the "Mother of All Islands," as there are in Puerto Rico, Cuba, New Jersey, New York, Florida, and other locations, where Taino festivals and traditions are honored and maintained. Even the church dedicated to Enrique by his wife is a tumbled-down, neglected ruin at this writing, though the great defender is honored by place names and statues. So, the story is completely fiction, as are the characters, but the spirit of the heritage lives on.

To create such a contemporary Taino world today for the Dominican Republic, we did much primary research across the island and have many sources to acknowledge for the data from which we selected details. In the western side of the country, where much of the action takes place, we owe a great debt of thanks to Jesús Manuel Garcia, then the director of the Hotel la Saladilla in Barahona, our inspiration for Los Diamantes del Mar Hotel. Thanks to Jesús and Ramon Emilio Cruz, who is himself of Taino heritage and knows the mountains intimately, we had the privilege to rappel up a couple of stories cliffside and explore a newly discovered cave of little faces, being among the first to enter it in its pristine form.

The scene where Lake Enriquillo engulfs the highway, stretching out to its Haitian counterpart, Etang Saumatre, is authentic and based on our own explorations, as are so many other scenes in the book, including having our rented cars pulled up backward at the Magnetic Pole, seeing the stately women processing in single file to lovely Lake Rincon to wash their clothing, exploring the real cities and villages, and sites with "little faces," and even negotiating the dry forest in several brief trips wherein we encountered both a legal and an illegal kiln. But, at the same time, we still owe a debt to many others to whom we turned for details.

The original history of the Tainos is found in Columbus's journals, but principally the story of Enrique is recorded by Bartolomé de las Casas in his *History of the Indies*. An accessible English version is translated and edited by Andrée Collard (New York: Harper & Row, 1971; see books 2.9–10, 3.122–127). Ramiro Matos González's *Azua Documental (y Apuntes*

Históricos) (Santo Domingo: Editora Alfa & Omega, 1995) is a treasure of information on the chiefs who faced the conquest and their domains and guided us as we adapted our simulation of a present division of the country into *cacicazgos*. Scott Doggett and Leah Gordon's *Dominican Republic & Haiti* (Oakland, CA: Lonely Planet, 1999) was also full of helpful data on the Haitian connection.

While acknowledging every person, site, and article that expanded our knowledge in all these years of research is impossible, certain ones left a lasting impact on the story. We found many excellent sources on the Tainos by a worthwhile investment of days in the Museo del Hombre Dominicano in Santo Domingo, Dominican Republic, and exploring the historical Taino sites in the Dominican Republic and Puerto Rico, including the enlightening Indian Ceremonial Center at Caguana, Puerto Rico, with its artifacts and batey field. Also in Puerto Rico, the Casa de la Cultura of the Municipality of Yabucoa with its indigenous museum, archaeological displays, and accessible archival articles yielded a wealth of material thanks to its kind and attentive staff.

On the internet, we were helped by a variety of informative sources, such as the United Confederation of Taino People, http://www.uctp.org/index.php?option=com_content&task=view&id=12&Itemid=26, accessed 27 March 2011. Many helpful articles such as "Taino Origins," "The Andean Culture of the Collas," "Taino Indian Fascinating Secrets, The Departure," etc., accessed 6 May 1999, we found at http://www.amdatel.com/blasinicreations/aj/tva.html. "The Taino World," accessed 4 January 2000, with many other insightful articles were shared on http://www.elmuseo.org/taino/tainoworld.html. The Guide to Caribbean Vacations (http://www.guidetocaribbeanvacations.com) offered much interesting data about the western side (e.g., how crocodiles got into the lake!) and the United Nations Educational Scientific and Cultural Organization (UNESCO) provided a scientific profile of the Jaragua-Bohoruca-Enriquillo Biosphere Reserve, cataloging the flora and fauna and other data. Also helpful were the *Boletin Informativo: Nacion Taina de las Antillas*, VIII:5 (Sept./Oct. 2000) out of New York/ New Jersey, which gave us good images for Jo's coronation festival and parade, and "The Invisible Boricua Indian" by Master Sergeant James "Running Fox" Lopez, http://www.indio.net/aymaco/Boricua%20.htm, accessed 27 March 2011, for ethos. Our story also benefited from "Taino Flags," http://www.crwflags.com/fotw/flags/xh-taino.html, accessed 27 March 2011; Tainos (Greater Caribbean, USA) Indigenous Caribbean Center, Information on Indigenous Peoples of the Caribbean, from the Guyenos to Central America, from the Antilles to North America, http://indigenouscaribbean.wordpress.com/directory/tainos-greater-caribbean-usa, accessed 27 March 2011; official website of the Aymaco Tribe, the Native American Indian Taino Tribe of Turabo, Borinken (Puerto Rico), Open Directory-Society=Ethnicity, http://www.indio.net/aymaco, accessed 27 March 2011; and The Americas: Indigenous: Caribbean: Tainos, http://www.dmoz.org/Society/Ethnicity/The_Americas/Indigenous/Caribbean/Tainos, accessed 27 March 2011. One of the best accounts of the wood contraband runners, Kirsis Díaz's "Contrabando de carbón a la vista de todo el mundo," we found in *Diario Libre* (14 May 2014:6), one of the island's excellent newspapers we read daily to keep up to date. Other insightful sources we consulted for Jo's research included: The World Bank Group 2012, "Fuel from the Fields: Alternative Charcoal," accessed 2 December 2014; "Deforestation in Haiti" from *Wikipedia*, accessed 2 December 2014; Willis Eschenbach, "How Environmental Organizations Are Destroying the Environment," accessed 25 June 2013; "Clean Cook Stove and Fuels Action Project for Haiti," web.mit.edu/d-lab, accessed 12 March 2012; and Gerald Murray, Matthew McPherson, Tim Schwartz, *Fading Frontier: An Anthropological Analysis of the Agroeconomy and Social Organization of the Haitian-Dominican Border* (Gainesville, FL: University of Florida), 2 April 1998, http:www.g . . . 970519,d.exy.

Our Glossary of Taino Terms was shaped by a variety of sources including the Taino Inter-Tribal Council Inc.'s superb *The Modern Taino Dictionary: The Dictionary of the Spoken Taino Language* (1st ed.) by Chief Pedro Guanikeyu Torres and the Taino TITC team of The Taino Language Project, http:www.taino-tribe.org/tedict.html. Also, we consulted Dr. José Barreiro's excellent glossary, *The Indian Chronicles* (Golden, CO: Fulcrum, 1993, 2012). Other helpful sources included the "Taino Vocabulary in the Dominican Republic [archive]" from the former Taino Pride website (http://www.anacaona.net); the Taino vocabulary list on the homepage of El Boricua: Un Poquito de Todo (A Monthly Bilingual, Cultural Publication for Puerto Rico, http://elboricua.com). The numbers we found on the "Taino Word Set" of www.nativelanguages.org/taino.htm. Translations of the Lord's Prayer in Taino from which we drew were by Dr. Cayetano Coll y Toste, posted by the Jatibonicu Taino Tribal Nation of Boriken (http://www.taino-tribe.org/taino-prayer.htm) , and by Prof. José Boriguex, passed on to us by our friend we will salute next.

Robert Felix, to whom we pay tribute in the book itself, is not only real, but one of the representatives to the United Nations when the Taino nation was reconfigured in the 1990s. To Robert, devout scholar, creative genius, world-class musician, we owe an inestimable debt for his theological and cultural insights and endless sharing of data, which richly informed this book and his great work on the compact disc, *Songs from the Cave, Ballads from the Papers* (most of which he produced, providing the vast majority of the instrumentation, creating the five instrumental tracks, and cowriting two of the songs) to help us provide a soundtrack of Bill's original music to enhance the reading experience of both *Cave of Little Faces* and *Name in the Papers,* Bill's previous novel. Also in that esteemed category of creative genius is our son, the vastly innovative Stephen Spencer, currently Program Director at Salem, Massachusetts Access TV. Consummate musician and producer, filmmaker, artist, and gourmet chef, Steve remastered the album, adding in a new vocal dimension, helped us bring Sierra Tepee's signature song, "High Sierra Nocturne," to you by creating its drum track and producing the song and video (see this video of "High Sierra Nocturne" on YouTube), and he even created our book's cover by melding his mom's on-location photograph of authentic "little faces" with his own photograph of Jasmine Myers's gracious modeling of Jo Archer, around which the splendid artist Shannon Carter then built her graphic design of our book cover. The wondrous Jasmine, our next creative genius to be applauded, is, like Jo, a woman who makes things happen. She is the founder and director of the award-winning Still Small Theatre Troupe, its spiritual leader, playwright, stage manager, director, costume designer, composer, lead or support actress, chief singer, whatever is needed, in short, the all-around go-to creative center. Jasmine not only enlivens our book's cover, her lovely voice enhances our album, and her flute interlude graces "High Sierra Nocturne." Those who wish to enjoy even more can listen to her own original album of flute compositions: *A Bathtub Full of Music.* Added to these dear folks are the excellent graphic artists, Saemi Kim, who designed the map of the Western Lands of the South, Deb Beatty Mel, our longtime friend who copyedited the novel to prepare it for Wipf and Stock Publishers and also designed our beautiful cd covers and booklet, our astute editorial team at Wipf and Stock, with whom it was a blessing to work, as it always is, and our perceptive outside readers: Dr. Robert Boenig, Dr. Jennifer Creamer, Anne Marie Cullen, Dawn Samsel, Kris Johnson, and Dr. Grace May, to whom we are deeply grateful. What a blessing to partner with such creativity.

With sincere appreciation, we dedicate this book to Rita Stobbe, who was the first champion of Bill's first novel, *Name in the Papers,* as well as this one. Rita and her husband, Les Stobbe, Bill's hardworking literary agent, though now semiretired, were an endless source of sound advice, inspiration, and friendship.

Finally, none of this would exist without the story that completes all stories, the great good news of Yeshua, YaYael, Jesucristo, Jesus Christ, Enrique's and our Lord and Savior, whose great act of restoration on our behalf pulses at the center of God's gracious eucatastrophe.

www.ingramcontent.com/pod-product-compliance
Lightning Source LLC
Chambersburg PA
CBHW071524120726
47907CB00012B/306